NIGHT PROBE!

CLIVE CUSSLER

NIGHT PROBE!

McCLELLAND AND STEWART

Night Probe!

Copyright © 1981 by Clive Cussler Enterprises, Inc.
Cover art copyright © 1981 by Bantam Books, Inc.
Illustrations by Errol Beauchamp
Book design by Barbara Cohen
All rights reserved

The Canadian Publishers
McClelland and Stewart Limited
25 Hollinger Road
Toronto M4B 3G2

Published simultaneously in the United States
by Bantam Books, Inc.

ISBN 0-7710-2503-3

Printed and bound in the United States of America

In gratitude to Jerry Brown, Teresa Burkert, Charlie Davis, Derek & Susan Goodwin, Clyde Jones, Don Mercier, Valerie Pallai-Petty, Bill Shea and Ed Wardwell, who kept me on the track.

Prologue

DEATHDAY

Wreck of the Empress of Ireland

Rimouski

QUEBEC

St. Lawrence River

NEW BRUNSWICK

MAINE

ONTARIO

VT.

Hudson River

N.H.

LAKE ONTARIO

MASS.

ATLANTIC OCEAN

NEW YORK

CONN.

R.I.

LAKE ERIE

Wreck of the
Manhattan Limited

NEW YORK

1

Streaks of lightning signaled a threatening thunderstorm as the *Manhattan Limited* hurtled over the ballasted rails piercing the New York countryside. Coal smoke burst from the locomotive's stack in a drumstick plume that dusted the stars stippling the night sky. Inside the cab, the engineer slipped a silver Waltham watch from the pocket of his coveralls, sprung the lid and studied the face in the glow from the firebox. It was not the approaching storm that worried him, but the relentless crawl of time that sought to rob him of his precious schedule.

Gazing out the right side of the cab, he watched the creosote ties sweep under the eight huge driving wheels of the 2-8-0 Consolidation-type locomotive. Like the captain of a ship who lived with his command, he had been at the same throttle for three years. He was proud of "Gallopin' Lena," as he affectionately called the 236,000 pounds of iron and steel. Built by Alco's Schenectady Works in 1911, she was burnished in gloss black with a red stripe and her number 88 neatly hand-painted in gold.

He listened to the steel wheels pounding out a moving rhythm against the rail joints, felt the momentum of the locomotive and the seven cars that followed.

Then he pulled the throttle up another notch.

In the seventy-foot private Pullman that brought up the rear, Richard Essex sat at a desk in the vestibuled library. Too tired to sleep and

3

bored with the tedium of the trip, he composed a letter to his wife to pass the time.

He described the ornate interior of the car, the elaborately carved Circassian walnut, the handsome brass electrical lamps, the red velvet revolving chairs and the potted palms. He even mentioned the beveled mirrors and ceramic tile floors in the lavatories of the four spacious sleeping compartments.

Behind him in a richly paneled observation parlor, five army guards in civilian dress played cards, the smoke from their cigars drifting in a blue cloud toward the brocade ceiling, their rifles laid casually about the furniture. Occasionally a player would lean over one of the brass spittoons dotting the Persian carpet. It was perhaps the highest level of luxury any of them had ever enjoyed, Essex speculated. The palatial transportation must have cost the government nearly seventy-five dollars a day, and all for the movement of a scrap of paper.

He sighed and finished his letter. Then he sealed it in an envelope, which he stuffed inside his breast pocket. Sleep still evaded him, so he sat and stared through the arched bay windows at the darkened landscape, listening for the wail of the engine's whistle just before a village depot or country crossing flashed past. Finally he stood up, stretched and walked to the elegant dining room, where he sat down at a mahogany table covered by a snowy cloth enhanced by crystal glasses and silver service. A glance at his watch told him it was a few minutes before two in the morning.

"What is your pleasure, Mr. Essex?" A black waiter had appeared as if by magic.

Essex looked up and smiled. "I know it's quite late, but I wonder if I might get a light snack."

"Happy to oblige, sir. What would you like to order?"

"Something that will help me close my eyes."

The waiter flashed a toothy grin. "May I suggest a small bottle of Pommard burgundy and a nice hot bowl of clam bouillon."

"That will be fine, thank you."

Later, as he sipped his wine, Essex couldn't help wondering if Harvey Shields was also finding sleep so elusive.

2

Harvey Shields was experiencing a nightmare.

His mind refused to accept any other explanation. The shriek of steel and the cries of agony and terror beyond the darkness that smothered him were too hellish for reality. He struggled to retreat from the devilish scene and drift back into a peaceful sleep, but then the pain began gnawing at his senses and he realized it was no dream.

Somewhere below he could hear the rush of water as though it was surging through a tunnel, followed by a gust of wind that squeezed the breath from his lungs. He tried to open his eyes, but the lids felt glued shut. He was not aware that his head and face were coated with blood. His body was gripped in an immovable fetal position against cold, ungiving metal. An acrid electrical smell stung his nostrils and combined with the increasing pain to prod him onto a higher plateau of consciousness.

He tried to move his arms and legs, but they refused to respond. A strange silence settled around him, broken only by the murmur of lapping water. He made another attempt at breaking clear of the unseen vise that clutched him. He took a great breath and then exerted every muscle in his limbs.

Suddenly an arm tore free and he gasped as a jagged piece of metal sliced his forearm. The agony swept him to complete awareness. He wiped the congealing wetness from his eyes and gazed about what had once been his stateroom aboard the Canadian luxury liner bound for England.

The large mahogany dresser was gone, as was the writing desk and the nightstand. Where the deck and starboard bulkhead should have been was a massive cavity, and across the twisted edge there was only the fog-shrouded darkness and the black water of the St. Lawrence River. It was as if he was looking into a bottomless void. Then his eyes caught and focused on a soft reflection of white and he knew he was not alone.

Almost within touching distance a young girl from the next

stateroom was buried in the debris with only her head and one pale shoulder protruding from the broken ceiling. Her hair was golden and rained in loose strands nearly three feet long. Her head was twisted at a grotesque angle and blood seeped from her lips, streaming down her face and slowly dyeing her cascading hair crimson.

Shields' initial shock receded and a spreading sickness took its place. Until now the specter of death had not crossed his mind, but in the lifeless corpse of the girl he could read his own diminishing future. Then a sudden thought burst inside him.

In despair his eyes vainly probed the debris for the hand case he had never let out of his sight. It was gone, swallowed up in the wreckage. Sweat erupted from his every pore as he fought to extricate his torso from its prison. The effort was fruitless, there was no feeling below his chest and he knew with fearful certainty that his back was crushed.

Around him the great liner was in its death throes, rapidly listing and settling into the cold water that would forever be its grave. Passengers, some in evening dress, most in sleeping clothes, were milling about the slanting decks trying to climb into the few lifeboats that were launched or leaping into the cold river, clutching anything that would float. Only minutes remained before the ship would take her final plunge a scant two miles from shore.

"Martha?"

Shields stiffened and turned his head toward the faint cry that sounded from beyond the demolished partition separating him from the inside corridor. He listened intently, and then it came again.

"Martha?"

"In here," Shields shouted. "Please help me."

There was no reply, but he heard sounds of movement through the pile of rubble. Soon a fallen piece of the ceiling was pushed aside and a face with a gray beard poked through.

"My Martha, have you seen my Martha?"

The intruder was in a state of shock and his words came hollow and without inflection. His forehead was badly lacerated and his eyes darted about frantically.

"A young girl with long blond hair?"

"Yes, yes, my daughter."

Shields motioned toward the body of the girl. "I'm afraid she's gone."

The bearded man feverishly forced a larger opening and crawled through. He approached the girl, his face numb with uncomprehension, and lifted the bloodstained head, smoothing back the hair. For several moments he did not utter a sound.

"She did not suffer," Shields offered gently.

The stranger did not reply.

"I'm sorry," Shields murmured. He could feel the ship listing sharply to starboard. The water was rising faster from below and there was little time left. He had to penetrate the father's grief and somehow persuade him to rescue the hand case.

"Do you know what happened?" he began.

"Collision," the answer came vaguely. "I was on deck. Another ship came out of the fog. Buried her bow in our side." The father paused, took out a handkerchief and dabbed the blood from the dead girl's face. "Martha begged me to take her to England. Her mother was reluctant, but I gave in. Oh God, if only I'd known . . ." His voice trailed off.

"There is nothing you can do," Shields said. "You must save yourself."

The father turned slowly and looked at him with unseeing eyes. "I killed her," he whispered hoarsely.

Shields was not getting through. Anger smoldered within him and ignited in a flame of desperation.

"Listen!" he cried. "Lost in the wreckage is a travel case with a document that must reach the Foreign Office in London!" He was shouting now. "Please find it!"

The water swirled in small eddies a few feet away. The flood that would engulf them was only seconds away. The rising tide was stained with the slime of oil and coal dust while the night air outside was torn by the screams of a thousand dying souls.

"Please listen to me while there is still time," Shields begged. "Your daughter is dead." He was beating at the restricting steel with clenched fists, uncaring of the pain as his skin shredded away. "Leave before it's too late. Find my travel case and take it with you. Give it to the captain, he'll know what to do."

The father's mouth trembled open. "I cannot leave Martha alone . . . she fears the dark . . ." He muttered as though he were speaking at an altar.

It was the deathblow. There was no moving the grief-stunned father as his mind entered delirium. He bent over his daughter and kissed her on the forehead. Then he dissolved into a fit of uncontrolled sobbing.

Strangely, the fury of frustration fell away from Shields. With the acceptance of failure and death, fear and terror no longer held meaning. In the few short moments left he slipped beyond the boundaries of reality and saw things with abnormal clarity.

There came an explosion deep in the bowels of the ship as her boilers burst. She rolled over on her starboard side and slid stern first onto the waiting riverbed. From the moment of the collision in the darkness of early morning until she vanished from view of the mass of humanity struggling to stay afloat in the icy water, less than fifteen minutes had elapsed.

The time was 2:10 a.m.

Shields did not try to fight it, to hold his breath staving off the inevitable for a few more seconds. He opened his mouth and gulped in the foul-tasting water, gagging as it poured down his throat. Into the airless tomb he sank. The choking and the suffering passed quickly, and his conscious mind blinked out.

And then there was nothing, nothing at all.

3

A night bred in hell, thought Sam Harding, ticket agent for the New York & Quebec Northern Railroad, as he stood on the platform of his station and watched the poplar trees bordering the track lean horizontal under the battering gusts of a violent windstorm.

He was experiencing the end of a heat wave that had baked the New England states; the hottest May since 1880, proclaimed Wacketshire's weekly newspaper in red-letter Bodoni typeface. Lightning hurtled through the predawn sky in jagged patterns, accompanied by a twenty-four-degree drop in temperature in one hour. Harding caught himself shivering at the sudden change as the breeze whipped at his cotton shirt, dampened by sweat from the oppressive humidity.

Down on the river he could see lights from a string of barges as they nosed their way against the downstream current. One by one their dim yellow glows blinked off and then on again as the barges passed under the foundation piers of the great bridge.

Harding's station sat on the outer perimeter of the town, village really, where the tracks of the railroad bisected in a cross. The main trunk ran north to Albany while the branch line swung east over the Deauville-Hudson River bridge to Columbiaville before forking south to New York City.

Though no drops had fallen, there was a definite smell of rain in the air. He walked over to his Model T Ford depot hack, untied a number of small cords under the edge of the roof and rolled down the leatherette side curtains over the oak side panels. Then he fixed them into place with the Murphy fasteners and reentered the station.

Hiram Meechum, the Western Union night man, was hunched over a chessboard, engaged in his favorite pastime of playing another telegrapher down the line. The panes in the windows rattled from the wind, keeping cadence with the staccato of the telegraph key screwed to the table in front of Meechum. Harding picked up a coffeepot from a kerosene stove and poured himself a cup.

"Who's winning?"

Meechum looked up. "I drew Standish down in Germantown. He's a damn tough customer." The key danced and Meechum moved one of the chess pieces. "Queen to knight four," he grunted. "It don't exactly look encouraging."

Harding pulled a watch from a vest pocket and studied the dial, knitting his eyebrows thoughtfully. "The *Manhattan Limited* is twelve minutes late."

"Probably behind schedule because of the storm," Meechum said. He tapped out his next move, placed his feet on the table and leaned his chair back on two legs awaiting his opponent's response.

Every clapboard on the station's walls creaked as a firebolt scorched the sky and struck a tree in a nearby pasture. Harding sipped at the steaming coffee and unconsciously stared at the ceiling, wondering if the lightning rod atop the roof was in good order. A loud clang from the telephone bell above his rolltop desk broke his thoughts.

"Your dispatcher with news on the *Limited*," Meechum predicted with unconcern.

Harding bent the swinging arm of the telephone upward to his standing position and pressed the small, circular receiver to his ear. "Wacketshire," he answered.

The dispatcher's voice from Albany was barely discernible through the storm-induced static on the circuit. "The bridge . . . can you see the bridge?"

Harding turned toward the east window. His vision carried no further than the end of the platform in the darkness. "Can't see. Have to wait for the next lightning flash."

"Is it still standing?"

"Why wouldn't it be standing?" Harding replied irritably.

"A tugboat captain just called from Catskill and raised hell," the dispatcher's voice crackled back. "Claims a girder dropped off the bridge and damaged one of his barges. Everyone here is in a panic. The agent in Columbiaville says the *Limited* is overdue."

"Tell them to relax. She hasn't reached Wacketshire yet."

"You sure?"

Harding shook his head in disbelief at the dispatcher's simple-minded question. "Dammit! Don't you think I'd know if a train passed my station?"

"Thank heavens we're in time." The relief in the dispatcher's tone came over the line despite the interference. "The *Limited* has ninety passengers on board not counting the crew and a special government car carrying some big-shot official to Washington. Flag it down and inspect the bridge at first light."

Harding acknowledged and hung up. He lifted a shuttered lantern with a red lens off a hook on the wall, shook it to see if the tank held kerosene and lit the wick. Meechum peered over his chess pieces questioningly.

"You flagging the *Limited?*"

Harding nodded. "Albany says a girder fell off the bridge. They want it checked before a train crosses over."

"Want me to light the semaphore lantern for you?"

A high-pitched whistle pierced the wind outside. Harding cocked an ear, measuring the sound. It came again only slightly louder.

"No time. I'll flash it down with this—"

Suddenly the door opened and a stranger stood on the threshold, his eyes ferreting the interior of the station. He was built like a jockey, rail-thin and short. A mustache was blond as was the hair that showed beneath the Panama straw hat cocked on his head. The clothes indicated a fastidious dresser; Weber and Heilbroner English-cut suit with silk stitching, the razor-creased pants stopping evenly above a pair of two-tone brown suede and leather shoes. His most eye-catching feature, however, was a Mauser automatic pistol held in a slim, effeminate hand.

"What in hell's going on?" Meechum mumbled in awe.

"A holdup, gentlemen," the intruder said with the tiniest hint of a smile. "I thought it was obvious."

"You're crazy," snapped Harding. "We've got nothing to rob."

"Your station has a safe," said the stranger, nodding toward the steel box standing on high castors in one corner of Harding's office area. "And safes contain valuable commodities, like payrolls perhaps?"

"Mister, robbing a railroad is a federal offense. Besides, Wacketshire is a farming community. There's no payroll shipments. Hell, we don't even have a bank."

"I'm in no mood to debate the economics of Wacketshire." The long hammer on the Mauser was pulled back. "Open the safe."

The whistle tooted again, much closer this time, and Harding knew from experience the sound came only a quarter mile up the track. "Okay, whatever you say, right after I flag the *Limited*."

The gun went off and Meechum's chessboard exploded, scattering the pieces about the linoleum floor. "No more stupid talk about stopping trains. I suggest you get on with it."

Harding stared at the robber, his eyes stricken with sudden horror. "You don't understand. The bridge might be out."

"I understand that you're trying to be clever."

"I swear to God—"

"He's telling the truth," Meechum cut in. "A warning just came over the line from Albany about the bridge."

"Please listen to us," Harding pleaded. "You could be murdering a hundred people." He paused, his face pale as the headlamp from the approaching engine beamed through the window. The whistle shrilled no more than two hundred yards away. "For God's sake—"

Meechum snatched the lantern from Harding's hand and lunged for the open doorway. The gun blasted again. A bullet thudded into his hip and he crashed to the floor a foot short of the threshold. He rolled to a kneeling position and cocked his arm to throw the lantern onto the track outside. The man in the straw hat grabbed his wrist and in the same motion brought the pistol barrel down on Meechum's head and kicked the door shut.

Then he whirled on Harding and snarled, "Open that damned safe."

Harding's stomach heaved at the sight of Meechum's blood spreading on the floor, and then he did as he was told. He clutched the combination dial, sick with helplessness as the train roared by on the track not twenty feet behind him, the lights from the Pullman coaches casting flickering reflections through the panes of the station windows. In less than a minute the clack from the last car's wheels on the rails had died away and the train was gone, heading up the grade to the bridge.

The tumblers dropped into place and Harding twisted the bolt arm, swung the heavy door open and stepped aside. Inside were a few small, unclaimed packages, old station logbooks and records, and a cashbox. The robber scooped up the box and counted out the contents.

"Eighteen dollars and fourteen cents," he said indifferently. "Hardly a munificent sum, but it should keep me eating for a few days."

He neatly folded the bills in a leather breast wallet and dropped the change in a pants pocket. Casually tossing the emptied cashbox on the desk, he stepped over Meechum and faded into the storm.

Meechum moaned and stirred. Harding knelt and lifted the telegrapher's head. "The train . . . ?" Meechum murmured.

"You're bleeding pretty bad," said Harding. He pulled a red bandana from his hip pocket and pressed it against the flowing wound.

Clenching his teeth against the burning agony of two injuries, Meechum stared dully at Harding. "Call the east bank . . . see if the train is safe."

Harding eased his friend's head to the floor. He grabbed for the phone and threw back the extension arm, opening the transmitter circuit. He shouted into the mouthpiece but silence was his only reply. He closed his eyes for a moment and prayed, then tried again. The line to the other side of the river was dead. Feverishly he turned the selector wheel on the Cummings-Wray sender and called the dispatcher at Albany. All he heard was static.

"I can't get through." He could taste the bitterness in his mouth. "The storm has disrupted the circuits."

The telegraph key began to click. "The telegraph lines are still open," muttered Meechum. "That's Standish with his chess move."

Painfully he dragged his body to the table and reached up and broke in the incoming message, tapping out an emergency line clearance. Then both men momentarily stared at each other, fearful of what they might learn in the morning light that was beginning to tint the eastern sky. The wind poured through the doorway and scattered loose papers and whipped at their hair.

"I'll alert Albany," Meechum said finally. "You see to the bridge."

As if in a dream, Harding jumped to the track bed, his panic mushrooming, and ran recklessly over the uneven rail ties. Soon his breath came in great gasps and his heart felt like it was thumping out of his rib cage. He topped the grade and hurried under the girders of the west bank's flanking span toward the center of the Deauville-Hudson bridge. He tripped and sprawled, gashing a knee on a rail spike. He picked himself up and stumbled on. At the outer edge of the center span, he stopped.

An icy nausea coursed through his body as he stood in numbed abhorrence and gazed through unbelieving eyes.

There was a great empty gap in the middle of the bridge. The center truss had vanished into the cold, gray waters of the Hudson River 150 feet below. Vanished too was the passenger train carrying a hundred men, women and children.

"Dead . . . all dead!" Harding cried in helpless rage. "All for eighteen dollars and fourteen cents."

Part I

ROUBAIX'S GARROTE

4

There was nothing unusual about the man slouched in the back seat of a nondescript Ford sedan driving slowly through the streets of Washington. To the pedestrians who scurried in front of the car at stoplighted intersections, he might have been a paper salesman being driven to work by his nephew. No one paid the slightest notice to the White House tag on the license plates.

Alan Mercier was a plump, balding character with a genial Falstaff face that masked a shrewd analytical mind. No clotheshorse, he was addicted to ever-rumpled, bargain-priced suits with white linen handkerchiefs stuffed sloppily in the breast pocket. They were trademarks that political cartoonists exaggerated with keen enthusiasm.

Mercier was no paper salesman. Recently appointed national security adviser to the country's new president, he was still unrecognized in the public eye. Widely respected in the academic community, he had built a reputation as a canny forecaster of international events. At the time he came under the eye of the President, he was director of the World Crisis Projection Commission.

Perching a pair of Ben Franklin specs on a bubble nose, he laid a briefcase across his lap and opened it. The underside of the lid held a visual display screen, and a keyboard console, bordered by two rows of colored lights, lay across the bottom. He typed out a combination of numbers and waited a brief moment while the signal was bounced by satellite to his corner office at the White House. There a computer, programmed by his aides, whirred into life and began relaying his workload for the day.

The incoming data arrived in code and was electronically deciphered in milliseconds by the battery-operated microprocessor on his lap, the final text reading out in green lowercase letters across the screen.

First came the correspondence, followed by a series of memos from his security council staff. Next came the daily reports from various governmental agencies, the Joint Chiefs of Staff and the director of Central Intelligence. He quickly digested them to memory before erasing their contents from the microprocessor's storage unit.

All except two.

He was still lingering over them when his car swung though the west gate of the White House. His eyes mirrored a curious perplexity. Then he sighed, pressed the off button and closed the case.

As soon as he arrived in his office and settled behind his desk, he dialed a private number at the Department of Energy. A man's voice answered in the middle of the first ring.

"Dr. Klein's office."

"This is Alan Mercier. Is Ron available?"

There was a slight pause, and then the voice of Dr. Ronald Klein, the director of energy, came on the line.

"Morning, Alan. What can I do for you?"

"I wonder if you could spare me a few minutes today."

"My schedule is pretty tight . . ."

"This is important, Ron. You name the time."

Klein wasn't used to being pushed, but the cement tone of Mercier's voice implied the security adviser was not about to be put off. He held his palm over the phone's mouthpiece while he checked with his administrative assistant. Then he came back on the line.

"How does between two thirty and three sound?"

"No problem," replied Mercier. "I have a lunch meeting at the Pentagon, so I'll swing by your office on the way back."

"You did say it was important."

"Let's put it another way," Mercier said, pausing for effect. "After I ruin the President's day, I'm going to screw up yours."

In the oval office of the White House, the President sat back from his desk and closed his eyes. He allowed his mind to wander from the pressures of the day for a minute or two. For a man who had been inaugurated to the nation's highest office only a few weeks before, he looked overly worn and tired. The election campaign had been long and exhausting, and he had yet to fully recover from it.

He was small in stature, with brown hair streaked with white and thinning; his features, once cheerful and crinkling, were set and solemn. He reopened his eyes as a sudden winter sleet rapped the floor-to-ceiling windows behind him. Outside on Pennsylvania Avenue, the traffic crawled at a slothlike pace as the pavement turned to ice. He longed for the warmer climate of his native New Mexico. He wished he could escape on a camping trip to the Sangre de Cristo Mountains near Santa Fe.

This man had never set out to become President. Never driven by blind ambition, he had served in the Senate during twenty years of conscientious effort and a solid record of accomplishments that did little toward making him a household name.

Nominated as a dark horse by his party's convention, he was elected by a wide popular margin when an investigative reporter dug up a series of shady financial dealings in his opponent's past.

"Mr. President?"

He looked up from his reverie at the sound of his aide's voice.

"Yes?"

"Mr. Mercier is here for your security briefing."

"All right, send him in."

Mercier entered the room and seated himself across the desk. He passed over a heavy folder.

"How goes the world today?" the President asked with a thin smile.

"Pretty grim, as always," replied Mercier. "My staff has completed the projections on the nation's energy reserves. The bottom line isn't exactly encouraging."

"You're not telling me anything I didn't know. What's the latest outlook?"

"The CIA gives the Middle East another two years before their fields scrape bottom. That will leave the world's known oil supply at less than fifty percent of demand. The Russians are hoarding their depleted reserves, and the Mexican offshore bonanza fell short of expectations. And as for our own oil deposits . . ."

"I've seen the figures," replied the President. "The hectic exploration several years ago brought in a few small fields at best."

Mercier surveyed the interior of a folder. "Solar radiation, windmills, electric autos, they're partial solutions of a sort. Unfortunately, their technology is at about the same state as television during the nineteen forties.''

"A pity the synthetic fuel programs got off to such a slow start.''

"The earliest target date before the oil-shale refineries can take up the slack is four years away. In the meantime, American transportation is up the polluted creek without locomotion.''

The President cracked a faint smile at Mercier's rare display of dry humor. "Surely there is some hope on the horizon.''

"There's James Bay.''

"The Canadian power project?''

Mercier nodded and reeled off the statistics. "Eighteen dams, twelve powerhouses, a work force of nearly ninety thousand people, and the rechanneling of two rivers the size of the Colorado. And, as the Canadian government literature states, the largest and most expensive hydroelectric project in the history of man.''

"Who operates it?''

"Quebec Hydro, the provincial power authority. They began work on the project in nineteen seventy-four. The price tag has been pretty hefty. Twenty-six billion dollars, the major share coming from New York money houses.''

"What's the output?''

"Over a hundred million kilowatts, with double that coming in the next twenty years.''

"How much flows across our borders?''

"Enough to light fifteen states.''

The President's face tensed. "I don't like being so heavily dependent on Quebec for electricity. I'd feel more secure if our nation's power came from our own nuclear plants.''

Mercier shook his head. "The sad fact is our nuclear facilities provide less than a third of our requirements.''

"As usual we dragged our feet,'' the President said wearily.

"The lag was partly due to escalating construction costs and expensive modifications,'' Mercier agreed. "Partly because the demands on uranium have put it in short supply. And then, of course, there were the environmentalists.''

The President sat in thoughtful silence.

"We banked on endless reserves that do not exist,'' Mercier continued. "And while our country consumed itself into a corner, the neighbors to the north went ahead and did something about it. We had no option but to tap their source.''

"Are their prices in line?''

Mercier nodded. ''The Canadians, bless their souls, have kept rates on a par with our own power companies.''

"A glimmer of sunshine after all.''

"There's a catch.''

The President sighed.

"We have to face the unpleasant fact,'' Mercier went on, ''that Quebec expects to pass a referendum for full independence by summer.''

"Prime Minister Sarveux has slammed the door on the Quebec separatists before. You don't think he can do it again?''

"No, sir, I don't. Our intelligence sources claim that Premier Guerrier of the Parti Québécois has the votes to make it stick next time around.''

"They'll pay a high price to break away from Canada,'' the President said. ''Their economy is already in chaos.''

"Their strategy is to rely on the United States to prop up their government.''

"And if we don't?''

"They can either raise electrical rates to an outrageous level or pull the plug,'' Mercier answered.

"Guerrier would be a fool to shut off our power. He knows we'd retaliate with massive economic sanctions.''

Mercier stared grimly at the President. ''Might take weeks, even months before the Quebeckers felt the pinch. In the meantime our industrial heartland would be paralyzed.''

"You paint a bleak picture.''

"That's only the background scene. You're familiar, of course, with the FQS.''

The President winced. The so-called Free Quebec Society was an underground terrorist movement that had assassinated several Canadian officials. ''What about them?''

"A recent CIA report claims they're Moscow-oriented. If they somehow gained control of the government, we'd have another Cuba on our hands.''

"Another Cuba,'' the President repeated in an expressionless tone.

"One with the capacity to force America to its knees.''

The President rose from his chair and walked to the window, staring at the sleet building on the White House grounds. He was silent for nearly half a minute. Finally he said, "We cannot afford a power play by Quebec. Especially in the months ahead." He turned and faced Mercier, his eyes grieved. "This country is broke and up to its ears in hock, Alan, and just between you and me and these walls, it's only a matter of a few years before we have no choice but to cut the stalling and declare national bankruptcy."

Mercier sagged into his chair. For a heavy man he appeared curiously hunched and shrunken. "I'd hate to see that occur during your administration, Mr. President."

The President shrugged resignedly. "From Franklin Roosevelt on, every chief executive has played a game of tag, pinning a multiplying financial burden on the office of his successor. Well the game is about to be called, and I'm *it*. If we lost electrical power to our northeastern states for twenty days or longer, the repercussions would be tragic. My deadline for the announcement of a new deflated currency would have to be drastically reduced. I need time, Alan, time to prepare the public and the business community for the ax. Time to make the transition to a new money standard as painless as possible. Time for our shale refineries to halt our dependence on foreign oil."

"How can we restrain Quebec from doing anything foolish?"

"I don't know. Our choices are limited."

"There are two options when all else fails," Mercier said, a thin line of tension forming around his mouth. "Two options as old as time to save an economy from sinking down the drain. One is to pray for a miracle."

"And the second?"

"Provoke a war."

At precisely 2:30 in the afternoon, Mercier entered the Forrestal Building on Independence Avenue and took the elevator to the seventh floor. Without fanfare he was ushered into the plush office of Ronald Klein, the secretary of energy.

Klein, a scholarly-looking man with long white hair and a large condor nose, unwound his slim six-feet-five-inches frame from one end of a littered conference table and came over to shake Mercier's hand.

"So what's this matter of dire importance?" asked Klein, skipping the cordial small talk.

"More odd than dire," replied Mercier. "I ran across a request from the General Accounting Office for data concerning the expenditure of six hundred and eighty million dollars in federal funding for the development of a doodlebug."

"A what?"

"Doodlebug," answered Mercier matter-of-factly. "That's a pet name given by geological engineers to any offbeat tool that's supposed to detect underground minerals."

"What's it got to do with me?"

"The money was earmarked for the Energy Department three years ago. There's been no accounting of it since. It might be wise to have your staff make a probe as to its whereabouts. This is Washington. Mistakes of the past have a nasty habit of falling on the heads of current officeholders. If the former energy secretary blew a staggering sum of money on a white elephant, you'd better be prepared with the facts in case some freshman congressman gets it in his head to grab headlines with an investigation."

"I'm grateful for the warning," Klein said sincerely. "I'll get my people busy sweeping the closets."

Mercier rose and extended his hand. "Nothing is ever simple."

"No," Klein said smiling. "It's never that."

After Mercier left, Klein walked over to a fireplace mantel and stared idly at a new log on the soot-coated grate, head bent, hands shoved in the side pockets of his coat.

"How incredible," he murmured to the empty room, "that anyone can lose track of six hundred and eighty million dollars."

5

The generator room of the James Bay hydroelectric project stunned the senses of Charles Sarveux as he surveyed the twelve square acres carved out of solid granite four hundred feet underground. Three rows of huge generators, five stories high and driven by water turbines, hummed with millions of kilowatts of electricity. Sarveux was suitably impressed, and displayed it to the pleasure of the Quebec Hydro Power directors.

This was his first visit to the project since his election as Prime Minister of Canada, and he asked all the expected questions.

"How much electrical energy does each generator produce?"

Percival Stuckey, the chief director, stepped forward. "Five hundred thousand kilowatts, Prime Minister."

Sarveux nodded and made a slight facial expression of approval. It was the appropriate gesture, a skill that had proved beneficial during his campaign for office.

A handsome man in the eyes of men as well as women, Sarveux could probably have won a contest over John F. Kennedy or Anthony Eden. His light blue eyes possessed a mesmeric quality and his sharp-cut facial features were enhanced by a thick mass of gray hair loosely styled in a fashionable but casual look. His trim, medium-height body was a tailor's dream, and yet he never called upon the services of tailors, preferring to buy his suits off the racks of department stores. It was only one of many twists of character precisely carried off so Canadian voters could identify with him.

A compromise candidate between the Liberals, the Party for Independent Canada and the French-speaking Party Québécois, he had walked a political tightrope his first three years of office, managing to keep his nation from falling apart at its provincial borders. Sarveux looked upon himself as another Lincoln, fighting to preserve unity and keep his house from dividing. It was only his threat of armed force that kept the radical separatists in check. But his plea for a strong central government was falling on a growing sea of deaf ears.

"Perhaps you would like to see the control center," suggested director Stuckey.

Sarveux turned to his principal secretary. "How is our time?"

Ian Jeffrey, a serious-faced man in his late twenties, checked his watch. "We're running tight, Prime Minister. We should be at the airport in thirty minutes."

"I think we can squeeze our schedule," Sarveux smiled. "It would be a pity if we missed anything worthwhile."

Stuckey nodded and motioned toward an elevator door. Ten floors above the generator chamber Sarveux and his entourage stepped out in front of a door marked SECURITY CARD PERSONNEL ONLY. Stuckey removed a plastic card that hung on a cord around his neck and inserted it in a slot beneath the door handle. Then he turned and faced the others.

"I'm sorry, gentlemen, but due to the narrow confines of the control center, I can only allow the Prime Minister and myself to enter."

Sarveux's security people started to protest, but he waved them to silence and followed Stuckey through the door and down a long corridor where the card process was repeated.

The power plant's control center was indeed small, and spartan as well. Four engineers sat in front of a console laced with a forest of lights and switches, peering at a panel of dials and gauges embedded in the facing wall. Except for a row of television monitors hanging from the ceiling, the only other fixtures were the chairs occupied by the engineers.

Sarveux looked around consideringly. "I find it incredible that such an awesome display of power is controlled by only four men and a modest amount of equipment."

"The entire plant and the transmission stations are operated by computers two floors beneath us," explained Stuckey. "The project is ninety-nine percent automated. What you see here, Mr. Sarveux, is the fourth-level manual monitoring system that can override the computers in the event of a malfunction."

"So humans still have a degree of control." Sarveux smiled.

"We're not obsolete quite yet." Stuckey smiled back. "There are a few areas left where electronic science can't be fully trusted."

"Where does this wealth of power terminate?"

"In a few days, when the project is fully operational, we'll service the whole of Ontario, Quebec and the northeastern United States."

A thought began to germinate in Sarveux's mind. "And if the impossible occurred?"

Stuckey looked at him. "Sir?"

"A breakdown, an act of God, sabotage."

"Nothing short of a major earthquake could put the power facilities entirely out of commission. Isolated damage or breakdown can be bypassed by two safety backup systems. If those fail, we still have manual control here in the booth."

"What about an attack by terrorists?"

"We've planned for exactly such a threat," said Stuckey confidently. "Our electronic security system is a marvel of advanced technology, and we have a five-hundred-man guard force to back it up. An elite division of assault troops couldn't reach this room in two months."

"Then someone here could cut the power."

"Not someone, singular." Stuckey shook his head resolutely. "It takes every man in this room, including myself, to close off the energy flow. Two, even three cannot do it. We each have a separate procedure unknown to the others that is built into the systems. Nothing has been overlooked."

Sarveux wasn't so sure.

He held out his hand. "A most impressive tour. Thank you."

Foss Gly had been meticulous in selecting the means and place for killing Charles Sarveux. Every drawback, however remote, had been taken into account and met with a counteraction. The angle of the plane's ascent was carefully measured, as was its speed. Many long hours were spent in practice sessions until Gly was satisfied that the gears of the plot meshed with exacting precision.

The site chosen was a golf course, one mile beyond the southwest end of the James Bay Airport's main runway. At that point, according to Gly's careful reckoning, the Prime Minister's government plane would have reached an altitude of 1500 feet at a speed of 180 knots per hour. Two British-manufactured hand-held Argo ground-to-air missile launchers, stolen from the army arsenal at Val Jalbert, were to be used for the attack. They were compact, weighing thirty pounds each when loaded, and easily concealed in a hiker's backpack when dismantled.

The entire plan, as calculated from start to finish, was a classic in efficiency. No more than five men were required, including three waiting on the golf course disguised as cross-country skiers, and one lookout on the observation balcony of the terminal building, with a concealed radio transmitter. After the heat-seeking missiles were launched at the target, the attack group was to ski casually toward the deserted clubhouse and leave in a four-wheel-drive station wagon, guarded by the fifth man who would be waiting in the parking lot.

Gly searched the sky with a pair of binoculars while his fellow conspirators assembled the launchers. A medium snow was falling, cutting his sight to a third of a mile.

It proved a mixed blessing.

The white curtain would shield their actions but leave them precious few seconds to aim and fire at a fast-moving object during the brief interval when it was visible. A British Airways jet passed over and Gly timed its passage before it was swallowed up by the weather. Barely six seconds. *Not good,* he thought grimly. Their chances of two direct hits were razor-thin.

He brushed the snow from a great mass of light sandy hair and lowered the binoculars, revealing a square, ruddy face. On first glance it was attractive in a boyish way. There were congenial brown eyes and a firm-cut chin, but on closer inspection it was the nose that upstaged the other features. Large and misshapen from numerous breaks suffered during brutal back-alley fights, it squatted between his cheeks with a strange beauty to its ugliness. For some inexplicable reason women thought it attractive, even sexy.

The tiny radio in the pocket of his down jacket beeped to life. "This is Dispatch to Field Foreman."

He pressed the transmit button. "Go ahead, Dispatch."

Claude Moran, a reed-thin, pockmarked Marxist who worked as a secretary for the governor-general, adjusted his earpiece receiver and began talking softly into a lapel microphone while gazing through the observation balcony window at the flight line below.

"I have that load of pipe, Field Foreman. Are you ready to receive it?"

"Say when," replied Gly.

"The truck will be along shortly, as soon as the dock crew unloads a shipment from the States."

The innocent-sounding conversation was contrived to throw off anyone who happened to be tuned to the same frequency. Gly interpreted Moran's double-talk as meaning the Prime Minister's plane was second in line for takeoff behind an American Airlines passenger jet.

"Okay, Dispatch. Let me know when the truck leaves the dock."

Personally, Gly felt no hatred toward Charles Sarveux. To him the Prime Minister was only a name in the newspapers. Gly was not even Canadian.

He was born in Flagstaff, Arizona, the result of a drunken coupling between a professional wrestler and a county sheriff's teenage daughter. His childhood was a nightmare of suffering and whippings dealt by his grandfather. In order to survive, Gly became very strong and hard. The day came when he beat the sheriff to death and fled the state. After that it had always been a fight to stay alive. He began by rolling drunks in Denver, led a ring of auto thieves in Los Angeles, hijacked gasoline tank trucks in Texas.

Gly did not look upon himself as a mere assassin. He preferred to be called a coordinator. He was the man who was called in when all others failed, a leader of specialists; he had a reputation for cold-blooded efficiency.

On the observation platform, Moran inched his face as close as he dared to the window before his breath fogged the glass. Sarveux's aircraft appeared to be dissolving into the falling snow on the taxi lane leading to the start of the runway.

"Field Foreman."

"Yes, Dispatcher."

"Sorry, but I cannot see my way clear of paperwork to give you an exact time for the pipe arrival."

"Understood," Gly answered. "Check with me after lunch."

Moran did not acknowledge. He took the escalator down to the main lobby and walked outside, where he hailed a cab. In the back seat he allowed himself the luxury of a cigarette and wondered what high appointment in the new Quebec government he should demand for his services.

On the golf course, Gly turned to the men aiming the missile launch-ers. Their eyes were pressed against the sighting lenses as each kneeled on one knee in the snow.

"One more takeoff to target," he cautioned them.

Nearly five minutes dragged by before Gly heard a set of jet engines roaring in the distance as they strained to lift their burden off the snowy asphalt. His eyes tried to penetrate the white wall in anticipation of seeing the red-and-blue insignia of the American airliner flash into view.

Too late, it dawned on him that aircraft belonging to heads of state took preference over commercial flights. Too late, the sight of the familiar red-and-white Canadian maple leaf burst through the blanket of snow.

"It's Sarveux!" he shouted. "Fire, for God's sake, fire!"

The two men pressed their firing buttons no more than a second apart. The first jerked his sights in the general direction of the plane, but his missile soared up and arched too far behind the tail structure for its heat-seeking mechanism to lock on target. The second man fired with more deliberation. He led the cockpit windows by a hundred yards before he let loose.

The explosive head, locking on to the exhaust of the outer starboard engine, homed in and struck aft of the turbine. To the men on the ground it seemed the muted explosion came long after the plane had vanished from sight. They waited for the sounds of a crash, but the fading whine of the engines remained unbroken. Quickly, they dismantled the launchers and skied to the parking lot. They were soon mingling with the southbound traffic on the James Bay-Ottawa highway.

The outboard engine burst into flame and the turbine blades broke loose and sprayed through the cowling, striking the inboard engine like shrapnel, slicing fuel lines and mangling the second-stage compressor.

Inside the cockpit the fire-warning bell sounded and the pilot, Ray Emmett, closed the throttle and pushed the button activating the freon fire extinguishers. His copilot, Jack May, began running through the emergency procedure checklist.

"James Bay Tower, this is Canada One. We have a problem here and are turning back," Emmett said in a calm monotone.

"Are you declaring an emergency?" the controller asked routinely.

"Affirmative."

"We will clear runway twenty-four. Can you make standard approach?"

"Negative, James Bay," answered Emmett. "I have two engines out, one on fire. I suggest you get out equipment."

"Fire, rescue equipment rolling, Canada One. You are cleared to land. Good luck."

The men in the control tower, knowing the pilot of Canada One was under severe stress, would not break his concentration with further talk. They could only stand by helplessly and await the outcome.

The aircraft was stalling and Emmett eased its nose down, increasing the airspeed to 210 knots, and turned into a wide, shallow bank. Fortunately the snow lessened and visibility rose to two miles, and he could see the flat farmland below and the beckoning end of the runway.

Back in the aft executive cabin, the two Royal Canadian Mounted Police, who guarded the Prime Minister twenty-four hours a day, went into action as soon as they felt the impact from the missile. They securely belted Sarveux to his seat and began building a mountain of loose cushions around his body. Up forward, his secretarial staff and the ever-present contingent of news reporters stared nervously at the smoldering engine that looked as though it was about to melt off the wing.

The hydraulic system was lost. May switched to manual. The pilots struggled together with the stiffened controls as the ground relentlessly reached up from below. Even at full throttle the two port engines were hard pressed to hold the giant airliner aloft. They were falling past the six-hundred-foot level now and still Emmett did not lower the landing gear, holding until the last possible moment to maintain what precious airspeed he still had.

The plane passed over the greenbelt surrounding the airport. It was going to be close. At two hundred feet Emmett dropped the wheels. Through the metronome sweep of the windshield wipers the ten-thousand-foot ribbon of runway twenty-four seemed to widen in slow motion. Then they swept over the leading lip of the asphalt, the tires no more than six feet from the ground. Emmett and May pulled the control yoke back with all their strength. A gentle landing would have been a miracle, any landing at all was a wonder. The impact came hard, jarring every rivet in the aluminum skin and blowing three tires.

The shattered starboard engine broke free of its mounts, and in a freakish gyration struck the ground and rebounded against the underside of the wing, ripping through the structural elements and gouging into the outer fuel cell. Five thousand gallons of jet fuel burst into a ball of flame that engulfed the right side of the aircraft.

Emmett threw the two good engines into reverse thrust and fought the plane's tendency to yaw to the left. Bits and pieces of rubber from the blown tires flayed away in shredded frenzy. Thirty feet of the blazing wing spun off and hurtled onto a taxi lane, narrowly missing a parked airliner. Not far behind, the fire trucks charged after the plane, sirens and red lights flashing.

Down the runway the dying plane rolled, like a fiery meteor leaving a tail of burning debris. Flames tore at the fuselage, which began to melt away. Inside, the heat grew to inferno proportions. The passengers were seconds away from burning alive as the insulation began to char, and clouds of smoke swirled down the aisle. One of the Mounties pulled open the emergency door opposite the fire while the other unclasped the Prime Minister's safety belt and unceremoniously shoved him toward the opening.

Ahead, in the main compartment over the wing, people were dying, their clothes smoldering as the intense heat seared their lungs. Ian Jeffery staggered screaming into the cockpit before he fell unconscious to the floor. Emmett and May took no notice; they were too busy fighting to keep the disintegrating plane on a straight course as it thundered down the rapidly diminishing runway.

The Mounties popped the emergency escape chute, but it flapped uselessly toward the tail of the aircraft after a piece of red-hot debris punctured its air sack. They turned and saw with horror that the forward bulkhead was torching itself into oblivion. Frantically, one of them snatched a blanket and wrapped it around Sarveux's head.

"Hold on to it!" he yelled.

Then he heaved the Prime Minister through the hatch.

The blanket saved Sarveux's life. He landed on a shoulder, dislocating it, and cartwheeled across the coarse surface of the runway, the blows about his head absorbed by the blanket. His legs splayed out and the left tibia twisted and snapped. He tumbled nearly thirty meters before skidding to a stop, his suit shredded in tatters that slowly stained crimson from a mass of skin abrasions.

Emmett and May died at the controls. They died with forty-two other men and three women as two hundred tons of aircraft erupted into a fiery coffin of orange and red. The forward momentum of the great shaft of flame scattered wreckage over a quarter of the runway. The fire fighters attacked the holocaust, but the tragedy was finished. Soon the blackened skeleton of the plane was buried under a sea of white foam. Asbestos-suited men probed the smoldering remains, forcing down the bile that rose in their throats when they came across roasted forms that were barely recognizable as human.

Sarveux, dazed and in shock, lifted his head and stared at the disaster. At first the paramedics did not identify him. Then one kneeled and studied his face.

"Holy Mother Mary!" he gasped. "It's the Prime Minister!"

Sarveux tried to answer, tried to say something meaningful. But no words came. He closed his eyes and gratefully accepted the blackness that enveloped him.

6

Flashbulbs flared and television cameras aimed their hooded lenses at the delicate features of Danielle Sarveux as she moved through a sea of reporters with the silent grace of a ship's figurehead.

She paused in the doorway of the hospital lobby, not from timidity but for effect. Danielle Sarveux did not simply enter a room, she inundated it like a monsoon. There was an inexpressible aura about her that made women stare in open admiration and envy. Men, she over-powered. World leaders and elder statesmen often regressed to self-conscious schoolboys in her presence.

To those who knew Danielle well, her cold poise and granite confidence were irritating. But to the great mass of people she was their symbol, a showcase almost, who proved that Canada was not a nation of homespun lumberjacks.

Whether hosting a social function or rushing to her injured husband's bedside, she dressed in a fashion that was showy elegance. She glided between the reporters, self-possessed and sensuous in a beige tip-tied crepe de chine with modest leg slit and a natural gray karakul jacket. Her raven hair swept downward in a cascade over the front of her right shoulder.

A hundred questions were shouted in chorus and a forest of microphones thrust at her, but she serenely ignored them. Four gargantuan Mounties forged a path to the hospital elevator. On the fourth floor the medical chief of staff stepped forward and introduced himself as Dr. Ericsson.

She looked at him, holding back the dreaded question. Ericsson anticipated her apprehension and smiled his best professional smile of reassurance. "Your husband's condition is serious, but not critical. He suffered abrasions over fifty percent of his body but there are no major complications. Skin grafts will take care of the heavy tissue loss on his hands. And, considering the degree and number of fractures, the surgery by a team of orthopedic specialists was very successful. It will be a matter of perhaps four months, however, before he can be up and about."

She read the evasion in his eyes. "Can you promise me that in time Charles will be as good as new?"

Cornered, Ericsson was forced to concede: "I must confess the Prime Minister will have a slight but permanent limp."

"I suppose you call that a *minor* complication."

The doctor met her eyes. "Yes, madame, I do. The Prime Minister is a most fortunate man. He has no complicated internal injuries, his mind and bodily functions are unimpaired, and the scars will eventually fade. At worst he will require the use of a cane."

He was surprised to see her mouth tighten in a grin. "Charles with a cane," she said in a cynical tone. "God, that's priceless."

"Pardon, madame?"

The limp will be worth twenty thousand votes was the reply that ran through her head, but with chameleon ease she transformed her facial expression back to that of the concerned wife. "Can I see him?"

Ericsson nodded and led her to a door at the end of the corridor. "The anesthetic from the operation has not entirely worn off yet, so you may find his speech a bit vague. He will also be experiencing some pain, so please keep your visit as brief as possible. The floor staff has made up an adjoining room if you wish to stay nearby during his recovery."

Danielle shook her head. "My husband's advisers think it best if I remain at the official residence where I can assist in carrying on the duties of office under his name."

"I understand." He opened the door and stood aside. The bedside was surrounded by several doctors and nurses and a vigilant Mountie. They all turned and separated as she approached.

The smells of antiseptic and the sight of Sarveux's unbandaged, reddened and raw arms made her feel nauseated. She hesitated a moment. Then he recognized her through half-opened eyes and his lips curved into a slight smile. "Danielle," he said, his voice slightly slurred. "Forgive me for not embracing you."

For the first time she saw Sarveux without the armor of his pride. She had never considered him vulnerable before and could not relate the broken, immobile body lying on the bed to the vain man she had lived with for ten years. The waxen face tempered with pain was not the face she knew. It was like looking at a stranger.

Hesitantly, she moved in and kissed him softly on both cheeks. Then she brushed the tumbled gray hair from his forehead, unsure of what to say.

"Your birthday," he said, breaking her silence. "I missed your birthday."

She looked confused. "My birthday is still months away, dearest."

"I meant to buy you a gift."

She turned to the doctor. "He's not making any sense."

Ericsson shook his head. "The lingering effects of the anesthetic."

"Thank God it was I who was hurt and not you," Sarveux rambled feebly. "My fault."

"No, no, nothing was your fault," Danielle said quietly.

"The road was icy, snow covered the windshield, I couldn't see. Took the curve too fast and stepped on the brakes. A mistake. Lost control . . ."

Then she understood. "Many years ago he was in an auto accident," Danielle explained to Ericsson. "His mother was killed."

"Not unusual. A drugged mind often takes one back in time."

"Charles," she said. "You must rest now. I'll be back in the morning."

"No, don't go." Sarveux's eyes looked past her shoulder to Ericsson. "I must talk to Danielle alone."

Ericsson thought a moment and then shrugged. "If you insist." He looked at Danielle. "Please, madame, no more than two minutes."

When the room was cleared, Sarveux started to say something, but then his body tautened in a spasm of pain.

"Let me get the doctor," she said, frightened.

"Wait!" he moaned through clenched teeth. "I have instructions."

"Not now, my dearest. Later when you are stronger."

"The James Bay project."

"Yes, Charles," she said humoring him. "The James Bay project."

"The control booth above the generator chamber . . . increase the security. Tell Henri."

"Who?"

"Henri Villon. He'll know what to do."

"I promise, Charles."

"There is great peril for Canada if the wrong people discover . . ." Suddenly his face contorted and he pressed his head deep into the pillow and moaned.

Danielle was not strong enough to watch his suffering. The room began to spin. She put her hands to her face and stepped back.

"Max Roubaix." His breath was coming in short gasps. "Tell Henri to consult Max Roubaix."

Danielle could stand no more. She turned and fled into the corridor.

Dr. Ericsson was sitting at his desk studying Sarveux's charts when the head nurse entered the office. She set a cup of coffee and a plate of doughnuts beside him.

"Ten minutes till show time, doctor."

Ericsson rubbed his eyes and glanced at his wristwatch. "I suppose the reporters are getting restless."

"More like murderous," the nurse replied. "They'd probably tear down the building if the kitchen didn't keep them fed." She paused to unzip a garment bag. "Your wife dropped off a clean suit and shirt. She insisted you look your best when you face the TV cameras to announce the Prime Minister's condition."

"Any change?"

"He's resting comfortably. Dr. Munson shot him with a narcotic right after Madame Sarveux left. A beautiful woman, but no stomach."

Ericsson picked up a doughnut and idly stared at it. "I must have been mad to allow the Prime Minister to talk me into administering a stimulant so soon after the operation."

"What do you suppose was in his mind?"

"I don't know." Ericsson stood up and removed his coat. "But whatever the reason, his delirious act was most convincing."

7

Danielle slipped out of the chauffeur-driven Rolls-Royce and peered up at the resident mansion of Canada's leader. In her eyes the three-story stone exterior was cold and morbid, like a setting of an Emily Brontë novel. She passed through the long foyer with its high ceiling and traditional furnishings and climbed the wide circular staircase to her bedroom.

It was her haven, the only room in the house Charles had allowed her to redecorate. A shaft of light from the bathroom outlined a raised hump lying on the bed. She closed the door to the hall and leaned against it, a fear mingled with a warmth that suddenly ignited within her stomach.

"You're crazy to come here," she murmured.

Teeth gleamed in a smile under the dim light. "I wonder how many other wives across the land are saying that very line to their lovers tonight."

"The Mounties guarding the residence . . . ."

"Loyal Frenchmen who have suddenly been struck blind and deaf."

"You must leave."

The hump unfolded into a shape of a nude man who stood up on the bed. He held out his hands. "Come to me, *ma nymphe.*"

"No . . . not here." The throaty tone in her voice gave away an awakening passion.

"We have nothing to fear."

"Charles lives!" she suddenly cried out. "Don't you understand? Charles still lives!"

"I know," he said without emotion.

The bedsprings creaked as he stepped to the floor and padded across the carpet. He possessed a formidable body; the huge, swollen muscles, symmetrically formed layer by layer over years of disciplined exercise, rippled and strained beneath his skin. He reached up, ran a hand through his hair and removed it. The skull was shaven, as was every inch of his body. The legs, chest, and pubic area glistened bare and smooth. He took her head between iron hands and pressed her face against the pectoral muscles of his chest. She inhaled the fragrant musky scent from the light coating of body oil he always applied before they made love.

"Do not think of Charles," he commanded. "He no longer exists for you."

She could feel the bestial power oozing from his pores. Her head was swimming as a burning desire for this hairless animal consumed her. The heat between her legs flared and she went limp in his arms.

The sun seeped through the half-open drapes and crept over the two figures entwined on the bed. Danielle lay with her breasts enfolding the nude head, her black hair fanned on the pillow. She kissed the smooth pate several times and then released it.

"You must go now," she said.

He stretched an arm across her stomach and turned the bedside clock to the light. "Eight o'clock. Still too early. I'll leave around ten."

Her eyes took on an apprehensive intensity. "Reporters are swarming everywhere. You should have left hours ago when it was dark."

He yawned and sat up. "Ten in the morning is a very respectable hour for an old family friend to be seen at the official residence. No one will notice my late departure. I'll be lost in the crowd of solicitous members of Parliament who are beating a path here this minute to offer their services to the Prime Minister's wife in her moment of anguish."

"You're a capricious bastard," she said, pulling the twisted bedclothes around her shoulders. "Warm and loving one moment, cold and calculating the next."

"How quickly women change their moods the morning after. I wonder if you would be half so shrewish if Charles had died in the crash?"

"The job was botched," she snapped angrily.

"Yes, the job was botched." He shrugged.

Her face took on a cold determined look. "Only when Charles lies in the grave will Quebec become an independent socialist nation."

"You want your husband dead for a cause?" he asked skeptically. "Has your love turned to such hatred that he has become nothing to you but a symbol to be eliminated?"

"We never knew love." She took a cigarette from a box on the nightstand and lit it. "From the beginning, Charles' only interest in me was a need for a political asset. My family's social standing provided him with entrée to society. I've supplied him with some sterling polish and style. But I've never been anything to Charles except a tool to enhance his public image."

"Why did you marry him?"

She drew on the cigarette. "He said he was going to be Prime Minister someday, and I believed him."

"And then?"

"Too late, I discovered Charles was incapable of affection. I once sought a passionate response. Now I cringe every time he touches me."

"I watched the news conference at the hospital on television. The doctor who was interviewed told how your anxiety and concern for Charles touched the hearts of the medical staff."

"Pure theatrics." She laughed. "I'm pretty good at it. But then I've had ten years of rehearsal."

"Did Charles have anything interesting to say during your visit?"

"Nothing that made any sense. They had just wheeled him out of the surgical recovery room. His mind was still numb from the anesthetic. He spoke mostly gibberish, raked up the past, a memory of an auto accident that killed his mother."

Danielle's lover slid out of bed and stepped into the bathroom. "At least he didn't babble away defense secrets."

She inhaled on the cigarette and let the smoke trickle from her nostrils. "Maybe he did."

"Go on," he said from the bathroom. "I can hear you."

"Charles instructed me to tell you to increase security at James Bay."

"Sheer nonsense." He laughed. "They have twice the amount of guards required to cover every square inch as it is."

"Not the whole project. Only the control booth."

He came to the doorway, wiping his bald head with a towel. "What control booth?"

"Above the generator chamber, I think he said."

He looked puzzled. "Did he elaborate?"

"Then Charles mumbled something about 'great peril for Canada if the wrong people discover . . .' "

"Yes, discover what?"

She made a helpless gesture. "He broke off because of the pain."

"That was all?"

"No, he wanted you to consult with somebody called Max Roubaix."

"Max Roubaix?" he repeated, his expression skeptical. "Are you certain that was the name he used?"

She stared at the ceiling, thinking back, then she nodded. "Yes, I'm positive."

"How odd."

Without further elaboration he reentered the bathroom, stood in front of a large full-length mirror and struck a pose known in muscle control jargon as a vacuum. Exhaling and sucking in his rib section, he expanded his rib cage, straining until the network of blood vessels seemed to erupt beneath the skin's surface. Next he did a side chest shot, left hand on right wrist, arm against upper torso.

Henri Villon studied his reflection with critical concern. His physique was as ideal as physically possible. Then he stared at the chiseled features of the face, the Roman-style nose, the indifferent gray eyes. When he dropped all expression the features became hard, with a satanic twist to the mouth. It was as though a savage was lurking beneath the sculptured marble of a statue.

The wife and daughter of Henri Villon, his Liberal party colleagues and half the population of Canada would never in their wildest fantasies have believed he was leading a double life. A respected member of Parliament and minister of internal affairs in the open, he walked the shadows as the veiled head of the Free Quebec Society, the radical movement dedicated to the full independence of French Quebec.

Danielle came up behind him, a sheet wrapped around her, toga-fashion, and traced his biceps with her fingers. "Do you know him?"

He relaxed and took a deep breath, slowly exhaling. "Roubaix?"

She nodded.

"Only by reputation."

"Who is he?"

"Better to ask that question in the past tense," he said, taking the brown-haired wig with graying sides and neatly placing it on his scalp. "If my memory serves me, Max Roubaix was a mass murderer who swung from the gallows over a hundred years ago."

FEBRUARY 1989
PRINCETON, NEW JERSEY

8

Heidi Milligan seemed out of place among the students grouped about the tables of the Princeton University archive reading room. The neatly tailored uniform of a navy lieutenant commander adorned a svelte body measuring six feet from manicured toenails to the roots of her naturally ash-blond hair.

To the young men in the room she was a welcome distraction from their studies. She knew instinctively that she was being stripped to her skin in their imaginations. But since she'd passed thirty, she'd become indifferent, though not too indifferent.

"Looks like you're on another all-nighter, Commander."

Heidi looked up into the ever-smiling face of Mildred Gardner, the matronly head archivist of the university. "All-nighter?"

"Late study. In my day we called it burning the midnight oil."

Heidi leaned back in her chair. "I've got to steal whatever time I can to work on my dissertation."

Mildred blew the bangs of her nineteen-fortyish pageboy hairstyle out of her eyes and sat down. "An attractive girl like you can't spend all your nights studying. You should find yourself a good man and live it up once in a while."

"First I'll get my doctorate in history, then I'll 'live it up.' "

"You can't get passionate with a piece of paper that says you're a Ph.D."

"Maybe the sound of Dr. Milligan turns me on," Heidi laughed. "If I'm to advance my career in the navy, I'll need the credentials."

"Sounds to me like you like to compete with the opposite sex."

"Sex has nothing to do with it. My first love is the navy. What's wrong with that?"

Mildred made a gesture of surrender. "No profit in arguing with a stubborn female, and hardheaded sailor to boot." She rose and looked down at the documents scattered on the table. "Anything I can pull from the shelves for you?"

"I'm researching Woodrow Wilson papers that deal with the navy during his administration."

"How horribly dull. Why that subject?"

"I guess you might say I'm intrigued by covering an untapped sideline of history."

"You mean subject matter no male has had the foresight to research before."

"You said it, not me."

"I don't envy the guy who marries you," said Mildred. "He'd come home from work and have to arm-wrestle. The loser cooking dinner and doing the dishes."

"I *was* married. Six years. To a colonel in the Marine Corps. I still carry the scars."

"Physical or mental?"

"Both."

Mildred dropped the subject and picked up the fiberboard case that housed the documents, and checked the file number. "You're in the ball park. This file contains the bulk of Wilson's naval correspondence."

"I've pretty much exhausted them," said Heidi. "Can you think of any avenue I might have missed?"

Mildred stared into space a moment. "A slim possibility. Give me ten minutes."

She returned in five, carrying another document case. "Unpublished material that hasn't been cataloged yet," she said with a pontifical grin. "Might be worth a look."

Heidi scrutinized the yellowed letters. Most were in the President's own hand. Advice to his three daughters, explanations of his stand against Tammany Hall to William Jennings Bryan during the Democratic convention of 1912, personal messages to Ellen Louise Axson, his first wife, and Edith Bolling Galt, his second.

Fifteen minutes before closing time Heidi unfolded a letter addressed to Herbert Henry Asquith, the Prime Minister of Britain. The paper appeared creased in irregular lines as though it had once been wadded up. The date was June 4, 1914, but there was no mark of acknowledgment, which suggested that the letter had never been sent. She began to read the neatly styled script.

Dear Herbert,

With the formally signed copies of our treaty seemingly lost and the heated criticism you are receiving from members of your cabinet, perhaps our bargain was never meant to be. And since formal transfer did not transpire, I have given my secretary instructions to destroy all mention of our pact. This uncustomary step is, I feel, somewhat reluctantly, warranted as my countrymen are a possessive lot and would never idly stand by knowing with certainty that—

A crease ran through the next line, obliterating the writing. The letter continued with a new paragraph.

At the request of Sir Edward, and with the concurrence of Bryan, I have recorded the funds deposited to your government from our treasury as a loan.

> Your friend,
>
> Woodrow Wilson

Heidi was about to set the letter aside because there was no reference to naval involvement when curiosity pulled her eyes back to the words "destroy all mention of our pact."

She hung on them for nearly a minute. After two years of in-depth study, she felt she had come to know Woodrow Wilson almost as well as a favorite uncle, and she'd discovered nothing in the former President's makeup to suggest a Watergate mentality during his years in public office.

The ten-minute warning sounded for the closing of the archives. She quickly transcribed the letter on a yellow legal pad. Then she checked in both file cases at the front desk.

"Run on to anything useful?" asked Mildred.

"A trail of smoke I didn't expect," replied Heidi vaguely.

"Where do you go from here?"

"Washington . . . the National Archives."

"Good luck. I hope you make a hit."

"Hit?"

"Discover a previously overlooked treasure of information."

Heidi shrugged. "You never know what might turn up."

She had not planned to pursue the meaning of Wilson's odd letter. But now that she had the door open a crack, she decided it was worth a further peek.

9

The Senate historian leaned back in his chair. "I'm sorry, commander, but we don't have room up here in the Capitol attic to store congressional documents."

"I understand," said Heidi. "You specialize in old photographs."

Jack Murphy nodded. "Yes, we maintain quite an extensive collection of government-related pictures going back as far as the eighteen forties." He idly fiddled with a paperweight on the desk. "Have you tried the National Archives? They have a massive storehouse of material."

"A wasted effort," Heidi shrugged. "I found nothing that related to my search."

"How can I help?"

"I'm interested in a treaty between England and America. I thought perhaps a photo might have been taken during the signing."

"We carry a wealth of those. The president has yet to be born who didn't call in an artist or photographer to record a treaty signature."

"All I can tell you is that it took place during the first six months of nineteen fourteen."

"I can't recall such an event off the top of my head," said Murphy, with a thoughtful look. "I'll be glad to make a search for you; might take a day or two. I have several research projects ahead of yours."

"I understand. Thank you."

Murphy hesitated, then stared at her, a quizzical look in his eyes.

"It strikes me odd that no mention of an Anglo-American treaty can be found in official archives. Do you have a reference to it?"

"I found a letter written by President Wilson to Prime Minister Asquith in which he alludes to a formally signed treaty."

Murphy rose from his desk and showed Heidi to the door. "My staff will give it a try, Commander Milligan. If there is a photograph, we'll find it."

Heidi sat in her room at the Jefferson Hotel, peering into a cosmetic case mirror at a crow's-foot that edged a widened eye. All things considered, she had accepted the merciless encroachment of age, and was keeping her youthful-looking face and a body that had yet to see an ounce of fat.

In the last three years she had weathered a hysterectomy, a divorce and a tender May-December affair with an admiral twice her age who recently died from a heart attack. Yet she still looked as vibrant and alive as when she graduated from Annapolis, fourteenth in her class.

She leaned closer to the mirror and studied a pair of Castilian brown eyes. The right one had a small imperfection at the bottom of the iris, a small pie-shaped splash of gray. Heterochromia iridis was the high-falutin term an ophthalmologist gave her when she was ten years old, and schoolmates had taunted her about possessing an evil eye. From then on she reveled in being different, especially later when boys found it appealing.

Since the death of Admiral Walter Bass she had felt no urge to search out and emotionally involve herself with another man. But before she realized what she was doing, the blue uniform was hanging in the closet and she was standing in the elevator in a bias-cut, coppery-colored slip dress of silk, piped in saffron that plunged devilishly low in back and front and was dashed with a silk flower at a V far below her breasts. Besides a matching purse, her only other accessory was a long feather and jeweled earring that dangled to her shoulder. For warmth against Washington's bleak winter air, she buried herself in a notch-collared greatcoat of dark brown-and-black synthetic fox.

The doorman sighed at the exhilarating view and opened the door to a cab.

"Where to?" asked the driver without turning.

The simple question took her by surprise. She had made up her mind to go out on the town; she hadn't planned where. She paused, and then opportunely her stomach growled.

"A restaurant," she blurted. "Can you recommend a nice restaurant?"

"What do you feel like eatin', lady?"

"I'm not sure."

"Steak, Chinese, seafood? You name it."

"Seafood."

"You got it," said the driver, punching the button on the digital meter. "I know just the place. Overlooks the river. Very romantic."

"Just what I need." Heidi laughed. "It sounds perfect."

Already the evening was a bust. Sitting by candlelight and sipping wine while watching the Capitol's lights sparkling on the Potomac River with no one to talk to only served to deepen her solitude. A woman dining by herself still seemed an odd sight to some people. She caught the discreet stares of the other diners and guessed their thoughts to pass the time. A date who's been stood up? A wife on the make? A hooker taking a dinner break? The latter was her favorite.

A man came in and was seated two tables behind her. The restaurant was dimly lit and all she could tell about him as he passed was that he was tall. She was tempted to turn around and give him an appraising gaze, but could not overcome her inbred standards of modesty.

Suddenly she sensed a presence standing at her side, and her nostrils picked up the vague scent of a man's shaving cologne.

"I beg your pardon, gorgeous creature," a voice whispered in her ear, "but could you see it in your heart to buy a poor, destitute wino a glass of muscatel?"

Startled, she cringed and looked up, her eyes wide.

The intruder's face was shadowed and indistinct. Then he came around and sat down opposite her. His hair was thick and black and the candlelight reflected a pair of warm sea-green eyes. His face was weathered and darkened by the sun. He stared at her as if anticipating a greeting, his features cool and expressionless, and then he smiled and the whole room seemed to brighten.

"Why, Heidi Milligan, can it be you don't remember me?"

She trembled as a tide of recognition swept over her.

"Pitt! Oh my God, Dirk Pitt!"

Impulsively she placed her hands on his temples and pulled him toward her until their lips touched. Pitt's eyes took on a bemused look, and when Heidi released him, he sat back and shook his head.

"Amazing how a man can misjudge a woman. All I expected was a handshake."

A blush tinted Heidi's cheeks. "You caught me in a weak moment. I was sitting here feeling sorry for myself, and when I saw a friend . . . well, I guess I got carried away."

He held her hands in a gentle grip and the smile faded. "I was saddened to hear of Admiral Bass's passing. He was a good man."

Her eyes grew dark. "The end was painless. After he went into a coma he just slipped away."

"God only knows how the Vixen affair might have turned out if he hadn't volunteered his services."

"Remember when we met?"

"I came to interview the admiral at his inn near Lexington, Virginia, where he retired."

"And I thought you were some government official who wanted to badger him. I treated you dreadfully."

Pitt paused and stared at her. "You two were very close."

She nodded. "We lived together for nearly eighteen months. He came from the old school, but he wouldn't consider marriage. Said it was stupid for a young woman to tie herself to a man with one foot in the grave."

Pitt could see the tears beginning to form and he quickly changed the subject. "If you don't mind my saying, you're the image of a high-school girl on her first prom date."

"The perfect compliment at the perfect moment." Heidi straightened and peered around the tables. "I don't mean to take you away from anything. You're probably meeting someone."

"No, I'm stag." He smiled with his eyes. "I'm between projects and decided to relax with a quiet supper."

"I'm glad we met," she said shyly.

"You have but to give the command, and I'm your slave till dawn."

She looked at him and the sights and sounds of the dining room faded into the background.

She stared demurely down at the table setting. "I'd like that very much."

When they entered Heidi's hotel room, Pitt tenderly picked her up and carried her to the bed.

"Do not move," he said. "I'll do everything."

He began to undress her, very slowly. She couldn't remember ever having a man undress her so completely, from her earrings to her shoes. He made as little contact with his fingers as possible and the anticipation mushroomed inside her to an exquisite agony.

Pitt was not to be hurried. She wondered how many other women he had sweetly tortured like this. The passion began to reflect in Pitt's depthless eyes and it excited her to an even higher level.

Suddenly his lips came down onto hers. They were warm and moist. She responded as his arms tightened around her hips and pulled her to him. She seemed to dissolve and a moan escaped her throat.

Just when the blood felt as though it would burst inside and her muscles pulsated uncontrollably, she opened her mouth to scream. It was then Pitt penetrated her and she came and came in a sweeping rage of pleasure that never seemed to end.

10

The most luxurious hour of sleep comes not in the beginning or middle but just prior to awakening. It is then that one dream falls upon another in a kaleidoscope of vivid fantasies. To be interrupted by the ringing of a telephone and thrust back to conscious reality is as tormenting as the scraping of fingernails across a blackboard.

Heidi's agony was compounded by an accompanying knock on her hotel room door. Her mind fogged from sleep, she lifted the receiver and mumbled, "Hold on a minute, please." Then she slid from bed and stumbled halfway across the room before realizing she was naked.

Grabbing a terrycloth robe from her suitcase, she threw it over her shoulders and cracked the door. A bellhop slipped around the barrier with the ease of an eel and set a large vase of white roses on a table. Still in a haze, Heidi tipped him and returned to the phone.

"Sorry for the delay. This is Commander Milligan."

"Ah, Commander," came the voice of Jack Murphy, the Senate historian, "did I wake you?"

"I had to get up anyway," she said, disguising the urge-to-kill tone in her voice.

"I thought you'd like to know your request triggered a recollection in my mind. So I ran a search last night after closing time and came up with something most interesting."

Heidi rubbed the cobwebs from her eyes. "I'm listening."

"There were no photographs on file of a treaty signing during nineteen fourteen," said Murphy. "I did find, however, an old shot of William Jennings Bryan, who was Wilson's secretary of state at the time; his undersecretary, Richard Essex; and Harvey Shields, indentified in a caption only as a representative of His Majesty's government, entering a car."

"I fail to see a connection," said Heidi.

"I'm sorry, I didn't mean to mislead you. The photograph itself tells us very little. But on the back there is a small penciled notation in the lower left corner that is barely legible. It gives the date, May twentieth, nineteen fourteen, and says: 'Bryan leaving White House with North American Treaty.' "

Heidi clutched the phone. "So it really existed."

"My guess is it was only a proposed treaty." Murphy's pride at successfully meeting a challenge was obvious in his tone. "If you would like a copy of the photograph we must charge a small fee."

"Yes . . . yes, please. Could you also make an enlargement of the writing on the back?"

"No problem. You can pick up the prints anytime after three o'clock."

"That will be terrific. Thank you."

Heidi hung up the phone and lay back on the bed, happily basking in the feeling of accomplishment. There was a connection after all. Then she remembered the flowers. A note was attached to one of the white roses.

You look ravishing out of uniform. Forgive me for not being near when you awoke.

Dirk

Heidi pressed the rose against her cheek and her lips parted in a lazy smile. The hours spent with Pitt returned as though observed through a pane of frosted glass, the sights and sounds fusing together in a dreamy sort of mist. He was like a phantom who had come and gone in a fantasy. Only the touch of their bodies lingered with clarity, that and a glowing soreness from within.

With reluctance she forced the reverie from her mind and picked up a Washington phone directory from the nightstand. Holding a long fingernail beneath a tiny printed number, she dialed and waited. On the third ring a voice answered.

"Department of State, can I help you?"

11

Shortly before two o'clock in the afternoon, John Essex pulled up his coat collar against a frigid north breeze and began to check the trays of his raft-culture grown mollusks. Essex's sophisticated farming operation, situated on Coles Point in Virginia, planted seed oysters, tending and cultivating them in ponds beside the Potomac River.

The old man was engrossed in taking a water sample when he heard his name called. A woman bundled in the blue overcoat of a naval officer stood on the pathway between the ponds, a pretty woman, if his seventy-five-year-old eyes were focusing properly. He packed his analysis kit and approached her slowly.

"Mr. Essex?" She smiled warmly. "I phoned earlier. My name is Heidi Milligan."

"You failed to mention your rank, Commander," he said, correctly identifying the insignia on her shoulder boards. Then his lips widened in a friendly smile. "I won't hold that against you. I'm an old friend of the navy. Would you like to come up to the house for a cup of tea?"

"Sounds marvelous," she replied. "I hope I'm not interrupting anything."

"Nothing that can't wait for warmer weather. I should be indebted to you for most likely saving me from a case of pneumonia."

She turned up her nose at the odor that pervaded the air. "It smells like a fish market."

"Are you an oyster lover, Commander?"

"Of course. They form pearls, don't they?"

He laughed. "Spoken like a woman. A man would have praised their gastronomic qualities."

"Don't you mean their aphrodisiac qualities?"

"An undeserved myth."

She made a sour face. "I'm afraid I never developed a fondness for raw oysters."

"Fortunately for me, many people do. Last year the ponds around us yielded over fifteen thousand tons per acre. And that was *after* extraction of the shells."

Heidi tried to look fascinated as Essex went on about the spawning and cultivation of oysters while leading her up a gravel path to a colonial brick house nestled in a grove of blooming apple trees. After settling her comfortably on a leather couch in his study, he produced a pot of tea. Heidi studied him carefully as he poured.

John Essex had twinkling blue eyes and prominent high cheekbones on the part of his face that showed; the bottom half was hidden in a luxuriant white mustache and beard. His body had no senior citizen fat. Even when he was dressed in old coveralls, mackinaw jacket and Wellington boots, the courtly manner that once graced the American embassy in London was still apparent.

"Well, Commander, is this an official visit?" he asked, handing her a cup and saucer.

"No, sir, I'm here on a personal matter."

Essex's eyebrows raised. "Young lady, thirty years ago I might have interpreted that as a flirtatious opening. Now, I'm sad to say, you've only excited an old derelict's inquisitive nature."

"I would hardly call one of the nation's most respected diplomats an old derelict."

"Times gone by." Essex smiled. "How may I be of service?"

"In doing research for my doctorate, I ran across a letter written by President Wilson to Herbert Asquith." She paused to pull a transcript from her purse and pass it to him. "In it he refers to a treaty between England and America."

Essex donned a pair of reading spectacles and read the letter twice. Then he looked up. "How can you be sure it's genuine?"

Without answering, Heidi handed him the two photographic enlargements and waited for a reaction.

William Jennings Bryan, portly and grinning, was bending to enter a limousine. Two men stood behind him in seemingly jovial conversation. Richard Essex, dapper and refined, wore a broad smile, while Harvey Shields had his head tilted back in a belly laugh, displaying two large protruding upper teeth, or what dentists termed an overbite, surrounded by a sea of gold inlays. The chauffeur who held open the car door stood stiffly unamused.

Essex's face remained impassive as he studied the enlargements. After several moments he looked up. "What is it you're fishing for, Commander?"

"The North American Treaty," she replied. "There is no hint of it in State Department records or historical archives. I find it incredible that all trace of such an important document can be so thoroughly lost."

"And you think I can enlighten you?"

"The man in the picture with William Jennings Bryan is Richard Essex, your grandfather. I traced your family tie in the hope that he may have left you papers or correspondence that might open a door."

Essex offered a tray of cream and sugar. Heidi took two lumps. "I'm afraid you're wasting your time. All of his personal papers were turned over to the Library of Congress after his death, every scrap."

"Never hurts to try," Heidi said dejectedly.

"Have you been to the library?"

"I spent four hours there this morning. A prolific man, your grandfather. The volume of his posthumous papers is overwhelming."

"Did you conduct a search of Bryan's writings also?"

"I drew a blank there too," Heidi admitted. "For all his religious integrity and inspiring oratory, Bryan was not a prodigious author of memoranda during his service as secretary of state."

Essex thoughtfully sipped his tea. "Richard Essex was a meticulous man, and Bryan leaned on him like a crutch to draft policy and prepare diplomatic correspondence. Grandfather's papers reflect an almost pathological attention to detail. Little passed through the State Department that didn't have his mark on it."

"I found him to be an obscure sort of person." The words came out before Heidi knew she had spoken them.

Essex's eyes clouded. "Why do you say that?"

"His record as undersecretary for political affairs is well documented. But there's no accounting for Richard Essex the man. Of course I found the usual condensed *Who's Who* type of biography, listing his birthplace, parents and schools, all in neat chronological order. But nowhere did I see a definitive description of his personality or character, his likes and dislikes. Even his papers are written in the third person. He's like the subject of a portrait the artist forgot to flesh out.''

''Are you suggesting he did not exist?'' Essex asked sarcastically.

''Why, no,'' Heidi said sheepishly. ''Quite obviously you're the living proof.''

Essex stared into his teacup as though seeing a vague picture on the bottom. ''It's true,'' he said finally. ''Besides his day-to-day observations of State Department procedure and a few photos in the family album, little remains of my grandfather's memory.''

''Can you recall him from your childhood?''

Essex solemnly shook his head. ''No, he died a young man of forty-two, the same year I was born.''

''Nineteen fourteen.''

''May twenty-eighth, to be exact.''

Heidi shot him a stunned look. ''Eight days after the treaty signing at the White House.''

''Think what you will, Commander,'' Essex said patiently. ''There was no treaty.''

''Surely you can't discount the evidence?''

''Bryan and my grandfather paid innumerable visits to the White House. The scribbling on the back of the photograph is undoubtedly an error. As to the letter, you've merely misconstrued its meaning.''

''The facts check out,'' Heidi persisted. ''The Sir Edward that Wilson writes of was Sir Edward Grey, Britain's foreign secretary. And a loan to Britain one week prior to the date on the letter for one hundred and fifty million dollars is a matter of record.''

''Granted that was a large sum at the time,'' Essex said knowledgeably. ''But prior to World War One, Great Britain was grappling with a program of social reform while purchasing armaments for the approaching conflict. Simply put, she needed a few bucks to tide her over until laws for higher taxation could be passed. The loan can hardly be called irregular. By today's international standards it would be considered a rather routine negotiation.''

Heidi stood up. ''I'm sorry to have troubled you, Mr. Essex. I won't take up any more of your afternoon.''

The twinkle returned in his eyes. ''You can trouble me anytime.''

At the door Heidi turned. ''One other thing. The library has a complete set of your grandfather's monthly desk diaries except the final one for May. It appears to be missing.''

Essex shrugged. "No great mystery. He died before he completed it. Probably lost in the shuffle when they cleaned out his office."

Essex stood at the window until Heidi's car disappeared into the trees. His shoulders drooped. He felt very tired and very old. He walked over to an ornately carved antique credenza and twisted the head of one of the four vacant-eyed cherubs adorning the corners. A small, flat drawer swung out from the bottom edge, a bare inch above the carpet. Inside rested a thin leatherbound book, its engraved cover cracked with age.

He sank into an overstuffed chair, adjusted his spectacles and began reading. It was a ritual, performed at varied intervals over the years. His eyes no longer saw the words on the pages; he had memorized them long ago.

He was still sitting there when the sun was gone and the shadows had stretched and melted into blackness. He clutched the book to his breast, his soul agonized by dread, his mind torn by indecision.

The past had caught up with a lonely old man in a darkened room.

12

Lieutenant Ewen Burton-Angus slipped his car into a parking stall at the Glen Echo Racquet Club, hoisted his tote bag from the passenger seat and hunched his shoulders against the cold. He hurried past the empty swimming pool and snow-coated tennis courts toward the warmth of the clubhouse.

He found the club manager seated at a table beneath a glass case stacked with rows of trophies.

"Can I help you?" asked the manager.

"Yes, my name's Burton-Angus. I'm a guest of Henry Argus."

The manager scrutinized a clipboard. "Right, Lieutenant Burton-Angus. Sorry, sir, but Mr. Argus called and said he couldn't make it. He told me to tell you he tried to catch you at the embassy, but you'd already left."

"A pity," said Burton-Angus. "As long as I'm here, do you have a racquetball court available where I can practice?"

"I had to reshuffle the reservations when Mr. Argus canceled. However, there is another gentleman who is playing alone. Perhaps you can pair up."

"Where can I find him?"

"He's seated in the bar. His court won't be free for another half hour. His name is Jack Murphy."

Burton-Angus found Murphy nursing a drink by a picture window overlooking the Chesapeake Canal. He introduced himself.

"Do you mind awfully having an opponent?"

"Not at all," said Murphy with an infectious smile. "Beats playing alone, providing you don't smear the court with me."

"Small chance of that."

"You play much racquetball?"

"Actually, squash is more my game."

"I'd guess that from your British accent." Murphy gestured to a chair. "Have a drink. Plenty of time before our court is free."

Burton-Angus welcomed the opportunity to relax and ordered a gin. "Beautiful countryside. The canal reminds me of one that runs near my home in Devon."

"Travels through Georgetown and into the Potomac River," Murphy said in his best tour-guide fashion. "When the water freezes in winter the local residents use it for skating and ice fishing."

"Do you work in Washington?" asked Burton-Angus.

"Yes, I'm the Senate historian. And you?"

"Aide to the naval attaché for the British embassy."

A detached expression crossed Murphy's face and it seemed to Burton-Angus that the American was staring right through him.

"Is something wrong?"

Murphy shook his head. "No, not at all. You being navy and British reminded me of a woman, a commander in the U.S. Navy who came to me searching for data concerning a treaty between our two countries."

"No doubt a trade treaty."

"I can't say. The strange part is that except for an old photograph, there is no record of it in Senate archives."

"A photograph?"

"Yes, with a notation about a North American Treaty."

"I'd be happy to have someone probe the embassy files for you."

"Please don't bother. It's not that important."

"No bother at all," insisted Burton-Angus. "Do you have a date?"

"On or about May twentieth, nineteen fourteen."

"Ancient history."

"Probably only a proposed treaty that was rejected."

"Nonetheless, I'll have a look," said Burton-Angus as his drink arrived. He held up the glass. "Cheers."

Sitting at his desk in the British embassy on Massachusetts Avenue, Alexander Moffat looked and acted like the archetype of a government official. With his hair trimmed short with an immaculately creased left-hand part, a ramrod spine and precise correctness in speech and mannerism, he and thousands of counterparts throughout the foreign service could have been stamped from the same cookie cutter. His desk was barren of all clutter; the only objects resting on its polished surface were his folded hands.

"I'm dreadfully sorry, Lieutenant, but I find nothing in the records department mentioning an Anglo-American treaty in early nineteen fourteen."

"Most peculiar," said Burton-Angus. "The American chap who gave me the information seemed reasonably certain such a treaty either existed or at least had been in the talk stage."

"Probably has his year wrong."

"I don't think so. He's the Senate historian. Not the type to muck up his facts and dates."

"Do you wish to pursue the matter?" asked Moffat in an official tone.

Burton-Angus clasped his hands thoughtfully. "Might be worth a check with the Foreign Office in London to clear the fog."

Moffat shrugged indifferently. "A vague clue to an unlikely event three-quarters of a century ago would hardly have a significant bearing on the present."

"Perhaps not. Still, I promised the fellow I'd see what I could find. Shall I make a formal request for an inquiry, in writing?"

"Not necessary. I'll phone an old school chum who heads up the signals department and ask him to have a run at the old records. He owes me a favor. Should have an answer this time tomorrow. Don't be disappointed if he fails to turn up anything."

"I won't," said Burton-Angus. "On the other hand, you never can tell what might be buried in Foreign Service archives."

13

Peter Beaseley knew more about the Foreign Office than any other man in London. As chief librarian in charge of records for over thirty years, he considered the entire history of British international affairs his private domain. He made a specialty of ferreting out policy blunders and scandalous intrigues, by diplomats past and present, that had been swept under the carpet of secrecy.

Beaseley ran a hand through a few strands of white hair and reached for one of several pipes littering a large circular tray. He sniffed at the official-looking paper on his desk as a cat might sniff at an uninviting meal.

"North American Treaty," he said aloud to the empty room. "Never heard of it."

In the minds of his staff it would have been a pronouncement from God. If Peter Beaseley had never heard of a treaty, it obviously did not exist.

He lit the pipe and idly watched the smoke. The year 1914 signaled the end of vintage diplomacy, he mused. After World War I the aristocratic elegance of international negotiation was replaced by mechanical maneuvers. It had become a shallow world indeed.

His secretary knocked and poked her head around the door. "Mr. Beaseley."

He looked up without really seeing her. "Yes, Miss Gosset."

"I'm going to lunch now."

"Lunch?" He took his watch from a vest pocket and gazed at it. "Oh yes, I'd lost all track of time. Where are you going to eat? Do you have a date?"

The two unexpected questions in sudden succession caught Miss Gosset by surprise. "Why, no, I'm eating quite alone. I thought I would try that new Indian restaurant on Glendower Place."

"Good, that settles it," Beaseley grandly announced. "You're lunching with me."

The invitation was a rare honor and Miss Gosset was surprised.

Beaseley caught her blank expression and smiled. "I have an ulterior motive, Miss Gosset. You may consider it a bribe. I need you to assist me in searching for an old treaty. Four eyes are faster than two. I don't want to waste too much time on this one."

She barely had time to slip on her coat before he hustled her outside and waved down a taxi with his umbrella.

"Sanctuary Building, Great Smith Street," Beaseley instructed the driver.

"With five buildings scattered about London crammed with old Foreign Office records," she said, adjusting a scarf, "it's a mystery to me how you know where to look."

"Correspondence dealing with the Americas during the year nineteen fourteen are shelved on the second floor of the east wing in the Sanctuary Building," he stated flatly.

Properly impressed, Miss Gosset remained silent until they reached their destination. Beaseley paid the driver, and they entered the lobby, showing their official credentials and signing in with the commissionaire. They took a rickety old elevator to the second floor. He walked unerringly to the correct section.

"You check April. I'll take May."

"You haven't told me what we're looking for," she said inquiringly.

"Any reference to a North American Treaty."

She felt there was more she needed to know, but Beaseley had already turned his back and was poring through a huge leather binder that held reams of yellowed official documents and department memoranda. She resigned herself to the inevitable and tackled the first volume of April 1914, wrinkling her nose at the musty odor.

After four hours, to the accompaniment of Miss Gosset's protesting stomach, they had turned up nothing. Beaseley replaced the binders and looked thoughtful.

"Excuse me, Mr. Beaseley, but about lunch?"

He looked at his watch. "I'm dreadfully sorry. I paid no attention to the time. Will you allow me to make that dinner?"

"I gratefully accept," sighed Miss Gosset.

They were signing out when Beaseley suddenly turned to the commissionaire.

"I'd like to examine the official secrets vault," he said. "My clearance allows me entry."

"But not the young lady," said the uniformed commissionaire, smiling politely. "Her pass only covers the library."

Beaseley patted Miss Gosset on the shoulder. "Please be patient a little longer. This shouldn't take but a few minutes."

He followed the commissionaire down three flights of stairs to the basement and up to a large iron door in a concrete wall. He watched as a pair of heavy brass keys turned the oiled tumblers of two immense antique padlocks without the least sound. The commissionaire pushed the door open and stood aside.

"I'll have to lock you in, sir," he said, parroting the book of regulations. "There is a telephone on the wall. Just ring three-two when you wish to leave."

"I'm aware of the procedure, thank you."

The file containing classified matter from the spring of 1914 was only forty pages thick and held no earth-shattering revelations. Beaseley was reinserting it in its slot when he noticed something odd.

Several of the files on each side protruded nearly half an inch from the rest of the neatly spaced row. He pulled them out.

Another file had somehow been shoved behind the others, keeping them from fitting evenly. He opened the cover. Across the title page of what looked to be a report were the words "North American Treaty."

He sat down at a metal table and began to read.

Ten minutes later, Beaseley had the look of a man who had been tapped on the shoulder in a cemetery at midnight. His trembling hands could scarcely punch out the correct telephone call buttons.

14

Heidi checked her boarding pass and looked up at the television monitor displaying the departure time of her flight.

"Another forty minutes to kill," she said.

"Time enough for a farewell drink," Pitt replied.

He steered her across the busy lobby of Dulles Airport to the cocktail lounge. Businessmen with loosened collars and wrinkled suits packed every corner. Pitt scrounged a small table and ordered from a passing waitress.

"I wish I could stay," she said wistfully.

"What's to stop you?"

"The navy frowns on officers who jump ship."

"When is your leave up?"

"I have to report to the Naval Communications Station in San Diego by noon tomorrow for assignment to sea duty."

He looked into her eyes. "It seems our romance is a victim of geography."

"We didn't give it much chance, did we?"

"Perhaps it was never meant to be," said Pitt.

Heidi stared at him. "That's what he said!"

"Who?"

"President Wilson in a letter."

Pitt laughed. "I'm afraid you've lost me."

"I'm sorry." She waved away the thought. "It was nothing."

"Sounds to me like your research is getting to you."

"Complications," she said. "I was sidetracked. It happens in research. You delve into one subject and find a fascinating bit of information that takes you on a totally different course."

The drinks came and Pitt paid the waitress. "You're sure you can't request an extension."

She shook her head. "If only I could. But I've used up all my accumulated leave time. It will be six months before I'm eligible again." Then suddenly her eyes came alive. "Why don't you come with me? We could have a few days together before I sail."

Pitt took her hand. "Sorry, dear heart, but my schedule won't permit it. I'm leaving myself, for a project in the Labrador Sea."

"How long will you be gone?"

"A month, maybe six weeks."

"Will we see each other again?" Her voice became soft.

"I'm a firm believer that good memories should be relived."

Twenty minutes later, after finishing their second drink, Pitt escorted Heidi to her boarding gate. Already the waiting area had cleared and the attendant behind the check-in counter was announcing the final call.

She set her purse and cosmetic case on a vacant chair and looked up at him through expectant eyes. He responded by kissing her. Then he tilted back his head and grinned. "There goes my macho reputation."

"How so?"

"As soon as word gets around that I was seen kissing a sailor, I'm through."

"You clown." She pulled his head down and kissed him long and hard. Finally she released him and blinked back the tears. "Goodbye, Dirk Pitt."

"Goodbye, Heidi Milligan."

She picked up her bags and walked toward the boarding ramp. Then she paused as though remembering something and returned. Fishing in her purse, she pulled out an envelope and pushed it into his hand.

"Listen! Read these papers," she said urgently. "They explain what's been sidetracking me. And . . . Dirk . . . There may be something here. Something important. See what you think. If you feel it's worth pursuing, call me in San Diego."

Before Pitt could reply, she had turned and was gone.

15

They say that after death, there is no more idyllic setting in which to await eternity than the graveyard of an English village. Nestled about the parish church in timeless tranquillity, the headstones stand moss-covered and mute, their carved names and dates eroded and seldom readable farther back than the nineteenth century.

Outside of London, in the tucked-away village of Manuden, a solitary bell tolled for a funeral. It was a chilly but beautiful day, the sun skirting rolling masses of pearl-tinted clouds.

Fifty or sixty people clustered about a flag-draped military coffin as the local vicar delivered the eulogy.

A regal-looking woman in her early sixties heard none of it. Her attention was focused on a man who stood alone, several paces away from the outer edge of the mourners.

He must be sixty-six, she thought. His black, carelessly brushed hair was sprinkled with gray and had receded slightly. The face was still handsome, but the ruthless look had softened. With a slight tinge of envy she noted that he maintained a trim and fit shape, while she had tended to spread. His eyes were aimed at the church steeple, his thoughts distant.

Only after the coffin was lowered into the ground and the crowd had dispersed did he step forward and stare into the grave as though piercing a window to the past.

"The years have treated you well," she said, coming up behind him.

He turned and recognized her presence for the first time. Then he smiled the old engaging smile she recalled so well and kissed her on the cheek.

"How incredible, you look even more sensuous than I remembered."

"You haven't changed," she laughed, self-consciously patting her gray hair with its few remaining sandy strands. "The same old flatterer."

"How long has it been?"

"You left the service twenty-five years ago."

"God, it seems two centuries at least."

"Your name is Brian Shaw now."

"Yes." Shaw nodded at the coffin waiting for the diggers to cover it. "He insisted I take a new identity when I retired."

"A wise move. You had more enemies than Attila the Hun. The SMERSH agent who assassinated you would have become a Soviet hero."

"No need to worry any longer." He smiled. "I doubt if my old adversaries are still alive. Besides, I'm an old has-been. My head isn't worth the price of a liter of petrol."

"You never married." It was a statement, not a question.

He shook his head. "Only briefly, but she was killed. You remember."

She flushed slightly. "I guess I never really accepted you as having a wife."

"And you?"

"A year after you left. My husband worked in the cryptographic analysis section. His name is Graham Huston. We live in London and manage nicely with our pensions and the profits of an antique shop."

"Not quite like the old days."

"Are you still living in the West Indies?"

"It became rather unhealthy, so I came home. Bought a small working farm on the Isle of Wight."

"I can't picture you as a gentleman farmer."

"Ditto for you selling antiques."

The gravediggers appeared from a pub across the road and took up their shovels. Soon the dirt was slapping against the wooden top of the coffin.

"I loved that old man," Shaw said wistfully. "There were times I wanted to kill him, and there were times I wished I could have embraced him as a father."

"He had a special affection for you too," she said. "He always fussed and worried when you were on an assignment. The other agents he treated more like chess pieces."

"You knew him better than anyone," he said softly. "A man has few secrets from his secretary of twenty years."

She gave a slight, perceptible nod. "It used to annoy him. I came to read his thoughts on many occasions . . ."

Her voice faltered and she could no longer bear to look at the grave. She turned away, and Shaw took her arm and led her from the churchyard.

"Have you time for a drink?"

She opened her handbag, picked out a tissue and sniffled into it. "I really must be getting back to London."

"Then it's goodbye, Mrs. Huston."

"Brian." She uttered the sound as if it stuck in her throat, yet she refrained from speaking his real name. "I will never get used to thinking of you as Brian Shaw."

"The two people we were died long before our old chief," Shaw said gently.

She squeezed his hand and her eyes were moist. "A pity we can't relive the past."

Before he could answer she pulled an envelope from her purse and slipped it into the side pocket of his overcoat. He said nothing, nor did he appear to notice.

"Goodbye, Mr. Shaw," she said in a voice he could hardly hear. "Take care of yourself."

A cold evening sleet lashed London as the diesel engine of a black Austin cab knocked to an idle in front of a large stone building in Hyde

Park. Shaw paid the driver and stepped out to the pavement. He stood for a few moments, ignoring the particles of wind-driven ice that pelted his face, staring up at the ugly edifice where he had once worked.

The windows were dirty and streaked and the walls bore soot and pollution from half a century of neglect. Shaw thought it odd that the building had never been sandblasted as had so many others around the city.

He climbed the steps and entered the lobby. A security guard matter-of-factly asked to see his identification and checked his name against a list of scheduled appointments.

"Please take the lift to the tenth floor," said the guard. "Someone will meet you."

The lift trembled and rattled as it always had, but the operator was gone, replaced by a panel of buttons. Shaw stopped the lift on the ninth floor and walked into the corridor. He found his old office and opened the door, expecting to see a secretary busily typing in the front area and a man sitting at his desk in the rear.

He was numbed to find the two rooms empty except for a few pieces of dusty litter.

He shook his head sadly. Who was it who said you can't go home again?

At least the stairway was where it was supposed to be, even though the security guard was no longer there. He climbed to the tenth floor and stepped out behind a blond girl, wearing a loose-fitting knit dress, who was facing the lift.

"I believe you're waiting for me," he said.

She whirled around startled. "Mr. Shaw?"

"Yes, sorry for the delay, but since this is a bit like old home week I thought I'd take a nostalgic tour."

The girl looked at him with ill-concealed curiosity. "The brigadier is waiting for you, please follow me."

She knocked on the familiar door and opened it.

"Mr. Shaw, sir."

Except for a different desk and the man rising behind it, the book-cases and fixtures were the same. At last he felt as though he was on home ground.

"Mr. Shaw, do come in."

Brigadier General Morris V. Simms extended a hand that was firm and dry. The peacock-blue eyes had a fluid friendliness to them, but

Shaw wasn't fooled. He could feel their gaze reading him like a computerized body scan.

"Please be seated."

Shaw sat in a tall-armed chair that was hard as marble. A rather unimaginative ploy, he thought, designed to place the brigadier's callers with an uncomfortable handicap. His former chief would have cursed such amateurish pettiness.

He noticed that the desk was untidy. Files were carelessly piled, several of their headings facing upside down. And there were indications of dust. Not spread evenly on the desk top, but in places where dust was not supposed to be. The upper rims of the In and Out baskets, under the receiver of the telephone, between the edges of papers protruding from their file covers.

Suddenly Shaw saw through the sham.

First there was the missing elevator operator who used to ensure that visitors went where they were sent. Then the missing security guards who had patrolled the stairways and acted as receptionists on every floor. Then there was his deserted office.

His former section of the British Secret Intelligence Service was no longer in this building.

The whole scene was a mock-up, a stage erected to act out a play for his benefit.

Brigadier Simms dropped stiffly into his chair and stared across at Shaw. There was no giveaway expression on the smooth soldier's face. It was as inscrutable as a jade Buddha.

"I suppose this is your first trip to the old haunt since you retired."

Shaw nodded. "Yes." He found it strange to sit in this room opposite a younger man.

"Must look about the same to you."

"There's been a few changes."

Simms' left eyebrow lifted slightly. "You no doubt mean in personnel."

"Time clouds one's memory," Shaw replied philosophically.

The eyebrow slipped back into place. "You must be wondering why I asked you to come?"

"Having an invitation stuck in my pocket during a funeral struck me as a bit theatrical," said Shaw. "You could have simply posted a letter or called on the telephone."

Simms gave him a frosty smile. "I have my reasons, sound reasons."

Shaw decided to remain aloof. He didn't like Simms and he saw no reason to be anything but civil. "You obviously didn't request my presence for a section reunion."

"No," Simms said, pulling out a bottom drawer and casually resting a highly polished shoe on it. "Actually I'd like to put you back in harness."

Shaw was stunned. What in hell was going on? He was amazed to feel a wave of excitement course through him. "I can't believe the service is so hard up it has to recall decrepit old agents from the rubbish heap."

"You're too hard on yourself, Mr. Shaw. You were perhaps the best the service ever recruited. You became something of a legend in your own time."

"A canker that led to my forced retirement."

"Be that as it may, I have an assignment that fits your talents like a glove. It requires a mature man with brains. There will be no call for physical agility or bloodletting. It's purely a case for investigative skill and wits. Despite your qualms about age, I have little question that a man of your experience can bring it off."

Shaw's mind was whirling. He was finding it difficult to make sense of Simms' statements. "Why me? There must be an army of other agents who are better qualified. And the Russians. They never throw out their files. The KGB will have me pegged an hour after I resurface."

"This is the era of electronic brains, Mr. Shaw. Section heads no longer sit in stuffy old offices and make opinionated decisions. All data on current assignments are now fed into computers. We leave it to their memory banks to tell us which agent is best suited to send out. Apparently they took a dim view of our present crop. So we programmed a list of retirees. Your name popped out at the top. As to the Russians, you are not to worry. You won't be dealing with them."

"Can you tell me what it is I'm so ideally suited for?"

"A watchdog job."

"If not the Russians, then who?"

"The Americans."

Shaw sat silent, not sure he heard right. Finally he said, "Sorry, Brigadier, but your robots made a mistake. Granted, I've never thought the Americans as civilized as the British, but they're a good

people. During my years in the service I formed many warm rela-
tionships with them. I've worked closely with men in the CIA. I refuse
to spy on them. I think you better find someone else."

Simms' face reddened. "You're overreacting. Listen to the facts,
Mr. Shaw. I'm not asking you to steal classified information from the
Yanks; only keep an eye on them for a few weeks. Not to sound
maudlin, but this is a matter which could very well threaten Her
Majesty's government."

"I stand rebuked," said Shaw. "Please continue."

"Thank you," Simms replied haughtily. "All right, then. Routine
investigation into something called the North American Treaty. A
rusty can of worms the Americans have dug up. You're to learn what
they know and if they intend to do anything about it."

"Sounds vague. What exactly is this treaty business?"

"I think it best if you weren't privy to its ramifications just yet,"
Simms said without elaboration.

"I understand."

"No, you don't, but that's neither here nor there. Care to give it a
go?"

Shaw was torn momentarily by indecision. His reflexes had faded,
his strength was half what it once had been. He could not read without
glasses. He could still bring down a grouse at fifty yards with a shotgun, but he had not fired a pistol in twenty years. Shaw did not dodge
the fact that he was an aging man.

"My farm . . . ?"

"Run by a professor of agronomy in your absence." Simms smiled.
"You'll find us more liberal with our purse strings than during your
day. I might add that the eighty acres you've been dickering for that
border your farm will be purchased in your name, courtesy of the
service, when you finish the assignment."

Times had changed, but the section's efficiency had not. Shaw was
never aware he was under surveillance. He was indeed getting old.

"You make it extremely difficult to say no, Brigadier."

"Then say yes."

The old line "In for a penny, in for a pound" ran through Shaw's
mind. Then he shrugged and spoke with the old self-assurance.

"I'll give it a try."

Simms rapped the desk with his fist. "Jolly good." He pulled open
a drawer and threw an envelope in front of Shaw. "Your airline

tickets, traveler's checks and hotel reservations. You'll go under your new identity, of course. Is your passport in order?''

"Yes," replied Shaw. "It will take me a fortnight to clean up my affairs.''

Simms waved a hand airily. "Your plane leaves in two days. Everything will be taken care of. Good hunting.''

Shaw's face tensed. "You were pretty damned sure of me.''

Simms' lips spread into a toothy smile. "I was betting on an old warhorse who yearns for one more battle.''

It was Shaw's turn to smile. He wasn't going to exit looking insipid. "Then why the clandestine crap?''

Simms stiffened. His face took on a cornered look. He said nothing.

"The masquerade," snapped Shaw. "This building hasn't been used for years. We could have just as easily met on a park bench.''

"It was that obvious?'' Simms said in a quiet voice.

"You might as well have posted a sign.''

Simms shrugged. "Perhaps I went to extremes, but the Americans have an uncanny way of knowing what goes on in British intelligence circles. Besides, it was necessary to see if you still possessed your powers of perception.''

"A test.''

"Call it what you will.'' Simms rose to his feet and walked around the desk. He offered his hand to Shaw. "I am sincerely sorry to have mucked up your schedule. I do not relish depending on someone who is out of his prime, but I am a blind man in a fog and you are my only hope to guide me out.''

Ten minutes later, Brigadier Simms and his secretary stood side by side in the lift as it rattled down to the lobby. She was adjusting a rain cap on her head while Simms seemed deep in thought.

"He was a strange one," she said.

Simms looked up. "I'm sorry.''

"Mr. Shaw. He moves like a cat. Gave me a fright the way he sneaked up behind me when I was expecting him to step out of the lift.''

"He came up the stairs?''

"From the ninth floor," she said. "I could tell from the pause in the indicator.''

"I rather hoped he'd do that," said Simms. "Makes it comforting to know he hasn't lost his devious touch.''

"He seemed a friendly old fellow."

Simms smiled. "That friendly old fellow has killed over twenty men."

"Would have fooled me."

"He'll need to fool a lot of people," Simms muttered as the lift door clanked open. "He has no idea of the massive stakes riding on his shoulders. It may well be we have thrown the poor bastard to the sharks."

16

An officer in a Royal Navy uniform stepped forward as Brian Shaw cleared airport customs.

"Mr. Shaw?"

"Yes, I'm Shaw."

"Lieutenant Burton-Angus, British embassy. Sorry about not seeing you through customs; I was held up in traffic. Welcome to Washington."

As they shook hands, Shaw cast a disapproving eye at the uniform. "A bit open, aren't we?"

"Not at all." Burton-Angus smiled. "If I suddenly showed up at the airport in mufti, someone might think I was playing cloak and dagger. Better to appear routine."

"Which way to the luggage claim?"

"Not necessary. Actually, I'm afraid your stay in the capital city has been cut rather short."

Shaw got the picture. "When does my plane leave and where am I going?"

"You depart for Los Angeles in forty minutes. Here is your ticket and boarding pass."

"Shall we discuss it?"

"Of course." Burton-Angus took Shaw by the arm. "I suggest we talk while mingling with the crowd. Makes it difficult for an eavesdropper, human or electronic."

Shaw nodded in understanding. "Been in the service long?"

"General Simms recruited me six years ago." Burton-Angus steered him to the book section of a gift shop. "You know of my involvement with your job."

"I read the report. You're the chap who discovered the first clue to the treaty."

"Yes, from the Senate historian."

"Jack Murphy."

Burton-Angus nodded.

"Were you able to get any more information out of him?" Shaw asked.

"General Simms thought it best not to press him. I told Murphy London had no record of the treaty."

"He bought it?"

"He had no reason not to."

"So we write Murphy off and begin somewhere else," said Shaw.

"The reason you're going to Los Angeles," Burton-Angus told him. "Murphy became aware of the treaty when a naval officer, a woman, made an inquiry. He found an old photograph and made her a copy. One of our people burglarized his office and scanned the file on research requests. The only female naval officer whose name appeared was a Lieutenant Commander Heidi Milligan."

"Any chance of reaching her?"

"Commander Milligan is communications officer on board an amphibious landing transport vessel bound for the Indian Ocean. It sailed from San Diego two hours ago."

Shaw stopped. "With Milligan out of reach, where does that leave us?"

"Fortunately, her ship, the U.S.S. *Arvada,* is under orders to lay over in Los Angeles harbor for three days. Something to do with modifications to the automated steering system."

They walked on. Shaw looked at the lieutenant with a growing respect. "You're very well informed."

"Part of the job." Burton-Angus shrugged modestly. "The Americans have few secrets from the British."

"That's a comforting thought."

Burton-Angus flushed slightly. "We better move along to the concourse. Your plane departs at gate twenty-two."

"Since there's been a change of plan," said Shaw, "I'd be interested in learning my new instructions."

"I thought it obvious," Burton-Angus replied. "You have approximately seventy-two hours to find out what Commander Milligan knows.''

''I'll need help.''

''After you've settled into your hotel, you'll be contacted by a Mr. Graham Humberly, a rather well-heeled Rolls-Royce dealer. He'll arrange for you to meet Commander Milligan.''

''He'll arrange for me to meet Commander Milligan,'' Shaw repeated, his tone sarcastic.

''Why, yes,'' said Burton-Angus, momentarily taken back by Shaw's evident skepticism. ''Humberly is a former British subject. The man cultivates an enormous channel of important contacts, particularly in the U.S. Navy.''

''And he and I are going to march up the gangplank of an American naval vessel, waving the Union Jack and whistling 'Brittania rules the waves,' and demand to interrogate a ship's officer.''

''If anybody can do it, Humberly can,'' Burton-Angus said resolutely.

Shaw drew deeply on his cigarette and stared at the lieutenant.

''Why me?'' he asked stonily.

''The way I understand it, Mr. Shaw, you were once the most able operative in the service. You know your way around Americans. Also, Humberly is planning on introducing you as a British businessman, an old friend from his Royal Navy days who also achieved fleet rank. Naturally, you're the right age.''

''Sounds logical.''

''General Simms is not expecting miracles. But we've got to go through the motions. The best we can hope from Milligan is that she proves to be a stepping-stone.''

''One more time,'' Shaw said. ''Why me?''

Burton-Angus stopped and looked up at the televised departure schedules. ''Your plane is on time. Here are your tickets. Don't worry about the luggage. It's been taken care of.''

''I assumed as much.''

''Well I guess what it came down to was your past record of . . . ah . . . shall we say, successful dealings with members of the opposite sex. General Simms thought it an asset. Of course, the fact that Commander Milligan recently had an intimate affair with an admiral twice her age rolled the dice in your favor.''

Shaw gave him a withering stare. ''Just goes to show what you've got to look forward to someday, laddy.''

"Nothing personal." Burton-Angus smiled wanly.

"You say you've been in the service six years?"

"And four months, to be more precise."

"Did they teach you how to detect a surveillance blind?"

Burton-Angus' eyes narrowed questioningly. "The class was mandatory. Why do you ask?"

"Because you flunked," Shaw said. He let it sink in a moment and then tilted his head to the left. "The man with the metal attaché case, staring innocently at his watch. He's been glued to us since we left the customs exit. Also, the stewardess in the Pan American uniform about twenty feet behind. Her airline is on another concourse. She's his backup. They'll have a third eye lurking ahead of us. I haven't fixed him yet."

Burton-Angus visibly paled. "Not possible," he muttered. "They can't be on to us."

Shaw turned and showed his ticket and passed it to the girl at the boarding entrance. Then he refaced the lieutenant.

"It would seem," he said in his best sardonic voice, "that the British have few secrets from the Americans."

He left Burton-Angus standing there looking like a drowning man.

Shaw sat back in his seat, relaxed, and felt in the mood for champagne. The stewardess brought him two small bottles with plastic glasses. The labels said California. He would have preferred a Tattinger, brut reserve vintage. California bubbly and plastic glasses, he mused. Would the Americans ever become civilized?

After he had polished off one bottle, he took stock. The CIA had put the finger on him the instant he boarded the plane in England, just as he knew General Simms knew they would.

Shaw was worried not at all. He operated better when things were out in the open. Skulking around alleys like an unperson was never to his liking. He felt exhilarated to be doing what he had once done so well. His senses had not left him—a shade slower perhaps, but still sharp enough.

He was playing his kind of game and he reveled in it.

17

The dingy gas station stood on a corner in the industrial outskirts of Ottawa. Erected soon after the Second World War, it was a square steel structure with one island containing three gas pumps that were scarred from years of hard use and badly in need of new paint. Inside the office, cans of oil and mummified flies littered dusty shelves while the windows, streaked with grime, displayed faded signs advertising some long forgotten tire sale.

Henri Villon turned his Mercedes-Benz sedan in over the driveway and stopped at the pumps. An attendant in grease-stained coveralls stepped out from under a car on the lube rack and approached, wiping his hands on a rag.

"What'll it be?" he asked with a bored expression.

"Fill it, please," answered Villon.

The attendant eyed an elderly man and woman sitting on a nearby bus bench, and then spoke in a tone they could not fail to overhear. "Five gallons is the government limit, you know, the oil shortage being what it is."

Villon nodded silently and the attendant pumped the gas. When he finished he went around to the front of the car and pointed. Villon pulled the release lever and the attendant raised the hood.

"You better take a look at your fan belt. She looks pretty worn."

Villon got out of the car and leaned on the fender opposite the attendant. He said in an undertone, "Do you have any idea of the unholy mess your bungling has caused?"

Foss Gly stared back across the engine. "What's done is done. The weather closed in at the last minute and the first missile lost the target. It's that simple."

"It's not that simple!" Villon snapped back. "Nearly fifty people killed for nothing. If the air safety inspectors discover the true cause of the crash, Parliament will be in an uproar demanding investigations into every organization, including the Boy Scouts. The news media will cry for blood after they learn twenty of their top political journalists were murdered. And the worst of it is, the Free Quebec Society will be suspected by all.''

"No one will trace the blame to the FQS." Gly's voice was cold and final.

"Damn!" Villon struck the fender with his fist. "If only Sarveux had died. The government would be in confusion and we could have made our move on Quebec."

"Your buddies in the Kremlin would have loved that."

"I won't be able to count on their support if we have another setback of this magnitude."

Gly extended a hand toward the engine as though he was working on it. "Why get cozy with the reds? Once they get their hooks in you, they never let loose."

"Not that it concerns you, but a government along Communist lines is Quebec's only hope of standing alone."

Gly shrugged indifferently and continued to pretend to work on the engine. "What do you want from me?"

Villon considered. "No percentage in panic. I think it best if you and your team of specialists, as you call them, continue your cover employment as usual. None of you are French, so it's doubtful you'll come under suspicion."

"I can't see the percentages in waiting around to get caught."

"You forget that since I am minister of internal affairs, all security matters pass through my office. Any leads pointing to you will be quietly lost in bureaucratic red tape."

"I'd still feel safer if we left the country."

"You underestimate events, Mr. Gly. My government is cracking at the seams. The provinces are snapping at one another's throats. The only question is, When will Canada shatter? I know it's coming, Charles Sarveux knows it, and so do those English stiff-necks who outspeech each other in that old stone relic by the Thames River. Soon, very soon, Canada, as the world knows her, will be no more. Believe me, you will be lost in the chaos."

"Lost and out of a job."

"A temporary situation," said Villon, his tone heavy with cynicism. "As long as there are governments, financial corporations and wealthy individuals who can afford your special bag of dirty tricks, Mr. Gly, your kind will never be forced to sell vacuum cleaners for a living."

Gly gave an indolent twist to his head and changed the subject. "How can I get in touch with you in case of a problem?"

Villon moved around the front of the car and clutched Gly's upper arm in an iron grip. "Two things you must remember. First, there will be no more problems. And second, under no circumstances are you to attempt contact with me. I cannot run the slightest risk of being tied to the FQS."

Gly's eyes closed for a brief instant of surprise and pain. He sucked in a breath and flexed the bicep as Villon increased the pressure. The two men stood there, neither giving an inch. Then, very slowly, a taut grin of satisfaction began to stretch Gly's lips and he glared into Villon's eyes.

Villon released his grasp and smiled grimly. "My compliments. Your strength and dimensions very nearly match mine."

Gly fought back an urge to massage the stabbing pain in his arm. "Lifting weights is as good a way as any to kill time between assignments."

"One can almost detect a faint resemblance between our facial features," said Villon, climbing behind the wheel of the Mercedes. "Except for your repulsive nose, we might be taken for brothers."

"Stick it in your ear, Villon!" The belligerence in Gly's voice was unmistakable. He glanced at the old couple still perched on the bench waiting for a bus, and then at the meter on the gas pump. "That'll be eighteen sixty."

"Charge it!" Villon snarled, and drove off.

18

Villon buttered a slice of breakfast toast and read the caption on page two of his morning newspaper.

NO LEADS IN TERRORIST ATTACK
ON PRIME MINISTER'S PLANE

Foss Gly had covered his tracks well. Villon kept his hand on the investigation, and he knew that with each passing day the scent grew colder. He subtly used the influence of his office to play down any connection between the assassins and the FQS unless definite proof was found. So far things were working smoothly.

His satisfaction faded to a chill as Villon thought of Gly. The man was nothing but a savage mercenary whose god was a fat price. There was no telling how a mad dog like Gly might run if he wasn't held on a tight leash.

Villon's wife came to the doorway of the breakfast room. She was a pretty woman with dark brown hair and blue eyes. "There's a phone call for you in the study," she said.

He entered the study, closed the door and picked up the phone. "This is Villon."

"Superintendent McComb, sir," came a voice as deep as a coal pit. "I hope I'm not interrupting your breakfast."

"Not at all," Villon lied. "You're the officer in charge of Mounted Police records?"

"Yes, sir," McComb replied. "The file you requested on Max Roubaix is on the desk in front of me. Shall I make a copy and send it to your office?"

"Not necessary," said Villon. "Please give me the basics over the phone."

"It's a bit bulky," McComb hedged.

"A five-minute capsule will do." Villon smiled to himself. He could almost imagine McComb's state of mind. No doubt a family man who was irritated as hell at having to leave a warm bed and a warm wife and a Sunday sleep-in to dig through old dusty records to satisfy the whim of a cabinet minister.

"The pages are over a hundred years old, so they're written in hand script, but I'll do my best. Let's see now, Roubaix's early life is sketchy. No date of birth. Listed as an orphan who drifted from family to family. First official record is age twelve. He was up before a local constable for killing chickens."

"You did say chickens?"

"Snipped off their heads with wire cutters in wholesale lots. He worked off damages to the farmer whose stock he had decimated. Then he moved to the next town and graduated to horses. Cut the throats of half a herd before he was apprehended."

"A juvenile psychopath with a bloodlust."

"People simply wrote him off as the village idiot in those days," said McComb. "Psychotic motivation was not in their dictionaries. They failed to understand that a boy who slaughtered animals for the hell of it was only one step away from doing the same to humans. Roubaix was sentenced to two years in jail for the horse bloodbath, but because of his age, fourteen, he was allowed to live with the constable, working off his time as a gardener and houseboy. Not long after his release, people in the surrounding countryside began to find the bodies of tramps and drunks who had been strangled."

"Where did all this take place?"

"A radius of fifty miles around the present city of Moose Jaw, Alberta."

"Surely Roubaix was arrested as a prime suspect?"

"The Mounties didn't work as fast in the nineteenth century as we do now," McComb admitted. "By the time Roubaix was tied to the crimes, he had fled into the virgin forests of the Northwest Territory and didn't turn up again until Riel's rebellion in eighteen eighty-five."

"The revolt by the descendants of French traders and Indians," said Villon, recalling his history.

"Métis, they were called. Louis Riel was their leader. Roubaix joined Riel's forces and enshrined himself in Canadian legend as our most prolific killer."

"What about the time he was missing?"

"Six years," McComb replied. "Nothing recorded. There was a rash of unsolved killings attributed to him, but no solid evidence or eyewitness accounts. Only a pattern that hinted of the Roubaix touch."

"A pattern?"

"Yes, all the victims were done in by injuries inflicted on the throat," said McComb. "Mostly from strangulation. Roubaix had turned away from the messy use of a knife. No great fuss was made at the time. People had a different set of moral codes then. They looked upon a scourge who eliminated undesirables as a community benefactor."

"I seem to remember he became a legend by killing a number of Mounties during Riel's rebellion."

"Thirteen, to be exact."

"Roubaix must have been a very strong man."

"Not really," replied McComb. "Actually he was described as frail of build and rather sickly. A doctor who attended him before his execution testified that Roubaix was racked by consumption—what we now call tuberculosis."

"How was it possible for such a weakling to overpower men who were trained for physical combat?" asked Villon.

"Roubaix used a garrote made from rawhide not much thicker than a wire. A nasty weapon that cut halfway into his victim's throat. Caught them unaware, usually when they were asleep. Your reputation is well known in body-building circles, Mr. Villon, but I daresay your own wife could choke you away if she slipped Roubaix's garrote around your neck some night in bed."

"You talk as if the garrote still exists."

"It does," said McComb. "We have it on display in the criminal section of the Mountie museum, if you care to view it. Like some other mass killers who cherished a favorite murder weapon, Roubaix lavished loving care on his garrote. The wooden hand grips that attach to the thong are intricately carved in the shape of timber wolves. It's really quite a piece of craftsmanship."

"Perhaps I'll have a look at it when my schedule permits," said Villon without enthusiasm. He pondered a moment, trying to make sense out of Sarveux's instructions to Danielle in the hospital. It didn't add up. A riddle of ciphers. Villon took a flyer on another tack. "If you had to describe Roubaix's case, how would you sum it up in a single sentence?"

"I'm not sure I know what you're after," said McComb.

"Let me put it another way. What was Max Roubaix?"

There was silence for a few moments. Villon could almost hear the gears turn in McComb's head. Finally the Mountie said, "I guess you could call him a homicidal maniac with a fetish for the stranglehold."

Villon tensed and then relaxed again. "Thank you, superintendent."

"If there is anything else . . ."

"No, you've done me a service, and I'm grateful."

Villon slowly replaced the receiver. He looked into space, focusing on the impression of a sickly man twisting a garrote. The stunned expression of incomprehension on the face of the prey. A final glimpse before the bulging eyes turned sightless.

Sarveux's delirious ravings to Danielle suddenly began to make a shred of sense.

19

Sarveux lay in the hospital bed and nodded as Deputy Prime Minister Malcolm Hunt was ushered into his hospital room. He smiled. "It was good of you to come, Malcolm. I'm well aware of the hell you're going through with the House of Commons."

Out of habit, Hunt held out his hand, but quickly withdrew it on seeing the salve-coated arms of the Prime Minister.

"Pull up a chair and get comfortable," Sarveux said graciously. "Smoke if you care to."

"The effects of my pipe might lose me the medical vote come next election," Hunt smiled. "Thank you, but I'd better pass."

Sarveux came straight to the point. "I have talked with the director of air safety. He assures me that the tragedy at James Bay was no accident."

Hunt's face whitened suddenly. "How can he be positive?"

"A piece of engine cowling was found a half mile beyond the runway," Sarveux explained. "Analysis showed fragments embedded in it that matched a type of rocket used by the army's Argo ground-to-air launcher. An inventory at the Val Jalbert Arsenal discovered two were missing, along with several warheads."

"Good lord." Hunt's voice trembled. "That means all those people on your aircraft were murdered."

"The evidence points in that direction," Sarveux said placidly.

"The Free Quebec Society," said Hunt, turning angry. "I can think of no one else who could be responsible."

"I agree, but their guilt may never be proved."

"Why not?" asked Hunt. "The FQS are either out of touch with reality or complete idiots to think they could get away with it. The Mounties will never permit the terrorists behind a crime of such magnitude to escape unpunished. As a radical movement they are finished."

"Do not be too optimistic, old friend. My attempted assassination does not fall into the same category as the bombings, kidnappings and slayings of the last forty years. Those were carried out by political amateurs, belonging to FQS cells, who were apprehended and convicted. The slaughter at James Bay was conceived and directed by professionals. That much is known by the fact they left no trace of their existence. The best guess by the chief commissioner of the Mounties is that they were hired from outside the country.''

Hunt's eyes were steady. ''The FQS terrorists might yet push us into a state of civil war.''

''That must not come to pass,'' Sarveux said quietly. ''I will not allow it.''

''It was you who threatened the use of troops to keep the separatists in line.''

Sarveux smiled a dry smile. ''A bluff. You are the first to know. I never intended a military occupation of Quebec. Repression of a hostile people would solve nothing.''

Hunt reached in his pocket. ''I believe I'll have that pipe now.''

''Please do.''

The two men sat silent while the deputy prime minister puffed his briar bowl to life. Finally he blew a blue cloud toward the ceiling.

''So what happens now?'' asked Hunt.

''The Canada we know will disintegrate while we stand helpless to prevent it,'' answered Sarveux sadly. ''A totally independent Quebec was inevitable from the start. Sovereignty-association was merely a half-assed measure. Now Alberta wants to go it alone. Ontario and British Columbia are making rumblings about nationhood.''

''You fought a good fight to keep us together, Charles. No one can deny you that.''

''A mistake,'' said Sarveux. ''Instead of a delaying action, you and I, the party, the nation, should have planned for it. Too late; we are faced with a Canada divided forever.''

''I can't accept your ominous forecast,'' Hunt said, but the life had gone out of his voice.

''The gap between your English-speaking provinces and my French Quebec is too great to span with patriotic words,'' said Sarveux, staring Hunt in the eyes. ''You are of British descent, a graduate of Oxford. You belong to the elite who have always dominated the political and economic structure of this land. You are the establishment. Your children study in classrooms under a photograph of the Queen. French Quebec children, on the other hand, are stared down upon by Charles de Gaulle. And, as you know, they have little opportunity for financial success or a prominent position in society.''

"But we are all Canadians," Hunt protested.

"No, not all. There is one among us who has sold out to Moscow."

Hunt was startled. He jerked the pipe from between his teeth. "Who?" he asked incredulously. "Who are you talking about?"

"The leader of the FQS," answered Sarveux. "I learned before my trip to James Bay that he has made deals with the Soviet Union that will take effect after Quebec leaves the confederation. What's worse, he has the ear of Jules Guerrier."

Hunt appeared lost. "The premier of Quebec? I can't believe that. Jules is French-Canadian to the core. He has little love for communism and makes no secret of his hate for the FQS."

"But Jules, like ourselves, has always assumed we were dealing with a terrorist from the gutter. A mistake. The man is no simple misguided radical. I'm told he holds a high position in our government."

"Who is he? How did you come by this information?"

Sarveux shook his head. "Except to say that it comes from outside the country, I cannot reveal my source, even to you. As to the traitor's name, I can't be certain. The Russians refer to him by various code names. His true identity is a well-kept secret."

"My God, what if something should happen to Jules?"

"Then the Parti Québécois would crumble and the FQS could step into the vacuum."

"What you're suggesting is that Russia will have a toehold in the middle of North America."

"Yes," Sarveux said ominously. "Exactly."

20

Henri Villon stared through the windows of the James Bay control booth, the grim smile of satisfaction on his face reflected in the spotless glass.

The riddle of Roubaix's garrote lay on the great generator floor below.

Behind him, Percival Stuckey stood in apprehensive confusion. "I must protest this act," he said. "It is beyond decency."

Villon turned and stared at Stuckey, his eyes cold. "As a member of Parliament and Mr. Sarveux's minister of internal affairs, I can assure you this test is of utmost concern to the country, and decency has nothing to do with it."

"It's highly irregular," Stuckey muttered stubbornly.

"Spoken like a true official," Villon said in a cynical tone. "Now then, can you do what your government asks of you?"

Stuckey pondered a moment. "The diversion of millions of kilowatts is quite complex and involves intricate lead and frequency control with correct timing. Though most of the excess power surge will be grounded, we'll still be throwing a heavy overload on our own systems."

"Can you do it?" Villon persisted.

"Yes." Stuckey shrugged in defeat. "But I fail to see the purpose in cutting power to every city between Minneapolis and New York."

"Five seconds," Villon said, ignoring Stuckey's probing remark. "You have only to shut off electrical energy to the United States for five seconds."

Stuckey gave a final glare of defiance and leaned between the engineers seated at the console and twisted several knobs. The overhead television monitors brightened and focused on varied panoramic views of city skylines.

"The contrast seems to lighten as you scan from left to right," noted Villon.

"The darker cities are Boston, New York and Philadelphia." Stuckey looked at his watch. "It's dusk in Chicago and the sun is still setting in Minneapolis."

"How will we know if full blackout is achieved with one city under daylight?"

Stuckey made a slight adjustment and the Minneapolis monitor zoomed to a busy intersection. The image was so clear that Villon could identify the street signs on the corner of Third Street and Hennepin Avenue.

"The traffic signals. We can tell when their lights go dark."

"Will Canadian power go off as well?"

"Only in towns near the border below our interconnect terminals."

The engineers made a series of movements over the console and paused. Stuckey turned and fixed Villon with a steady stare. "I will not be held responsible for the consequences."

"Your objections are duly noted," Villon replied.

He gazed at the monitors as a cold finger of indecision tugged his mind, followed by a torrent of last-second doubts. The strain of what he was about to do settled heavily about his shoulders. Five seconds. A warning that could not be dismissed. Finally he cast off all fears and nodded.

"You may proceed."

Then he watched as one-quarter of the United States blinked out.

Part II
THE
DOODLEBUG

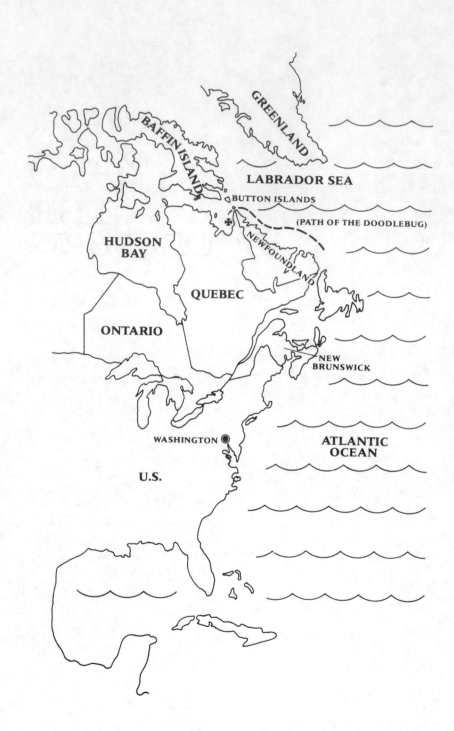

GREENLAND

BAFFIN ISLAND

LABRADOR SEA

BUTTON ISLANDS

(PATH OF THE DOODLEBUG)

NEWFOUNDLAND

HUDSON
BAY

QUEBEC

ONTARIO

NEW
BRUNSWICK

WASHINGTON ◉

ATLANTIC
OCEAN

U.S.

21

There was a feeling of helplessness, almost fear in Alan Mercier's mind as he worked late into the night, sifting through a stack of military recommendations relating to national security. He couldn't help wondering if the new president was capable of grasping realities. Declaring national bankruptcy was asking for impeachment, no matter how desperately the nation required the act.

Mercier sat back and rubbed his tired eyes. No longer were these simply typewritten proposals and predictions on eight-by-ten bond paper. Now they became decisions affecting millions of flesh-and-blood human beings.

Suddenly he felt impotent. Matters of vast consequences stretched beyond his view, his comprehension. The world, the government had grown too complex for a mere handful of men to control adequately. He saw himself being swept along on a tidal wave that was racing toward the rocks.

His depression was interrupted by an aide who entered his office and motioned toward the telephone. "You have a call, sir, from Dr. Klein."

"Hello, Ron, I take it you don't have enough hours in the day either."

"Right you are," Klein came back. "I thought you might like to know I have a lead on your expensive gizmo."

"What is it exactly?"

"I can't say. No one around here has the vaguest idea."

"You'll have to explain."

"The funding came to the Department of Energy all right. But then it was immediately siphoned off to another government agency."

"Which one?"

"The National Underwater and Marine Agency."

Mercier did not respond. He went silent, thinking.

"You there, Alan?"

"Yes, I'm sorry."

"Seems we were only the middleman," Klein went on. "Wish I could give you more information, but that's all I found."

"Sounds devious," mused Mercier. "Why would Energy quietly switch such a large sum of money to an agency concerned with marine science?"

"Can't say. Shall I have my staff pursue it further?"

Mercier thought a moment. "No, better let me handle it. A probe from a neutral source might encounter less hassle."

"I don't envy you, tangling with Sandecker."

"Ah, yes, the director of NUMA. I've never met him, but I hear he's a testy bastard."

"I know him," Klein said. "That description is an understatement. You nail his hide on the barn door and I guarantee half of Washington will present you with a medal."

"Talk has it he's a good man."

"The guy is no idiot. He skirts politics but keeps the right company. He won't hesitate to step on feet, 'damn the torpedoes' and all that, to get a job done. No one who ever picked a fight with him came out a winner. If you have evil thoughts in his direction, I suggest you have a strong case."

"Innocent until proved guilty," said Mercier.

"He's also a tough man to catch. Almost never returns his phone calls or sits around his office."

"I'll think of a way to pin him down," Mercier said confidently. "Thanks for your help."

"Not at all," said Klein. "Good luck. I have a feeling you'll need it."

22

Every afternoon at exactly five minutes to four, Admiral James Sandecker, the chief director of the National Underwater and Marine Agency, left his office and took the elevator down to the tenth-floor communications department.

He was a bantam-size man, a few inches over five feet with a neatly trimmed red beard matching a thick head of hair that showed little indication of white. At age sixty-one, he was a confirmed health nut. He nurtured a trim body by downing daily doses of vitamins and garlic pills supplemented by a six-mile morning run from his apartment to the tall, glassed headquarters of NUMA.

He entered the immense, equipment-laden communications room, which covered fifteen thousand square feet and was manned by a staff of forty-five engineers and technicians. Six satellites, dispersed in hovering orbits above the earth, interconnected the agency with weather stations, oceanographic research expeditions, and a hundred other ongoing marine projects around the world.

The communications director looked up at Sandecker's entry. He was quite familiar with the admiral's routine.

"Projection room B, if you please, Admiral."

Sandecker acknowledged with a curt nod and stepped into what appeared to be a small movie theater. He sank into a soft chair and patiently waited until an image began to focus on the screen.

A tall, lanky man three thousand miles away stared out of the screen from piercing eyes. His hair was black and he grinned from a face that looked like a rock that dared ocean surf to crash over it.

Dirk Pitt was sitting tilted back in a chair with his feet planted irreverently on an electronic console. He held up a sandwich that displayed a missing bite and made an open gesture.

"Sorry, Admiral, you caught me in the middle of a snack."

"You've never stood on formality before," Sandecker grumbled good-naturedly. "Why start now?"

"It's colder than a polar bear's rectum inside this floating abortion. We burn off a ton of calories just trying to keep warm."

"The *Doodlebug* is not a cruise ship."

Pitt set the sandwich aside. "Maybe so, but next trip the crew would appreciate a little more thought being given to the heating system."

"How deep are you?"

Pitt consulted a dial. "Seven hundred and thirty feet. Water temperature is twenty-nine degrees. Conditions not exactly conducive to a game of water polo."

"Any problems?"

"None," Pitt answered, his grin still in place. "The *Doodlebug* is performing like a perfect lady."

"We're running out of time," said Sandecker evenly. "I expect a call from the new president at any moment, demanding to know what we're up to."

"The crew and I will stick around until the fuel is gone, Admiral. I can promise you no more."

"Any mineral contacts?"

"We've passed over large iron deposits, commercially obtainable uranium, thorium, gold and manganese. Almost every mineral except our primary target."

"Does the geology still look promising?"

"Strengthening indications, but nothing that looks like a structural uplift, anticline or salt dome."

"I'm hoping for a stratigraphic trap. It's got the greatest potential."

"The *Doodlebug* can't produce a paying sandbar, Admiral, only find one."

"Not to change the subject, but keep a sharp eye in your rearview mirror. I can't bail you out if you're caught trespassing on the wrong side of the street."

"I've been meaning to ask you, what's to stop an audience from triangulating my video transmissions?"

"One shot in forty."

"Sir?"

"NUMA's satellite communications network has a direct link with forty other stations. They all receive and instantaneously relay your transmissions. The lag is less than a millisecond. To anyone tuned into this sending frequency your voice and image come from forty different locations around the globe. There is no way they can single out the original."

"I think I can live with those odds."

"I'll leave you to your sandwich."

If Pitt felt pessimistic he didn't show it. He put on a confident face and threw a lazy wave. "Hang loose, Admiral. The law of averages is bound to catch up."

Sandecker watched as Pitt's figure faded from the screen. Then he rose from his chair and left the projection room. He walked up two flights of stairs to the computer section and passed through security. In a glass-enclosed room set away from the rest of the humming machines a man in a white lab coat studied a stack of computer printout sheets. He peered over the rims of his glasses as the admiral approached.

"Good afternoon, doc," greeted Sandecker.

Dr. Ramon King indolently replied by holding up a pencil. He had a light-skinned narrow, gloomy face, with jutting jaw and barbed-wire eyebrows—the kind of face that mirrors nothing and rarely displays a change of expression.

Doc King could afford a sour countenance. He was the creative genius behind the development of the *Doodlebug*.

"Everything functioning smoothly?" asked Sandecker, trying to make conversation.

"The probe is functioning perfectly," answered King. "Just as it did yesterday, the day before that and the previous two weeks. If our baby develops teething problems, you'll be the first to be notified."

"I'd prefer good news to no news."

King laid aside the printout sheets and faced Sandecker. "You're not only demanding the moon but the stars as well. Why continue this risky expedition? The *Doodlebug* is a qualified success. It penetrates deeper than we had any right to expect. The doors of discovery it throws open stagger the mind. For God's sake, cut the subterfuge and make its existence known."

"No!" Sandecker snapped back. "Not until I damn well have to."

"What are you trying to prove?" King persisted.

"I want to prove that it's more than a highfalutin dowser."

King readjusted his glasses and went back to scanning the computer data. "I'm not a gambling man, Admiral, but since you're carrying the bulk of the risk on your shoulders, I'll tag along for the ride, knowing full well I'll go on the Justice Department's shit list as an accomplice." He paused and peered at Sandecker. "I have a vested interest in the *Doodlebug*. I'd like to see it make a score as much as anyone. But if something fouls up and those guys out there in the ocean are caught like thieves in the night, then the best you and I can hope for is to be tarred and feathered and exiled to Antarctica. The worst, I don't want to think about.''

23

The Washington athletic community looked askance at Sandecker's running habits. He was the only jogger anyone had ever seen pounding along the sidewalk with an ever-present Churchill-style cigar stub protruding from his mouth.

He was puffing along toward the NUMA building under an early morning overcast sky when a rotund man in a rumpled suit, sitting on a bus bench, looked up over a newspaper.

''Admiral Sandecker, may I have a word with you?''

Sandecker turned out of curiosity, but not recognizing the President's security adviser, he kept his stride. ''Call me for an appointment,'' he panted indifferently. ''I don't like to break my pace.''

''Please, Admiral, I'm Alan Mercier.''

Sandecker stopped, his eyes narrowing. ''Mercier?''

Mercier folded the newspaper and stood. ''My apologies for interrupting your morning exercise, but I understand you're a hard man to trap for conversation.''

''Your office supersedes mine. You could have simply ordered me to come to the White House.''

''I'm not fanatical on official protocol,'' Mercier replied. ''An informal meeting such as this has its advantages.''

''Like catching your quarry off his home ground,'' said Sandecker, cannily sizing up Mercier. ''A sneaky tactic. I use it myself on occasion.''

''According to rumors, you're a master of sneaky tactics.''

Sandecker's expression went blank for an instant. Then he burst into a laugh, pulled a lighter from a pocket of his sweat suit and lit the cigar stub. ''I know when I'm licked. You didn't ambush me for my wallet, Mr. Mercier. What's on your mind?''

''Very well, suppose you tell me about the doodlebug.''

"Doodlebug?" The admiral gave a faint tilt to his head—a movement equivalent to stunned surprise in any other man. "A fascinating instrument. I assume you're familiar with its purpose."

"Why don't you tell me?"

Sandecker shrugged. "I guess you could say it's a kind of water dowser."

"Water dowsers don't cost six hundred and eighty million taxpayer dollars."

"What exactly do you want to know?"

"Does such an exotic instrument exist?"

"The Doodlebug Project is a reality, and a damned successful one, I might add."

"Are you prepared to explain its operation and account for the money spent on its development?"

"When?"

"At the earliest opportunity."

"Give me two weeks and I'll lay the doodlebug in your lap neatly wrapped and packaged."

Mercier was not to be taken in. "Two days."

"I know what you're thinking," said Sandecker earnestly. "But I promise you there is no fear of scandal, far from it. Trust me for at least a week. I simply can't put it together in less."

"I'm beginning to feel like an accomplice in a con game."

"Please, one week."

Mercier looked into Sandecker's eyes. My God, he thought, the man is actually begging. It was hardly what he expected. He motioned to his driver who was parked a short distance away and nodded.

"Okay, Admiral, you've got your week."

"You drive a tough bargain," said Sandecker, with a sly grin.

Without another word the admiral turned and resumed his morning jog to NUMA headquarters.

Mercier watched the little man grow even smaller in the distance. He seemed not to notice his driver standing patiently beside the car, holding the door open.

Mercier stood rooted, a maddening certainty growing within him that he'd been had.

24

It had been an exhausting day for Sandecker. After his unexpected meeting with Mercier he fenced with a congressional budget committee until eight in the evening, hawking the goals and accomplishments of NUMA, appealing for, and in a few cases, demanding additional funding for his agency's operations. It was a bureaucratic chore he detested.

After a light dinner at the Army and Navy Club, he entered his apartment at the Watergate and poured himself a glass of buttermilk.

He took off his shoes and was beginning to unwind when the phone rang. He would have ignored it if he hadn't turned to see which line held the incoming call. The red light on the direct circuit to NUMA blinked ominously.

"Sandecker."

"Ramon King here, Admiral. We've got a problem on the *Doodlebug*."

"A malfunction?"

"No such luck," replied King. "Our sweep systems have picked up an intruder."

"Is he closing with our vessel?"

"Negative."

"A chance passing by one of our own subs then," Sandecker suggested optimistically.

King sounded concerned. "The contact is maintaining a parallel course, distance four thousand meters. It appears to be shadowing the *Doodlebug*."

"Not good."

"I'll have a firmer grasp on the situation when the computers spit out a more detailed analysis of our unknown caller."

Sandecker went silent. He sipped at the buttermilk, his mind meditative. Finally, he said, "Call the security desk and tell them to track down Al Giordino. I want him in on this."

King spoke hesitantly. "Is Giordino acquainted with . . . ah, does he . . . ?"

"He knows," Sandecker assured King. "I personally briefed him on the project during its inception in the event he had to substitute for Pitt. You'd better get on with it. I'll be there in fifteen minutes."

The admiral hung up. His worst fear had put in its appearance. He stared at the white liquid within the glass as if he could visualize the mysterious craft stalking the defenseless *Doodlebug*.

Then he set the glass aside and hurried out the door, unaware that he was still in his stocking feet.

Deep beneath the surface of the Labrador Sea not far from the northern tip of Newfoundland, Pitt stood in stony silence, studying the electronic readout across the display screen as the unidentified submarine skirted the outer fringes of the *Doodlebug*'s instrument range. He leaned forward as a line of data flashed on. Then, suddenly, the display screen blinked out as contact was lost.

Bill Lasky, the panel operator, turned to Pitt and shook his head. "Sorry, Dirk, our visitor is a shy one. He won't sit still for a scan."

Pitt put his hand on Lasky's shoulder. "Keep trying. Sooner or later he's bound to step on our side of the fence."

He moved across the control room through the maze of complex electronic gear, his feet silent on the rubber deck covering. Dropping down a ladder to a lower deck, he entered a small room not much bigger than a pair of adjoining phone booths.

Pitt sat on the edge of a folding bunk, spread a blueprint on a small writing desk and studied the guts of the *Doodlebug*.

A *diving deformity* was the less than endearing term that ran through his mind when he first laid eyes on the world's most sophisticated research vessel. It looked like nothing previously built to prowl beneath the seas.

The *Doodlebug*'s compact form lay somewhere south of ludicrous. The best descriptions anybody had come up with were "the inner half of an aircraft wing standing on end" and "the conning tower of a submarine that has lost its hull." In short, it was a slab of metal that traveled in a vertical position.

There was a reason for the unorthodox lines of the *Doodlebug*. The concept was a considerable leap in submersible technology. In the past, all mechanical and electronic systems had been built to conform within the space limitations of a standard cigar-shaped hull. The *Doodlebug*'s aluminum shell, on the other hand, had been built around its instrument package.

There were few creature comforts for the three-man crew. Humans were essential only for emergency operation or repairs. The craft was automatically operated and piloted by the computer brain center at NUMA headquarters in Washington, almost three thousand miles away.

"How about a little medicine to clear the cobwebs?"

Pitt lifted his head and looked into the mournful bloodhound eyes of Sam Quayle, the electronics wizard of the expedition. Quayle held up a pair of plastic cups and a half pint of brandy, whose remaining contents hardly coated the floor of the bottle.

"For shame," said Pitt, unable to suppress a grin. "You know NUMA regulations forbid alcohol on board research vessels."

"Don't look at me," Quayle replied with mock innocence. "I found this work of the devil, or what's left of it, in my bunk. Must have been forgotten by an itinerant construction worker."

"That's odd," said Pitt.

Quayle looked at him questioningly. "How so?"

"The coincidence." Pitt reached under his pillow and pulled out a fifth of Bell's Scotch and held it up. The interior was half full. "An itinerant construction worker left one in my bunk too."

Quayle smiled and handed the cups to Pitt. "If it's all the same to you, I'll save mine for snakebite."

Pitt poured and handed a cup to Quayle. Then he sat back in the bunk and spoke slowly: "What do you make of it, Sam?"

"Our evasive caller?"

"The same," answered Pitt. "What's stopping him from dropping in and giving us the once-over? Why the cat-and-mouse game?"

Quayle took a healthy belt of the Scotch and shrugged. "The *Doodlebug*'s configuration probably won't compute on the sub's detection system. The skipper is no doubt contacting his command headquarters for a rundown on underwater craft in his patrol area before he pulls us over to the curb and cites us for trespassing." Quayle finished his drink and gazed longingly at the bottle. "Mind if I have seconds?"

"Help yourself."

Quayle poured himself a generous shot. "I'd feel much safer if we could pin a name tag on those guys."

"They won't come within range of our scan. What beats me is how they can walk such a fine line. They seem to dip in and out as if they were taunting us.''

"No miracle,'' said Quayle, making a face as the Scotch seared his throat. "Their transducers are measuring our probes. They know within a few meters of where our signals die out.''

Pitt sat up, his eyes narrowed. "Suppose . . . just suppose . . . ?''

He didn't finish. He left his quarters at a half run, clawing his way up the ladder to the control room. Quayle took another swallow and followed. Only he didn't run.

"Any change?'' Pitt asked.

Lasky shook his head. "The uninvited are still playing cagey.''

"Gradually fade the probes. Maybe we can draw them closer. When they step into our yard, hit them with every sensing device we've got.''

"You expect to sucker a nuclear sub, manned by a first-rate professional crew, with a kindergarten trick like that?'' Quayle asked incredulously.

"Why not?'' Pitt grinned fiendishly. "I'll bet my snake medicine against yours they'll fall for it.''

Quayle looked like a salesman who had just sold a waterfront lot in the Gobi Desert. "You're on.''

For the next hour it was business as usual. The men went about their chores of monitoring the instruments and checking the equipment. At last Pitt looked at his watch and gestured in Lasky's direction.

"Systems standby,'' he directed.

"Ready systems,'' Lasky acknowledged.

"Okay, nail the bastard!''

The data unit in front of them burst into life and the remote display swept across the screen.

> *Contact: 3480 meters.*
> *Course: Bearing one zero eight.*
> *Speed: Ten knots.*

"He bit the hook!'' Quayle couldn't keep the excitement out of his voice. "We've got him!''

> *Overall length: 76 meters.*
> *Beam (approximate): 10.7 meters.*
> *Probable submerged displacement: 3650 tons.*

Power: One water-cooled nuclear reactor.
Design: Hunter-killer.
Class: Amberjack.
Flag: U.S.A.

"It's one of ours," Lasky said with obvious relief.

"At least we're among friends," Quayle muttered.

Pitt's eyes were intent. "We're not out of the woods yet."

"Our snoopy friend has altered his course to zero seven six. Speed increasing," Lasky read aloud from the screen. "He's moving away from us now."

"If I didn't know better," Quayle said thoughtfully, "I'd say he was setting for an attack."

Pitt looked at him. "Explain."

"Several years ago, I was a member of a design team that developed underwater weapons systems for the navy. I came to learn that a hunter-killer sub will come to flank speed and break away from the target prior to a torpedo launch."

"Kind of like firing your six-shooter over a shoulder at the villain while riding out of town at full gallop."

"A fair parallel," Quayle allowed. "The modern torpedo is crammed with ultrasonic, heat and magnetic sensors. Once fired, it goes after a target with ungodly tenacity. If it misses on the first pass, it circles around and keeps trying until it makes contact. That's why the mother sub, figuring the target has weapons of the same capability, gets off the mark early and takes evasive action."

A concerned look came over Pitt's face. "How far to the bottom?"

"Two hundred and thirty meters," Lasky answered.

The metric system had never quite caught on with Pitt. Out of habit he converted the reading to about 750 feet. "And the contour?"

"Looks rough. Rock outcroppings, some fifteen meters high."

Pitt walked over to a small plotting table and studied a chart of the seafloor. Then he said, "Switch us on override and take us down."

Lasky looked at him questioningly. "NUMA control won't take kindly to us cutting off their reins."

"We're here, Washington is three thousand miles away. I think it best if we command the vessel until we know what we're facing."

Confusion showed in Quayle's face. "You don't seriously think we're going to be attacked?"

"As long as there's a one percent probability I'm not about to ignore it." Pitt nodded at Lasky. "Take us down. Let's hope we can get lost in the seafloor geology."

"I'll need sonar to avoid striking an outcropping."

"Keep it locked on the sub," Pitt ordered. "Use the lights and TV monitors. We'll eyeball it."

"This is insane," said Quayle.

"If we were hugging the coast of Siberia do you think the Russians would hesitate to boot us where it hurts?"

"Holy mother of Christ!" Lasky gasped.

Pitt and Quayle froze, their eyes suddenly taking on the fear of the hunted as they stared at the green letters glowing on the display screen.

> *Emergency: CRITICAL.*
> *New contact: Bearing one nine three.*
> *Speed: Seventy knots.*
> *Status: Collision imminent.*
> *Time to contact: One minute, eleven seconds.*

"They've gone and done it," Lasky whispered with the look of a man who had seen his tomb. "They've fired a torpedo at us."

Giordino could almost smell the foreboding, and he could see it in the eyes of Dr. King and Admiral Sandecker as he burst through the door of the computer room.

Neither man acknowledged his arrival or so much as glanced in the direction of the swarthy little Italian. Their full concentration was fixed on the huge electronic display covering one wall. Giordino quickly scanned and absorbed the readout on the impending disaster.

"Reverse their forward motion," he said calmly.

"I can't." King lifted his hands in a helpless gesture. "They've switched to control override."

"Then tell them!" Giordino said, his tone suddenly sharp.

"No way." Sandecker's words came strained and hollow. "There's a breakdown in voice transmission from the communications satellite."

"Make contact through the computers."

"Yes, yes," King murmured, a faint gleam of understanding in his eyes. "I still command their data input."

Giordino watched the screen, counting the remaining seconds of the torpedo's run as King spoke into a voice response unit that relayed the message to the *Doodlebug*.

"Pitt anticipated you," said Sandecker, nodding at the screen. They all felt a brief surge of relief as the forward speed of the submersible began to fall off.

"Ten seconds to contact," said Giordino.

Sandecker grabbed a telephone and bellowed at the shaken operator on duty. "Get me Admiral Joe Kemper, chief of naval operations!"

"Three seconds . . . two . . . one . . ."

The room fell into hushed silence; all were afraid to speak, to be the first to utter the words that might become the epitaph of the submersible and its crew. The screen remained dark. Then the readout came on.

"A miss," King sighed heavily. "The torpedo passed astern with ninety meters to spare."

"The magnetic sensors can't get a firm lock-in on the *Bug*'s aluminum hull," commented Sandecker.

Giordino had to grin at Pitt's reply.

> *Round one. Ahead on points.*
> *Any bright ideas for round two?*

"The torpedo's circling for another try," said King.

"What's its trajectory?"

"Appears to be running a flat path."

"Have them turn the *Doodlebug* on her side, angling to a horizontal plane, keeping the keel toward the torpedo. That will reduce the strike area."

Sandecker got through to one of Kemper's aides, a lieutenant commander who told him the chief of naval operations was asleep and couldn't be disturbed. The aide might as well have thrown a pie at a freight train.

"You listen to me, sonny," Sandecker said in the intimidating tone he was famous for. "I happen to be Admiral James Sandecker of NUMA and this is an emergency. I strongly suggest you put Joe on the phone or your next tour of duty will be at a weather station on Mount Everest. Now move it!"

In a few moments, Admiral Kemper's yawning voice slurred over the phone. "Jim? What in hell is the problem?"

"One of your subs has just attacked one of my research vessels, that's the problem."

Kemper reacted as if he'd been shot. "Where?"

"Ten miles off the Button Islands in the Labrador Sea."

"That's in Canadian waters."

"I've no time for explanations," said Sandecker. "You've got to order your sub to self-destruct their torpedo before we have a senseless tragedy on our hands."

"Stay on the line," said Kemper. "I'll be right back to you."

"Five seconds," Giordino called out.

"The circle has narrowed," King noted.

"Three seconds . . . two . . . one . . ."

The next interval seemed to drag by as if in molasses while they waited. Then King announced, "Another miss. Only ten meters above this time."

"How close are they to the seafloor?" Giordino asked.

"Thirty-five meters and closing. Pitt must be trying to hide behind a formation of rock outcroppings. It looks hopeless. If the torpedo doesn't get them on the next pass, there's an odds-on chance it'll tear a hole in the hull."

Sandecker stiffened as Kemper returned on the line. "I've talked with the chief of arctic defense. He's putting through a priority signal to the sub's commander. I only hope he's in time."

"You're not alone."

"Sorry about the mix-up, Jim. The U.S. Navy doesn't usually shoot first and ask questions afterward. But it's open season on unidentified undersea craft caught that close to the North American shoreline. What was your vessel doing there anyway?"

"The navy isn't the only one who conducts classified missions," said Sandecker. "I'm grateful for your assist." He rang off and gazed up at the screen.

The torpedo was barreling through the depths with murder on its electronic mind. Its detonator head was fifteen seconds away from the *Doodlebug.*

"Get down," King pleaded aloud. "Twelve meters to the bottom. Lord, they're not going to make it."

Giordino's mind raced in search of options, but none were left. There was no escaping the inevitable this time. Unless the torpedo destructed in the next few moments, the *Doodlebug* and the three men inside her would lay in the sea forever.

His mouth felt dry as a sandpit. He did not count down the seconds this time. In times of stress men perceive strange things that are out of place with unusual clarity. Giordino idly wondered why he hadn't noticed before that Sandecker wasn't wearing any shoes.

"It's going to strike this time," King said. It was a simple statement of fact, no more. His face was drained of all emotion, the skin pale as he raised his hands over his eyes and shut out all sight of the screen.

No sound came over the computers as the torpedo bore in on the *Doodlebug*. No explosion or shriek of metal bursting into twisted scrap came through the impassive computers. They were immune to the choked-off cries of men dying in the black and icy depths.

One by one the soulless machines shut down. Their lights blinked out and their terminals went cold. They stood silent.

To them, the *Doodlebug* no longer existed.

25

Mercier felt no sense of elation about what he must do. He liked James Sandecker, respected the man's candor and forthright manner of organization. But there was no dodging an immediate inquiry into the loss of the *Doodlebug*. He dared not wait and run the risk of a security breach that would bring the news media circling like vultures. He had to quickly formulate plans for bringing the admiral, and the White House, through the mess without a national outcry.

His secretary's voice came over the intercom. "Admiral Sandecker is here, sir."

"Show him in."

Mercier half expected to see a man haggard from lack of sleep, a man saddened by death and tragedy, but he was mistaken.

Sandecker strode into the room resplendent in gold braid and beribboned uniform. A newly lit cigar was firmly anchored in one corner of his mouth, and his eyes twinkled with their usual gleam of cockiness. If he was going under the magnifying glass, he was obviously going in style.

"Please have a seat, Admiral," said Mercier, rising. "The Security Council meets in a few minutes."

"You mean the inquisition," said Sandecker.

"Not so. The President simply wants to learn the facts behind the *Doodlebug*'s development and place the events of the last thirty-six hours in proper perspective."

"You're not wasting any time. It hasn't been eight hours since my men were murdered."

"That's a bit harsh."

"What else would you call it?"

"I'm not a jury," said Mercier quietly. "I want you to know I truly regret that the project didn't work out."

"I'm prepared to shoulder all blame."

"We're not looking for a scapegoat, only the facts, which you've been most reluctant to reveal."

"I've had my reasons."

"We'll be most interested in hearing them."

The intercom beeped.

"Yes?"

"They're ready for you."

"On our way." Mercier motioned toward the door. "Shall we?"

They stepped into the White House cabinet room. A blue rug matched the drapes and on the north wall a portrait of Harry Truman peered from above the fireplace. The President sat at the center of a huge oval mahogany table, his back to the terrace overlooking the rose garden. Directly opposite, the vice-president scratched notes on a pad. Admiral Kemper was present as was Secretary of Energy Dr. Ronald Klein, Secretary of State Douglas Oates and the Director of Central Intelligence, Martin Brogan.

The President came over and greeted Sandecker warmly. "It's a pleasure to see you, Admiral. Please sit down and get comfortable. I believe you know everyone present."

Sandecker nodded and took a vacant chair at the end of the table. He sat alone and distant from the others.

"Now then," the President said for openers, "suppose you tell us about your mysterious *Doodlebug*."

Dirk Pitt's secretary, Zerri Pochinsky, walked into the computer room with a cup of coffee and a sandwich on a tray. The rims of her hazel eyes were watery. She found it difficult to accept the fact of her boss's death. The shock of losing someone so close had not fully settled about her. It would come later, she knew, when she was alone.

She found Giordino straddling a chair, his elbows and chin nestled on the backrest. He was staring at the row of inert computers.

She sat down next to him. "Your favorite," she said softly. "Pastrami on wheat."

Giordino shook his head at the sandwich but drank the coffee. The caffeine did little to relieve the frustration and anger of having had to watch Pitt and the others die while he stood helpless to prevent it.

"Why don't you go home and get some sleep," Zerri said. "Nothing can be accomplished by staying here."

Giordino spoke as if in a trance. "Pitt and I went back a long way."

"Yes, I know."

"We played high-school football together. He was the shrewdest, most unpredictable quarterback in the league."

"You forget, I've been present when you two reminisced. I can almost give you an instant replay."

Giordino turned to her and smiled. "Were we that bad?"

Zerri smiled back through her tears. "You were that bad."

A team of computer technicians came through the door. The man in charge came over to Giordino. "Sorry to interrupt, but I have orders to break down the project and move the equipment to another section of the department."

"Erase-the-evidence time, is it?"

"Sir?"

"Did you clear this with Dr. King?"

The man solemnly nodded his head. "Two hours ago. Before he left the building."

"Speaking of home," said Zerri. "Come along. I'll do the driving."

Obediently Giordino rose to his feet and rubbed his aching eyes. He held the door open and gestured for Zerri to exit first. He started to follow her, but suddenly stopped on the threshold.

He came within a hair of missing it. Later, he could never explain why an unfathomable urge made him turn for one final look.

The wink of light was so brief he would have missed it if his eyes hadn't been aimed in the right direction at the right moment. He shouted at the technician who had just switched off the circuits.

"Turn them back on!"

"What for?" demanded the technician.

"Damn it, turn the circuits back on!"

One look at Giordino's scowling features was enough. There was no argument this time. The technician did as he was told.

Suddenly the room lost all dimension. Everyone recoiled as though witnessing the birth of some grotesque apparition. Everyone except Giordino. He stood immobile, his lips spreading in a surprised, joyous smile.

One by one, the computers returned to life.

"Let me get this straight," said the President, his face clouded with doubt. "You say this *Doodlebug* of yours can see through ten miles of solid rock?"

"And identify fifty-one different minerals and metal traces within it," Sandecker replied without blinking an eye. "Yes, Mr. President, I said exactly that."

"I didn't think it was possible," said CIA Director Brogan. "Electromagnetic devices have had limited success measuring the electrical resistivity of underground minerals, but certainly nothing of this magnitude."

"How is it a project of such importance was researched and developed without presidential or congressional knowledge?" asked the vice-president.

"The former president knew," Sandecker explained. "He had a fancy for supporting futuristic concepts. As I'm sure you're aware of by now, he secretly funded an undercover think tank called Meta Section. It was Meta Section scientists who designed the *Doodlebug*. Wrapped in security, the plans were given to NUMA. The President arranged the bankroll, and we built it."

"And it actually works?" the President pressed.

"Proof positive," Sandecker answered. "Our initial test runs have pinpointed commercially obtainable deposits of gold, manganese, chromium, aluminum and at least ten other elements including uranium."

The men around the table had a varied display of expressions. The President looked at Sandecker strangely. Admiral Kemper's face was impassive. The rest stared in open disbelief.

"Are you suggesting you can determine the extent of the deposit as well as an appraisal of its worth?" Douglas Oates asked dubiously.

"Within a few seconds of detecting the element or mineral, the

Doodlebug computes a precise evaluation of ore reserve data, projected mining costs and operating profits and, of course, the exact coordinates of the location.''

If Sandecker's audience had appeared skeptical before, they looked downright incredulous now. Energy Secretary Klein asked the question that was on everyone's mind.

"How does the thing work?"

"The same basic principle as radar or marine depth sounders, except that the *Doodlebug* transmits a sharply focused, concentrated pulse of energy straight down into the earth. This high-energy beam, similar in theory to a radio station that broadcasts different sound tones over the air, throws out various signal frequencies that are reflected by the geological formations it encounters. My engineers refer to it as sweep modulation. You can compare it to shouting across a canyon. When your voice hits a rock wall, you get a distinct echo. But if there are trees or foliage in the way, the echo comes back muffled.''

"I still don't understand how it can identify specific minerals," said a confused Klein.

"Each mineral, each element in the makeup of the earth resonates at its own peculiar frequency. Copper resonates at about two thousand cycles. Iron at twenty-two hundred. Zinc at four thousand. Mud, rock and sand shale each have an individual signature that determines the quality of the signal that strikes and reflects off its surface. On a computer display, the readout looks like a vivid cross-section of the earth, because the various formations are color-coded.''

"And you measure the depth of the deposit by the signal's time lag," Admiral Kemper commented.

"You're quite right.''

"Seems to me the signal would weaken and become distorted the deeper it goes," said Mercier.

"It does," admitted Sandecker. "The beam loses energy as it passes through the different earth layers. But by recording each encounter during the penetration, we've learned to expect and recognize the deviant reflections. We call this density tracking. The computers analyze the effect and transmit the corrected data in digital form.''

The President shifted restlessly in his chair. "It all sounds unreal.''

"It's real, all right," said Sandecker. "What it boils down to, gentlemen, is that a fleet of ten *Doodlebug*s could chart and analyze every geological formation under every cubic foot of seafloor in five years.''

The room fell silent for several moments. Then Oates murmured reverently. "God, the potential is inconceivable."

CIA Director Brogan leaned over the table. "Any chance the Russians may be onto a similar instrument?"

Sandecker shook his head. "I don't think so. Until a few months ago we didn't have the technology to perfect the high-energy beam. Even with a crash program starting from scratch, they'd need a decade to catch up."

"One question that needs answering," said Mercier. "Why the Labrador Sea? Why didn't you test the *Doodlebug* on our own continental shelf?"

"I thought it best to conduct the trials in an isolated area far from normal shipping traffic."

"But why so close to the Canadian shore?"

"The *Doodlebug* stumbled on indications of oil."

"Oil?"

"Yes, the trail appeared to lead toward the Hudson Strait north of Newfoundland. I gave the order for the *Doodlebug* to deviate from its original course and follow the scent into Canadian waters. The responsibility for the loss of a very dear friend, his crew and the research vessel is mine and mine alone. No one else is to blame."

An aide entered the room like a wraith and offered coffee. When he reached Sandecker he laid a note at his elbow. It read,

URGENT I SEE YOU.

Giordino

"If I may beg a short interruption," said Sandecker. "I believe one of my staff is outside with updated information on the tragedy."

The President gave him an understanding look and nodded in the direction of the doorway. "Of course. Please have him join us."

Giordino was shown into the cabinet room, his face beaming like a lighthouse.

"The *Doodlebug* and everyone on board came through," he blurted without preamble.

"What happened?" demanded Sandecker.

"The torpedo struck a rock outcropping fifty meters from the submersible. The concussion short-circuited the main terminals. It took

Pitt and his men until an hour ago to make emergency repairs and reopen communications.''

"No one was injured?" asked Admiral Kemper. "The hull remained tight?''

"Bumps and bruises," Giordino replied like a telegram. "One broken finger. No leaks reported.''

"Thank God they're safe," said the President, suddenly all smiles.

Giordino could no longer continue to play it cool. "I haven't mentioned the best part.''

Sandecker looked at him quizzically. "Best part?''

"Right after the computers came on line, the output analyzers went crazy. Congratulations, Admiral. The *Doodlebug* ran onto the granddaddy of stratigraphic traps.''

Sandecker tensed. "Are you saying they found oil?''

"Initial indications suggest a field extending nearly ninety-five miles by three-quarters of a mile wide. The yield appears staggering. Projections put the paying sandbar at two thousand barrels per acre foot. The reserve could conceivably bring in eight billion barrels of oil.''

No one around the table could say a word. They could only sit there, soaking up the enormous consequences of it all.

Giordino opened an attaché case and handed Sandecker a sheaf of papers. "I didn't have time to tie it with a ribbon, but here are preliminary figures, calculations and projections, including the estimated costs of drilling and production. Dr. King will have a more concise report when the *Doodlebug* has better surveyed the field.''

"Where exactly is this strike?" asked Klein.

Giordino unrolled a chart and spread it on the table in front of the President. He began to outline the *Doodlebug*'s course with a pencil.

"After the near miss by the torpedo, the crew of the *Doodlebug*, took evasive action. They didn't know the sub's attack had been called off. Swinging on a northwest arc from the Labrador Sea, they hugged the seabed through Gray Strait south of the Button Islands and moved into Ungava Bay. It was here," Giordino paused to make a mark on the chart, "they discovered the oil field.''

The excitement abruptly faded from the President's eyes. "Then it wasn't near the coast of Newfoundland?''

"No, sir. Newfoundland's provincial border ends at a point of land at the entrance of Gray Strait. The oil strike was in the waters off Quebec.''

The President's expression turned to a look of disappointment. He and Mercier stared at each other in stricken understanding.

"Of all the places in all the northern hemisphere," the President said barely above a whisper, "it had to be Quebec."

Part III

THE NORTH AMERICAN TREATY

26

Pitt slipped Heidi's notes on the North American Treaty into a briefcase and nodded as the airline stewardess checked to see if his seat belt was clasped and his back rest was in an upright position. He massaged his temples, trying vainly to relieve a headache that had persisted since he changed planes at St. John's, Newfoundland.

Now that the *Doodlebug*'s hectic sea trials were over, the little research vessel had been hoisted aboard its mother ship and transported to Boston for repairs and modifications. Bill Lasky and Sam Quayle left immediately for a week's vacation with their families. Pitt envied them. He was not afforded the luxury of a rest. Sandecker ordered him back to NUMA headquarters for a firsthand report on the expedition.

The plane's tires thumped onto the runway at Washington's National Airport a few minutes before seven. Pitt remained in his seat while the other passengers crowded prematurely into the aisles. One of the last to debark, he took his time, rightly figuring that no matter how slowly he wandered to the baggage claim, he always arrived before his luggage.

He found his car, a red 1966 AC Ford Cobra, in the VIP section of the parking lot where it had been left by his secretary earlier in the afternoon. A note was tucked in the steering wheel.

Dear Boss,

Welcome home.

Sorry I couldn't hang around to greet you, but I have a date. Get a good night's sleep.

I told the admiral your plane wouldn't arrive till tomorrow night. Have a day off on me.

Zerri

P.S. Almost forgot what it's like to drive a big old brute. Fun, fun, but oh what awful gas mileage.

Pitt smiled and engaged the starter, listening with pleasure as the 427-cubic-inch engine kicked into life with an obscene roar. While waiting for the temperature gauge to creep into the WARM, he reread the note.

Zerri Pochinsky was the lively type, her pretty face seldom without a contagious smile, hazel eyes mischievous and warm. She was thirty, never married, a mystery to Pitt, full-bodied, with long fawn-colored hair that fell below her shoulders. He'd thought more than once of having an affair with her. The invitation had been demurely signaled often enough. But with regret, he adhered to a law burned in the concrete of an office building somewhere, and learned the hard way during his younger, less disciplined days, that grief always comes to the man who plays games with his staff.

He shook off an erotic image of her inviting him between the sheets and crammed the Cobra into gear. The aging two-seater convertible leaped out of the parking lot and squeaked rubber as it swung onto the highway leading from the airport. He turned from the capital city and headed south, remaining on the Virginia side of the Potomac River. The Cobra's engine loafed along without effort as Pitt passed a stream of minicars that made up the tail end of the evening traffic rush.

At a small town called Hague he turned off the highway and took a narrow road until he reached Coles Point. When the river came into sight he began studying names on the rural mailboxes beside the road's shoulder. His headlights picked out an elderly woman walking a large Irish setter.

He stopped and leaned toward the passenger window. "I beg your pardon, can you direct me to the Essex place?"

She gave Pitt a wary look and pointed behind the car. "You missed the Essex gate about a half mile back. The one with the iron lions."

"Yes, I recall seeing it."

Before Pitt could begin a U-turn, the woman bent down to the open window. "Won't find him home. Mr. Essex left four, maybe five weeks ago."

"Do you know when he'll return?" Pitt asked.

"Who's to say?" She shrugged. "He often closes down his house and goes to Palm Springs this time of year. Lets my son tend his oyster ponds. Mr. Essex just comes and goes; easy for him, being alone and all. Only way to tell he's gone to the desert is when his mailbox overflows."

Of all people to ask directions, Pitt thought, he had to pick the neighborhood busybody. "Thank you," he said. "You've been most helpful."

The woman's lined face suddenly became a mask of friendliness and her voice turned to molasses. "If you have a message for him, you can give it to me. I'll see that he gets it. I pick up all his mail and newspapers anyway."

Pitt looked at her. "He didn't stop his newspaper?"

She shook her head. "The man is as absentminded as they come. When my boy was working the ponds the other day he said he saw steam coming from the Essex house heating vents. Imagine going away and leaving the heat in the house on. Pure waste, considering the energy shortage."

"You said Mr. Essex lives alone?"

"Lost his wife ten years ago," answered busybody. "His three children are scattered all over. Hardly ever write the poor man."

Pitt thanked her again and rolled up the window before the woman could prattle on. He didn't have to look in the rearview mirror to know she had kept her eye on the car as he turned into the Essex drive.

He rolled through the trees, parked the Cobra in front of the house and switched off the ignition, but left the headlights on. He sat there a few moments, listening to the engine crackle from its heat, nearing a siren on the other side of the river in Maryland. It was a beautiful night. Clear and brisk. Lights sparkled on the river like Christmas ornaments.

The house stood dark and silent.

Pitt climbed out of the sports car and walked around the garage. He lifted the main door on its well-oiled hinges and peered at the two cars facing frontward, the bright work on their grills and bumpers gleaming under the Cobra's lights. One was a compact, a tiny, gas-saving, front-engined Ford. The other was an older Cadillac Brougham, one of the last of the big cars. They were both covered with a light layer of dust.

The interior of the Cadillac was immaculate and the odometer only showed 6400 miles. Both cars looked showroom new; even the underside of the fenders had been kept free of road grime. Pitt had begun to penetrate Essex's world. Judging from the loving care the former ambassador lavished on his automobiles, he was a meticulous and orderly man.

He eased the garage door back down and turned to face the house. The woman's son had been right. Wisps of whitish vapor drifted out of the vents on the roof and faded into the blackened sky. He stepped onto the front porch, found the chime button and pushed it. There was no reply, no movement on the other side of the picture windows whose drapes were tied open. Purely because it seemed the thing to do, he tried the door.

It opened.

Pitt stood there in momentary surprise. An unlocked front door was not in the script; neither was the rank stink of putrefaction that wafted over the threshold and invaded his nostrils.

He stepped inside, leaving the door open behind him. Then he groped for the light switch and flicked it on. The foyer was empty, as was the adjoining dining room. He moved swiftly through the house, beginning with the upstairs bedrooms. The terrible odor seemed everywhere. There was no pinning it down to a particular area. He returned downstairs and checked the living room and kitchen, quickly scanning their interiors before moving on. He almost missed the study, thinking the closed door merely opened to a closet.

John Essex sat in the overstuffed chair, his mouth agape, head twisted over and to the side in agony, a pair of glasses hanging grotesquely from a leathered ear. His once twinkling blue eyes had collapsed and depressed into the skull. Decomposition had been rapid because the thermostat in the room was set at 75°. He had been sitting there, strangely undiscovered for a month, struck dead, so the coroner would state, by a blood clot in the coronary artery.

Pitt could read the signs. During the first two weeks the body had turned green and bloated, popping the buttons from Essex's shirt. Then after the internal fluids had expelled and evaporated, the corpse began to shrivel and dry out, the skin stiffening to the consistency of tanned hide.

Sweat began to seep from Pitt's forehead. The stuffiness of the room, together with the stench, spun him to the verge of sickness. Holding a handkerchief over his nose, he struggled against the urge to vomit, and knelt in front of John Essex's corpse.

A book lay in the lap; one clawlike hand was clamped on the engraved cover. The cold finger of dread etched a path down Pitt's neck. He had seen death close up before, and his reaction was always the same: a feeling of repugnance that slowly gave way to a frightening realization that he too would someday look like the rotting thing in the chair.

Hesitantly, as though he half expected Essex to awake, he pried the book loose. Then he switched on a desk lamp and flipped through the pages. It looked to be some sort of diary or personal journal. He turned to the front heading. The words seemed to rise up from the yellowed paper.

PERSONAL OBSERVATIONS
BY
RICHARD C. ESSEX
FOR
APRIL OF 1914

Pitt sat down behind the desk and began reading. After about an hour he stopped and looked at the remains of John Essex, his expression of revulsion replaced with one that was filled with pity.

"You poor old fool," he said with sadness in his eyes.

Then he turned off the light and left, leaving the former ambassador to England alone once again in a darkened room.

27

The air was heavy with the smell of gunpowder as Pitt moved behind a row of muzzle-loading gun enthusiasts at a shooting range outside

Fredericksburg, Virginia. He stopped at a bald-headed man who sat hunched over a bench, peering intently down the iron sights of a rifle barrel that was fully forty-six inches in length.

Joe Epstein, a columnist for the *Baltimore Sun* during working hours and an avid black powder rifleman on weekends, gently squeezed the trigger. The report came like a sharp thump, followed by a small whiff of dark smoke. Epstein checked his hit through a telescope and then began pouring another powder charge down the long barrel.

"The Indians will be all over you before you've reloaded that antique," Pitt said with a grin.

Epstein's eyes brightened in recognition. "I'll have you know I can get off four shots a minute if I hurry." Using pillow ticking as wadding, he rammed a lead ball past the muzzle. "I tried to call you."

"I've been on the go," Pitt said briefly. He nodded at the gun. "What is it?"

"A flintlock. Seventy-five-caliber Brown Bess. Carried by British soldiers during the Revolutionary War." He handed the gun to Pitt. "Care to try it?"

Pitt sat down at the bench and sighted on a target two hundred yards away. "Were you able to dig up anything?"

"The newspaper morgue had bits and pieces on microfilm." Epstein placed a small amount of powder in the flintlock's priming pan. "The trick is not to flinch when the flint ignites the powder in the pan."

Pitt pulled the lock mechanism back. Then he aimed and eased the trigger. The primer flashed almost in his eyes and carried down the touchhole. The charge in the barrel exploded an instant later and his shoulder felt as if it had been rammed by a pile driver.

Epstein stared through the telescope. "Eight inches, two o'clock of dead center. Not bad for a city dude." A voice over a loudspeaker announced a cease-fire and the shooters laid down their pieces and began walking across the range to replace their targets. "Come along and I'll tell you what I found."

Pitt nodded silently and followed Epstein down a slope toward the target area.

"You gave me two names, Richard Essex and Harvey Shields. Essex was undersecretary of state. Shields was his British counterpart, deputy secretary of the Foreign Office. Both career men, the workhorse type. Very little publicity on either man. Carried out their work behind the scenes. Apparently they were rather shadowy figures."

"You're only icing the cake, Joe. There has to be more."

"Not much. As near as I can tell, they never met, at least in their official roles."

"I have a photograph showing them coming out of the White House together."

Epstein shrugged. "My four hundredth mistaken conclusion for the year."

"What became of Shields?"

"He drowned on the *Empress of Ireland*."

"I know about the *Empress*. A passenger liner that sank in the St. Lawrence River after colliding with a Norwegian coal collier. Over a thousand lives were lost."

Epstein nodded. "I'd never heard of her until I read Shields' obituary. The sinking was one of the worst maritime disasters of the age."

"Strange. The *Empress*, the *Titanic* and the *Lusitania* all went under within three years of one another."

"Anyway, the body was never found. His family held a memorial service in some unpronounceable little village in Wales. That's all I can tell you about Harvey Shields."

They reached the target and Epstein studied the hits. "A six-inch grouping," he said. "Pretty good for an old smoothbore muzzle-loader."

"A seventy-five-caliber ball makes a nasty hole," said Pitt, eyeing the shredded target.

"Think what it would do on flesh."

"I'd rather not."

Epstein replaced the target and they began walking back to the shooting line.

"What about Essex?" asked Pitt.

"What can I tell you that you don't already know?"

"How he died, for starters."

"A train wreck," answered Epstein. "Bridge collapsed over the Hudson River. A hundred dead. Essex was one of them."

Pitt thought a moment. "Somewhere, buried in old records in the county where the accident occurred, there must be a report listing the effects found on the body."

"Not likely."

"Why do you say that?"

"Now we've touched on an intriguing parallel between Essex and Shields." He paused and looked at Pitt. "Both men were killed on the same day, May twenty-eighth, nineteen fourteen, and neither of their bodies were ever recovered.''

"Great," Pitt sighed. "It never rains . . . but then I didn't expect it to be cut-and-dried.''

"Investigations into the past never are.''

"The coincidence between the deaths of Essex and Shields seems unreal. Could there have been a conspiracy?''

Epstein shook his head. "I doubt it. Stranger things happen. Besides, why sink a ship and murder a thousand souls when Shields could have simply been tossed over the side somewhere in the middle of the Atlantic?''

"You're right, of course.''

"You mind telling me what this is all about?''

"I'm not sure where any of this is leading, myself.''

"If it's newsworthy, I hope you'll let me in on it.''

"Too early to throw in the open. It may be nothing.''

"I've known you too long, Dirk. You don't involve yourself with nothing.''

"Let's just say I'm a sucker for historical mysteries.''

"In that case I've got another one for you.''

"Okay, lay it on me.''

"The river under the bridge was dragged for over a month. Not a single body of a passenger or crewman ever turned up.''

Pitt stopped and stared evenly at Epstein. "I don't buy that. It doesn't figure that a few bodies wouldn't have drifted downriver and beached on the shoreline.''

"That's only the half of it," Epstein said with a cagey look. "The train wasn't found either.''

"Jesus!''

"Out of professional curiosity I read up on the *Manhattan Limited*, as it was called. Divers went down for weeks after the tragedy, but turned up zero. The locomotive and all the coaches were written off as having sunk in quicksand. Directors of the New York & Quebec Northern Railroad spent a fortune trying to recover a trace of their crack train. They failed, and finally threw in the towel. A short time later, the line was absorbed by the New York Central.''

"And that was the end of it.''

"Not quite," Epstein said. "It's claimed that the *Manhattan Limited* still makes its ghostly run.''

"You're kidding.''

"Scout's honor. Local residents in the Hudson River valley swear to seeing a phantom train as it turns from the shore and heads up the grade of the old bridge before it vanishes. Naturally, the apparition only appears after dark."

"Naturally," Pitt replied sarcastically. "You forgot the full moon and the howling of banshees."

Epstein shrugged and then laughed. "I thought you'd appreciate a touch of the macabre."

"You have copies of all this?"

"Sure. I figured you'd want them. There's five pounds of material on the sinking of the *Empress* and the investigation following the Hudson River bridge failure. I also scrounged up the names and addresses of a few people who make a hobby out of researching old ship and train disasters. It's all neatly packaged in an envelope out in the car." Epstein motioned toward the parking lot of the shooting range. "I'll get it for you."

"I appreciate your time and effort," said Pitt.

Epstein stared at him steadily. "One question, Dirk, you owe me that."

"Yes, I owe you that," Pitt acquiesced.

"Is this a NUMA project or are you on your own?"

"Strictly a personal show."

"I see." Epstein looked down on the ground and idly kicked a loose rock. "Did you know that a descendant of Richard Essex was recently found dead?"

"John Essex. Yes, I know."

"One of our reporters covered the story." Epstein paused and nodded in the direction of Pitt's Cobra. "A man matching your description, driving a red sports car, and asking directions to Essex's house was seen by a neighbor an hour before an anonymous phone call to the police tipped them off about his death."

"Coincidence," Pitt shrugged.

"Coincidence your ass," said Epstein. "What in hell are you up to?"

Pitt took a few steps in silence, his face set in a grim expression. Then he smiled slightly, and Epstein could have sworn the smile was tinged with foreboding.

"Believe me, my friend, when I say you don't want to know."

28

Graham Humberly's house sprawled over the top of a hill in Palos
Verdes, a posh bedroom community of Los Angeles. The architecture
was a blend of contemporary and California Spanish with rough coated
plaster walls and ceilings, laced with massive weathered beams covered by a roof of curved red tile.

A large fountain splashed on the main terrace and spilled into a
circular swimming pool. A spectacular panoramic view overlooked a
vast carpet of city lights to the east, while the rear faced down on the
Pacific Ocean and Catalina Island to the west.

Music from a mariachi band and the tidal current of babble from a
hundred voices greeted Shaw as he entered Humberly's home. Bar-
tenders were feverishly mixing gallons of tequila margaritas while the
caterers busily replenished spicy Mexican dishes on a buffet table that
seemed to stretch into infinity.

A small man with a head too large for his shoulders approached. He
was wearing a black dinner jacket with an oriental dragon embroidered
on the back.

"Hello, I'm Graham Humberly," he said with a glossy smile.
"Welcome to the party."

"Brian Shaw."

The smile remained glossy. "Ah, yes, Mr. Shaw. Sorry for not
recognizing you, but our mutual friends didn't send me a photograph."

"You have a most impressive home. Nothing quite like it in England."

"Thank you. But the credit belongs to my wife. I preferred something more provincial. Fortunately, her taste surpassed mine."

Humberly's accent, Shaw guessed, hinted of Cornwall. "Is Commander Milligan present?"

Humberly took his arm and led him away from the crowd. "Yes,
she's here," he said softly. "I had to invite every officer of the ship to
make sure she'd come. Come along, I'll introduce you around."

"I'm not much for social dribble," said Shaw. "Suppose you point her out and I'll handle things on my own."

"As you wish." Humberly studied the mass of bodies milling around the terrace. Then his gaze stopped and he nodded toward the bar. "The tall, rather attractive woman with blond hair in the blue dress."

Shaw easily picked her out in an admiring circle of white-uniformed naval officers. She looked to be in her mid-thirties and radiated a warmth that escaped most women. She seemed to accept the attention naturally without any sign of caprice. Shaw liked what he saw at first glance.

"Perhaps I can smooth the way by separating her from the horde," said Humberly.

"Don't bother," replied Shaw. "By the way, do you have a car I might borrow?"

"I have a fleet. What have you got in mind, a chauffeured limousine?"

"Something with more spirit."

Humberly thought a moment. "Will a Rolls Royce Corniche convertible be appropriate?"

"It should do nicely."

"You'll find it in the drive. A red one. The keys will be in the ignition."

"Thank you."

"Not at all. Good hunting."

Humberly returned to his duties as host. Shaw moved toward the bar and shouldered his way up to Heidi Milligan. A blond young lieutenant gave him an indignant stare.

"A bit pushy, aren't you, dad?"

Shaw ignored him and smiled at Heidi. "Commander Milligan, I'm Admiral Brian Shaw. May I have a word with you . . . alone."

Heidi studied his face a moment, trying to place him. She gave up and nodded. "Of course, Admiral."

The blond lieutenant looked as if he'd discovered his fly was open. "My apologies, sir. But I thought . . ."

Shaw flashed him a benevolent smile. "Always remember, lad, it pays to know the enemy."

"I like your style, Admiral," Heidi shouted over the roar of the wind.

Shaw's foot pressed the accelerator another half inch, and the Rolls surged north along the San Diego freeway. He'd had no specific destination in mind when he left the party with Heidi. Thirty years had passed since he last saw Los Angeles. He drove aimlessly, depending only on the direction signs, not at all sure where they would take him.

He glanced at her out of the corner of his eye. Her eyes were wide and sparkling from exhilaration. He felt her hand grip his arm.

"You better slow down," she yelled, "before you're stopped by a cop."

That he didn't need. Shaw eased off the gas pedal and let the car coast down to the legal speed limit. He turned on the FM radio and a Strauss waltz settled over the car. He started to change the station, but she touched his hand.

"No, leave it." She leaned back in the seat and gazed up at the stars. "Where are we going?"

"An old Scottish ploy," he laughed. "Abduct females to distant places . . . that way they must become interested in you if they want to get home."

"Won't work." She laughed. "I'm already three thousand miles away from home."

"Without a uniform too."

"Naval regulation: Lady officers are allowed to dress in civilian attire for social functions."

"Three cheers for the American navy."

She looked at him speculatively. "I've never known an admiral who drove a Rolls-Royce."

He smiled. "There are dozens of us on-the-beach, old British seadogs who wouldn't be caught in any other car."

"Three cheers for your navy," she laughed.

"Seriously, I made a few wise investments when I commanded a naval depot in Ceylon."

"What do you do now that you're retired from service?"

"Write mostly. Historical books. *Nelson at the Battle of the Nile, The Admiralty in World War I,* that sort of thing. Hardly the stuff best-sellers are made of, but there's a certain amount of prestige attached to it."

She looked at him strangely. "You're putting me on."

"I beg your pardon."

"Do you really write historical naval books?"

"Of course," he said innocently. "Why should I lie?"

"Incredible," murmured Heidi. "I do too, but I've yet to be published."

"I say, that is incredible," Shaw said, doing his best to appear properly amazed. Then he groped for her hand, found it and gave a light pressure. "When must you return to your ship?"

He could feel her tremble slightly. "There's no rush."

He glanced at a large green sign with white letters as it flashed past. "Have you ever been to Santa Barbara?"

"No," she said in almost a whisper. "But I hear it's beautiful."

In the morning it was Heidi who ordered breakfast from room service. As she poured the coffee, she experienced a glowing warmth of delight. Making love to a stranger only a few hours after meeting him gave her an inner thrill she had not known before. It was a sensation that was peculiar to her.

She could easily recall the men she'd had: the frightened midshipman at Annapolis, her ex-husband, Admiral Walter Bass, Dirk Pitt, and now Shaw . . . she could see them all clearly, as if they were lined up for inspection. Only five, hardly enough to make up an army, much less a platoon.

Why is it, she wondered, the older a woman becomes, the more she regrets not having gone to bed with more men. She became annoyed with herself. She had been too careful in her single years, afraid to appear overly eager, never able to bring herself to indulge in a casual affair.

How silly of her, she thought. After all, she often felt she'd had ten times the physical pleasure of any man. Her ecstasy mushroomed from within. Men she knew had felt a sensation that was merely external. They seemed to rely more on imagination and were frequently disappointed afterward. Sex to them was often no different from going to a movie; a woman demands much more . . . too much.

"You look pensive this morning," said Shaw. He pulled up her hair and kissed the nape of her neck. "Suffering remorse in the cold light of dawn?"

"More like entranced in fond remembrance."

"When do you sail?"

"Day after tomorrow."

"Then we still have time together."

She shook her head. "I'll be on duty until we cast off."

Shaw walked over and stared through the sliding glass doors of their hotel room overlooking the ocean. He could only see a few hundred feet. The Santa Barbara coastline was covered by a mantle of fog.

"A damned shame," he said wistfully. "We have so much in common."

She came over and slipped her arm around his waist. "What do you have in mind? Making love at night and researching by day?"

He laughed. "Americans and their direct humor. Not a bad idea though. We might very well complement each other. What exactly is it you're writing at the moment?"

"My thesis for a doctorate. The navy under President Wilson's administration."

"Sounds terribly dull."

"It is." Heidi went silent, a thoughtful look in her face. Then she said, "Have you ever heard of the North American Treaty?"

There it was. No coaxing, no intrigue or torture; she simply came out with it.

Shaw did not answer immediately. He chose his reply carefully.

"Yes, I recall running across it."

Heidi looked at him, her mouth half open to speak, but nothing came out.

"You have a strange expression on your face."

"You're familiar with the treaty?" she asked in astonishment. "You've actually seen references to it?"

"I've never actually read the wording. Fact is I've forgotten its purpose. It was of little consequence as I remember. You can find material relating to it in most any archive in London." Shaw had kept his tone nonchalant. He calmly lit a cigarette. "Is the treaty part of your research project?"

"No," Heidi answered. "By chance I stumbled on a brief mention. I pursued it out of curiosity, but turned up nothing that proved it ever truly existed."

"I'll be happy to make a copy and send it to you."

"Don't bother. Just knowing it wasn't a figment of my imagination is enough to soothe my inquisitive soul. Besides, I turned my notes over to a friend in Washington."

"I'll send them to her."

"She's a he."

"All right, *he,*" he said, trying to mute the impatience in his voice. "What's his name and address?"

"Dirk Pitt. You can reach him at the National Underwater and Marine Agency."

Shaw had what he came for. A dedicated agent would have whisked Heidi back to her ship and rushed aboard the first flight to Washington.

Shaw had never considered himself dedicated in the gung ho sense. There were times it did not pay, and this was one of them.

He kissed Heidi hard on the mouth.

"So much for research. Now let's go back to bed."

And they did.

29

An early afternoon breeze blew steadily out of the northeast. A cold breeze full of little needles that jabbed exposed skin into numbness. The temperature was three degrees Celsius, but to Pitt, as he stood looking out over the waters of the St. Lawrence River, the windchill factor made it feel closer to minus ten.

He inhaled the smells of the docks jutting into the little bay a few miles from the Quebec Province city of Rimouski, his nostrils sifting out the distinct tangs of tar, rust and diesel oil. He walked along the aging planks until he came to a gangway that led down to a boat resting comfortably in the oily water. The designer had given it no-nonsense lines, about fifteen meters, spacious flush decks, twin screw and diesel engines. There was no attempt at flashy chrome; the hull was painted black. It was built to be functional, ideal for fishing trips, diving excursions or oil surveys. The topside was squared away and spotless, the sure signs of an affectionate owner.

A man emerged from the wheelhouse. He wore a stocking cap that failed to restrain a thicket of coarse black hair. The face looked as though it had been battered by a hundred storms, but the eyes were sad and watchful as Pitt hesitated before stepping onto the afterdeck.

"My name is Dirk Pitt. I'm looking for Jules Le Mat."

There was a slight pause, and then strong white teeth flashed like a theater marquee in a hearty smile. "Welcome, Monsieur Pitt. Please come aboard."

"She's a smart boat."

"No beauty, maybe, but like a good wife it's sturdy and loyal." The hand clasp was like a vise. "You've picked a fine day for your visit. The St. Lawrence is cooperating. No fog and only a mild chop over deep water. If you'll give me a hand and cast off, we can get under way."

Le Mat went below and started the diesels as Pitt unwrapped the bow and stern lines from the dock cleats and coiled them on the deck. The green water of the bay slid past the hull almost unwrinkled and slowly altered to an unruly blue as they entered the mainstream of the river. Twenty-eight miles away, the rising hills on the opposite shore were painted white by the winter snows. They passed a fishing boat heading toward the docks with a week's catch, its skipper waving in reply to Le Mat's squawk on the boat's horn. Astern, the spires of Rimouski's picturesque cathedrals stood out in sharp detail under the March sun.

The icy breeze increased its bite as they left the shelter of the land and Pitt ducked into the saloon.

"A cup of tea?" inquired Le Mat.

"Sounds good," said Pitt, smiling.

"The pot is in the galley." Le Mat spoke without turning, his hands loosely gripped on the wheel, his gaze straight ahead. "Please help yourself. I have to keep a sharp eye for ice floes. They're thicker than flies on manure this time of year."

Pitt poured a steaming cup. He sat on a high swivel chair and looked out at the river. Le Mat was right. The water was littered with ice floes about the same size as the boat.

"What was it like the night the *Empress of Ireland* went down?" he asked, breaking the silence.

"Clear skies," Le Mat answered. "The river was calm, its waters a few degrees above freezing, no wind to speak of. A few patches of fog, common in the spring when the southern warm air meets the cold river."

"The *Empress* was a good ship?"

"One of the best." Le Mat replied seriously to what he considered a naive question. "Built to the finest standards of the day for her owners, the Canadian Pacific Railway. She and her sister ship, the *Empress of Britain,* were handsome liners, fourteen thousand tons and five hundred and fifty feet long. Their accommodations were not as elegant, perhaps, as those on the *Olympic* or the *Mauritania,* but they achieved a solid reputation for providing their passengers with a comfortable sort of luxury on the Atlantic crossing.''

"As I recall, the *Empress* departed Quebec bound for Liverpool on its final voyage.''

"Cast the mooring lines close to four thirty in the afternoon. Nine hours later she lay on the river bottom, her starboard side stove in. It was the fog that wrote the ship's epitaph.''

"And a coal collier called the *Storstad.*''

Le Mat smiled. ''You've done your homework, Mr. Pitt. The mystery was never completely laid to rest how the *Empress* and the *Storstad* collided. Their crews sighted each other eight miles apart. When they were separated by less than two miles a low fogbank drifted across their path. Captain Kendall, master of the *Empress,* reversed his engines and stopped the ship. It was a mistake; he should have kept underway. The men in the wheelhouse on the *Storstad* became confused when the *Empress* vanished in the mists. They thought the liner was approaching off their port bow when indeed, it was drifting with engines stopped to their starboard. The *Storstad*'s first mate ordered the wheel to the right and the *Empress of Ireland* and her passengers were condemned to disaster.''

Le Mat paused to point at an ice floe nearly an acre in size. ''We had an unseasonably cold winter this year. The river is still frozen solid a hundred and fifty miles upstream.''

Pitt kept silent, slowly sipping the tea.

"The six-thousand-ton *Storstad,*'' Le Mat continued, ''laden with eleven thousand tons of coal, cut into the *Empress* amidships, slicing a gaping wound twenty-four feet high and fifteen feet wide. Within fourteen minutes the *Empress* fell to the bed of the St. Lawrence, taking over a thousand souls with her.''

"Strange how quickly the ship vanished into the past,'' Pitt said pensively.

"Yes, you ask anyone from the States or Europe about the *Empress* and they'll tell you they never heard of her. It's almost a crime the way the ship was forgotten.''

"You haven't forgotten her.''

"Nor has Quebec Province,'' said Le Mat, pointing toward the east. ''Just behind Pointe au Père, 'Father's Point' in English, lie eighty-eight unidentified victims of the tragedy in a little cemetery still maintained by the Canadian Pacific Railroad." A look of great sorrow came on Le Mat's face. He spoke of the terrible mathematics of the dead as though the sinking had happened yesterday. "The Salvation Army remembers. Out of a hundred and seventy-one who were going to London for a convention, only twenty-six survived. They hold a memorial service for their dead at Mount Pleasant Cemetery in Toronto on the anniversary of the sinking."

"I'm told you've made the *Empress* a life's work."

"I have a deep passion for the *Empress*. It's like a great love that overwhelms some men in seeing the painting of a woman who died long before they were born."

"I lean more on flesh than fantasy," said Pitt.

"Sometimes fantasy is more rewarding," Le Mat replied, a dreamlike expression on his face. Suddenly he came alert and spun the wheel to avert an ice floe that loomed in the path of the boat. "Between June and September, when the weather warms, I dive on the wreck twenty, maybe thirty times."

"What is the condition of the *Empress*?"

"A fair amount of disintegration. Though not as bad as you might think after seventy-five years of submersion. I think it's because the fresh water from the river dilutes the salinity from the eastern sea. The hull lies on its starboard side at a list of forty-five degrees. Some of the overhead bulkheads have fallen in on the upper superstructure, but the rest of the ship is pretty much intact."

"Its depth?"

"About a hundred and sixty-five feet. A bit deep for diving on compressed air, but I manage it." Le Mat closed the throttles and shut down the engines, allowing the boat to drift in the current. Then he turned and faced Pitt. "Tell me, Mr. Pitt, what is your interest in the *Empress*? Why did you seek me out?"

"I'm searching for information on a passenger by the name of Harvey Shields, who was lost with the ship. I was told that no one knows more about the *Empress* than Jules Le Mat."

Le Mat considered Pitt's reply for some time, then said: "Yes, I recall a Harvey Shields was one of the victims. There is no mention of him during the sinking by survivors. I must assume he was one of nearly seven hundred who still lie entombed within the rotting hulk."

"Perhaps he was found but never identified, like those buried in Father's Point cemetery."

Le Mat shook his head. "Mostly third-class passengers. Shields was a British diplomat, an important man. His body would have been recognized.''

Pitt set aside the teacup. ''Then my search ends here.''

''No, Mr. Pitt,'' said Le Mat, ''not here.''

Pitt looked at him, saying nothing.

''Down there,'' Le Mat went on, nodding toward the deck. ''The *Empress of Ireland* lies beneath us.'' He pointed out a cabin window. ''There floats her marker.''

Fifty feet off the port side of the boat an orange buoy rose and fell gently on the icy river, its line stretching through the dark waters to the silent wreck below.

30

Pitt swung his rented minicar off the state thruway and entered a narrow paved road adjoining the Hudson River shortly after sunset. He passed a stone marker designating a Revolutionary War site and was tempted to stop and stretch his legs, but decided to press on to his destination before it became dark. The scenic river was beautiful in the fading light, the fields that dipped to the water's edge glistened under a late winter snowfall.

He stopped for gas at a small station below the town of Coxsackie. The attendant, an elderly man in faded coveralls, stayed inside the office, his feet propped on a metal stool in front of a woodburning stove. Pitt filled the tank and entered. The attendant peered around him at the pump.

''Looks like twenty dollars even,'' he said.

Pitt handed him the cash. ''How much further to Wacketshire?''

His eyes squinted in suspicion as they studied Pitt like probes. ''Wacketshire? It ain't been called that in years. Fact of the matter is, the town don't exist no more.''

''A ghost town in upstate New York? I'd have thought the southwest desert a more likely place.''

''No joke, mister. When the railroad line was torn up back in '49, Wacketshire gave up and died. Most of the buildings were burned down by vandals. Nobody lives there anymore except some fella who makes statues.''

"Is anything left of the old track bed?'' Pitt asked.

"Most of it's gone,'' said the old man, his expression turning wistful. "Damned shame, too.'' Then he shrugged. "At least we didn't have to see them smelly diesels come through here. The last train over the old line was pulled by steam.''

"Perhaps steam will return someday.''

"I'll never live to see it.'' The attendant looked at Pitt with growing respect. "How come you're interested in a deserted railroad?''

"I'm a train nut,'' Pitt lied without hesitation. He seemed to be getting quite good at it lately. "My special interest is the classic trains. At the moment I'm researching the *Manhattan Limited* of the New York & Quebec Northern system.''

"That's the one that fell through the Deauville Bridge. Killed a hundred people, you know.''

"Yes,'' Pitt said evenly, "I know.''

The old man turned and gazed out the window. "The *Manhattan Limited* is special,'' he said. "You can always tell when it comes down the line. It has a sound all its own.''

Pitt wasn't sure he heard right. The attendant was speaking in the present tense. "You must be talking about a different train.''

"No, sir. I've watched the old *Manhattan Limited* come hootin' and clankin' down the track, whistle a-blowin', headlight a-glowin', just like it did the night it went in the river.''

The old-timer spoke of seeing the phantom train as nonchalantly as if he were describing the weather.

It was dusk when Pitt stopped his car at a small turnout in the road. A cold wind was rolling in from the north, and he zipped an old leather driving jacket to his neck and turned up the collar. He slipped a knit ski cap over his head and stepped out of the car, locking the doors.

The colors in the western sky were altering from orange to a blue-purple as he trudged across a frozen field toward the river, his boots crunching on a four-inch layer of snow. He realized that he had forgotten his gloves, but rather than return to the car and lose minutes of the ebbing daylight, he jammed his hands deeper in his pockets.

After a quarter of a mile he reached a belt of hickory trees and low shrubs. He picked his way around the frozen branches, which sprouted strange growths of ice crystals, and came to a high embankment. The slopes were steep and he had to use his hands to claw his way up the wind-glazed slippery surface to the top.

At last, his fingers frozen numb, he stood on the long abandoned track bed. It was badly eroded in places and covered by tangles of dead and ice-stiffened weeds protruding from the snow.

The once busy railroad was only a distant memory.

In the dimming light Pitt's eyes picked out the telltale relics of the past. A few rotting crossties half buried in the ground, an occasional rusty spike, scattered rock from the track ballast. The telegraph poles still stood, stretching off into infinity like a line of straggling, battle-weary soldiers. Their weathered crossbeams were still bolted in place.

Pitt took his bearings and began trudging along a slight curve that led up the grade to the empty bridge crossing. The air was sharp and tingled his nostrils. His breath formed shapeless mists that quickly vanished. A rabbit darted in front of him and leaped down the embankment.

Dusk had deepened to night. He no longer cast a shadow when he stopped and stared down at the icy river 150 feet below. The stone abutment of the Deauville-Hudson bridge seemed to lead to nowhere.

Two solitary piers rose like forlorn sentinels from the water that swirled around their base. There was no sign of the 500-foot truss they had once supported. The bridge had never been rebuilt; the main track was constructed further south to cross over a newer and stronger suspension span.

Pitt knelt on his haunches for a long while trying to visualize that fateful night, almost seeing the red lights on the last coach grow smaller as the train rolled onto the great center truss, hearing the shriek of tortured metal, the great splash in the uncaring river.

His reverie was interrupted by another sound, a high-pitched wailing in the distance.

He rose to his feet and listened. For a few moments all he could hear was the whisper of the wind. Then it came again from somewhere to the north, echoing and reechoing off the forbidding cliffs along the Hudson, the naked limbs of the trees, the darkened hills of the valley.

It was a train whistle.

He saw a faint, swelling yellow glow moving steadily toward him. Soon other sounds touched his ears, a grinding clatter and the hissing of steam. Unseen birds, startled by the sudden noise, flapped into the black sky.

Pitt could not bring himself to believe the reality of what he apparently saw; it was impossible for a train to be speeding over the nonexistent rails of the forsaken track bed. He stood unfeeling of the cold, searching for an explanation, his mind refusing to accept his senses, but the scream of the whistle grew louder and the light brighter.

For maybe ten seconds, maybe twenty, Pitt stood as frozen as the trees bordering the track bed. The adrenaline surged through his bloodstream, and the floodgates of fear burst open and swept away all established thoughts of logic. He began to lose reality as fingers of panic tightened around his stomach.

The shrill whistle shattered the night again as the horror laid into the curve and pounded up the grade to the missing bridge, the headlamp transfixing him in a blinding glare.

Pitt never remembered how long he watched petrified at what deep down he knew to be a superstitious apparition. Faintly the cry of self-preservation broke through and he looked around for a way to flee. The narrow sides of the abutment dropped off in the blackness; behind him was the sheer drop to the river.

He felt trapped on the brink of a void.

The ghostly locomotive was lunging closer with a vengeance, the clang of its bell audible now above the roar of the exhaust.

Then suddenly anger replaced the fear in Pitt, an anger that stemmed partly from his own helplessness, partly from his slowness to act. The moment it took him to make a decision seemed a lifetime. Only one practical direction was open to him and he grabbed it.

Like a sprinter off the mark at the starter's gun, he charged down the grade on a collision course with the unknown.

31

The blazing light abruptly blinked out and the clamor melted into the night.

Pitt stopped and stood stock-still, swept by incomprehension, straining to readjust his eyes to the darkness. He cocked his head, listening. No sound was to be heard except the whisper of the north wind again.

He became aware of the burning cold on his exposed hands and the pounding of his heart.

Two full minutes passed, and nothing happened. He began jogging slowly along the barren track bed, halting every few yards and studying the carpet of snow. Except for his footprints heading in the opposite direction, the white was unmarred.

Confusion in his gut, he continued for half a mile, stalking warily, half expecting but somehow doubtful of finding a trace of the mechanical specter. Nothing struck his eye. It was as if the train had never been.

He stumbled over a rigid object in his path, sprawling awkwardly on a wind-scoured patch of gravel. Cursing his clumsiness, he groped around in a circle, his fingers coming in contact with two parallel ribbons of cold metal.

My God, they're rails.

He jerked to his feet and pushed on. After rounding a sharp bend, he saw the blue glow of a television set through the windows of a house. The rails appeared to run past the front porch.

A dog barked from within the house and soon a square of light spread through an opened door. Pitt merged into the shadows. A huge, shaggy sheep dog jumped down on the crossties, sniffed the frigid air, and not wishing to linger, hoisted his hind leg and did his thing before tearing back into the comfort of a fireplace-warm living room. Then the door closed.

As Pitt came closer he distinguished a great black hulk parked on a sidetrack. It proved to be a locomotive with a stoker car and caboose attached behind. Cautiously he climbed into the cab and touched the firebox. The metal was ice cold. Rust came away in his hands—the boilers had not been lit for a long time.

He crossed over the tracks to the house and knocked on the front door.

The dog dutifully rasped out a series of barks and soon a man in a rumpled bathrobe stood on the threshold. The light was at his back and his facial features were shadowed. He was almost as wide as the doorway and carried his weight like a wrestler.

"Can I help you?" he asked in a bottom-of-the-barrel voice.

"I'm sorry to trouble you," replied Pitt with a down-home smile, "but I wonder if I might have a word with you?"

The man gave Pitt a chilly once-over and then nodded. "Sure, come on in."

"My name is Pitt, Dirk Pitt."

"Ansel Magee."

The name struck a chord with Pitt but before he could tie it down, Magee turned and bellowed, "Annie, we got a visitor."

A woman came out of the kitchen. She carried herself languidly and stood tall. Her shape was pencil thin, the exact opposite of Magee. Pitt guessed she'd been a fashion model at one time. Her hair was salt and pepper and gracefully styled. She wore a tight-fitting red housecoat with a matching apron, and she held a dishtowel in one hand.

"My wife Annie." Magee made the appropriate gestures with his hand. "This is Mr. Pitt."

"How do you do?" Annie said warmly. "You look like you could use a cup of coffee."

"I'd love one," said Pitt. "Black, thank you."

Her eyes widened. "Did you know your hands were bleeding?"

Pitt looked at the skin abrasions on his palms. "I must have scraped them when I tripped over the rails outside. They're so numb from the cold I didn't notice."

"You just sit down here by the fire," said Annie, guiding him to a circular sofa. "I'll get them fixed up for you." She hurried into the kitchen and filled a bowl with warm water. Then she went to the bathroom for the antiseptic.

"I'll get the coffee," Magee volunteered.

The sheep dog stayed and stared blankly at Pitt. At least he thought the dog was staring at him. Its eyes were curtained by thick tufts of hair.

He regarded the interior of the living room. The furniture appeared to be individually designed along contemporary lines. Each piece, including the lamps and numerous art objects, was elegantly contoured in poly resin and painted either red or white. The room was a livable art gallery.

Magee returned with a cup of steaming coffee.

In the light Pitt identified the kindly, elflike face. "You're Ansel Magee, the sculptor."

"I'm afraid there are certain art critics who would disagree with that label." Magee laughed good-naturedly.

"You're modest," said Pitt. "I once stood in a block-long line waiting to view your exhibit at the National Art Gallery in Washington."

"Are you a modern-art connoisseur, Mr. Pitt?"

"I'd hardly qualify even as a dilettante. Actually, my love affair is with antique machinery. I collect old cars and airplanes." That part was true. "I also have a passion for steam locomotives." That part was another lie.

"Then we have a common meeting ground," said Magee. "I'm an old train buff myself." He reached over and turned off the television.

"I noticed your private railroad."

"An Atlantic type four-four-two," Magee said as if reciting. "Rolled out of the Baldwin Works in nineteen oh-six. Pulled the *Overland Limited* from Chicago to Council Bluffs, Iowa. It was quite a speedster in its day."

"When was the last time it was operated?" Pitt sensed immediately that he'd used the wrong terminology by the sour expression on Magee's face.

"I stoked it up two summers ago after I laid in about a half mile of track. Ran the neighbors and their kids back and forth on my private line. Gave it up after my last heart attack. It's sat idle ever since."

Annie returned and began bathing his cuts. "Sorry, but all I could find was an old bottle of iodine. It'll sting."

She was wrong: Pitt's hands still had no feeling. He watched silently while she tied the bandages. Then she sat back and appraised her handiwork.

"Won't win a medical award, but I guess it will do until you get home."

"It will do just fine," Pitt said.

Magee settled into a tulip-shaped chair. "Now then, Mr. Pitt. What's on your mind?"

Pitt came right to the point. "I'm accumulating data on the *Manhattan Limited*."

"I see," said Magee, but it was plain he didn't. "I assume your interest lies more in the nature of its last run rather than its track history."

"Yes," Pitt admitted. "There are several aspects of the disaster that have never been explained in depth. I've gone over the old newspaper accounts, but they raise more questions than they answer."

Magee eyed him suspiciously. "Are you a reporter?"

Pitt shook his head. "I'm special projects director for the National Underwater and Marine Agency."

"You're with the government?"

"Uncle Sam pays my wages, yes. But my curiosity concerning the Deauville-Hudson bridge disaster is purely personal."

"Curiosity? More like obsession, I'd say. What else would drive a man to wander about the countryside in freezing weather and in the dead of night?"

"I'm on a tight schedule," Pitt explained patiently. "I must be in Washington by tomorrow morning. This was my only chance to view the bridge site. Besides, it was still daylight when I arrived."

Magee seemed to relax. "My apologies for forcing an inquisition on you, Mr. Pitt, but you're the only stranger who's stumbled onto my little hideaway. Except for a few select friends and business associates, the public thinks I'm some sort of weird recluse feverishly pouring molds in a rundown warehouse on New York's east side. A sham contrived for a purpose. I value my seclusion. If I had to contend with a constant stream of gawkers, critics and newspeople pounding at my door all day, I would never get any work done. Here, hidden away in the Hudson valley, I can create without hassle."

"More coffee?" asked Annie. With feminine astuteness she had picked the opportune time to interrupt.

"Please," replied Pitt.

"How about some hot apple pie?"

"Sounds great. I haven't eaten since breakfast."

"Let me make you something, then."

"No, no, the pie will be fine."

As soon as she left, Magee continued the conversation. "I hope you understand what I'm driving at, Mr. Pitt."

"I have no reason to sell out your privacy," said Pitt.

"I shall trust you not to."

Feeling was beginning to return to Pitt's hands and they ached like hell. Annie Magee brought him the apple pie and he attacked it with the ravenousness of a farmhand.

"Your fascination with trains," Pitt said between bites. "Living practically on top of the bridge site, you must have an insight on the disaster that can't be found in old files."

Magee stared into the fire a long moment, then began speaking in a vacant tone. "You're right, of course. I *have* studied the strange incidents surrounding the wreck of the *Manhattan Limited*. Dug into local legends, mostly. I was lucky and interviewed Sam Harding, the station agent who was on duty the night it happened, a few months before he died at a rest home in Germantown. Eighty-eight he was. Had a memory like a computer bank. God, it was like talking with history. I could almost see the events of that fatal night unfold in front of my eyes."

"A holdup at the exact moment the train came through," said Pitt. "The robber refusing to let the station agent flag the engineer and save a hundred lives. It reads like fiction."

"No fiction, Mr. Pitt. It occurred just the way Harding described it to the police and newspaper reporters. The telegrapher, Hiram Meechum, had a bullet hole in his hip as proof."

"I'm familiar with the account." Pitt nodded.

"Then you know the robber was never caught. Harding and Meechum positively identified him as Clement Massey, or Dapper Doyle as he was called in the press. A natty dresser who had pulled off some pretty ingenious heists."

"Odd that the ground split and swallowed him."

"Times were different before the war to end all war. The law authorities weren't nearly as sophisticated as they are now. Doyle was no moron. A few years behind bars for robbery is one thing. Indirectly causing the deaths of a hundred men, women and children is quite another. If he had been caught, a jury would have taken all of five minutes to send him to the gallows."

Pitt finished off the pie and leaned back in the sofa. "Any guesses as to why the train was never recovered?"

Magee shook his head. "Supposedly it sank in quicksand. Local scuba-diving clubs still search for artifacts. A few years ago an old locomotive headlamp was pulled from the river a mile downstream. Folks generally assumed that it came from the *Manhattan Limited*. I feel it is only a matter of time before the riverbed shifts and reveals the wreckage."

"More pie, Mr. Pitt?" asked Annie Magee.

"I'm tempted, but no, thank you," said Pitt, rising. "I'd best be leaving. I have a plane to catch at Kennedy in a few hours. I'm grateful for your hospitality."

"Before you go," said Magee, "I'd like to show you something."

The sculptor pushed himself from the chair and walked over to a door set in the middle of the far wall. He opened it to a darkened room and disappeared inside. He reappeared a few moments later, holding a flickering kerosene lamp.

"This way," he said, motioning.

Pitt entered, his nose sorting out the musty smells of aged wood and leather from the kerosene vapor, his eyes scanning the shadows that quivered under the soft flame of the lamp.

He recognized the interior as an office furnished with antiques. A potbellied stove squatted in the middle of the floor, its flue sprouting straight through the roof. The orange glow revealed a safe backed into a corner, its door decorated with the painting of a covered wagon crossing the prairie.

Two desks sat against a wall of windows. One was a rolltop with an old-fashioned telephone perched on its surface, the other was long and flat and supported a large cabinet filled with pigeonholes. On the edge, in front of a leather-cushioned tilt-back chair, there was a telegraph key whose wires angled up and through the ceiling.

The walls held a Seth Thomas clock, a poster touting the Parker and Schmidt traveling amusement show, a framed picture of an overripe girl holding a tray stacked with bottles of beer advertising the Ruppert Brewery on 94th Street in New York City, and a Feeney & Company insurance calendar dated May 1914.

"Sam Harding's office," Magee said proudly. "I've re-created it exactly as it was on the night of the robbery."

"Then your house . . ."

"Is the original Wacketshire station," Magee finished. "The farmer I bought the property from used it to store feed for his cows. Annie and I restored the building. A pity you haven't seen it in daylight. The architecture has a distinctive design. Ornate trimmings around the roof, graceful curves. Dates back to the eighteen eighties."

"You've done a remarkable job of preservation," Pitt complimented him.

"Yes, it's been given a better fate than most old railroad stations," said Magee. "We made a few changes. What used to be the freight area is now bedrooms, and our living room is the former waiting room."

"The furnishings, are they original?" Pitt asked, touching the telegraph key.

"For the most part. Harding's desk was here when we bought the place. The stove was salvaged from a trash pile, and Annie rescued the safe from a hardware store in Selkirk. The real prize, though, was this."

Magee lifted a leather dustcover, revealing a chessboard. The hand-carved ebony and birch pieces were cracked and worn by the years.

"Hiram Meechum's chess set," explained Magee. "His widow gave it to me. The bullet hole from Massey's pistol was never patched."

Pitt studied the board for a few moments in silence. Then he looked out the windows at the blackness.

"You can almost sense their presence," he said finally.

"I often sit alone here in the office and try to visualize that fateful night."

"Do you see the *Manhattan Limited* as it roars past?"

"Sometimes," Magee said dreamily. "If my imagination flows freely . . ." He stopped and stared at Pitt suspiciously. "A strange question. Why do you ask?"

"The phantom train," answered Pitt. "They say it still makes its spectral run over the old track bed."

"The Hudson valley is a breeding ground for myths," Magee scoffed. "There are those who even claim to have seen the headless horseman, for God's sake. What starts as a tall tale becomes a rumor. Embellished with age and exaggerated by local folklore, the rumor turns into a full-blown legend bending the outer fringe of reality. The phantom train hauntings began a few years after the bridge failure. Like a ghost of a guillotined man who wanders about searching for his head, the *Manhattan Limited,* so its disciples believe, will never enter that great depot in the sky until it finally crosses over the river."

Pitt laughed. "Mr. Magee, you are a card-carrying skeptic."

"I won't deny it."

Pitt looked at his watch. "I really must be on my way."

Magee showed him outside and they shook hands on the old station platform.

"I've had a fascinating evening," said Pitt. "I'm grateful to you and your wife for your hospitality."

"Our pleasure. Please come back and visit us. I love to talk trains."

Pitt hesitated. "There is one thing you might keep in mind."

"What's that?"

"A funny thing about legends," Pitt said, searching Magee's eyes. "They're usually born from a truth."

In the light from the house, the kindly face was somber and thoughtful, no more. Then Magee shrugged noncommittally and closed the door.

32

Danielle Sarveux warmly greeted Premier Jules Guerrier of Quebec Province in the corridor of the hospital. He was accompanied by his secretary and Henri Villon.

Guerrier kissed Danielle lightly on both cheeks. He was in his late seventies, tall and slender with unkept silver hair and thick tangled beard. He could have easily accommodated an artist's conception of Moses. As Premier of Quebec he was also the leader of the French-speaking Parti Québécois.

"How marvelous to see you, Jules," said Danielle.

"Better for old eyes to behold a beautiful woman," he answered gallantly.

"Charles is looking forward to seeing you."

"How is he getting along?"

"The doctors say he is doing fine. But the healing process will take a long time."

Sarveux was propped up by pillows, his bed parked beside a large window with a view of the Parliament building. A nurse took their hats and coats, and then they grouped around the bed on a chair and sofa. Danielle poured a round of cognac.

"I'm allowed to serve a drink to my visitors," said Sarveux. "But unfortunately alcohol won't mix with my medication so I can't join you."

"To your speedy recovery," toasted Guerrier.

"A speedy recovery," the others responded.

Guerrier set his glass on an end table. "I'm honored that you asked to see me, Charles."

Sarveux looked at him seriously. "I've just been informed you're calling a referendum for total independence."

Guerrier gave a Gallic shrug. "The time is long overdue for a final break from the confederation."

"I agree, and I intend to give it my full endorsement."

Sarveux's statement fell like a guillotine blade.

Guerrier visibly tensed. "You'll not fight it this time?"

"No, I want to see it done and over with."

"I've known you too long, Charles, not to suspect an ulterior motive behind your sudden benevolence."

"You misread me, Jules. I'm not rolling over like a trained dog. If Quebec wants to go it alone, then let it be. Your referendums, your mandates, your incessant negotiations. That's in the past. Canada has suffered enough. The confederation no longer needs Quebec. We will survive without you."

"And we without you."

Sarveux smiled sardonically. "We'll see how you do starting from scratch."

"We expect to do just that," said Guerrier. "Quebec Parliament will be closed and a new government installed. One patterned after the French republic. We will write our own laws, collect our own taxes, and establish formal relations with foreign powers. Naturally, we'll maintain a common currency and other economic ties with the English-speaking provinces."

"You'll not get your cake and eat it too," said Sarveux, his voice hard. "Quebec must print its own money, and any trade agreements must be renegotiated. Also, customs inspection stations will be erected along our common borders. All Canadian institutions and government offices will be withdrawn from Quebec soil."

A look of anger crossed Guerrier's face. "Those are harsh actions."

"Once Quebeckers have turned their backs on the political freedoms, wealth and future of a united Canada, the severance must be unconditional and complete."

Guerrier got to his feet slowly. "I would have hoped for more compassion from a fellow Frenchman."

"My fellow Frenchmen murdered fifty innocent people in an attempt to assassinate me. Consider yourself lucky, Jules, that I don't lay the blame on the doorstep of the Parti Québécois. The outrage and whiplash would cause irreparable damage to your cause."

"You have my solemn word, the Parti Québécois played no part in the plane crash."

"What about the terrorists of the FQS?"

"I have never condoned the actions of the FQS," Guerrier said defensively.

"Mere lip service. You've done nothing to stop them."

"They're like ghosts," Guerrier protested. "No one even knows who their leader is."

"What happens after independence and he comes out in the open?"

"When Quebec becomes free the FQS no longer has a reason to exist. He and his organization can only wither away and die."

"You forget, Jules, terrorist movements have a nasty habit of turning legitimate and forming opposition parties."

"The FQS will not be tolerated by Quebec's new government."

"With you at its head," Sarveux added.

"I should expect so," Guerrier said without a trace of ego. "Who else has the mandate of the people for a glorious new nation?"

"I wish you luck," Sarveux said skeptically. There was no arguing with Guerrier's fervor, he thought. The French were dreamers. They thought only of a return to romantic times when the fleur-de-lis waved majestically throughout the world. The noble experiment would be a failure before it began. "As Prime Minister I will not stand in your way. But I warn you, Jules, no radical upheavals or political unrest that will affect the rest of Canada."

"I assure you, Charles," Guerrier said confidently, "the birth will be peaceful."

It was to prove an empty promise.

Villon was furious; Danielle knew all the signs. He came and sat beside her on a bench outside the hospital. She shivered silently in the cool spring air, waiting for the eruption she knew would come.

"The bastard!" he finally growled. "The underhanded bastard gave Quebec to Guerrier without a fight."

"I still can't believe it," she said.

"You knew, you must have known what Charles had in the back of his mind."

"He said nothing, gave me no indication—"

"Why?" he interrupted her, his face flushed with rage. "Why did he make an abrupt about-face on his stand for a united Canada?"

Danielle turned silent. She had an instinctive fear of his anger.

"He's pulled the rug from under us before we could build a strong base. When my partners in the Kremlin learn of it, they'll withdraw their commitments."

"What can Charles possibly gain? Politically, he's committing suicide."

"He's playing the canny fox," said Villon, coming back on keel. "With a senile old fool like Guerrier at the helm, Quebec will be little more than a puppet regime to Ottawa, begging for handouts, long-term loans and trade credits. Quebec will be worse off as a nation than as a province."

She looked at him, her expression turning hard. "It doesn't have to be that way."

"What are you saying?"

She clutched his arm. "Bury the FQS. Come out in the open and campaign against Guerrier."

"I'm not strong enough to take on Jules."

"The French desperately need a younger, aggressive leader," she persisted. "The Henri Villon I know would never bow to English Canada or the United States."

"Your husband cut me off in midstep. Without the time to build a proper organization it would be impossible."

"Not if Jules Guerrier dropped dead."

For the first time Villon laughed. "Not likely. Jules may have every malady in the medical books, but he has the fortitude to outlive us all."

A curious intensity showed in Danielle's face. "Jules must die to save Quebec."

The inference was crystal. Villon turned inward to his thoughts and did not speak for nearly a minute.

"Killing the others was different, they were strangers. Their deaths were political necessity. Jules is a loyal Frenchman. He has fought the fight longer than any of us."

"For what we stand to gain, the price is small."

"The price is never small," he said, like a man immersed in a dream. "Lately, I find myself wondering who will be the last man to die before it's all over."

33

Gly leaned over the stained washbasin toward the mirror and re-arranged his face.

He placed a prosthesis made from white foam rubber latex over his battered nose, lengthening the tip and raising the bridge. The false addition was kept in place by spirit gum and tinted with a special makeup for coating rubber. His reshaped beak was dusted with a bit of translucent powder to remove the shine.

His original eyebrows had been plucked out. He peeled away their replacements and began attaching crepe hair with the spirit gum, dabbing the tiny tufts in place with tweezers. The new brows were arched higher and thickened to a bushier look.

He paused and stood back a few moments, comparing his handiwork with the photographs taped to the lower edge of the mirror. Satisfied with his progress, he took a highlight makeup a few shades darker than white and drew it from a point on the chin along the jawline to a point under each ear. Next, a lowlight earth tone was blended under the chin. The finished artistry gave his oval jaw more of a squared, chiseled appearance.

He realigned his mouth by covering it with a base makeup and then brushing a line under the lower lip with a matching colored lipstick so that it seemed fatter and more protruding.

The contact lenses followed. This was the only part he detested. Changing the color of his eyes from brown to gray was like changing his soul. He could no longer distinguish Foss Gly under the disguise after the lenses went in.

The final touch was the brown wig. He lowered it over his nude head with both hands as though it was a crown.

At last, he stood back and scrutinized full face and profiles while holding a small lamp at different lighting angles. It was near perfect, he judged, as near perfect as possible, considering the primitive conditions in the dingy bathroom of the fleabag hotel where he was registered.

The night clerk was not at the desk when he passed through the lobby. Two side streets and an alley later, he sat behind the wheel of a Mercedes-Benz sedan. He had stolen it from the parking lot of a bank earlier that afternoon and switched the license plates.

He drove through the old section of Quebec City called Lower Town, hugging the curbing of the quaint narrow streets and honking at the occasional pedestrian, who gave way only after fixing Gly with a belligerent stare.

It was a few minutes past nine and the lights of Quebec sparkled on the ice lingering over the St. Lawrence. Gly passed below the famed

Chateau Frontenac hotel and swung onto the expressway bordering the river. The traffic moved along rapidly and soon he was abreast of the Battlefields Park on the Plains of Abraham where the British army triumphed over the French in 1759 and gained Canada for the empire.

He turned off into the fashionable suburban community of Sillery. Great stone houses sat ageless and fortlike, protecting the wealthy and social celebrities of the province. Gly could not identify with such security. To him the houses looked like monstrous crypts inhabited by people who did not know they were dead.

He stopped at a heavy iron gate and identified himself to a speaker. There was no reply. The gate swung open and he drove up a circular drive to an imposing granite mansion surrounded by several acres of lawn. He parked the car under the front portal and rang the door chime. Premier Jules Guerrier's chauffeur-bodyguard bowed Gly into the foyer.

"Good evening, Monsieur Villon, this is an unexpected pleasure."

Gly was pleased. His facial alteration had passed its first test. "I was visiting friends in Quebec and thought I would drop by and pay my respects to Monsieur Guerrier. I'm told he isn't feeling well."

"A bout with the flu," said the chauffeur, taking Gly's coat. "The worst is over. His temperature has dropped, but it will be a while before he can get back in harness again."

"If he's not up to a late visit perhaps I should run along and call tomorrow."

"No please. The premier is watching television. I know he'll be glad to see you. I'll take you up to his room."

Gly waved him off. "Don't bother. I know the way."

He went up the vast circular staircase to the second floor. At the top he paused to orient himself. He had memorized the plans for the entire house, fixed every exit in his mind as a precaution for hurried escape. Guerrier's bedroom, he knew, was the third door on the right. He entered quietly without knocking.

Jules Guerrier was slouched in a large overstuffed chair, slippered feet propped on an ottoman, peering at a television set. He was wearing a silk paisley robe thrown carelessly over his pajamas. He didn't notice Gly's intrusion; his back was to the door.

Gly moved silently across the carpet to the bed. He picked up a large pillow and approached Guerrier from behind. He started to lower the pillow over Guerrier's face, but he hesitated.

He must see me, Gly thought. His ego needed to be pacified. He had to prove to himself again that he could indeed become Henri Villon. Guerrier seemed to sense a presence. He turned slowly and his eyes came level with Gly's beltline. They trailed up his chest to his face and then they widened, not from fear but from astonishment.

"Henri?"

"Yes, Jules."

"You can't be here," Guerrier said dumbly.

Gly moved around behind the television set and faced the premier. "But I am here, Jules. I'm right here inside the TV."

And so he was.

An image of Henri Villon filled the center of the screen. He was making an address at the opening of Ottawa's new performing arts center. Danielle Sarveux was seated behind him, and next to her was Villon's wife.

Guerrier was unable to comprehend, to fully conceive what his eyes reflected to the cells of his brain. The broadcast was live. He had no doubt of it. As a formality he had received an invitation and recalled the scheduled events of the ceremony. Villon's speech was set for now. He stared into Gly's face, his jaw slack in shock.

"How?"

Gly did not answer. In the same motion he straddled the chair and pressed the pillow into Guerrier's face. The beginning of a terrified cry became scarcely more than a muffled animal sound. The premier had little strength for the uneven struggle. His hands found Gly's thick wrists and feebly tried to pull them away. His lungs felt as if they ignited into a ball of flame. Just before the final darkness, a great blaze of light burst in his head.

After thirty seconds the hands loosened their grip and fell away, dangling awkwardly over the armrests of the chair. The aging body went limp, but Gly maintained the pressure for another three full minutes.

Finally he turned off the TV set, bent down and listened for a heartbeat. All life functions had ceased. The premier of Quebec was dead.

Swiftly Gly crossed the room and checked the hall outside. It was empty. He returned to Guerrier, removed the pillow and threw it back on the bed. Gently, to keep from causing a tear in the fabric, he removed the robe and laid it over the back of the chair. He was relieved to see that the premier had not wet himself. Next came the slippers. They were casually dropped beside the bed.

Gly felt no disgust, nor even the smallest measure of distaste as he picked up the corpse and placed it on the bed. Then with clinical composure he forced open the mouth and began probing.

The first thing a police pathologist examined if he suspected induced asphyxiation was the victim's tongue. Guerrier had cooperated; his tongue bore no teeth marks.

There were, however, slight indications of bruises inside the mouth. Gly took a small makeup kit from his pocket and selected a soft pinkish grease pencil. He could not make the discolorations disappear completely, but he could blend them in with the surrounding tissue. He also darkened the paleness around the interior of the lips, removing another hint of suffocation.

The eyes stared unseeing, and Gly closed them. He massaged the contorted face until it took on a relaxed, almost peaceful expression. Then he fixed the body in a restful position of sleep and pulled up the bedcovers.

A tiny, nagging doubt ticked in the back of his mind as he walked from the bedroom. It was the doubt of a perfectionist who always sensed a detail undone, an indefinable overlooked detail that refused to focus. He was descending the upper flight of stairs when he saw the bodyguard emerge from the pantry carrying a tray with a porcelain teapot.

Gly stopped in midstep. He abruptly realized an oversight that he should have realized before. Guerrier's teeth were too perfect. It dawned on him that they must have been false.

He crouched out of vision of the approaching bodyguard and ran back to the bedroom. Five seconds and he held them in his hand. Where did the old man keep them until morning? He must soak them in a cleaning solution. The bedside table was bare except for a clock. He found a plastic bowl filled with blue liquid on the bathroom counter. There was no time for him to analyze the contents. He dropped in the dentures.

Gly opened the bedroom door just as the bodyguard was reaching for the knob from his side in the hall.

"Oh, Monsieur Villon, I thought you and the premier might like some tea."

Gly nodded over his shoulder toward the lump on the bed. "Jules said he felt tired. I think he was asleep as soon as his head hit the pillow."

The bodyguard took his word for it. "Would you like a cup before you leave, sir?"

Gly closed the door. "Thank you, no. I must be getting along."

They returned to the foyer together. The bodyguard set down the tray and helped him into his coat. Gly lingered on the threshold, making certain Guerrier's man saw the Mercedes.

He bid a good-night and started the car. The gate opened and he swung onto the deserted street. Eight blocks away he parked at the curb between two large homes. He locked the doors and stomped the ignition key into the ground with his heel.

What could be more common than a Mercedes-Benz sitting in a stylish residential district, he figured. People who lived in mansions seldom talked to their neighbors. Each would probably think the car belonged to friends visiting next door. The car would be ignored for days.

Gly was on a bus back to Quebec at ten past ten. The exotic poison he had concocted was still in his pocket. It was a foolproof method of murder, used by the Communist intelligence service. No pathologist could detect its presence in a corpse with certainty.

The decision to use the pillow was a spur-of-the-moment afterthought. It seemed a fitting tool for Gly's fetish for inconformity.

Most murderers followed a pattern, developed a routine modus operandi, preferred a particular weapon. Gly's pattern was that he didn't have one. Every kill was completely different in execution from the last. He left no strings to connect him with the past.

He felt a flush of excitement. He had cleared the first hurdle. One more remained, the trickiest, most sensitive one of them all.

34

Danielle lay in bed and watched the smoke of her cigarette curl toward the ceiling. She was only dimly aware of the warm little bedroom in the remote cottage outside Ottawa, the gathering darkness of the evening, the firm, smooth body beside her.

She sat up and looked at her watch. The interlude was over, and she felt a regret that it could not go on indefinitely. Responsibility beckoned and she was compelled to reenter reality.

"Time for you to go?" he asked, stirring beside her.

She nodded. "I must play the dutiful wife and visit my husband in the hospital."

"I don't envy you. Hospitals are nightmares in white."

"I've become used to it by now."

"How is Charles coming along?"

"The doctors say he can come home in a few weeks."

"Come home to what?" he said contemptuously. "The country is rudderless. If an election were held tomorrow, he would surely be defeated."

"All to our advantage." She rose from the bed and began dressing. "With Jules Guerrier out of the way the timing is perfect for you to resign from the cabinet and publicly announce your candidacy for President of Quebec."

"I'll have to draft my speech carefully. The idea is to come on like a savior. I cannot afford to be cast as a rat jumping a sinking ship."

She came over and sat down beside him. The faint smell of his maleness aroused her again. She placed a hand on his chest and could feel his heartbeat.

"You were not the same man this afternoon, Henri."

His face seemed to take on a concerned look. "How so?"

"You were more brutal in your lovemaking. Almost cruel."

"I thought you'd enjoy the change."

"I did." She smiled and kissed him. "You even felt different inside me."

"I can't imagine why," he said casually.

"Neither can I, but I loved it."

Reluctantly she pushed herself away and stood up. She put on her coat and gloves. He lay there, watching her.

She paused and looked down, giving him a penetrating look. "You never told me how you arranged to make Jules Guerrier's death appear natural."

A chilling expression came into his eyes. "There are some things you are better off not knowing."

She looked as though she'd been slapped in the face. "We never had secrets between us before."

"We do now," he said impassively.

She did not know how to react to his sudden coldness. She had never seen him like this and it stunned her.

"You sound angry. Is it something I've said?"

He glanced at her uninterestedly and shrugged. "I expected more from you, Danielle."

"More?"

"You've told me nothing about Charles that I can't read in a newspaper."

She looked at him questioningly. "What do you want to know?"

"The man's inner thoughts. Conversations with other cabinet ministers. How does he intend to deal with Quebec after the separation? Is he thinking of resigning? Damn it, I need information, and you're not delivering."

She held out her hands expressively. "Charles has changed since the plane crash. He's become more secretive. He doesn't confide in me as before."

His eyes went dark. "Then you've become useless to me."

She averted her face, the hurt and anger swelling in her breast.

"Don't bother contacting me again," he went on icily, "unless you have something important to say. I'm taking no more risks for boring sex games."

Danielle ran for the door, and then she turned. "You son of a bitch!" she choked through a sob.

How odd, she thought, that she had never seen the monster in him before. She suppressed a shudder and wiped at the tears with the back of her hand as she fled.

His laughter followed her to the car and rang in her ears during the drive to the hospital.

She could not know that back in the bedoom of the cottage Foss Gly lay highly pleased with himself for passing his final test with flying colors.

35

The President's chief of staff nodded an indifferent greeting and remained seated behind his desk as Pitt was ushered into his office. He glanced up without smiling. "Take a chair, Mr. Pitt. The President will be with you in a few minutes."

There was no offer of a handshake, so Pitt set his briefcase on the carpet and took a couch by the window.

The chief of staff, a young man in his late twenties with the grandiloquent name of Harrison Moon IV, swiftly answered three phone calls and adroitly shuffled papers from one bin to another. Finally he condescended to look in Pitt's direction.

"I want you to be fully aware, Mr. Pitt, that this meeting is highly irregular. The President has precious little time for pithy chats with third-level civil servants. If your father, Senator George Pitt, hadn't made the request and implied that it was urgent, you wouldn't have gotten past the front gate."

Pitt gave the pompous ass an innocent look. "Gosharootie, I'm flattered all to hell."

The chief of staff's face clouded. "I suggest you show respect for the office of the President."

"How can one be impressed with the President," said Pitt with a sardonic smile, "when he hires assholes like you."

Harrison Moon IV stiffened as though shot. "How dare you—!"

At that moment the President's secretary came into the office. "Mr. Pitt, the President will see you now."

"No!" shouted Moon, leaping to his feet, his eyes glazed in rage. "The appointment is canceled!"

Pitt approached Moon and grabbed him by the lapels of his coat and jerked him halfway across the desk. "My advice to you, kid, is not to let the job go to your head." Then he shoved Moon backward into his swivel chair. But Pitt had shoved a bit too hard. The momentum of Moon's weight tipped the chair over and he spilled onto the floor.

Pitt smiled cordially at the stunned presidential secretary and said,

"You needn't bother showing me the way, I've been to the oval office before."

Unlike his chief of staff, the President greeted Pitt courteously and held out his hand. "I've often read of your exploits on the *Titanic* and *Vixen* projects, Mr. Pitt. I was particularly impressed with your handling of the *Doodlebug* operation. It's an honor to meet you at last."

"The honor is mine."

"Won't you please sit down," the President said graciously.

"I may not have the time," said Pitt.

"I'm sorry?" The President lifted an eyebrow questioningly.

"Your chief of staff was rude and treated me damned shabbily, so I called him an asshole and roughed him up a bit."

"Are you serious?"

"Yes, sir. I should imagine the Secret Service will burst in here any second and drag me off the premises."

The President walked over to his desk and punched an intercom button. "Maggie, I want no interruptions for any reason until I say so."

Pitt was relieved when the President's face stretched into a wide smile. "Harrison gets carried away at times. Perhaps you may have shown him an overdue lesson in humility."

"I'll apologize on my way out."

"No need." The President dropped into a highbacked chair across a coffee table from Pitt. "Your dad and I go back a long way. We were both elected to Congress in the same year. He told me over the phone you had stumbled on a revelation, as he put it, that boggles the mind."

"Dad's earthy rhetoric," Pitt laughed. "But in this case he's one hundred percent right."

"Tell me what you've got."

Pitt opened the briefcase and began laying papers on the coffee table. "I'm sorry to bore you with a history lesson, Mr. President, but it's necessary to lay the groundwork."

"I'm listening."

"In early nineteen fourteen," Pitt began, "there were no doubts in British minds that war with Imperial Germany was just around the corner. By March, Winston Churchill, who was then first lord of the admiralty, had already armed some forty merchant ships. The War Department forecast the opening of hostilities for September after the European harvest was in. Field Marshal Lord Kitchener, the secretary of state for war, realizing the coming conflict was going to be a colossal drain of men and resources, was shocked to find only enough ammunition and supplies for a three-month campaign.

"At the same time the United Kingdom had been busy on a crash program of social reform that had already caused a substantial increase in taxation. It didn't take a clairvoyant to see that mushrooming armament costs, interest on debts, welfare and pension payments would break the back of the economy."

"So Britain was scraping the bottom of its treasury when it entered World War I," said the President.

"Not quite," replied Pitt. "Shortly before the Germans poured into Belgium, our government had loaned the British one hundred and fifty million dollars. At least it went into the records as a loan. In reality it was a down payment."

"I'm afraid I've lost the trail."

"The Prime Minister, Herbert Asquith, and King George V met in a closed-door emergency session on May second and came up with a solution born of desperation. They secretly approached President Wilson with their proposal and he accepted. Richard Essex, undersecretary of state under William Jennings Bryan, and Harvey Shields, deputy secretary of the British Foreign Office, then drafted what was to be briefly known as the North American Treaty."

"And what was the gist of this treaty?" asked the President.

There was a cold silence of perhaps ten seconds while Pitt hesitated. Finally he cleared his throat.

"For the sum of one billion dollars Great Britain sold Canada to the United States."

Pitt's words flew over the President's head. He sat blank, unbelieving of what he heard.

"Say again," he demanded.

"We bought Canada for one billion dollars."

"That's absurd."

"But true," said Pitt firmly. "Before the war broke out there were many members of Parliament who doubted loyal support by the colonies and dominions. There were liberals as well as conservatives who openly stated that Canada was a drain on the empire."

"Can you show me proof?" asked the President, his eyes skeptical.

Pitt handed him a copy of Wilson's letter. "This was written by Woodrow Wilson to Prime Minister Asquith on June fourth. You'll note that it was creased through part of one sentence. I ran a spectrograph test on it and found the missing words cause the line to read: 'my countrymen are a possessive lot and would never idly stand by knowing with certainty that our neighbor to the north and our own beloved country had become one.' "

The President studied the letter for several minutes, then he set it on the coffee table. "What else do you have?"

Without comment Pitt passed over the photograph of Bryan, Essex and Shields leaving the White House with the treaty. Then he played his trump card.

"This is the desk diary of Richard Essex for the month of May. The entire scope of the conferences leading to the North American Treaty is set down in scrupulous detail. The last entry is dated May twenty-second, nineteen fourteen, the day Essex left the capital for Canada and the final signing of the treaties."

"You said treaties, plural."

"There were three copies, one for each country involved. The first to sign were Asquith and King George. Shields then carried the historic papers to Washington where, on May twentieth, Wilson and Bryan added their names. Two days later, Essex and Shields departed together by train to Ottawa where the Canadian prime minister, Sir Robert Borden, affixed the last signature."

"Then why was it no formal transfer of Canada into the Union took place?"

"A series of unfortunate circumstances," explained Pitt. "Harvey Shields, in company with a thousand other souls, went down with the transatlantic liner *Empress of Ireland* after it collided with a coal collier and sank in the St. Lawrence River. His body and the British copy of the treaty were never recovered."

"But surely Essex reached Washington with the American copy."

Pitt shook his head. "The train carrying Essex plunged off a bridge into the Hudson River. The disaster became something of a classic mystery when neither the crew and the passengers, nor any trace of the train, was ever found."

"That still left one copy in Canadian hands."

"The trail goes cold at this point," said Pitt. "The rest is speculation. Apparently Asquith's cabinet rebelled. The ministers, including no doubt Churchill, must have been furious when they discovered the Prime Minister and the King had tried to sell off their largest dominion behind their backs."

"I doubt the Canadians were overly fond of the deal either."

"With two copies of the treaty gone it would have been a simple matter for Sir Robert Borden, a loyal Englishman, by the way, to have destroyed the third, leaving Wilson with no tangible evidence to advance an American claim.''

''It doesn't seem possible official records concerning negotiations of such magnitude could be so conveniently lost,'' said the President.

''Wilson states in his letter he instructed his secretary to destroy all mention of the pact. I can't speak for the Foreign Office, but it seems a safe bet to say they're collectors. Traditionally, the British aren't given to throwing away or burning documents. Whatever treaty papers survive are probably buried under a ton of dust in some old Victorian warehouse.''

The President rose and began pacing. ''I wish I could have studied the wording of the treaty.''

''You can.'' Pitt smiled. ''Essex penned a draft in his desk diary.''

''May I keep it?''

''Of course.''

''How did you happen onto this diary?''

''It was in the possession of his grandson,'' Pitt answered without elaboration.

''John Essex?''

''Yes.''

''Why did he keep it a secret all these years?''

''He must have been afraid its exposure would cause an international upheaval.''

''He may have been right,'' said the President. ''If the press blasted this discovery on a slow news week, there is no predicting the grassroots reaction by people on both sides of the border. Wilson was right: the Americans are a possessive lot. They might demand a takeover of Canada. And God only knows the hell Congress would raise.''

''There is a catch,'' said Pitt.

The President stopped his pacing. ''And that is?''

''There is no record of payment. The initial deposit was converted to a loan. Even if a copy of the treaty turned up, the British would reject it by claiming, and rightfully so, they were never compensated.''

''Yes,'' the President said slowly, ''nonpayment could void the treaty.''

He moved to the tall windows and gazed across the winter-brown grass of the White House lawn, saying nothing, struggling with his thoughts. Finally he turned and stared directly at Pitt.

''Who knows about the North American Treaty besides you?''

"Commander Heidi Milligan, who began the preliminary research after finding the Wilson letter, the Senate historian who uncovered the photographs, my father, and of course, Admiral Sandecker. Since he is my immediate superior I only felt it fair he should know what I was investigating."

"No one else?"

Pitt shook his head. "I can't think of anyone."

"Let's keep it a select club, shall we?"

"Whatever you say, Mr. President."

"I deeply appreciate your bringing this matter to my attention, Mr. Pitt."

"Would you like me to pursue it?"

"No, I think it best if we drop the treaty back in its coffin for now. There is no purpose in damaging our relations with Canada and the United Kingdom. I see it as a simple case of what nobody knows, won't hurt them."

"John Essex would have agreed."

"And you, Mr. Pitt, would you agree?"

Pitt closed his briefcase and stood up. "I'm a marine engineer, Mr. President. I steer well clear of political involvement."

"A wise course," said the President with an understanding smile. "A wise course indeed."

Five seconds after the door closed behind Pitt, the President spoke into his intercom.

"Maggie, get me Douglas Oates on the holograph."

He settled behind his desk and waited.

Soon after taking up residence in the White House he had ordered a holographic communications system installed in his office. He took an almost childlike interest in studying his cabinet members' expressions, body movements and outward emotions while he visually talked to them miles away.

The three-dimensional image of a man with wavy auburn hair and conservatively attired in a gray pinstripe suit materialized in the middle of the oval office. He was seated in a leather executive chair.

Douglas Oates, the secretary of state, nodded and smiled. "Good morning, Mr. President. How goes the battle?"

"Douglas, how much money has the United States given away to Britain since nineteen fourteen?"

Oates stared quizzically. "Given?"

"Yes, you know, war loans written off, economic aid, contributions, whatever."

Oates shrugged. "A pretty substantial sum, I should imagine."

"Over a billion dollars?"

"Easily," replied Oates. "Why do you ask?"

The President ignored the question. "Arrange for a courier. I have something of interest for my friend in Ottawa."

"More data on the oil bonanza?" Oates persisted.

"Even better. We've just been dealt a wild card on the Canadian solution."

"We need all the luck we can get."

"I guess you might call it a red herring."

"Red herring?"

The President had the look of a cat with a mouse under its paw.

"The perfect ploy," he said, "to divert British attention from the real conspiracy."

36

The President sidestroked to the edge of the White House pool and pulled himself up the ladder as Mercier and Klein came from the dressing room.

"I hope an early morning swim doesn't disrupt your schedules."

"Not at all, Mr. President," said Mercier. "I can use the exercise."

Klein peered around the indoor pool room. "So this is the famous swimming pool. I understand the last president who used it was Jack Kennedy."

"Yes," replied the President. "Nixon had it covered over and held press conferences here. Me, I'd rather swim than face a horde of drooling reporters."

Mercier grinned. "What would the Washington press corps say if they heard you refer to them as a drooling horde?"

"Strictly off the record." The President laughed. "What say we break in the new hot tub? The workmen finished installing it yesterday."

They settled into a small circular area built into the shallow end of the pool. The President turned on the circulating pumps and set the temperature at 105 degrees Fahrenheit. As the water heated, Mercier felt sure he was being scalded to death. He began to sympathize with lobsters.

Finally the President relaxed and said, "This is as good a place as any to conduct business. Suppose you gentlemen tell me where we stand on the Canadian energy situation."

"The news looks grim," said Mercier. "Our intelligence sources have learned that it was a parliamentary minister, Henri Villon, who ordered the blackout from James Bay."

"Villon." The name rolled off the President's tongue as though it had a bad taste. "He's that double-talking character who bad-mouths the United States every time he buttonholes a reporter."

"The same," replied Mercier. "There's talk he may run for President of the new Quebec republic."

"With Guerrier dead, there is an ugly chance he might win," added Klein.

A frown crossed the President's face. "I can't think of anything worse than Villon dictating price and supply policies for James Bay and the new oil discovery by NUMA."

"It's frustrating as hell," grumbled Mercier. He turned to Klein. "Is the reserve as vast as Admiral Sandecker predicts?"

"He came in on the low side," Klein answered. "My experts went over NUMA's computer data. It appears ten billion barrels is closer to the mark than eight."

"How is it possible the Canadian oil companies missed it?"

"A stratigraphic trap is the most difficult of all oil deposits to find," explained Klein. "Seismic equipment, gravity meters, magnetometers, none of them can detect the presence of hydrocarbons in that geological state. The only surefire means is by random drilling. The Canadians sank a well within two miles of the *Doodlebug*'s strike but came up dry. The position was inserted on the oil maps with the symbol denoting a dry hole. Other exploration teams have stayed clear of the area."

Mercier waved the rising steam from in front of his eyes. "It would appear we've made Quebec a very wealthy new nation."

"Provided that we tell them," said the President.

Klein looked at him. "Why keep it a secret? It's only a matter of time before they stumble onto the field themselves. By pointing the way and cooperating in the development, the Quebec government, out of gratitude, will surely sell us the crude oil at reasonable prices.''

"A false optimism," said Mercier. "Look what happened in Iran and the OPEC nations. Let's face it, half the world thinks the United States is fair game when it comes to price gouging."

The President tilted his head back and closed his eyes. "Suppose we possessed a piece of paper establishing that Canada belongs to the United States?"

Mercier and Klein sat in bewildered silence, uncertain of what the President had in mind. Finally Mercier spoke the words that were on their minds.

"I can't imagine such a document."

"Nor I," said Klein.

"Wishful thinking," the President said, airily waving his hand. "Forget it, we've got more down-to-earth problems to discuss."

Mercier looked into the water. "The greatest danger to our national security is a fragmented Canada. I feel we must do whatever is possible to assist Prime Minister Sarveux in preventing Quebec from going it alone."

"You make a sound case," said the President. "But I'm going to ask you to shelve it."

"Sir?"

"I want you to coordinate a top secret program with the State Department and Central Intelligence to make certain that Quebec independence becomes a reality."

Mercier looked like he'd been bitten by a shark. "I don't think you realize—"

"My decision is final," the President interrupted. "I'm asking you as a friend to follow through for me."

"May I ask why?"

A faraway look came into the President's eyes and Mercier felt a chill run through him at the sudden hardening that entered the man's voice.

"Trust me when I say that a divided Canada is in the best interests of North America."

Klein buttoned up his raincoat as he stood on the south portico of the White House awaiting his car and driver. The threatening gray skies did little to relieve his uneasy mood.

"I can't help wondering if the President is as mad as Henri Villon," he said.

"You misinterpret them," replied Mercier. "Crafty perhaps, but neither man is mad."

"Odd, his fairy tale of combining Canada with the U.S."

"He stepped out of character on that one. What in hell can he have on his mind?"

"You're the national security adviser. If anyone should know, it's you."

"You heard. He's keeping something from me."

"So what happens now?"

"We wait," Mercier answered in a hollow tone. "We wait until I can figure what the President has up his sleeve."

37

"Sold!"

The auctioneer's voice roared through the amplifiers like a shotgun blast. The usual rumblings from the crowd followed as they marked their programs with the high bid on a 1946 Ford coupe.

"Can we have the next car, please?"

A pearl-white 1939 540K Mercedes-Benz with a Freestone & Webb custom body purred quietly onto the center stage of the Richmond, Virginia, Coliseum. A crowd of three thousand people murmured approval as the beams from the overhead spotlights highlighted the gleaming paint on the elegant coachwork. Bidders milled around the stage, some down on their hands and knees eyeballing the suspension and running gear, others examining every detail of the upholstery, while still others probed about the engine compartment with the savvy of Kentucky horse trainers contemplating a potential derby winner.

Dirk Pitt sat in the third row and rechecked the numerical order in his program. The Mercedes was listed fourteenth in the annual Richmond Antique and Classic Car Auction.

"This is truly a beautiful and exotic automobile," touted the auctioneer. "A queen among classics. Will somebody start the bidding at four hundred thousand?"

The ringmen in tuxedos wandered among the crowd, prodding the bidders. Suddenly one raised his hand. "I have one hundred and fifty."

The auctioneer went into his unintelligible singsong spiel, and the bidding became brisk as car buffs began the ritual of competing for the prize. Quickly, the mark of two hundred thousand was reached and passed.

Absorbed in the action, Pitt did not notice a young man in a three-piece suit slip into the empty seat next to him.

"Mr. Pitt?"

Pitt turned and looked into the babyish face of Harrison Moon IV.

"Funny," Pitt said without surprise, "you didn't strike me as the type who would be interested in old cars."

"Actually, I'm interested in you."

Pitt gave him an amused look. "If you're gay, you're wasting your time."

Moon frowned and looked around to see if anyone seated nearby was tuned to their conversation. They were all wrapped up in the bidding. "I'm here on official government business. Can we go someplace private and talk?"

"Give me five minutes," said Pitt. "I'm bidding on the next car."

"Now, if you please, Mr. Pitt," said Moon, trying to look commanding. "My business with you is far more important than watching grown men throw money away on obsolete junk."

"I have two hundred and eighty thousand," the auctioneer droned. "Will someone give me three hundred."

"At least you can't call it cheap," said Pitt calmly. "That car happens to be a mechanical work of art, an investment that appreciates from twenty to thirty percent a year. Your grandchildren won't be able to touch it for less than two million dollars."

"I'm not here to argue the future of antiques. Shall we go?"

"Not a chance."

"Perhaps you might curb your obstinacy if I were to tell you I'm here on behalf of the President."

Pitt's expression had turned to stone. "Big goddamned deal. Why is it every punk who goes to work for the White House thinks he can intimidate the world? Go back and tell the President you failed, Mr.

Moon. You might also inform him that if he wants something from me to send a messenger boy who can demonstrate a degree of class.''

Moon's face turned pale. This wasn't going the way he'd planned, not at all.

"I . . . I can't do that,'' he stammered.

"Tough.''

The auctioneer raised his gavel. "Going once . . . twice for three hundred and sixty thousand.'' He paused, scanning the audience. "If there is no further advance . . . sold to Mr. Robert Esbenson of Denver, Colorado.''

Moon had been cut down, coldly, unmercifully. He took the only avenue left open to him. "Okay, Mr. Pitt, your rules.''

The Mercedes was driven off and a four-door, two-tone straw-and-beige convertible took its place. The auctioneer fairly glowed as he described its features.

"And now, ladies and gentlemen, number fifteen on your program. A 1950 British-built Jensen. A very rare car. The only model of this particular coachwork known to exist. A real beauty. May we open the bidding at fifty thousand?''

The first bid came in at twenty-five thousand. Pitt sat in silence as the price climbed.

Moon studied him. "Aren't you going to bid?''

"All in good time.''

A stylishly dressed woman in her late forties waved her bidder's card. The auctioneer nodded and ordained her with a smile. "I have twenty-nine thousand from the lovely Ms. O'Leery of Chicago.''

"Does he know everybody?'' Moon asked, showing a spark of interest.

"Collectors form a loose clique,'' replied Pitt. "Most of us usually show up at the same auctions.''

The bidding slowed at forty-two thousand. The auctioneer sensed the peak had come. "Come now, ladies and gentlemen, this car is worth much, much more.''

Pitt raised his bidder's card.

"Thank you, sir. I now have forty-three. Will anyone raise it to forty-four?''

Ms. O'Leery, wearing a designer double-breasted wool checked jacket and a slim taupe flannel skirt with a revealing front slit, signaled for an advance.

Before the auctioneer could announce her bid, Pitt's card was in the air. "Now she knows she's got a fight on her hands," he said to Moon.

"Forty-four and now forty-five. Who will make it forty-six?"

The bidding stalled. Ms. O'Leery conversed with a younger man sitting next to her. She seldom showed up with the same consort at two auctions. She was a self-made woman who had built a tidy fortune merchandising her own brand of cosmetics. Her collection was one of the finest in the world and numbered nearly one hundred cars. When the ringman leaned down to solicit a bid, she shook her head and then turned around and winked at Pitt.

"That was hardly the wink of a friendly competitor," observed Moon.

"You should try an older woman sometime," said Pitt as though lecturing a schoolboy. "There's little they don't know about men."

An attractive girl maneuvered down Pitt's aisle and asked him to sign the sales agreement.

"Now?" asked Moon hopefully.

"How did you get here?"

"My girlfriend drove me down from Arlington."

Pitt came to his feet. "While you round her up, I'll go to the office and settle my account. Then she can follow us."

"Follow us?"

"You wanted to talk in private, Mr. Moon. So I'm going to give you a treat and drive you back to Arlington in a real automobile."

The Jensen rolled effortlessly over the highway toward Washington. Pitt kept one eye out for the traffic patrol and the other on the speedometer. His foot held the accelerator at a steady seventy miles an hour.

Moon buttoned his overcoat up to the neck and looked miserable. "Doesn't this relic have a heater?"

Pitt hadn't noticed the cold seeping in through the cloth top. As long as the engine hummed, he was in his element. He turned a knob on the dashboard and soon a thin wisp of warm air spread through the Jensen's interior.

"Okay, Moon, we're alone. What's your story?"

"The President would like you to lead fishing expeditions into the St. Lawrence and Hudson rivers."

Pitt jerked his eyes off the road and stared at Moon. "You're joking?"

"I couldn't be more serious. He thinks you're the only qualified man to take a stab at finding the copies of the North American Treaty.''

"You know about it?''

"Yes, he took me into his confidence ten minutes after you left his office. I'm to act as liaison during your search.''

Pitt slowed the car down to the legal speed limit and was silent for several seconds. Then he said, "I don't think he knows what he's asking.''

"I assure you the President has looked at it from every angle.''

"He's asking the impossible and expecting a miracle.'' Pitt's expression was incredulous, his voice quiet. "There's no way a piece of paper can remain intact after being immersed in water for three-quarters of a century.''

"I admit the project sounds unpromising,'' agreed Moon. "And yet, if there is one chance in ten million a copy of the treaty exists, the President feels we must make an effort to find it.''

Pitt stared down the road that split the Virginia countryside. "Suppose for a minute we got lucky and laid the North American Treaty on his lap? What then?''

"I can't say.''

"Can't or won't?''

"I'm only a special aide to the President . . . a messenger boy as you so rudely put it. I do what I'm told. My orders are to give you every assistance and see that your requests for funds and equipment are met. What happens if and when you salvage a readable document is none of my business and certainly none of yours.''

"Tell me, Moon,'' said Pitt, a faint smile edged on his lips. "Have you ever read *How to Win Friends and Influence People?*''

"Never heard of it.''

"I'm not surprised.'' Pitt ran up the rear end of an electric minicar that refused to yield the fast lane and blinked the Jensen's lights. The other driver finally signaled and gave way. "What if I say no deal?''

Moon stiffened almost imperceptibly. "The President would be most disappointed.''

"I'm flattered.'' Pitt drove along, lost in thought. Then he turned and nodded. "Okay, I'll give it my best shot. I presume we're to begin immediately.''

Moon simply nodded, vastly relieved.

"Item one on your list,'' said Pitt. "I'll need NUMA's manpower and resources. Most important, Admiral Sandecker must be informed of the project. I won't work behind his back.''

"What you're about to attempt, Mr. Pitt, falls under the trite term of 'delicate situation.' The fewer people who know about the treaty, the less chance the Canadians get wind of it.''

"Sandecker must be informed,'' Pitt repeated firmly.

"All right, I'll set up a meeting and acquaint him with the project.''

"Not good enough. I want the admiral briefed by the President. He deserves that.''

Moon had the look of a man who has had his wallet picked. He kept his eyes straight ahead when he replied. "Okay, consider it done.''

"Item two,'' Pitt continued. "We'll need a pro to handle the historical research.''

"There are several top men around Washington who have taken on government assignments. I'll send you their résumés.''

"I was thinking of a woman.''

"Any particular reason?''

"Commander Heidi Milligan did the preliminary research on the treaty. She knows her way through archives, and she'd be one less to initiate into the club.''

"Makes sense,'' said Moon thoughtfully, "except that she's somewhere out in the Pacific.''

"Ring up the chief of naval operations and get her back, providing, of course, you carry the clout.''

"I carry the clout, Mr. Pitt,'' Moon replied coolly.

"Item three. One of the treaty copies went down with the *Empress of Ireland*, which lies in Canadian waters. There's no way we can keep our diving operations a secret. Under existing salvage laws we're required to notify their government, the Canadian Pacific Railroad, which owned the vessel, and the insurance companies that paid off the claims.''

The subdued expression on Moon's face turned smug. "I'm ahead of you on that score. The necessary paperwork is in the mill. Your cover story is that you're an archaeological team searching for artifacts that will be preserved and donated to American and Canadian maritime museums. You should be able to bring up enough trash during the operation to pacify any prying eyes.''

"Item four,'' said Pitt. "The money.''

"Ample funds will be placed at your disposal to see the job through.''

Pitt hesitated before he spoke again, listening to the steady purr of the Jensen's 130-horsepower engine. The sun had dropped below the tops of the trees and he turned on the lights.

"I make no guarantees," he said at last.

"Understood."

"How do we stay in touch?"

Moon took out a pen and wrote on the back of Pitt's auction program. "I'll be available at this number on a twenty-four-hour basis. We won't meet face to face again unless you run into an unexpected crisis." He paused and looked at Pitt, trying to fathom the man. But Pitt could not be read. "Any other questions?"

"No," said Pitt, wrapped in thought. "No more questions."

There were a hundred questions swirling in Pitt's mind; none that could be answered by Moon.

He tried to visualize what he might find beneath the forbidding currents of the Hudson and St. Lawrence rivers, but nothing jelled. And then he began to wonder what was behind the mad, unfathomable scheme that was hurling him into the unknown.

38

"The time for decision."

Sandecker spoke to no one in particular as he gazed at the hydrographic charts, photo-enlarged to cover the far wall of the NUMA operations room. He rapped a knuckle against the one depicting a section of the Hudson River.

"Do we tackle the *Manhattan Limited* first?" He paused and gestured at the adjoining chart. "Or the *Empress of Ireland?*" He refaced the room and studied the four people seated around the long table. "Which one should take priority?"

Heidi Milligan, whose face showed the fatigue of a long flight from Honolulu, started to say something, but held back.

"Ladies first," Al Giordino said, grinning.

"I'm not qualified to voice an opinion on underwater salvage," she said hesitantly. "But I believe the ship offers the best chance of finding a readable treaty."

"Care to state your reasons?" asked Sandecker.

"Before the days of air travel," Heidi explained, "it was standard procedure for diplomatic couriers who sailed across the oceans to seal documents inside several layers of oilcloth as a protection against water damage. I recall one incident where important papers were found intact on a British Foreign Office courier when his body washed ashore six days after the *Lusitania* sinking."

Sandecker smiled and nodded at her in satisfaction. She would be a good woman to have around. "Thank you, Commander. You've given us our first ray of hope."

Giordino yawned. He had spent most of the night being briefed on the project by Pitt, and it was all he could do to stay awake. "Perhaps Richard Essex wrapped his copy of the treaty in oilcloth too."

Heidi shook her head. "Most likely he would have carried it in a leather traveling bag."

"Little chance of that surviving," Sandecker acknowledged.

"My vote still goes to the train," said Giordino. "The *Empress* lies in a hundred and sixty-five feet—well below the safe depth for air diving. The train, on the other hand, can be no deeper than forty feet. After seven decades the ship must be eaten away by saltwater flowing in from the St. Lawrence Gulf. The train would be better preserved by fresh river water."

Sandecker turned to a small man whose owlish brown eyes peered through a large pair of horn-rimmed glasses. "Rudi, how do you see it?"

Rudi Gunn, NUMA's director of logistics, looked up from a pad filled with scribbles and unconsciously scratched one side of his nose. Gunn rarely gambled or played the angles. He dealt his cards from solid facts, never vague percentages.

"I favor the ship," he said quietly. "The only advantage of salvaging the *Manhattan Limited* is that it rests on home ground. However, the current of the Hudson River is three-and-a-half knots. Far too strong for divers to work with any level of efficiency. And, as Al suggested, chances are, the engine and coaches are buried in the silt. This calls for a dredging operation. The worst kind."

"The salvage of a ship in open water is far more complex and time-consuming than bringing up a Pullman car from shallow depths," Giordino argued.

"True," Gunn conceded. "But we know where the *Empress* lies. The grave of the *Manhattan Limited* has never been found."

"Trains don't dissolve. We're looking at a confined area less than a mile square. A sweep with a proton magnetometer should make contact within a few hours."

"You talk as if the locomotive and coaches are still attached by their couplings. After the fall from the bridge they probably were scattered all over the riverbed. We could spend weeks excavating the wrong car. I can't accept the odds. It's too hit-or-miss."

Giordino did not retreat. "What would you calculate the odds are against finding a small packet inside a crumbling fourteen-thousand-ton vessel?"

"We ignore the odds." Dirk Pitt spoke quietly and for the first time. He sat at the end of the table, hands folded behind his head. "I say we try for both simultaneously."

Silence settled over the operations room. Giordino sipped at his coffee, mulling over Pitt's words. Gunn peered speculatively through his thick-lensed glasses.

"Can we afford the complications of dividing our efforts?"

"Better to ask, can we afford the time?" Pitt answered.

"Do we have a deadline?" Giordino queried.

"No, we're not held to a set schedule," said Sandecker. He moved away from the charts and sat on one corner of the table. "But the President made it clear to me that if a copy of the North American Treaty still exists, he wants it damned quick." The admiral shook his head. "What in hell good a soggy scrap of seventy-five-year-old paper is to our government, or what the urgency of finding it is, was not explained. I wasn't offered the luxury of reasoning why. Dirk is right. We don't have the time to conduct leisurely search projects in tandem."

Giordino looked at Pitt and sighed. "Okay, we shoot for two birds with one stone."

"Two stones," Pitt corrected him. "While a salvage expedition forces its way inside the ship's hull, a survey team probes the Hudson for the *Manhattan Limited,* or specifically, for the government railroad coach that carried Richard Essex."

"How soon can we get the show on the road?" asked Sandecker.

Pitt's eyes took on a detached look, as though they were focused on an object beyond the walls of the room. "Forty-eight hours to assemble a crew and gear, twenty-four to load and outfit a vessel. Then allowing for good sailing weather, we should be moored over the *Empress* in five days."

"And the *Manhattan Limited?*"

"I can put a boat equipped with magnetometer, side-scan sonar and a sub-bottom profiler on site by this time the day after tomorrow," Giordino replied positively.

The time estimates seemed optimistic to Sandecker, but he never questioned the men in front of him. They were the best in the business and they rarely disappointed him. He stood up and nodded at Giordino.

"Al, the *Manhattan Limited* search is yours. Rudi, you'll head the salvage operation on the *Empress of Ireland.*" He turned to Pitt. "Dirk, you'll act as combined projects director."

"Where would you like *me* to start?" asked Heidi.

"With the ship. The builder's blueprints, deck plans, the exact area of Harvey Shields' stateroom. Any relevant data that will lead us to the treaties."

Heidi nodded. "The public inquiry into the disaster was held in Quebec. I'll begin by digging into the transcript of the findings. If your secretary will book me on the next flight, I'll be on my way."

She looked mentally and physically exhausted, but Sandecker was too pressured for time to voice a gentlemanly offer of a few hours' sleep. He paused a few moments, staring into each determined face.

"All right," he said without emotion. "Let's do it."

39

General Morris Simms, casually attired as a fisherman, felt oddly out of character carrying a bamboo rod and wicker creel as he walked down a worn path to the River Blackwater near the village of Seward's End, Essex. He stopped at the edge of the bank under a picturesque stone bridge and nodded a greeting to a man who was seated on a folding chair, patiently contemplating a bobber on the surface of the water.

"Good morning, Prime Minister."

"Good morning, Brigadier."

"Frightfully sorry to trouble you on your holiday."

"Not at all," said the Prime Minister. "The bloody perch aren't biting anyway." He tilted his head toward the portable table beside him that held a bottle of wine and what looked to Simms like a ham-and-veal pie. "There's extra glasses and plates in the basket. Help yourself to the sherry and pie."

"Thank you, sir, I think I shall."

"What's on your mind?"

"The North American Treaty, sir." He paused as he poured the sherry. "Our man in the States reports the Americans are going to make an all-out effort to find it."

"Any chance they might?"

"Very doubtful." Simms held up the bottle. "More sherry?"

"Yes, thank you."

Simms poured. "At first I thought they might make a few simple probes. Nothing elaborate, of course, a small operation to convince themselves there was little hope of a document surviving. However, it now seems they're going after it in deadly earnest."

"Not good," the Prime Minister grunted. "That indicates, to me at least, that if they're remotely successful, they intend to exercise the terms set down in the treaty."

"My thought also," Simms agreed.

"I can't picture the Commonwealth without Canada," said the Prime Minister. "The entire framework of our overseas trade organization would begin an inevitable collapse. As it is, our economy is in shambles. The loss of Canada would be a disaster."

"As bad as all that?"

"Worse." The Prime Minister stared into the stream while he spoke. "If Canada goes, Australia and New Zealand would follow in three years. I don't have to tell you where that would leave the United Kingdom."

The enormity of the Prime Minister's dire prediction was beyond Simms' comprehension. England without an empire was inconceivable. And yet, sadly, deep down he knew British stoicism could find a way to accept it.

The bobber made a couple of quick dips but became still again. The Prime Minister sipped at the sherry thoughtfully. He was a formidably heavy-featured man with unblinking blue eyes and a mouth that ticked up at the edges in a perpetual smile.

"What instructions are your people working under?" he asked.

"Only to observe and report the Americans' actions."

"Are they aware of the treaty's potential threat?"

"No, sir."

"You'd better inform them. They must be aware of the danger to our nation. Where do we stand otherwise?"

"Using the National Underwater and Marine Agency as a cover, the President has ordered an intensive salvage operation on the *Empress of Ireland.*"

"This thing must be nipped in the bud. We've got to keep them off the *Empress.*"

Simms cleared his throat. "By . . . ah what measures, sir?"

"It's time we told the Canadians what the Americans are about. Offer our cooperation within the framework of Commonwealth law. Request they revoke permission for NUMA to operate on the St. Lawrence. If the President persists in this folly, blow up the wreck and destroy the British treaty copy once and for all."

"And the American copy that was lost on the train? We can't very well order them off their own river."

The Prime Minister shot Simms an acid look. "Then you'll just have to think of something a bit more drastic, won't you?"

Part IV

THE EMPRESS OF IRELAND

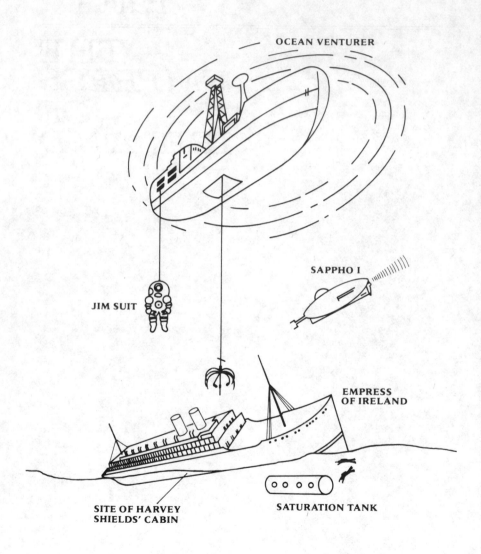

OCEAN VENTURER

SAPPHO I

JIM SUIT

EMPRESS
OF IRELAND

SITE OF HARVEY
SHIELDS' CABIN

SATURATION TANK

40

Villon closed the file cover and shook his head.

"Nonsense."

"I assure you," said Brian Shaw, "it is not nonsense."

"What does it all mean?"

"Exactly what you read in the report," said Shaw, staring directly at Villon. "The Americans have launched a search for evidence of a treaty that gives the whole of Canada to them."

"Until now, I've never heard of such a treaty."

"Few people have." Shaw paused to light a cigarette. "Immediately after the documents were lost, all but a few references to the negotiations were secretly destroyed."

"What proof do you have the Americans are actually out to lay their hands on this treaty?"

"I followed a string through a labyrinth. It led to a chap by the name of Dirk Pitt who holds a high level position with the National Underwater and Marine Agency. I had him watched closely by embassy personnel. They discovered he is leading two search expeditions: one to the spot on the Hudson River where Essex's train was lost, and the other to the *Empress of Ireland*. I can assure you, Mr. Villon, he is not looking for treasure."

Villon sat silently for a moment. Then he shifted in his chair and leaned forward. "How can I help you?"

"For starters, you could order Pitt and his crew off the St. Lawrence."

Villon shook his head. "I can't do that. Permission for the salvage operation went through the proper channels. There is no telling what the Americans might do if we suddenly revoked their license. They could easily retaliate by shutting off our fishing rights in their waters."

"General Simms considered that prospect. So he came up with another option." Shaw paused a moment. "He suggests that we destroy the wreck of the *Empress*."

"You could do that without causing a nasty incident?"

"Provided that I can reach the wreckage before Pitt does."

Villon sat back, coldly analyzing how the information Shaw had put before him could be exploited to his advantage. He let his eyes drift across the room to a painting on the wall of a clipper ship under full sail before the wind. At last, his thoughts arranged, he nodded.

"I shall give you every cooperation."

"Thank you," Shaw replied. "I'll require the services of five men, a boat and the proper diving equipment."

"You'll need a good man to coordinate your plans."

"Do you have someone in mind?"

"I do," said Villon. "I'll see that he gets in touch with you. He is a Mountie, well trained for this sort of work. His name is Gly, Inspector Foss Gly."

41

The expedition to locate the *Manhattan Limited* seemed jinxed from the start. Giordino was frustrated to the gills. Already he was four days behind on his promised schedule.

After a hurried dockside loading of men and equipment, the trim new research boat, the *De Soto*, sixty feet long and especially designed by NUMA engineers to cruise inland waterways, churned upriver and headed toward near destruction.

The helmsman kept a keen eye on the channel buoys and passing pleasure craft. His main concern, however, was the falling barometer and a light splattering of rain on the wheelhouse windows. Together they promised a first-class storm by nightfall.

As darkness settled, the river's chop began throwing spray over the *De Soto*'s foredeck. Suddenly the wind howled down over the steep palisades bordering the shoreline, gusting from twenty miles an hour to over sixty. The force of the blast pushed the speeding boat out of the main channel. Before the helmsman could literally muscle it back on course, it had driven into shallow waters, ripping a two-foot gash under its port bow on what was believed to be a submerged log.

For the next four hours, Giordino drove his crew with the heavy hand of a Captain Bligh. The sonar operator insisted later that the feisty Italian's tongue lashed about his ears like a bullwhip. It was a masterful performance. The hole was plugged until there were only a few small trickles, but not before the water had risen above the bilges and was sloshing ankle deep on the lower deck.

Laden with two tons of water, the *De Soto* handled sluggishly. Giordino ignored it in his fury and crammed the throttles to their stops. The sudden burst of speed raised the splintered wound above the waterline and the vessel hurtled back down the river toward New York.

Two days were lost while the boat was drydocked and its hull repaired. No sooner had they gotten underway again than the magnetometer was found to be defective and a new unit rushed from San Francisco. Two more days down the drain.

At last, under the light of a full moon, Giordino watched cautiously as the *De Soto* slipped under the massive stone abutment that had once supported the Hudson-Deauville bridge. He poked his head in the open wheelhouse window.

"What do you read on the fathometer?"

Glen Chase, the taciturn, balding captain of the boat, cast an eye at the red digital numerals. "About twenty feet. Looks safe enough to park here till morning."

Giordino shook his head at Chase's land talk. The captain stoutly refused to voice the language of the sea, using left for port and right for starboard, claiming that ancient tradition did not fit the modern scheme of the times.

The anchor was dropped and the boat secured by lines running to a convenient tree on shore and the rusting remains of the bridge pier in the river. The engines were shut down and the auxiliary power unit fired up. Chase stared up at the crumbling abutment.

"Must have been quite a structure in its day."

"Fifth longest in the world when it was built," said Giordino.

"What do you suppose caused it to fall?"

Giordino shrugged. "According to the inquiry report, the evidence was inconclusive. The best theory was high winds combined with lightning strikes weakened a supporting truss."

Chase nodded his head toward the river. "Think it's waiting down there?"

"The train?" Giordino gazed at the moonlit waters. "It's there all right. The wreckage wasn't found in 1914 because all salvage men had at their command were copper-helmeted divers in clumsy canvas suits, groping in zero visibility, and grapples dragged by small boats. Their equipment was too limited and they looked in the wrong place."

Chase lifted his cap and scratched his head. "We should know in a couple of days."

"Less, with any luck."

"How about a beer?" Chase asked, smiling. "I always buy for an optimist."

"I believe I will," said Giordino.

Chase disappeared down a stairwell and made his way to the galley. In the main dining salon the crew could be heard joking among themselves as they adjusted the television dish antenna to pick up signals from a passing relay satellite.

A sudden chill raised goose bumps on Giordino's hairy arms, and he reached inside the wheelhouse for a windbreaker. As he was pulling up the zipper he hesitated and cocked an ear.

Chase appeared and handed him a beer can. "I didn't bother with glasses."

Giordino held up his hand for silence.

"You hear that?"

Chase's brow furrowed. "Hear what?"

"Listen."

Chase tilted his head, his eyes locked in the unseeing stare of a man concentrating on sounds.

"A train whistle," he announced indifferently.

"You sure?"

Chase nodded. "I can hear it plainly. Definitely a train whistle."

"Don't you find that odd?" asked Giordino.

"Why should I?"

"Diesel locomotives have air horns. Only the old steam engines blew whistles, and the last one was retired thirty years ago."

"Could be one of those kids' rides at an amusement park somewhere up the river," Chase surmised. "Sound can carry for miles over water."

"I don't think so," Giordino said, cupping his ears and swinging his head back and forth like a radar antenna. "It's getting louder . . . louder and closer."

Chase ducked into the wheelhouse and returned with a land road map and a flashlight. He unfolded the paper over the deck railing and beamed the light.

"Look here," he said pointing to the tiny blue lines. "The main rail line cuts inland twenty miles south of here."

"And the nearest track?"

"Ten, maybe twelve miles."

"Whatever is making that sound is no more than a mile away," Giordino said flatly.

Giordino tried to fix the direction. The blazing moon illuminated the landscape with crystal clarity. He could distinguish individual trees two miles away. The sound was approaching along the west bank of the river above them. There was no movement of any kind, no lights except those of a few distant farmhouses.

Another shriek.

New sounds now. The clangor of heavy steel, the throaty, pulsating exhaust of steam and combustion split the night. Giordino felt as if he was suspended in air. He stood rigid. He waited.

"It's turning—turning toward us," Chase rasped as though he was still trying to convince himself. "God, it's coming off the ruins of the bridge."

They both stared upward at the top of the abutment, unable to breathe, unable to grasp what was happening. All at once the deafening noise of the invisible train exploded out of the dark above them. Giordino instinctively ducked. Chase froze, his face a ghastly corpse-white, the enlarged pupils of his eyes black pits you could fall into.

And then, abruptly, silence—a silence deathlike and ominous.

Neither man spoke, neither moved. They stood rooted to the deck like wax figures without hearts or lungs. Slowly Giordino gathered his thoughts and took the flashlight from Chase's unresisting hand. He shone its beam on the top of the abutment.

There was nothing to see but time-worn stone and impenetrable shadows.

42

The *Ocean Venturer* lay anchored over the wreck of the *Empress of Ireland*. A light rain had passed in the early morning hours and the *Venturer*'s white hull glistened orange under the new sun. In contrast, a tired old fishing boat, its faded blue paint scarred and chipped, lazily trolled its nets two hundred yards away. To the fishermen the *Ocean Venturer,* silhouetted against the brightening horizon, looked as if it had been created by an artist with a warped sense of humor.

Its hull lines were aesthetic and contemporary. Beginning with its gracefully rounded bow, the main deck line traveled in an eye-pleasing curve to the oval fantail. There were none of the sharp edges associated with most other ships; even the egg-shaped bridge rested on an arched spire. But there the beauty ended. Like a Cyrano's repulsive nose, a derrick similar to those erected in new oil fields protruded incongruously from the *Ocean Venturer*'s midsection.

Functional, if not attractive, the derrick possessed the capability of lowering a variety of scientific packages through the hull to the seafloor or of raising heavy objects such as salvage debris straight into the ship's bowels. The *Ocean Venturer* was the perfect vessel to act as a work platform for the treaty search.

Pitt stood on the stern, clutching a Portuguese fisherman's cap tightly to his head as the blades of a NUMA helicopter whipped the air around him. For a few moments the pilot hovered while he tested the wind currents. Then he dropped the chopper slowly until the skids settled firmly on the painted markings of the flight pad.

Pitt hunched over, jogged up to the craft and opened the door. Heidi Milligan, dressed in a jumpsuit of cotton painter's cloth in dazzling azure blue, hopped out. Pitt helped her down and took a suitcase that was passed to him by the pilot.

"On your next taxi run," Pitt yelled above the whine of the turbines, "bring us a case of peanut butter."

The pilot waved a casual salute and shouted back, "Shall do."

Pitt escorted Heidi across the deck as the helicopter lifted from the pad and dipped its nose toward the south. She turned to him and smiled.

"Does the project director always double as baggage porter?"

"Like the man said," Pitt laughed, "I get no respect."

Several minutes after he showed her to her quarters, she entered the dining salon carrying a packet of papers and sat down beside him.

"How was your trip?"

"Productive," she replied. "How's your end?"

"We arrived on site yesterday afternoon, eighteen hours ahead of schedule, and positioned the *Ocean Venturer* above the wreck."

"What's your next move?"

"A small unmanned remote sub with cameras will be lowered to survey the *Empress*. The video data it relays to our monitors will be studied and analyzed."

"What angle does the ship lie?"

"Forty-five degrees to starboard."

Heidi frowned. "Lousy luck."

"Why?"

She began to spread the papers over the table. Some were quite large and had to be unfolded.

"Before I answer that, here's a copy of the passenger list from the *Empress* on its final sailing. At first I thought I hit a dead end when I couldn't find Harvey Shields' name among the first-class passengers. Then it occurred to me that he might have traveled in a lower class to avoid advertising his presence. Most transatlantic liners provided plush accommodations on second-class decks for wealthy but frugal eccentrics or high-level government officials who wanted to cross the oceans in low profile. That's where I found him. Upper deck D, cabin forty-six."

"Nice work. You put a fix on the needle in the haystack. Now we don't have to tear the whole ship apart."

"That's the good news," said Heidi. "Now the bad news."

"Let's have it."

"The *Storstad*, the Norwegian coal collier that sank the *Empress*, struck the liner starboard amidships almost directly between the funnels, gouging a wedge-shaped hole over fifteen feet wide and nearly fifty feet in height. The collier's bow sliced into the boiler rooms below the waterline with a section of the second-class accommodations straight above."

"You're suggesting that the *Storstad* obliterated Shields' cabin?"

"We have to consider the worst possibility." Heidi spread a copy of the *Empress of Ireland*'s plans over the charts. She pointed a pencil tip at a small circled area. "Number forty-six was an outside starboard cabin. It was either damned close or directly in the middle of the impact point."

"That could explain why Shields' body was never found."

"He was probably crushed to death in his sleep."

"What did you mean by 'lousy luck' when I gave you the wreck's angle?"

"A forty-five-degree list to starboard would put cabin forty-six in the riverbed," Heidi replied. "The interior must be buried in silt."

"Back to square one. The silt would preserve the treaty's covering but make it almost impossible to find."

Heidi sat silently watching Pitt as he slowly tapped his fingers on the table, his mind rummaging through the data laid before him. His deep green eyes took on a faraway look.

She reached over and touched his hand. "What are you thinking about?"

"The *Empress of Ireland*," Pitt said quietly. "It's the ship the world forgot. A tomb of a thousand souls. God only knows what we'll find when we get inside her."

43

"I hope you don't mind seeing me on such short notice," said the President as he strode from the elevator.

"Not at all," replied Sandecker without fanfare. "Everything has been constructed. Please step this way."

The President motioned his Secret Service men to wait by the elevator. Then he followed the admiral down a carpeted hallway to a large cedar double door. Sandecker opened it and stood aside.

"After you, Mr. President."

The room was circular and the walls were covered by a dark purple fabric. There were no windows and the only piece of furniture was a large kidney-shaped table that stood in the center. Its surface was illuminated by blue and green overhead spotlights. The President approached and stared at a three-foot-long object resting on a bed of fine-grained sand.

"So this is how it looks," he said in a reverent tone.

"The grave of the *Empress of Ireland,*" Sandecker acknowledged. "Our miniature craftsman worked from video pictures relayed by the *Ocean Venturer*."

"Is that the salvage ship?" the President asked, pointing to another model that was suspended on a clear plastic plate about two feet above the *Empress*.

"Yes, the models are in exact proportion to each other. The distance between them represents the depth from the surface to the riverbed."

The President studied the *Empress* model for several seconds. Then he shook his head in wonderment. "The treaty is so small and the ship so large. Where do you begin to look?"

"Our researcher had a breakthrough on that score," said Sandecker. "She was able to pinpoint the location of Harvey Shields' cabin." He motioned to an area amidships on the buried starboard hull. "It lies somewhere about here. There is, unfortunately, a good possibility that the cabin was mangled in the collision with the coal collier."

"How will you go about reaching the cabin?"

"After the crew conducts a survey of the interior of the ship by an unmanned remote search vehicle," replied Sandecker, "the salvage operation will start on the lifeboat deck and excavate downward to the target site."

"It looks like they're going about it the hard way," said the President. "Me, I'd enter from outside the lower hull."

"Easier said . . . As near as we can figure, Shields' cabin lies under tons of silt. Take my word for it, Mr. President, dredging through river mud is a dangerous, exhausting, time-consuming procedure. By attacking from inside the ship the men will have a firm platform from which to work, and most important, they'll be able to orient the exact direction of their penetration from the shipbuilder's plans at any time during the operation."

"You've made your case," the President acquiesced.

Sandecker went on: "We're relying on four different systems to tunnel through the guts of the ship. One is the derrick you see on the *Ocean Venturer*. Designed for a lifting load of fifty tons, it will remove the heavier debris. Second, a two-man submersible with mechanical arms will function as an all-purpose backup unit."

The President picked up a detailed miniature and studied it. "I take it this represents the submersible?"

Sandecker nodded. "The *Sappho I*. It was one of four deepwater recovery vehicles used on the *Titanic* project last year."

"I didn't mean to interrupt. Please continue."

"The third system is the keystone of the operation," said Sandecker. He held up a doll-like figure that resembled a mechanical polar bear with portholes in a bulbous head. "An articulated, deepwater atmospheric diving system, more commonly called a JIM suit. It is constructed of magnesium and fiberglass, and a man inside it can work at tremendous depths for hours at a time while eliminating the need for decompression. Two of these suits will enable six men to work on the wreck around the clock."

"Looks heavy and cumbersome."

"In air, with an operator inside, it weighs eleven hundred pounds. Under water, only about sixty. It's surprisingly agile. You might say it puts hiking on the seafloor in a class with hiking on the Sahara."

The President took the figure from Sandecker's offered hand and moved the tiny articulated arms and legs. "It also makes aqualung divers obsolete."

"Not entirely," answered Sandecker. "A diver with three-dimensional mobility is still the backbone of any salvage operation. The fourth and final system is called saturation diving." He gestured at a model in the form of a cylindrical tank. "A team of divers will live in this pressurized chamber while breathing a mixture of helium and oxygen. This prevents the narcotic effects of inhaling nitrogen under pressure. The chamber permits men to work underwater for long stretches of time without the danger of lung gases dissolving into the bloodstream, forming bubbles and causing the bends. Also, they don't have to decompress until the job is finished."

The President fell silent. By education and occupation he was an attorney, a precise and analytical man—and yet scientific data was beyond him. He did not wish to appear stupid in front of the admiral. He chose his words carefully.

"Surely your people don't intend to literally claw a path through an acre of steel."

"No, there is a better method."

"Like explosives perhaps?"

"Too risky." Sandecker replied matter-of-factly. "The steel in the wreck has been under attack by corrosive elements for seventy-five years. It has become porous and its tensile strength is greatly reduced. A charge in the wrong place or one too strong, and the whole ship could collapse in on itself. No, we'll cut our way through.''

"With acetylene cutting torches, then.''

"With pyroxone.''

"Never heard of it.''

"A pliable incendiary substance that can burn under water at an incredibly high temperature for precontrolled lengths of time. Once pyroxone is molded against the surface to be separated, it is ignited by an electronic signal. At three thousand degrees Celsius it will melt any barrier in its way, including rock.''

"It's hard to imagine.''

"If I can answer any more questions . . .''

The President made a disparaging gesture. "No, I'm satisfied. You and your people are doing a remarkable job.''

"If we don't come up with the treaty, you'll know we did all that was technically possible.''

"I gather you're not too hopeful.''

"Frankly, Mr. President, I think we have about as much chance as a titmouse in a buzzard's beak.''

"What are your feelings concerning the treaty on the *Manhattan Limited?*''

"I'll save any comment until we find the train.''

"At least I know your position,'' the President said, smiling.

Sandecker suddenly looked wolfish. "Sir, I have a question.''

"Go ahead.''

"May I respectfully ask just what in hell this is all about?''

It was the President's turn to look wolfish. "You may well ask, Admiral, but all I'm going to tell you is that the scheme is crazy,'' he said with an ill-boding look in his eyes. "The craziest scheme ever hatched by a president of the United States.''

44

The silence in the dense green depths of the St. Lawrence River was broken by a strange whirring sound. Then a thin shaft of bright bluish light sliced into the cold water, slowly increasing in dimension until it became a large rectangle. A school of curious fish, attracted by the brilliant glow, swam toward it in languid circles, seemingly uncaring of the blurred shadows that wavered above them.

Inside the huge center well of the *Ocean Venturer* a team of engineers readied a remote-search vehicle that hung suspended by a cable from a small crane. One man adjusted the light source units for the three cameras while another linked up the battery power supply.

The RSV was shaped like an elongated teardrop, only three feet long and ten inches in diameter, and showed no protrusions on its smooth titanium skin. Steering and propulsion were provided by a small hydrojet pump with variable thrusters.

Heidi stood on the edge of the well opening and peered at the fish below.

"A strange feeling," she said. "Looking at water inside a ship and wondering why we're not sinking."

"Because you're standing four feet above the surface," Rudi Gunn answered her with a grin. "So long as the river can't penetrate below the waterline, we stay afloat."

One of the engineers waved his hand. "It's buttoned up."

"No umbilical cable for electronic control?" asked Heidi.

"Baby responds by remote sound impulses up to three miles under water," explained Gunn briefly.

"You call it Baby?"

"That's because it's usually wet," Pitt laughed.

"Men and their juvenile humor," she said, shaking her head.

Pitt turned to the well. "Diver in," he ordered.

A man encased in a thermal diving suit adjusted his face mask and slipped over the side. He guided the RSV as it was lowered into the well and released it when they both had fallen below the *Venturer*'s keel.

"Now let's move along to the control room and see what's down there," Pitt said.

A few minutes later they were watching three different viewing screens, mounted horizontally. On the opposite side of the room several technicians studied dials and noted instrument readings on clipboards. Against another wall a bank of computers began recording the data transmissions.

A cheerful fat man with curly strawberry hair and freckles stippling his face grinned with a great flash of teeth as Pitt introduced him to Heidi.

"Doug Hoker, meet Heidi Milligan," Pitt said, dropping Heidi's naval rank. "Doug plays mother to Baby."

Hoker half rose out of his chair in front of a large console and shook her hand. "Always glad to have a beautiful audience."

She smiled at the compliment. "This is one opening I didn't want to miss."

Hoker turned back to his console and immediately became all business. "Passing eighty feet," he droned, his right hand on an aircraft control grip. "Water temperature thirty-four degrees."

"Circle Baby in from the stern," said Pitt.

"Acknowledged."

At 165 feet the river bottom appeared on the color video screens, a drab, washed-out brown, devoid of life except for an occasional crab and scattered bits of weed. Visibility under the RSV's high-intensity lights was little more than ten feet.

Gradually a dark shape began to grow from the top of the screen, slowly enlarging until its huge pintles could be clearly seen.

"Nice sense of direction," Pitt said to Hoker. "You laid it dead on the rudder."

"Something else coming up," Gunn announced. "The propeller, by the looks of it."

The four great bronze blades that once had driven the 14,000-ton ship from Liverpool to Quebec on many crossings moved at a funereal pace past the camera eyes of the RSV.

"About twenty feet from tip to tip," Pitt judged. "Must weigh at least thirty tons."

"The *Empress* was a twin-screw vessel," said Heidi softly. "The one on the port side was salvaged in nineteen hundred and sixty-eight."

Pitt turned to Hoker. "Come up fifty feet and travel forward along the starboard boat deck."

Deep beneath their feet the little sub obeyed its impulse commands and swam over the stern railing, narrowly missing the staff that had once flown the ensign of the *Empress'* home port.

"The aft mast is down," Pitt said in a monotone. "The rigging appears to be gone."

Then the boat deck came into view. A few of the davits hung empty, but some still held steel lifeboats frozen for eternity in their chocks. The ventilators stood in silent agony, their buff-colored paint long flaked away, but the two funnels had vanished, fallen decades before into the silt.

No one spoke for a few minutes. It was as though they could somehow reach into the past and sense the hundreds of frightened men, women and children milling the decks in confusion, helplessly feeling the ship sink beneath them with terrible swiftness.

Heidi's heart began to pound against her breast. There was a morbid aura about the scene. Seaweed, clinging to the rust-eaten hulk, swayed eerily to and fro with the current. She shivered involuntarily and clasped her hands together to keep them from trembling.

Finally Pitt broke the silence. "Take it inside."

Hoker took a handkerchief from his pocket and wiped the nape of his neck.

"The two upper decks have collapsed," he murmured as if conversing in a church. "We can't penetrate."

Pitt spread the ship's interior drawings on a chart table and traced a line with his finger. "Drop down to the lower promenade deck. The first-class lobby entrance should be clear."

"Is Baby actually going to enter the ship?" Heidi asked.

"That's what it was designed for," replied Pitt.

"All those people dead in there. Somehow it almost seems sacrilegious."

"Men have been diving on the *Empress* for half a century," Gunn said gently, as though talking to a child. "The museum at Rimouski is filled with artifacts taken from inside the wreck. Besides, it's imperative to see what we'll be up against when we begin cutting through—"

"I have penetration," Hoker interrupted.

"Take it slow," Pitt acknowledged. "The wooden ceilings have probably fallen and clogged the passageways."

For the next few seconds only the floating particles in the water showed on the monitors. Then the RSV's light source fell on a fan-shaped stairway. The curled lines of the banisters were still evident, held erect by sagging support columns. The Persian carpeting that had once graced the lower landing had long since rotted away, as had the chairs and sofas.

"I think I can negotiate the aft passageway," said Hoker.

"Make entry," Pitt instructed tersely.

The stateroom doorways marched by the cameras in wraithlike procession as the RSV threaded its way through the fallen rubble. After thirty feet the passageway looked clear and they made an inspection of a cabin. The luxurious comfort for which the ill-fated ship was famous had deteriorated into pitiful scraps. The spacious bunk-style beds and ornate dressers had long ago surrendered to the ravages of the callous waters.

The journey into time passed with agonizing slowness. It took nearly two hours for the RSV to break into a lounge area.

"Where are we?" asked Gunn.

Pitt consulted the drawings again. "We should be coming on the entrance of the main dining saloon."

"Yes, there it is," Heidi pointed excitedly. "The large doorway to the right of the screen."

Pitt looked at Gunn. "It's worth checking out. According to the plans, Shields' cabin lies on the deck directly below."

The lights of the RSV played over the huge room, casting phantom shadows beyond the columns that supported the remains of the sculptured ceilings above the dining alcoves. Only the oval mirrors on the walls, their glass coated with decades of slime, bore mute testimony to the opulent decor that had once enhanced the passengers' dining pleasure.

Suddenly there was a movement on the fringe of the light beams.

"What in hell is that?" blurted Gunn.

Spellbound, everyone in the control room started at the etheric cloud that floated into camera range.

For a long moment it seemed to hover, the outer edges vague and wavering in slow motion. Then, as if encased within a milky translucent shroud, a human form reached out for the RSV, an indistinct, disembodied form like two photographic negatives overlaying one another and producing a double exposure.

Heidi fell silent; her blood turned to ice. Hoker sat like a chunk of granite at the console, his face dazed with disbelief. Oddly, Gunn tilted his head to one side and studied the apparition with the clinical look of a surgeon contemplating an X-ray.

"In my wildest dreams," he said in a hoarse voice, "I never really thought I'd see a ghost."

Gunn's apparent composure didn't fool Pitt. He could see the little man was in a near state of shock. "Reverse Baby," he said calmly to Hoker.

Fighting a fear he had never experienced before, Hoker gathered his senses and moved his fingers over the controls. At first the undulating shape receded in the background, and then it began to grow larger again.

"Oh, lord, it's following," whispered Heidi.

A quick glance at the strained, stunned faces showed the same realization on every mind. They stood paralyzed, their attention transfixed on the monitors.

"For God's sake, what is it doing?" rasped Gunn.

No one answered, no one in the control room possessed the power of speech. No one except Pitt.

"Turn Baby around and get it out of there, fast!" he snapped.

Hoker forced himself to tear his eyes from the unearthly sight and pushed the power setting to FULL.

The little survey craft was not designed for speed. At maximum, its thrusters could only propel it at three knots. It began a tight turn. The cameras in the bow panned away from the undulating menace, past the open portholes glowing weirdly from the filtered light from the surface, past the faces of the mirrors that reflected no more. The 180-degree maneuver seemed to take an endless time.

And it came too late.

A second transparent specter drifted above the threshold of the doorway to the lounge, its shadowy arms outstretched and beckoning.

45

"Damn!" Pitt cursed. "Another one!"

"What should I do?" Hoker's voice was pleading, almost desperate.

It would be an understatement to say that Pitt held the undivided attention of everyone in the control room. They were awed by his glacial concentration. It was beginning to seep through to them why he was held in such high esteem by Admiral Sandecker. If ever a man was in the right place at the right time, it was Dirk Pitt standing on the deck of a salvage ship calling the shots against the unnatural.

Given a century, they could never have guessed the thought running through his mind. All they could detect from his expression was that anger had replaced studied contemplation.

If "Attack and be damned" worked with the phantom train, Pitt reasoned, there was little to lose by repeating the play. He nodded to Hoker.

"Ram the bastard!"

The mood abruptly changed now. Everyone took their strength from Pitt. Their fear gradually altered to growing determination to expose what their imaginations suggested were dead souls haunting the decaying ocean liner.

The RSV zeroed in and struck the spectral barrier in the doorway. There seemed to be no resistance at first. The blurred figure gave way, but then it floated forward and its shroud enveloped the craft. All focus was lost from the cameras and the monitors projected only vague shadows.

"It appears our hosts have substance," Pitt said conversationally.

"Baby is not responding to command," Hoker called out. "The controls react as if it's immersed in cooked oatmeal."

"Try reversing the thrusters."

"No go." Hoker shook his head. "Whatever those things are, they've immobilized it."

Pitt walked across to the control console and peered over Hoker's head at the instruments. "Why is the directional indicator vascillating?"

"It's like they're wrestling with Baby," answered Hoker. "Trying to drag it somewhere, I would guess."

Pitt gripped his shoulder. "Shut down all systems except the cameras."

"What about the lights?"

"Shut them down too. Let those heavy-handed ghosts think they've damaged Baby's power source."

The monitors dimmed until their screens showed only blackness. They looked cold and dead, but occasionally a faint, undefined movement showed through. If a stranger had walked into the control room he would have written everyone off as mentally incompetent; finding a group of people standing enraptured by dark TV screens was a psychologist's dream.

Ten minutes became twenty, and twenty became thirty. There was no change. Anticipation hung heavy in the air. Nothing and still nothing. Then very gradually, so gradually nobody noticed it at first, the screens began to lighten.

"What do you make of it?" Pitt asked Hoker.

"No way of telling. Without power, I can't read the systems."

"Activate the instruments, but only long enough for the computers to record the data."

"You're talking in microseconds."

"Then go for it."

The dexterity in Hoker's index finger ran a poor second to the incomprehensible speed of the data system as he flicked the switch. The demand signals were received by the RSV and returned to the computers, which in turn relayed their readout across the digital dials on the console before the switch clicked to OFF.

"Position, four hundred meters, heading zero-twenty-seven degrees. Depth, thirteen meters."

"It's coming up," Gunn said.

"Surfacing about a quarter mile off our starboard stern," Hoker verified.

"I can make out color now," said Heidi. "A dark green becoming a deep blue."

The haze in front of the camera lenses began to shimmer. Then a bright orange glare burst from the video screens. Human forms could be distinguished now, blurred as though animated through a frosted window.

"We have sun," declared Hoker. "Baby is on the surface."

Without a word, Pitt ran from the room up a companionway to the bridge. He snatched a pair of binoculars hanging by the helm and aimed them across the river.

The sky was free of clouds and the late morning sun reflected off the waters. A light breeze came in from the sea and nudged the short furrows upriver. The only vessels in sight were a tanker steaming from the direction of Quebec and a fleet of five fishing boats to the northeast, fanned out on different headings.

Gunn came up behind Pitt. "See anything?"

"No, I was too late," Pitt said shortly. "Baby is gone."

"Gone?"

"Perhaps kidnapped is a better word. Baby has probably been taken aboard one of those fishing boats out there." He paused and handed the glasses to Gunn. "My guess is the old blue trawler, or maybe the red one with the yellow wheelhouse. Their nets are hung so they block off all view of any activity on the far side of their decks."

Gunn stared silently across the water for a few moments. Then he lowered the binoculars. "Baby is a two-hundred-thousand-dollar piece of equipment," he said angrily. "We've got to stop them."

"I'm afraid the Canadians would not take kindly to a foreign vessel forcibly boarding boats inside their territorial limits. Besides, we've got to keep a low profile on our operation. The last thing the President needs is a messy incident over a piece of gear that can be replaced at the expense of the taxpayers."

"It doesn't seem right," grumbled Gunn.

"We'll have to forget righteous indignation," said Pitt. "The problem we have to face is who and why. Were they simply thieving sport divers or persons with more relevant motives?"

"The cameras might tell us," said Gunn.

"They might at that," Pitt said with a faint smile. "Providing the kidnappers didn't pull Baby's plug."

There was a strange atmosphere in the control room when they returned, thick and acrid and almost electrical. Heidi was sitting in a chair shuddering; all color was drained from her face, her eyes were blank. A young computer technician had produced a glass of brandy and was coaxing her to drink it. She looked for all the world as if she'd seen her third ghost of the day.

Hoker and three other engineers were bent over a circuit panel, checking the rows of indicating lights gone dark, fruitlessly manipulating knobs and switches. It was obvious to Pitt that all communications with the RSV had gone dead.

Hoker looked up when he saw Pitt. "I've got something interesting to show you."

Pitt nodded toward Heidi. "What's wrong with her?"

"She saw something that knocked hell out of her."

"On the monitors?"

"Just before transmission was cut off," Hoker explained. "Take a look while I replay the videotape."

Pitt watched. Gunn came and stood beside him, staring. The darkened screens slowly lightened and once again they saw the RSV break into sunlight. The glare lessened and then flashed in several sequences.

"This is when Baby was lifted from the water," observed Pitt.

"Yes," Hoker agreed. "Now catch the next action."

A series of distortion lines swept horizontally across the monitors, and then abruptly the left one blinked out.

"The clumsy nerds," Hoker complained bitterly. "They didn't know a delicate piece of gear when they saw it. They dropped Baby on its port camera and broke the color pickup tube."

At that moment the shroud was pulled back, coming into focus. The material could now be clearly seen for what it was.

"Plastic," exclaimed Gunn. "A thin sheet of opaque plastic."

"That explains the protoplasm," said Pitt. "And there are your neighborhood spooks."

Two figures in rubber diving suits knelt down and appeared to study the RSV.

"A pity we can't see their faces under the face masks," said Gunn.

"You'll see one soon enough," said Hoker. "Watch."

A pair of legs clad in Wellington boots and denim pants walked into camera range. Their owner stopped behind the divers and bent down and peered into the camera lenses.

He wore a British-style commando sweater with leather patches over the shoulders and elbows. A knit stocking cap was set at a casual side angle; graying hair along the temples was brushed fastidiously above the ears. He seemed to be in his late fifties, Pitt figured, or perhaps middle sixties. He had the look about him of a man who might be older than he appeared.

The face possessed a cruel, self-assured quality, found in men who are familiar with hazard. The dark eyes had the detached interest of a sniper peering through a telescopic sight at his impending victim.

Suddenly there was a slight, discernible widening of the eyes and the intense expression turned to anger. His mouth twisted with silent words and he spun quickly from view.

"I'm not a lip-reader," said Pitt, "but it looked as if he said 'You fools.' "

They remained, watching, as what looked like a canvas tarpaulin was thrown over the RSV and the monitors turned dark for the last time.

"That's all she wrote," said Hoker. "Contact was lost a minute later when they destroyed the transmission circuitry."

Heidi rose from the chair and moved forward as if she was in a trance. She pointed at the dead monitors, her lips quivering.

"I know him," she said, her voice barely audible. "The man in the picture . . . I know who he is."

46

Dr. Otis Coli inserted a du Maurier cigarette in a gold-tipped filter, clamped it between his dentures and lit it. Then he resumed poking through the open access panel into the electronic heart of the RSV.

"Damned clever, the Americans," he said, impressed with what he saw. "I've read scientific papers on it, but never seen one up close."

Coli, director of the Quebec Institute of Marine Engineering, had been recruited by Henri Villon. He was a gorilla of a man, barrel-chested, and had a rounded, heavy-browed face. His white hair passed his collar, and his mustache, beneath a thin, sloping nose, looked as if it had been clipped with sheep shears.

Brian Shaw stood beside Coli, his face clouded with concern. "What do you make of it?"

"An ingenious bit of technology," said Coli in the tone of a young man engrossed in a *Playboy* foldout. "Visual data is translated and sent by ultrasonic sound waves to the mother ship where it is encoded and enhanced by computers. The resulting imagery is then transferred to videotape with rather amazing clarity."

"So what's the scam?" grunted Foss Gly. He perched boredly atop a rusty winch mounted on the blue fishing boat's foredeck.

Shaw fought to hold down his temper. "The scam, as you so apathetically put it, is that these cameras were transmitting pictures when you brought them on board. Not only have the people on the NUMA ship been alerted to the fact they're being watched, they also have our faces recorded on videotape."

"How does that concern us?"

"Their project director is probably whistling up a helicopter this minute," Shaw replied. "Before nightfall the tape will be in Washington. And by this time tomorrow they'll probably have identification."

"On you maybe," Gly said grinning. "My partner and I kept our face masks on. Remember?"

"The damage has been done. The Americans will know we're not local divers looting a wreck. They'll be aware of who and what they're up against and will take every precaution."

Gly shrugged and began unzipping his diving suit. "If that mechanical fish hadn't interrupted us, we could have laid the charges, blown the hulk and left them precious little to salvage."

"Bad luck on our part," said Shaw. "How far did you get?"

"We'd barely started when we saw lights coming from over the stern."

"Where are the explosives?"

"Still on the forecastle of the wreck, where we stored them."

"How many pounds?"

Gly thought a moment. "Harris and I made six trips each, towing two hundred-pound sealed containers."

"Twenty-four hundred pounds," Shaw totaled. He turned to Doc Coli. "What if we detonated?"

"Right now?"

"Right now."

"Weight for weight, Trisynol is three times as powerful as TNT." Coli paused to stare across the water at the *Ocean Venturer*. "The pressure waves from its explosion would break the back of the NUMA ship."

"And the *Empress of Ireland?*"

"Demolish the bow section and smash in the forepart of the superstructure. At that point the main force would be absorbed. Further aft, a few bulkheads might buckle, a few decks cave in."

"But the central section of the wreck would remain intact."

"Quite correct," nodded Coli. "Your only accomplishment would be the mass death of innocent men."

"Little sense in pursuing that quarter," Shaw said thoughtfully.

"I'd certainly want no part in it."

"So. Where does that leave us?" asked Gly.

"For the moment, we tread softly," replied Shaw. "Sit back and observe, also find us another boat. The Americans are no doubt on to this one."

A look of contempt crossed Gly's face. "Is that the best you can come up with?"

"I'm satisfied. Unless you've got other ideas."

"I say blow the bastards to bits and end it now," Gly said coldly. "If you lack the stomach, old man, I'll do it."

"Enough!" Shaw snapped, his eyes fixed on Gly. "We're not at war with the Americans, and there is nothing in my instructions that condones murder. Only carnal idiots kill unnecessarily or wantonly. As for you, Inspector Gly, no more debates. You'll do as you're told."

Gly shrugged smugly in acquiescence and said nothing. He didn't have to waste words. What Shaw didn't know, what no one knew, was that he had inserted a radio detonator in one of the Trisynol containers.

With the press of a button he could set off the explosives anytime the mood struck him.

47

Mercier ate lunch with the President in the family dining room of the White House. He was thankful that his boss, unlike other chief executives, served up cocktails before five o'clock. The second Rob Roy tasted even better than the first, though it didn't exactly complement the Salisbury steak.

"The latest intelligence says the Russians have moved another division up to the Indian border. That makes ten, enough for an invasion force."

The President wolfed down a boiled potato. "The boys in the Kremlin burned their fingers by overrunning Afghanistan and Pakistan. And now they've got a full-fledged Muslim uprising on their hands that has spilled into Mother Russia. I wish they would invade India. It's more than we could hope for."

"We couldn't sit on the sidelines and not become militarily involved."

"Oh, we'd rattle our sabers and make fiery speeches in the United Nations denouncing another example of Communist aggression. Send a few aircraft carriers into the Indian Ocean. Launch another trade embargo."

Mercier picked at his salad. "In other words, the same reaction as we've always given. Stand by and watch—"

"—the Soviets dig their own grave," interrupted the President. "Marching on seven hundred million people who live in poverty would be like General Motors buying a vast welfare department. Believe me, the Russians would lose by winning.''

Mercier did not agree with the President, but deep down he knew the nation's leader was probably right. He dropped the subject and turned to a problem closer to home.

"The Quebec referendum for total independence comes up next week. After going down to defeat in '80 and '86, it looks like the third time may be the lucky charm.''

The President appeared unconcerned as he scooped up a forkful of peas. "If the French think full sovereignty leads to utopia, they're in for a rude awakening.''

Mercier put out a feeler. "We could stop it with a show of force.''

"You never give up, do you, Alan?''

"The honeymoon is over, Mr. President. It's only a question of time before congressional opposition and the news media begin labeling you an indecisive leader. The very opposite of what you promised during the campaign.''

"All because I won't go to war over the Middle East or send troops into Canada?''

"There are other measures, less drastic, to show a determined front.''

"There is no reason to lose one American life over a dwindling oil field in the desert. As for Canada, things will work themselves out.''

Mercier came straight out with it. "Why do you want to see a divided Canada, Mr. President?''

The chief executive looked across the table at him coolly. "Is that what you think? That I want to see a neighboring country torn apart and turned into chaos?''

"What else am I to believe?''

"Believe in me, Alan.'' The President's expression turned cordial. "Believe in what I am about to do.''

"How can I?'' asked a confused Mercier, "when I don't know what it is?''

"The answer is simple,'' replied the President with a trace of sadness in his voice. "I'm making a desperate play to save a critically ill United States.''

It had to be bad news. From the sour look on Harrison Moon's face, the President knew it couldn't be anything else. He laid aside the speech he was editing and sat back in his chair.

"You look like a man with a problem, Harrison."

Moon laid a folder on the desk. "I'm afraid the British have tagged the game."

The President opened the file and found himself staring at an eight-by-ten glossy of a man who gazed back at the camera.

"This was just flown in from the *Ocean Venturer*," explained Moon. "An underwater survey vehicle was probing the wreck when it was ripped off by a pair of unknown divers. Before communications were broken, this face appeared on the monitors."

"Who is he?"

"For the last twenty-five years he's been living under the name of Brian Shaw. As you can see in the report, he's a former British secret agent. His record makes interesting reading. Achieved quite a bit of notoriety back in the fifties and early sixties. He became too well known to operate; couldn't step on the sidewalk without a Soviet agent from their SMERSH assassination unit waiting to cut him down. His cover, as they say in the intelligence circles, was blown. Forced his secluded retirement. Their secret service buried his old identity by listing him as killed on duty in the West Indies."

"How did you put a make on him so fast?"

"Commander Milligan is on board the *Ocean Venturer*. She recognized him from the monitors. The CIA tracked down his true identity in their files."

"She knew Shaw?" the President asked incredulously.

Moon nodded. "Met him at a party in Los Angeles a month ago."

"I thought she was shipped out to sea."

"A foul-up. It never occurred to anyone to check out the fact that her ship was ordered to lay over three days in Long Beach for modifications. Also, nothing was said about not allowing her on shore."

"Their meeting? Could it have been a setup?"

"Seems so. The FBI spotted Shaw when he arrived from Britain. A usual procedure when embassy staff members greet overseas visitors. Shaw was escorted to a plane bound for LA. There the party was thrown by Graham Humberly, a well-known jet setter on the payroll of British intelligence."

"So Commander Milligan spilled her knowledge of the treaty."

Moon shrugged. "She had no instructions to keep her mouth shut."

"But how did they get wind of our knowledge of the treaty in the first place?"

"We don't know," Moon admitted.

The President read through the report on Shaw. "Odd that the British would trust an assignment of such magnitude to a man crowding seventy."

"At first glance it seems MI6 has given our treaty search low priority. But when you think about it, Shaw might well be the perfect choice to operate undercover. If Commander Milligan hadn't recognized his face, I doubt if we'd have tied him to British intelligence."

"Times have changed since Shaw was on the active list. He may be out of his element on this one."

"I wouldn't bet on it," Moon said. "The guy is no slouch. He's pegged us every step of the way."

The President sat very still for a moment. "It would appear that our neatly hatched concept has been penetrated."

"Yes, sir," Moon nodded somberly. "It's only a question of days, maybe hours, before the *Ocean Venturer* is ordered off the St. Lawrence. The stakes are too high for the British to gamble on us not finding the treaty."

"Then we write off the *Empress of Ireland* as a lost cause."

"Unless . . ." Moon said as if thinking out loud. "Unless Dirk Pitt can find the treaty in what precious time he has left."

48

Pitt scanned the screens, which showed the salvage team going about their business on the hulk below. Like two moon creatures cavorting in slow motion, the JIM suits and their human occupants carefully placed the Pyroxone on the upper superstructure. The men worked comfortably under the surface-equal atmosphere within their articulated enclosures. While outside, the bodies of the scuba divers were squeezed by seventy-five pounds of pressure per square inch. Pitt turned to Doug Hoker, who was fine-tuning a monitor.

"Where's the submersible?"

Hoker turned and studied a chart unreeling from a sonar recorder. "The *Sappho I* is cruising twenty meters off the port bow of the

Empress. Until we're ready to begin removing debris, I've ordered its crew to patrol a quarter-mile perimeter around the wreck.''

"Good thinking," said Pitt. "Any sign of trespassers?"

"Negative."

"At least we'll be ready for them this time."

Hoker made a dubious gesture. "I can't give you a perfect detection system. Visibility is too lousy for the cameras to see very far."

"What about side-scan sonar?"

"Its transducers cover a three-hundred-sixty-degree spread for three hundred meters, but again, no guarantees. A man makes an awfully small target."

"Any surface ships prowling about?"

"An oil tanker passed by ten minutes ago," answered Hoker. "And what looks to be a tug with a trash barge under tow is approaching from upriver."

"Probably going to dump its load further out in the gulf," Pitt surmised. "Won't hurt to keep a sharp eye on it."

"Ready to burn," announced Rudi Gunn, who stood looking up at the monitors, a pair of earphones with an attached microphone clamped on his head.

"Okay, clear the divers off the site," ordered Pitt.

Heidi entered the control room wearing a tan corduroy jump suit, a tray with ten steaming coffee cups held carefully in front of her. She passed them around to the engineering crew, offering the last one to Pitt.

"Have I missed anything?" she asked.

"Perfect timing. We're going for the first burn. Keep your fingers crossed that we laid the right amount of Pyroxone in the right place."

"What will happen if you didn't?"

"Not enough, and we accomplish nothing. Too much in the wrong place, and half the side of the ship caves in, costing us days we can't afford. You might compare us with a wrecking crew which is demolishing a building floor by floor. Explosives have to be set in strategic positions for the interior structure to collapse within a prescribed area."

"Flasher is set and counting," reported Gunn.

Pitt anticipated the question in Heidi's mind. "A flasher is an electronically timed incendiary device that ignites the Pyroxone."

"Divers are free of the ship and we are counting," said Gunn. "Ten seconds."

Everyone in the control room focused their eyes on the monitors. The countdown dragged by while they tensely awaited the results. Then Gunn's voice broke the heavy atmosphere.

"We are burning."

A bright glare engulfed the *Empress of Ireland*'s starboard topside, and two ribbons of white incandescence curled out from the same source and raced around the deck and bulkheads, joining together and forming a huge circle of superheat. A curtain of steam burst above the fiery arc and swirled toward the surface.

Soon the framework in the center began to sag. It hung there for nearly a minute, refusing to give way. Then the Pyroxone melted the last tenacious bond and the aging steel fell silently inward and vanished onto the deck below, leaving an opening twenty feet in diameter. The molten rim of the ring turned red and then gray, hardening again under the relentless cold of the water.

"Looking good!" said Gunn excitedly.

Hoker threw his clipboard in the air and whooped. Then they all began laughing and applauding. The first burn, the crucial burn, was a critical success.

"Lower the grappling claw," Pitt said sharply. "Let's not waste a minute clearing that rubble out of there."

"I have a contact."

Not everyone's focus had been on the monitors. The shaggy-haired man at the side-scan sonar recorder had kept his eyes on the readout chart.

In three steps Pitt was behind him. "Can you identify?"

"No, sir. Distance is too great to enhance with any detail. Looked like something dropped off that barge passing to port."

"Did the target glide out on an angle?"

The sonar operator shook his head. "Dropped straight down."

"Doesn't read like a diver," said Pitt. "The crew probably heaved a bundle of scrap or weighted trash overboard."

"Shall I stay on it?"

"Yes, see if you can detect any movement." Pitt turned to Gunn. "Who's manning the submersible?"

Gunn had to think a moment. "Sid Klinger and Marv Powers."

"Sonar has a strange contact. I'd like them to make a pass over it."

Gunn looked at him. "Think our callers might be back?"

"The reading is doubtful," Pitt shrugged. "But then, you never know."

As soon as he dropped over the side of the barge, Foss Gly swam straight to the bottom. Dragging an extra set of air tanks with him wasn't the easiest of chores, but he would need them for the return trip and the necessary decompression stops before he could resurface. He leveled off and hugged the riverbed, kicking his flippers with a lazy rhythm. He had a long way to go and much to do.

He had traveled only fifty meters when he heard a sustained droning coming from somewhere in the black void. He froze, listening.

The acoustics of the water scattered the sound and there was no way his ears could accurately detect the direction of the source. Then his eyes distinguished a dim yellow glow that grew and expanded above and to his right. There was no uncertainty in his mind. The *Ocean Venturer*'s manned submersible was homing in on him.

There was no place to hide on the flat and barren riverbed, no rock formations, no forest of kelp to shield him. Once the submersible's high-intensity beam picked him out, he would become as conspicuous as an escaping convict flattened against a prison wall under the harsh glare of a spotlight.

He dropped the spare air tanks and pressed his body into the silt, imagining the crew's faces pressed against the viewing ports, eyes trying to pierce the unending darkness. He held his breath so no telltale air bubbles would issue from his regulator.

The craft passed behind him and moved on. Gly inhaled a great breath, but didn't congratulate himself. He knew the crew would double back and keep looking.

Then he realized why he'd been missed. The silt had billowed up and clouded his figure. He lashed out with his fins and watched with relief as the submersible's light became lost in a great swirl of sediment. He grabbed up handfuls and waved the ooze about him. Within seconds he was totally cloaked. He switched on his diving light, but the floating muck reflected its ray. If he was blind, so were the men inside the submersible.

He groped around until his hands touched the spare air tanks. He checked his luminous wrist compass for the direction of the *Empress* and started to swim, stirring up the bottom in his wake.

"Klinger reporting in from the *Sappho*," said Gunn.

Pitt stepped back from the monitors. "Let me talk to him."

Gunn pulled off the headset and held it out. Pitt adjusted it to his head and spoke into the tiny microphone.

"Klinger, this is Pitt. What did you find?"

"Some sort of disturbance on the riverbed," Klinger's voice came back.

"Could you make out the cause?"

"Negative," Klinger repeated. "Whatever it was must have sunk in the silt."

Pitt looked over at the side-scan sonar. "Any contacts?"

The operator shook his head. "Except for a cloudlike smudge this side of the sub, the chart reads clear."

"Shall we return and give a hand with the salvage?" asked Klinger.

Pitt subsided into momentary silence. Oddly, Klinger's query annoyed him. Deep down inside he felt that an indefinable something was being overlooked.

Cold logic dictated that the human mind was far less infallible than machines. If the instruments detected nothing, then chances were, nothing was there to detect. Against his own nagging doubts, Pitt acknowledged Klinger's request.

"Klinger."

"Go ahead."

"Come on back, but take it slow and run a zigzag course."

"Understood. We'll keep a sharp eye. *Sappho* out."

Pitt handed the communications link back to Gunn. "How's it going?"

"Beautifully," replied Gunn. "See for yourself."

The clearing of the gallery was proceeding at a furious rate, or as furiously as was possible under the gluelike hindrance of deepwater pressure. The team of divers from the saturation chamber sliced away at the smaller pieces of scrap, working with acetylene torches and hydraulic cutters. Two of them propped up the teetering bulkheads with aluminum support pillars to prevent a cave-in.

The men in the JIM suits were guiding the grappling claw, dangling from the *Ocean Venturer*'s derrick above, to the heaviest sections of twisted debris. While one manhandled the lift cable, twisting it to the best angle, the other man held a small box in his hand-operated manipulator clamps that controlled the huge claw. When they were satisfied that they had a good, healthy bite, the pincers were closed, and the winch operator on the derrick took over, gently easing the load out of what had come to be known affectionately as the pit.

"At the rate they're going," said Gunn, "we'll be ready to make the final burn over the area of Shields' stateroom in four days."

"Four days," Pitt said turning over the words slowly. "God only knows if we'll still be here—" Suddenly he stiffened and stared at the screens.

Gunn looked at him. "Is something wrong?"

"How many divers are supposed to be out of the chamber this shift?"

"Four at a time," replied Gunn. "Why do you ask?"

"Because I count five."

49

Gly cursed himself for taking such a foolish risk, but lying under one of the rusting lifeboats he could not observe in any detail the activity taking place down in the hole where the salvage team was laboring. The idea of mingling with them seemed absurdly simple, though dangerous.

He noted there was only a slight difference in the style of his thermal exposure suit and theirs. The air tanks strapped to his back were of an earlier model, but the color was the same. Who would notice a near-lookalike interloper in the murk?

He swam down and approached from one side until his fins scraped against something solid: a steel hatch cover torn loose and resting on the deck. Before he could figure out his next move, one of the salvage crew drifted over and pointed down at the hatch. Gly gave an exaggerated nod of his head in understanding, and together the two of them wrestled the heavy steel plate to the bulwarks and heaved it over the side.

There were no invisible perils here. Gly recognized the threat and kept a wary eye. He pitched in with the others as though he had been doing it from the start. It was to his way of thinking a classic case of the most obvious being the least obvious.

They were much farther along than he had imagined. The NUMA people were like miners who seemed to know exactly where the mother lode was located, and they dug their shaft accordingly. By his calculation they were removing a ton of scrap every three hours.

He kicked across the cavity, taking an approximate measurement of its width. The next two questions were, how deep were they going and how long would it take them to get there?

Then he sensed that something was out of place, an impression more fancied than evident. Nothing looked to be out of the ordinary. The salvage men seemed too involved with their work to notice Gly. Yet there was a subtle change.

Gly moved into the shadows and floated immobile, breathing shallowly and evenly. He listened to the magnified underwater sounds and watched the animated movements of the JIM suits. His overworked sixth sense told him it was time to fade away.

But he was too late.

What was imperceptible a moment before came through with glassy transparency now. The other divers looked busy, but they were accomplishing nothing. The grappling claw had not returned after snatching its last load. The saturation divers lazily poked at the debris but did not transfer any of it over the side.

Slowly, with clairvoyant cooperation, they had gradually formed a crescent around Gly. Then it dawned on him. His presence had been detected from the mother ship. He had failed to catch the TV cameras attached to the lights because they were hidden by the glare, nor did he realize until now that the salvagers could receive instructions from a command center through miniaturized receivers inside their hoods.

He retreated until his back flattened against a bulkhead. The JIM suits formed a barrier in front of him while the other divers hovered on the flanks, closing off the final avenues of escape. They were all gazing at him now, and unemotional.

Gly unsheathed an eight-inch knife and crouched, thrusting it palm up in the nonprofessional but still lethal stance of a street fighter. It was a futile gesture born from a reflex action. The other divers carried knives too, nasty stainless steel blades strapped to their legs. And the manipulator clamps of the JIM suits possessed an inhuman strength to make painful wounds indeed.

They gathered around him motionless, like statues in a graveyard. Then one of the divers took a plastic slate from his weight belt and briefly wrote on it with a yellow grease stick. He finished and held the slate in front of Gly's nose.

The message was short and to the point. It simply read,

KISS OFF

For a moment Gly was stunned.

This was not the reception he expected. Not waiting to be cajoled, he flexed his knees and launched his body upward, swimming strongly over the NUMA divers' heads. They made not the slightest effort to stop him, moving only to turn and watch him melt into the blackness.

"You let him go," Gunn said quietly.

"Yes, I let him go."

"Do you think it was wise?"

Pitt stood impassive and did not immediately answer, his incredible green eyes narrowed in conjecture. There was a smile but not a smile. The expression was almost menacing, that of a lion waiting in cover for a passing meal.

"You saw the knife," Pitt said at last.

"He didn't have a prayer. Our boys would have fed him to the fish."

"The man was a killer." It was a simple statement, nothing more.

"We can still pick him up when he surfaces," Gunn persisted. "He would be helpless then."

"I don't think so."

"Any particular thought in mind?"

"Elementary," said Pitt. "We use a small fish to catch a big one."

"So that's it, eh?" Gunn said, unconvinced. "Wait until he meets up with his buddies, form a posse and round up the lot. Then turn them over to the authorities."

"For all we know, they are the authorities."

Gunn was more confused than ever. "So what's the percentage?"

"Our visitor was only on a scout mission. Next time he might bring some friends and really get nasty. We need to buy time. I think it would be worth our while to stop their clock."

Gunn made a peculiar twist with his lips and nodded. "I'm with you, but we had better get a move on. That guy will be boarding the next boat that passes by."

"No rush," Pitt said, quite relaxed. "He'll have to decompress for at least a half an hour. Probably has a spare set of air cylinders stashed on the river bottom somewhere."

Another question formed in Gunn's mind. "You said the gate-crasher was a killer. What made you say that?"

"He was too quick with the knife, too anxious to use it. Those who are born with a killer instinct never hesitate."

"So we're up against people with a license to kill," said Gunn thoughtfully. "Not exactly a cozy thought."

50

In the basin of the port of Rimouski, along the two deserted docks and the long warehouses, the predawn atmosphere was quiet and desolate, the stillness accented by the absence of wind.

It was too early for the appearance of the dockworkers, the eternally squawking seagulls, and the diesel locomotives that hauled the unloaded cargo to a nearby industrial park.

Tied to one dock was the tug that had towed an empty barge up and down the river past the *Ocean Venturer* only a few hours earlier. It was streaked with red rust, and the ravages from thirty years of hard use lay heavily on its uncompromising lines. A light streamed from the portholes of the master's cabin directly below the pilothouse, dimly reflecting across the black water.

Shaw checked his watch and pushed a tiny switch on what could have passed for a pocket calculator. He closed his eyes in thought a moment, and then began punching the rows of buttons.

Nothing like the old days, he mused, when an agent had to hide in an attic and mutter in low tones into the microphone of a radio transmitter. Now digital signals were relayed by satellite to a computer in London. There the message was decoded and sent to its proper destination by fiber optical transmission.

When he finished, he laid the electronic unit on the table and stood up to stretch. His muscles were stiff and his back sore. The bane of advancing age. He reached into his suitcase and pulled out the bottle of Canadian Club he had purchased after arriving at the Rimouski airport.

The Canadians called it whiskey, but to his British taste it seemed little different from American bourbon. It struck him as primitive to drink it warm—only the Scots preferred to down their liquor that way—but then, decrepit tugboats lacked such modern conveniences as icemakers.

He sat down in a chair and lit one of his specially ordered cigarettes. At least something remained of the past. All he lacked was a warm companion. It was times like these, when he was alone with a bottle and reflecting on his life, that he regretted not having remarried.

His reverie was interrupted when the little device on the table gave off a muted beep. Then a fine slip of paper, no more than a quarter of an inch in width, began to issue from one end. A marvel of advanced technology; it never failed to amuse him.

He donned a pair of reading glasses, another curse of the creeping years, and began studying the diminutive wording on the paper. The full text consumed nearly half a meter. At the end he removed his glasses, switched off the transmitter-receiver and replaced it in his pocket.

"The latest news from jolly old England?"

Shaw looked up to find Foss Gly standing in the doorway.

Gly made no move to enter. He just stared at Shaw from under questioning eyebrows and the expression in the eyes was that of a jackal sniffing the air.

"Merely an acknowledgment of my report on what you observed," replied Shaw casually. He began idly wrapping the message strip around his index finger in a roll.

Gly had changed from his thermal exposure suit into dungarees and a heavy turtleneck sweater. "I've still got the shivers. Mind if I help myself to a shot of your booze?"

"Be my guest."

Gly emptied half a water glass of the Canadian Club in two swallows. He reminded Shaw of an immense trained bear he'd once seen gulping a bucket of ale.

Gly expelled a long sigh. "Makes me feel almost human again."

"By my reckoning," said Shaw conversationally, "your decompression stage was five minutes on the down side. Are you feeling any ill effects?"

Gly made as if to pour himself another drink. "A slight tingling sensation, nothing more—" In a lightning movement his hand shot across the table and clutched Shaw's wrist in a steel grip. "That message wouldn't happen to concern me, now would it, dad?"

Shaw tensed as the nails dug into him. He flattened his feet on the floor, planning to thrust his body backward out of the chair. But Gly anticipated his thoughts.

"No tricks, dad, or I'll snap your bone."

Shaw sagged. Not from fear. From anger at being caught at a disadvantage.

"You overrate yourself, Inspector Gly. Why should the British secret service bother itself about you?"

"A thousand apologies," Gly sneered, maintaining the pressure. "I'm the suspicious type. Liars make me edgy."

"A crude accusation from a crude mind," said Shaw, coming back on balance. "I'd expect little else, considering the source."

Gly's lips twisted. "Clever words, Superspy. Suppose you tell me you didn't contact your boss in London and receive an acknowledgment over two hours ago."

"And if I say you're mistaken?"

"No good. I had a little chat with Doc Coli in the galley. Is your memory so rotten you've forgotten he helped you compose your report on that little gizmo? Or that you added a postscript after Coli left. A request for a rundown on Foss Gly. You know it, I know it. The reply is there in your hand."

The trapdoor had sprung and Shaw had fallen through. He cursed his transparency. He had little doubt that the ugly man across the table would murder if given the slightest opportunity. His only hope was to stall and throw Gly off his stride. He tried a long shot.

"Mr. Villon mentioned in passing that you might prove unstable. I should have taken him at his word."

The angry widening of the eyes told Shaw he had struck a nerve. He continued to turn the screw.

"I believe he even used the term 'psycho.' "

The reaction was not what he expected. Not what he expected at all.

Instead of cold wrath, Gly's expression was suddenly transformed to one of enlightenment. He released Shaw's wrist and sat back. "So the double-talking scum stabbed me in the back," Gly muttered. "I might have guessed he'd eventually wise up to my scheme." He paused and looked at Shaw curiously. "I get the story now. Why I was always sent to do the underwater dirty work. Somewhere along the line you were to see to it I was conveniently drowned by an unfortunate accident."

Shaw was at a loss. None of this was going in the direction he intended. He flat out didn't know what Gly was talking about. He had no option but to string along. Very carefully he removed the message from his finger with his free hand and flipped it on the table in front of

Gly and studied his eyes. There was a fractional glace downward, no more than a second. But it was enough.

"What puzzles me is why you're risking your life for a government and a man who wants you dead."

"Maybe I like the company benefits."

"Wit doesn't become you, Mr. Bogus Inspector Gly."

"How much did Villon tell you about me?"

"He didn't elaborate," said Shaw, mashing out his cigarette in an ashtray and noting that Gly's eyes followed the movement. "He only suggested that I would be doing Canada a favor by removing you. Frankly, I wasn't keen to play the role of a hired assassin, especially without knowing why you deserved to die."

"What changed your mind?"

"You did." Shaw had Gly's interest at a peak, but he still had no idea where it was taking him. "I began to study you. Your French-Canadian tongue is letter perfect. But your English: now there hangs another tale. Not the accent, mind you, but the terminology. Words like 'booze' and 'gizmo,' expressions such as 'What's the scam?' Pure Americanese. Curiosity got the better of me and I asked London to run a check on you. The answer is there on the table. You *do* deserve to die, Mr. Gly. No man deserves it more."

Gly's face turned menacing and his grinning teeth glistened yellow under the cabin light. "Do you think you're man enough to take me, dad?"

Shaw clutched the edge of the table with his hands and wondered how Gly intended to kill him. Gly would have to use a gun with a silencer or perhaps a knife. A loud report would bring Coli and the crew of the tug rushing into the cabin. Gly sat with his arms crossed casually in front of him. He looked relaxed, too relaxed.

"I don't have to bother. Mr. Villon had a change of heart. He's decided to turn you over to the Mounties."

Shaw had taken a wrong turn. He could read the mistake on Gly's face.

"Nice try, dad, but you blew it. Villon can't afford to keep me alive. I could put him behind bars until the next ice age."

"Just testing the water," said Shaw with feigned indifference. "The report is on Villon, not you." He nodded at the tabletop. "Read it yourself."

Gly's eyes flicked downward.

Shaw threw every ounce of his strength against the table in a twisting motion and rammed the corner edge into the sweater just above the beltline.

A sharp grunt was the only reaction. Gly absorbed the momentum and scarcely recoiled. It would have knocked any other man across the room in agony. He clamped a great ham of a fist around a table leg and effortlessly lifted the heavy oak fixture to the ceiling.

Shaw was stunned. The thing must have weighed a hundred and fifty pounds.

Gly slowly lowered the table, and set it aside as easily as a child laying a doll in a baby carriage and rose to his feet. Shaw picked up his chair and brought it down in a violent arc, but Gly simply grabbed it in midair, wrenched it away and placed it neatly under the table.

There was no anger, no savage glare in Gly's eyes as they stared unblinkingly into Shaw's only three feet away.

"I have a gun," said Shaw, fighting to keep his voice controlled.

"Yes, I know," replied Gly, grinning satanically. "A quaint, old-fashioned twenty-five-caliber Beretta. I found it stashed in a boot beside your bunk. In fact, it's still there. I made sure before I came in here."

Shaw realized he wasn't going to feel the hammer impact of a bullet or the cut of a knife. Gly was going to do the job with his bare hands.

Shaw fought off a wave of mental nausea and lashed out with a vicious judo kick. He might just as well have stubbed his toe on a tree. Gly spun sideways and neutralized the thrust to his groin, taking the blow on his hip. He moved forward, taking no precaution to cover himself. He had the blank look of a butcher approaching a side of beef.

Retreating until his back met a bulkhead, Shaw glanced wildly around for a weapon, a lamp, or a book he could hurl, anything to slow two hundred pounds of muscle. But tugboat cabins are conceived for austere living; except for a picture screwed into a panel, there was nothing in reach.

Shaw pressed the flats of his hands together and whipped them in a scything chop to the side of Gly's neck. It was, he knew with sickening certainty, his last act of defiance. The result was the same as striking concrete, and he gasped in shock and pain. It felt as if both his palm bones had cracked.

Gly, showing no ill effects, reached around the small of Shaw's back with one massive arm and pulled, while the other forearm pressed into Shaw's chest. Then Gly slowly increased the opposing pressures and Shaw's spine began to bend.

"So long, you limey twit."

Shaw gnashed his teeth together as the agony suddenly mushroomed inside him. The air was squeezed from his lungs and he could feel his heartbeat pounding in his head as the cabin began to dim and waver before his eyes. A final scream tried to force its way through clenched teeth, but died. There was nothing left now but the gruesome snap of his back. Death was the only release.

Somewhere in the distance, it seemed miles off, came the sound of a loud crack, and Shaw thought it was all over. The relentless pressure fell away and the agony dropped by several degrees. He went limp and crumpled to the deck.

Shaw wondered what would happen next. A long walk down a dark tunnel before reaching a blinding light? He was vaguely disappointed that there was no music. He began to itemize his sensations. It struck him odd that he could still feel pain. His ribs ached and his spine felt as though it was on fire. Apprehensively he opened his eyes. It took them a few moments to focus properly.

The first objects he distinguished were a pair of cowboy boots.

He blinked, but they were still there. Calfskin with stitched design on the sides, high heel and modified pointed toe. He turned his head and looked up into a craggy face with eyes that seemed to smile.

"Who are you?" he mumbled.

"Pitt. Dirk Pitt."

"Strange, you don't look like the devil." Shaw had never doubted where he would eventually wind up.

Now the lips smiled. "There are some who would disagree." He knelt and hooked his hands under Shaw's arms. "Here, let me help you up, dad."

"God, how I wish," Shaw murmured irritably, "that people would stop calling me dad."

51

Gly lay like a dead man. His arms were loosely outflung, his legs twisted and slightly bent. He looked like a deflated rubber balloon.

"How did you manage that?" asked a dazed Shaw.

Pitt held up a very large wrench. "Equally good for turning bolts and denting skulls."

"Is he dead?"

"I doubt it. Nothing less than a cannon could wipe him out."

Shaw took several deep breaths and massaged his aching hands. "I'm grateful for your timely intervention, Mr. . . . er . . ."

"The name is Pitt, Mr. Shaw. And you can cut the charade. We both know all about each other."

Shaw shifted his mind from first gear into second. Through luck he had barely survived one opponent, and now he was facing another.

"You're taking quite a chance, Mr. Pitt. My crew could come marching through the door any second."

"If anybody comes marching in here," Pitt said nonchalantly, "it'll be my crew. While you were waltzing with that walking muscle on the floor, your crew got securely stowed away in the engine room."

"My compliments," replied Shaw. "You walk softly and carry a big wrench."

Pitt shoved the tool into the side pocket of his windbreaker and sat down. "They were very cooperative. But I guess that happens to men when they stare into the business end of an automatic rifle."

Pain waves shot up and down Shaw's back. His lips pressed together and his face paled. He tried a few bending exercises, but they only made matters worse.

Pitt watched him. "I suggest you see an osteopath after you notify MI6 of recent events."

"Thank you for your concern," Shaw muttered. "How do you come to know so much?"

"You became an instant celebrity when you looked into the cameras

214

of our survey vehicle. Heidi Milligan recognized your face, and the CIA fleshed out your past.''

Shaw's eyes narrowed. ''Commander Milligan is on board your ship?''

''You're old friends, she tells me. A lovely girl, and savvy too. She conducts our historical research.''

''I see,'' said Shaw. ''She laid out the path for your salvage operation.''

''If you mean that Heidi pointed out the location of Harvey Shields' cabin, yes.''

Shaw was always amazed at the frankness of the Americans. Pitt, on the other hand, was always irritated by the British preference for fencing around.

''Why are you here, Mr. Pitt?''

''I felt the time had come to warn you to lay off.''

''Lay off?''

''There's no law that says you can't sit in the bleachers as a spectator, Mr. Shaw. But keep your boys out of our salvage area. The last one tried to play rough.''

''You must be talking about Mr. Gly there.''

Pitt looked down at the inert body. ''I should have guessed.''

''There was a time when I might have made him a good match,'' said Shaw wistfully.

Pitt smiled a smile that warmed the room. ''I only hope I'm in as good a shape as you when I'm sixty-six.''

''Good guess.''

''Weight one hundred and seventy pounds; height six feet one inch, right-handed, numerous scars. No guess, Mr. Shaw. I have a copy of your biography. You've led an interesting life.''

''Perhaps, but your accomplishments far outstrip mine.'' Shaw smiled for the first time. ''You see, I have a file on you too.''

Pitt looked at his watch. ''I must be getting back to the *Ocean Venturer*. It was a pleasure meeting you.''

''I'll see you to your boat. It's the least I can do for a man who saved my life.''

Two men stood guard on the deck outside. They were about the size and shape of polar bears. One of them spoke with a voice that seemed to come up from his socks when he spotted Shaw.

''Any problems, sir?''

Pitt shook his head. "None. Are we ready to shove off?"

"Everyone is aboard except us."

"Go ahead. I'll follow."

Both men gave Shaw a don't-try-anything-funny look and climbed over the side to a launch moored beside the tug.

Pitt turned and said, "Give my regards to General Simms."

Shaw peered at Pitt with continued respect. "Is there anything you don't know?"

"There's lots I don't know." Pitt's expression turned devilish. "For one thing, I never took the time to learn backgammon."

God, Shaw thought, the man is beyond wonder, but he was too much the professional not to see the icy shrewdness beneath the outer layer of friendly warmth. "I shall be happy to teach you sometime. I'm rather good at the game."

"I'll look forward to it."

Pitt held out his hand.

In all his years in the deadly business of espionage, this was the first time Shaw ever recalled shaking hands with the enemy. He stared into Pitt's eyes for a long moment.

"Forgive me for not wishing you luck, Mr. Pitt, but you cannot be allowed to find the treaty. Your side has everything to gain. Mine has everything to lose. You must understand that."

"We both know the score."

"I would very much regret having to kill you."

"I wouldn't like it much either." Pitt straddled the railing, paused and threw a wave. "Break a leg, Mr. Shaw." And then he dropped onto the foredeck of the launch.

Shaw stood for several minutes, watching the tiny boat until it became lost in the darkness. Then he wearily walked down to the engine room and released Dr. Coli and the tug's crew.

When he returned to his cabin, Foss Gly was gone.

52

A crowd of nearly one thousand people stood outside the residence of the Prime Minister, applauding and waving placards and hand-painted banners in French and English, wishing Charles Sarveux well as he arrived home from the hospital. The doctors had insisted that he be transported by ambulance, but he firmly ignored their advice and rode home in the official limousine, impeccably dressed in a newly purchased suit, his scarred hands concealed by a pair of oversize kid gloves.

One of his party advisers suggested he keep his bandages in plain view to evoke public sentiment. But Sarveux would have no part of gimmicky politics. It was not his way.

The pain in his hip was excruciating. His arms were stiff with scar tissue and exploded in agony every time he attempted to move them. He was thankful the crowds and reporters were too distant to see the sweat that ran down his face as he smiled through tight lips and waved to their cheers.

The car passed through the gate and stopped at the front steps. Danielle rushed up to the door and threw it open.

"Welcome home, Charles—"

The words stuck in her throat when she saw the tortured face, deep-etched in ashen suffering.

"Help me inside," he whispered.

"Let me get a Mountie—"

"No," he cut her off. "I will not be taken for an invalid."

He twisted in the back seat and placed his feet on the ground, his body half in, half out of the car. He took a moment to steel himself against the torment, then hooked one arm around Danielle's waist and swayed to a standing position.

She nearly went down under his weight. It took all her strength to hold him upright. She could almost feel the agony emanate from him as they shuffled up the steps of the landing. At the doorway he turned and flashed the famous Charles Sarveux smile at a bevy of reporters across the drive and made a thumbs-up sign.

Once the front door closed, his iron will gave out and he began to sink to the carpet. A Mountie swiftly pushed Danielle aside and grabbed him around the shoulders. A doctor and two nurses materialized, and together they gently carried him up the stairs to his room.

"You were mad to play hero," the doctor reprimanded Sarveux after settling the Prime Minister in bed. "Your fracture is far from fully healed. You might have caused serious damage and set back your recovery."

"A small risk to assure the people that their leader is not a vege-
table." Sarveux smiled weakly.

Danielle came and sat on the edge of the bed. "You've made your
point, Charles. There is no need to exert yourself."

He kissed her hand. "I beg your forgiveness, Danielle."

She looked at him in confusion. "Forgiveness?"

"Yes," he said softly so the others in the room did not hear. "I
undervalued your spirit. I always looked upon you as a wealthy child
whose only aim in life was to nurture a great beauty and indulge in
Cinderella fantasies. I was wrong."

"I'm not sure I understand . . ." she said hesitantly.

"In my absence you stepped into my shoes and took up the reins of
office with dignity and determination," he said sincerely. "You have
truly proven that Danielle Sarveux is the first lady of the land."

Suddenly she felt a deep sadness for him. In certain respects he was
perceptive, and in others he seemed naive. Only now was he beginning
to appreciate her capabilities. And yet her desires completely eluded
him. He could not see that she was an illusion, could not guess the
extent of her deceit.

By the time he came to know her fully, she thought, it would be too
late.

Sarveux was in his robe, seated on the sofa and staring at the
television set, when Henri Villon entered his room later that night. A
news commentator was standing in the middle of Quebec Street, surrounded by a huge crowd of cheering people.

"Thank you for coming, Henri."

Villon looked at the TV. "It's done," he said quietly. "The referendum for full independence has passed. Quebec is a nation."

"Now the chaos begins," said Sarveux. He punched the OFF button
on the control box and the TV set went dark. Then he turned to Villon
and motioned to a chair. "How do you see it?"

"I'm certain the transition will be smooth."

"You're overly optimistic. Until a general election can be held to
install a new government, Quebec's parliament will be in turmoil, a
golden opportunity for the FQS to rise up out of their sewer and make a
power play." He shook his head sadly. "Jules Guerrier's death could
not have come at a worse time. He and I could have worked together in
softening the road. Now I don't know."

"Surely you feel that the vacuum left by Jules can be filled?"

"By whom? You perhaps?"

A hardness came into Villon's eyes. "No man is better qualified. My efforts were instrumental in putting across the referendum. I have the backing of the trade unions and financial institutions. I am a respected party leader, and most important, I am a Frenchman who is highly regarded by the rest of Canada. Quebec needs me, Charles. I shall run for president and I'll win."

"So Henri Villon is going to lead Quebec out of the wilderness," said Sarveux caustically.

"French culture is more alive today than ever before. My sacred duty is to nourish it."

"Stop waving the fleur-de-lis, Henri. It doesn't become you."

"I have deep feelings for my native land."

"You have deep feelings for only Henri Villon."

"You think so little of me?" snapped Villon.

Sarveux stared him in the eye. "I had a high opinion of you once. But I watched as blind ambition transformed a dedicated idealist into a devious schemer."

Villon glared back. "I think you should explain yourself."

"For starters, what possessed you to black out a third of the United States at the James Bay power project?"

Villon's expression turned impassive. "I felt it was necessary. The blackout was meant as a warning to the Americans to keep their hands off of French affairs."

"Where did you get such an insane idea?"

Villon gave him a bemused look. "From you, of course."

Sarveux's expression went blank.

Suddenly Villon began to laugh. "You really don't remember, do you?"

"Remember what?" Sarveux asked mechanically.

"In the hospital after the plane crash, your mind was confused from the anesthetic. You raved about Canada being in great peril if the wrong people discovered the vulnerability of the control booth at James Bay. You were vague on the meaning. But then you instructed Danielle to tell me to consult Max Roubaix, the long-dead garrote murderer."

Sarveux sat mute, his face unreadable.

"A damned clever riddle, considering it came from a scrambled brain," Villon continued. "It took me a while to figure the parallel between Roubaix's favorite weapon and an energy stranglehold. I thank you for that, Charles. You unwittingly showed me how to make the Americans dance to the mere flip of an electrical switch.''

Sarveux sat in silence for a moment, then he looked up at Villon and said, ''Not unwittingly.''

Villon missed the point. ''Pardon?''

''Danielle did not hear the raving of a delirious man. There was a great deal of pain, but my mind was clear when I told her I wanted you to consult Max Roubaix.''

''Playing some sort of childish game, Charles?''

Sarveux ignored him. ''A very old and dear friend said you would betray my trust and the faith the Canadian people had in you. I could not bring myself to believe you were a traitor, Henri. But I had to be sure. You took the bait and threatened the United States with energy blackmail. A grave mistake on your part, antagonizing a superpower in the next yard.''

Villon's mouth tightened in an ugly grin. ''So you think you know something. To hell with you and to hell with the United States. As long as Quebec controls the St. Lawrence River and the hydroelectricity from James Bay it will be we who dictate to them and western Canada for a change. The Americans' righteous and holy preaching has made them clowns in the eyes of the world. They sit smug in their stupid morality, caring only about their private assets and bank accounts. America is a fading power on the way out. Inflation will finish their economic system. If they dare try and ram sanctions down Quebec's throat, we'll cut their circuits.''

''Brave talk,'' said Sarveux. ''But like so many others, you'll find that underestimating their resolve never pays. When their backs are to the wall, the Americans have a habit of coming out fighting.''

''The guts have gone out of them,'' Villon sneered.

''You're a fool.'' Sarveux could not suppress the chill that ran through him. ''For the good of Canada I will unmask and break you.''

''You couldn't break a shop clerk,'' Villon mocked him. ''You haven't got a shred of solid evidence against me. No, Charles, soon the English-speaking bastards will kick you out of office, and I'll see to it you're not welcome in Quebec. It's about time you woke up to the fact that you're a man without a country.'' Villon rose and pulled a sealed envelope from his breast pocket and dropped it rudely in Sarveux's lap. ''My resignation from the cabinet.''

''Accepted,'' Sarveux said with grim finality.

Villon could not leave without one parting insult. ''You're a pitiful creature, Charles. You haven't come to grips with it yet, but you have nothing left, not even your precious Danielle."

At the doorway Villon turned for a last look at Sarveux, expecting to see a man drowning in despair and defeat, his hopes and dreams shattered beyond repair.

Instead, he saw a man who was inexplicably smiling.

Villon went direct to his office in the Parliament building and began cleaning out his desk. He saw no purpose in waiting for morning and suffering through a multitude of goodbyes from men he neither respected nor liked.

His chief aide knocked and entered. "You have several messages—"

Villon waved a hand and cut him off. "I'm not interested. As of one hour ago I am no longer minister of internal affairs."

"There is one from Mr. Brian Shaw that sounded quite urgent. Also, General Simms has been personally trying to reach you."

"Yes, that North American Treaty affair," Villon said without looking up. "They're probably begging for more men and equipment."

"Actually it's a request for our navy to escort the American ship off the wreckage of the *Empress of Ireland*."

"Fill out the necessary papers and sign my name to them. Then contact the commanding naval officer of the St. Lawrence District and have him carry out the request."

The aide turned and started for his office.

"Wait!" Villon's French fervor suddenly welled up within him. "One more thing. Instruct General Simms and Mr. Shaw that the sovereign nation of Quebec no longer relishes British meddling in her territory, and they are to cease all surveillance activities at once. Then get a message to our mercenary friend, Mr. Gly. Tell him there's a fat bonus for giving the NUMA ship a rousing farewell party. He'll understand."

53

They came late the following morning, ensigns flying and half the crew smartly turned out to stare at the *Ocean Venturer*. The foam fell away from the bow to a gentle wave; the beat of the engines slowed as the Canadian destroyer eased to a stop on a parallel heading two hundred yards to the south.

The radio operator came up to Pitt and Heidi who were standing on the bridge wing. "From the captain of the destroyer H.M.C.S. *Huron*. He requests permission to board."

"Nice and courteous," mused Pitt. "At least he asked."

"What do you think is on his mind?" asked Heidi.

"I *know* what's on his mind," replied Pitt. He turned to the radio operator. "Extend my compliments to the captain. Permission to board granted, but only if he honors us by staying for lunch."

"I wonder what he's like?" Heidi murmured.

"Who else but a woman would care?" Pitt laughed. "Probably a spit-and-polish type, cool, precise and very official, who talks in Morse code."

"You're just being nasty." Heidi smiled.

"You wait." Pitt grinned back. "I bet he climbs up the ladder whistling 'Maple Leaf Forever.' "

Lieutenant Commander Raymond Weeks did nothing of the sort. He was a jolly-looking man with laughing gray-blue eyes and a warm face. He had a pleasant ringing voice that came out of a short body with a noticeable paunch. With the right stuffing and a costume he'd have made a perfect department store Santa Claus.

He leaped lightly over the railing and walked unerringly up to Pitt, who was standing slightly off to one side of the welcoming committee.

"Mr. Pitt, I'm Ray Weeks. This is indeed an honor. I was absorbed by your work on the *Titanic* raising. You might even say I'm a fan of yours."

Charmingly disarmed, Pitt could only mumble, "How do you do."

Heidi nudged him in the ribs. "Spit and polish, heh?"

Weeks said, "Beg your pardon."

"Nothing," Heidi said brightly. "An inside joke."

Pitt recovered and made the introductions. It was, to his way of thinking, a wasted formality. That Weeks had been well briefed was obvious. He seemed to know everything about everybody. He expounded on a marine archaeological project that Rudi Gunn had nearly forgotten, even though he had been its field director. Weeks was especially solicitous to Heidi.

"If all my fellow officers looked like you, Commander Milligan, I might never retire from service."

"Flattery deserves a reward," said Pitt. "Perhaps I can persuade Heidi to give you a tour of the ship."

"I'd like that very much." Then Weeks' expression turned serious. "You may not be so hospitable when you learn the nature of my visit."

"You've come to tell us the ball game has been called because of political rain."

"Your vernacular is most appropriate." Weeks shrugged. "I have my orders. I'm sorry."

"How much time have we got to retrieve our men and equipment?"

"How much do you need?"

"Twenty four hours."

Weeks was no fool. He knew enough about salvage to know Pitt was conning him. "I can give you eight."

"We can't bring up the saturation chamber in less than twelve."

"You'd make a good merchant in a Turkish bazaar, Mr. Pitt." Weeks' smile returned. "Ten hours should see you through."

"Providing you begin counting after lunch."

Weeks threw up his hands. "My God, you never give up. All right, after lunch it is."

"Now that's settled, Commander Weeks," said Heidi, "if you'll follow me, I'll show you the operation."

Accompanied by two of his ship's officers, Weeks trailed Heidi down a stairway to the work platform inside the center well. Pitt and Gunn turned and slowly made their way to the control room.

"Why the VIP treatment for a character who's kicking us out of the park?" Gunn asked irritably.

"I bought ten hours," Pitt said in a low voice. "And I'm going to buy every minute I can to keep those guys below working on the wreck."

Gunn stopped and looked at him. "Are you saying you're not discontinuing the project?"

"Hell, yes," said Pitt earnestly.

"You're nuts." Gunn shook his head in wonder. "We need at least two more days to break through to Shields' cabin. You don't stand a prayer of stalling that long."

Pitt smiled crookedly. "Maybe not, but by God, I'm going to try."

Through the heavy veil of sleep, Moon felt someone shaking him. He had remained in his office around the clock since the *Ocean Venturer* had moored over the *Empress of Ireland*. Normal sleeping hours were forgotten and he took to catching up on his sleep with short catnaps. When he finally opened his eyes he found them looking into the grim features of the White House communications director.

He yawned and sat up. "What's the latest?"

The communications director handed him a sheet of paper. "Read it and weep."

Moon studied the wording. Then he looked up. "Where's the President?"

"He's speaking to a group of Mexican-American labor leaders out in the rose garden."

Moon slipped on his shoes and hurried down the hallway, pulling on his coat and straightening his tie as he went. The President had just finished a round of handshaking and was returning to the oval office when Moon caught up with him.

"More bad news?" asked the President.

Moon nodded and held up the message. "The latest word from Pitt."

"Read it to me as we walk back to my office."

"He says, 'Have been ordered out of the St. Lawrence by the Canadian navy. Granted a ten-hour grace period to pack the suitcases. Destroyer is standing by . . .' "

"Is that all?"

"No, sir, there's more."

"Then let's have it."

Moon read on. " 'Intend to disregard eviction notice. Salvage continues. We are preparing to repel boarders. Signed Pitt.' "

The President stopped in mid-stride. "What was that?"

"Sir?"

"The last part, read it again."

" 'We are preparing to repel boarders.' "

The President shook his head in astonishment. "Good lord, the order to repel boarders hasn't been given in a hundred years."

"If I'm any judge of character, Pitt means what he says."

The President looked thoughtful.

"So the British and Canadians have slammed the door."

"I'm afraid that's the verdict," said Moon. "Shall I contact Pitt and order him to break off the salvage? Any other action might provoke a military response."

"It's true we're walking a tightrope, but good old-fashioned guts deserve a reward."

Moon suppressed a sudden fear. "You're not suggesting we throw Pitt a lifeline."

"I am," said the President. "It's time we showed some guts of our own."

54

They stood together tenderly as though it was the first time and watched a young moon rise in the east, guessing the destinations of the ships beating steadily downriver. Overhead the two red lights, signifying a vessel moored over a wreck, burned from the mast, giving them just enough glow to make out each other's faces.

"I never knew it would come to this," Heidi said softly.

"You created a ripple effect," Pitt responded, "and it's still spreading."

She leaned against him. "Strange how the discovery of an old crumpled letter in a university archive could touch so many lives. If only I'd left well enough alone," she whispered.

Pitt put his arm around her and gently squeezed. "We can't look back on the ifs. There's no profit in it."

Heidi gazed across the water at the Canadian destroyer. The decks and boxlike superstructure were brightly lit, and she could hear the hum of the generators. She shivered as a drifting patch of fog crept in across the river.

"What will happen when we overstep Commander Weeks' deadline?"

Pitt held up his watch to the dim mast lights. "We'll know in another twenty minutes."

"I feel so ashamed."

Pitt looked at her. "What is this, cleanse-the-soul hour?"

"That ship wouldn't be out there if I hadn't blabbed to Brian Shaw."

"Remember what I said about ifs."

"But I slept with him. That makes it worse. If anyone is hurt . . . I . . ." The words escaped her and she fell silent as Pitt held her tight.

They did not speak again until, a few minutes later, a low, polite cough tugged them back to reality. Pitt turned to see Rudi Gunn standing on the bridge wing above.

"You'd better come up, Dirk. Weeks is getting pretty insistent. Claims he sees no evidence of our departure. I'm running out of excuses."

"Did you tell him the ship is swept by bubonic plague and mutiny?"

"No time for humor," Gunn said seriously. "We also have a contact on radar. A ship steering out of the main channel in our direction. I fear our luncheon guest has called up reinforcements."

Weeks stared through the bridge windows at the incoming mist. He held a cup of coffee in one hand that was half full and turning cold. His normally easygoing disposition was stretched to the limits by the annoying indifference of the NUMA ship to his requests for information. He turned to his first officer, who was bent over a radarscope.

"What do you make of it?"

"A large ship, nothing more. Probably a coastal tanker or a containership. Can you see its lights?"

"Only when they climbed over the horizon. The fog has cut them off."

"The curse of the St. Lawrence," said the first officer. "You never know when the fog decides to shroud this part of the river."

Weeks trained a pair of binoculars on the *Ocean Venturer,* but already its lights were beginning to blur as the fogbank rolled in. Within a few minutes the *Venturer* would be completely obscured.

The first officer straightened up and rubbed his eyes. "If I didn't know better, I'd say the target was on a collision course."

Weeks picked up a microphone. "Radio room, this is the Captain. Patch me in on the safety call frequency."

"The contact is slowing," said the first officer.

Weeks waited until he heard the bridge speaker come on and emit a low crackle of static. Then he began transmitting.

"To the ship on an upriver course, bearing zero-one-seven degrees off Pointe-au-Père. This is the H.M.C.S. *Huron*. Please respond. Over."

His only reply was the muted static.

He called two more times, but there was still no reply.

"Down to three knots and still closing. Range twelve hundred yards."

Weeks ordered a seaman to sound the inland waterway fog signal for a ship at anchor. Four blasts of the *Huron*'s horn whooped over the black water: one short, two long, one short.

The answer was a prolonged shriek that cut through the fog.

Weeks stepped to the doorway, his eyes straining into the night. The approaching intruder remained invisible.

"He appears to be slipping between us and the *Ocean Venturer*," the first officer reported.

"Why in hell don't they answer? Why don't the fools stay clear?"

"Maybe we'd better throw a scare into them."

A devious gleam came into Weeks' eyes. "Yes, I think that might do the trick." He pressed the mike's transmit button and said, "To the ship off my port stern. This is the H.M.C.S. destroyer *Huron*. If you do not identify yourself immediately, we shall open fire and blow you out of the water."

Perhaps five seconds passed. Then a voice rasped out of the bridge speaker in a pronounced Texas drawl.

"This is the U.S.S. guided missile cruiser *Phoenix*. Draw when you're ready, pardner."

55

Local farmers may have welcomed the rain that poured onto the Hudson River valley, but it only further depressed the crew of the *De Soto*. Their search for the *Manhattan Limited* had turned up nothing but the twisted, rusting remains of the Hudson-Deauville bridge, which lay on the river bottom like the scattered bones of an extinct dinosaur.

Hour followed hour, the crew keyed to the instruments, the helmsman steering over the same grids five and six times, everyone trying to spot something they might have overlooked. Three times the probes that trailed behind the boat's stern hung up on underwater obstructions, creating delays of several hours before divers could work them free again.

The line of Giordino's mouth tightened as he pored over the grid charts, sketching in the debris shown by the side-scan sonor. Finally he turned to Glen Chase.

"Well, we may not know where it is, but we sure as hell know where it ain't. I'm hoping the diving team will get lucky." He looked up at the large brass chronograph on the wheelhouse wall. "They should be surfacing about now."

Chase idly thumbed through the historical report on the *Manhattan Limited* wreck that Heidi Milligan had compiled and sent from Canada. He stopped at the last two pages and read them in silence.

"Is it possible the train was salvaged years later when it was 'old news,' and no one bothered notifying the newspapers?"

"I don't think so," replied Giordino. "The disaster was too big an event in these parts for a successful recovery to go unnoticed and unrecorded."

"Any truth to the claims by individual divers that they discovered the locomotive?"

"None that can be verified. One guy even swears he sat in the cab and rang the engine's bell. Another says he swam through a Pullman car filled with skeletons. Show me an unsolved mystery, and I'll show you a certified weirdo with all the answers."

A figure in a dripping exposure suit materialized in the doorway and stepped into the wheelhouse. Nicholas Riley, chief diver for the project, sank to the deck, his back pressed against a bulkhead, and exhaled a great sigh.

"That three-knot current is murder," he said tiredly.

"Did you find anything?" Giordino asked impatiently.

"A veritable junkyard," Riley answered. "Sections of the bridge are strewn all over the riverbed. Some of the girders look shredded, as if they were blown apart."

"That's explained in here," said Chase, holding aloft the report. "The Army Corps of Engineers blasted off the top of the wreckage in nineteen seventeen because it was a menace to navigation."

"Any sign of the train?" Giordino persisted.

"Not even a wheel." Riley paused to blow his nose. "Bottom geology is fine sand, very soft. You could sink a thin dime in it."

"How deep is bedrock?"

"According to our laser probe," replied Chase, "bedrock lies at thirty-seven feet."

"You could blanket a train and still have twenty feet to spare," said Riley.

Giordino's eyes narrowed. "If geniuses were awarded roses and idiot skunks, I'd get about ten skunks."

"Well, maybe seven skunks," Chase needled him. "Why the self-flagellation?"

"I was too dumb to see the solution to the enigma. Why the proton magnetometer can't get a solid reading. Why the sub-bottom profiler can't distinguish an entire train under the sediment."

"Care to share your revelation?" queried Riley.

"Everyone takes for granted that the weakened bridge collapsed under the weight of the train and they dropped together, the locomotive and coaches entangled with steel girders, into the water below," Giordino said briskly. "But what if the train fell through the center span first, and then the entire bridge dropped down on top and blanketed it?"

Riley stared at Chase. "I think he's got something. The weight of all that steel could well have pressed all trace of the train deep into the soft sand."

"His theory also explains why our detection gear has struck out," Chase agreed. "The broken mass of the bridge structure effectively distorts and shields our probe signals from any objects beneath."

Giordino faced Riley. "Any chance of tunneling under the wreckage?"

"No way," grunted Riley. "The bottom is like quicksand. Besides, the current is too strong for my divers to accomplish much."

"We'll need a barge with a crane and dredge to yank that bridge off the bottom if we expect to lay our hands on the train," said Giordino.

Riley rose wearily to his feet. "Okay, I'll get my boys to shoot some underwater survey photos so we'll know where to lay the jaws of the crane."

Giordino took off his cap and wiped a sleeve over his forehead. "Funny how things work out. Here I thought we'd have the easy time of it, while Pitt and his crew got the short end of the stick."

"God knows what they're up against in the St. Lawrence," said Chase. "I wouldn't trade places with them."

"Oh, I don't know," Giordino shrugged. "If Pitt is running true to form, he's probably sitting in a deck chair with a beautiful woman on one side and a mai tai on the other, lapping up the Canadian sun."

56

A strange mist, a swirling, reddish mist curtained off the light and swam thickly in front of Pitt's eyes. Once, twice, several times he tried desperately to struggle through to the other side, reaching out in front of him like a blind man.

There had been no time to prepare for the shock, no time for his mind to comprehend, no time even to wonder. He wiped away the claret that trickled over his brows and probed a gash on his forehead four inches long and thankfully not skull-deep.

Pitt dragged himself to his feet, staring in disbelief at the litter of bodies around him.

Rudi Gunn's pale face looked up at Pitt, eyes lost and uncomprehending, and devoid of expression. He swayed on hands and knees, muttering softly.

"Oh, God! Oh, God! What happened?"

"I don't know," Pitt answered in a strained voice, foreign even to himself. "I don't know."

On shore Shaw froze in hunched paralysis, lips compressed until his mouth no longer showed, face contorted in blind and bitter rage, a bitterness directed at his own sense of guilt.

Ignoring Villon's order to leave Canada, he had set up camp on the eastern tip of Father's Point, two-and-a-half miles from the salvage site. He had assembled a British army S-66 long-range reconnaissance scope that could read a newspaper headline at five miles, and had begun the tedious routine of observing the small fleet of ships moored over the *Empress of Ireland.*

Launches were charging back and forth between the two naval vessels like ferries held to a schedule. Shaw amused himself by imagining the heated negotiations going on between the American and Canadian officers.

The *Ocean Venturer* appeared still and dead. No one moved about its decks, but he could clearly see that the derrick was still in operation as its huge winch pulled up slime-covered scrap from the hulk below.

Shaw sat back to rest his eyes for a moment and munch a couple of candy bars that passed for breakfast. He noticed a small outboard hydroplane coming down the river at great speed, somewhere between ninety and a hundred miles an hour as it blasted off the wave tops and trailed a ten-foot rooster tail in its wake.

His curious nature aroused, he turned the scope on it.

The hull was painted a metallic gold with a burgundy stripe that flared at the stern. The effect was that of an arrow as it banked and tracked into the sun. Shaw waited until the glare subsided and then he zeroed in on the driver. The single figure behind the windscreen wore goggles, but Shaw recognized the squat nose, the cold, hard face.

It was Foss Gly.

Shaw gazed fascinated as the hydroplane cut a large circle around the three ships, leaping clear of the water with only the props submerged, then thumping down with a kettledrum impact that carried to where Shaw was standing.

It was difficult to keep the scope trained on the bouncing boat, but he locked in when it swung on an opposite course and gave him a clear view of the exposed cockpit over the transom.

Gly was clutching the wheel with his right hand while his left hand held aloft a small box. A thin shaft gleamed in the sun, and Shaw identified it as an antenna.

"No!" he shouted to the unhearing wind as the awful truth of Gly's intent struck him. "No, damn you, no!"

Suddenly the stillness of the morning was shattered by a rumbling thunder that seemed to come from far away and then heighten with terrible swiftness, and a caldron of boiling water erupted and burst toward the sky around the *Ocean Venturer* as the explosives on the bow of the *Empress* detonated.

The research vessel seemed to porpoise above the maelstrom, hang suspended for a few seconds, and then fall back on its starboard side, down, down until it seemed to drown under the massive column of water.

Even on shore the violence of the explosion was shocking. Shaw steadied himself on the tripod of the scope and stared, numb with disbelief.

The spray rose whitely in a vast cloud, swirling above the masts of *Huron* and *Phoenix,* fighting gravity and finally raining in a drenching torrent that entirely saturated the superstructures of both ships. There wasn't a man left standing on any deck. They were all knocked flat or overboard by the force of the blast.

When Shaw retrained the scope of Gly, the hydroplane was hurtling far up the river toward Quebec. Stony-faced, bitter at his helplessness, Shaw could only watch in agonized frustration as Gly once again escaped.

He turned back to the *Ocean Venturer*.

It looked like a dead ship. Its stern had settled ominously and its hull was heeled far over to starboard. Slowly and frighteningly the derrick teetered crazily sideways, hung, then ponderously toppled over the side with a great splash, leaving an incredible tangle of debris and cable heaped on the decks. God only knew how many men had been killed or maimed inside the steel walls.

Shaw could not bear to see any more. He picked up the scope and walked heavily away from the shoreline, the deep rumble of the explosion rolling across the river and echoing back in his ears.

57

For some inexplicable reason the *Ocean Venturer* refused to die.

Perhaps it was the heavy double hull, especially designed for ramming through ice, that saved the ship. Many of the outer plates were smashed, the seams split and the keel twisted. The damage was extensive and severe, but still the ship survived.

Pitt had watched the derrick go over. He stared numbly through the shattered windows of the control room, released his grip on a doorway and staggered uncontrollably into Hoker's console, his sense of balance telling him what his eyes refused. The deck was tilting at an angle of thirty degrees.

His first thought was the grim appreciation that the ship was mortally hurt. Hard on the heels of that came the sickening realization of what the frightful blast must have done to the divers on the wreck. He shook off the fog and the dull ache that tried to creep back in his mind. He logically categorized the steps to be taken. Then he went into action.

He grabbed the phone and rang up the chief engineer. Nearly a minute crawled by before an impersonal voice replied in dazed shock. "Engine room."

"Metz, is that you?"

"You'll have to speak louder, I can't hear."

It dawned on Pitt that to the men on the lower decks and in the engine room, the roar and concussion must have been ear-shattering. He shouted into the mouthpiece.

"Metz, this is Pitt!"

"Okay, that's better," Metz replied in a metallic monotone. "What in hell is going on?"

"My best guess, my only guess is an explosion from below."

"Damn, I thought the Canadians stuck a torpedo in us."

"Report on damage."

"It's like working under a hundred running faucets down here. Water is gushing in everywhere. I doubt if the pumps have the capability to handle it. That's all I can tell you until I sound the hull."

"What about injuries?"

"We were catapulted around like drunken gymnasts. I think Jackson has a broken knee, and Gilmore a skull fracture. Beyond that, a few battered eardrums and a gang of bruises."

"Come back to me every five minutes," Pitt ordered. "And whatever you do, keep the generators turning."

"I don't have to be reminded. If they go, we go."

"You got the idea."

Pitt crammed the phone in its receiver and looked worriedly at

Heidi. Gunn was kneeling over her, cradling her head in his arms. She lay crumpled against the chart table, barely conscious, staring through vacant eyes at her left leg. It lay at a queer angle.

"Funny," she whispered. "It doesn't hurt a bit."

The pain would come, thought Pitt. Already her face was flour-white from shock. He took her hand. "Just lie still until we can get a stretcher."

He wanted to say more, to comfort her, but there was no time. Reluctantly he turned away at the anguished interruption of Hoker's voice.

"The board is out." Hoker was fighting to recover, picking his fallen chair off the deck, staring dumbly at his darkened console panel and monitors.

"Then fix the damned thing!" Pitt rapped out. "We've got to know what happened to the underwater crew."

He took a headset and patched himself into all the stations of the *Ocean Venturer*. On and below decks the scientists and engineers of NUMA began pulling their senses together and toiling like madmen to save their ship. The more seriously injured were carried to the hospital bay, where they soon overfilled the facilities and were placed in rows outside in the hallway. Those who did not have critical jobs labored to tear aside the wreckage of the derrick or seal the cracks in the hull as they stood in waist-high frigid water. A team of divers was hurriedly assembled to go below.

The messages kept pouring in as Pitt directed the recovery. A still bewildered radio operator turned to him. "Just in from the captain of the *Phoenix*. He wishes to know if we need assistance?"

"Hell, yes, we need assistance!" Pitt shouted. "Request he bring his ship alongside. We need every available pump he's got and all the damage control men he can spare."

He broke off and dabbed a damp towel on his forehead, waiting impatiently for the answer.

"The message is: 'Hold the fort,' " said the radio operator excitedly. " 'We will tie up on your starboard side.' " Then a few seconds later: "Commander Weeks on the *Huron* asks if we're abandoning ship."

"He'd like that," Pitt growled. "It would solve all his problems."

"Standing by for an answer."

"Tell him we'll abandon ship when we can step off on the bottom. Then repeat the request for men and pumping equipment—"

"Pitt?" Metz' voice broke in over the headset.

"Go ahead."

"Looks like the stern took the brunt of the blast. From midships forward the hull is tight and dry. From there back it's got more cracks than a jigsaw puzzle. I'm afraid we've had it."

"How long can you keep us afloat?"

"At the rate the water's rising it should reach and short the generators in twenty or twenty-five minutes. Then we lose the pumps. After that, maybe ten minutes."

"Help is on the way. Open the side loading doors so that damage control men and pumping equipment can be transferred from the naval vessels."

"They'd better hustle, or we won't be around to throw a welcome party."

The radio operator gestured and Pitt made his way toward him across the slanting deck.

"I've reestablished contact with *Sappho I*," he said. "I'll tie you in on the phone."

"*Sappho I*, this is Pitt, please reply."

"This is Klinger on *Sappho I*, or what's left of us."

"What is your condition?"

"We're lying about a hundred and fifty meters southeast of the wreck with our bow buried in the mud. The hull stood up to the concussion—it was like sitting inside a clanging bell—but one of the view ports cracked and we're taking on water."

"Are your life-support systems functioning?"

"Roger. They should keep us healthy for a while yet. The problem is, we'll drown a good fifteen hours before our oxygen supply goes."

"Can you make a free ascent?"

"I might," replied Klinger. "I only lost a tooth from the jolt. Marv Powers, though, is in a bad way. Both his arms are busted and he took a bad crack on the head. He'd never make it to the surface."

Pitt closed his eyes for a moment. He did not relish playing God with men's lives, designating priorities over who was saved first or last. When he looked up again, he had made his decision.

"You'll have to hold on for a while, Klinger. We'll get to you just as soon as we can. Keep me posted every ten minutes."

Pitt stepped out on the bridge wing and peered down. Four divers were disappearing over the side.

"I have a picture," said Hoker in triumph as one of the video monitors brightened into life.

The monitor showed a view of the excavation pit as seen from the upper promenade deck. The support columns were collapsed and the decks below had fallen inward. There was no sign of the two JIM suits or the saturation divers.

The cold, abstract eye of the camera saw only a crater ringed with grotesquely distorted steel, but to Pitt it was as though he was staring into an open grave.

"God help them," Hoker muttered under his breath. "They must all be dead."

58

Seventy miles away, Captain Toshio Yubari, a solid, weatherworn man in the prime of his early forties, sat erect in a bridge chair, intent on the small boat traffic that dotted the water ahead. The tide was running home toward the sea, and the 665-foot containership *Honjo Maru* loafed along at a steady fifteen knots. Yubari had decided to wait and ring for twenty knots once the ship had rounded Cape Breton Island.

The *Honjo Maru* had carried 400 new electric minicars from Kobe, Japan, and was making the return voyage with a cargo of newsprint paper from the great pulp mills of Quebec. The massive rolls that filled the containers were far heavier per unit volume than the small cars, and the hull rode low in the water, a scant three inches above the waterline.

First Officer Shigaharu Sakai stepped from the wheelhouse and stood beside the captain. He stifled a yawn and rubbed his reddened eyes.

"Fun night ashore?" Yubari asked, smiling.

Sakai mumbled an unintelligible reply and changed the subject.

"Lucky we didn't cast off on a Sunday," he said, nodding at a fleet of sailing sloops that were racing around a buoyed course about a mile off their port bow.

"Yes, I'm told the traffic is so heavy on weekends you can almost walk across the river on the yachts."

"Shall I take the bridge, captain, while you enjoy a noonday meal?"

"Thank you," replied Yubari, keeping his gaze straight ahead, "but I prefer to remain until we reach the gulf. You might ask the steward, though, to bring me a bowl of noodles with duck and a beer."

Sakai started to comply and then stopped in mid-turn, pointing down the river. "There comes a brave soul or a very reckless one."

Yubari had already spotted the hydroplane and stared with the fascination men have with high speed. "He must be doing close to ninety knots."

"If he hits one of those sloops, there won't be enough left to make a pair of chopsticks."

Yubari came to his feet. "The fool is heading straight for them."

The hydroplane charged into the massed sloops like a coyote through a flock of chickens. The skippers wildly slewed their boats in all directions, losing the wind, full sails suddenly collapsing and flapping uncontrollably.

The inevitable occurred as the hydroplane slashed across the bow of one yacht, tearing away its bowsprit and losing a windshield in the bargain. Then it was free, leaving the fleet scattered and rolling heavily in its whipping wake.

Yubari and Sakai were entranced by the mad antics of the hydroplane as it made a sweeping curve and set a course for the *Honjo Maru*. The small, darting craft was close enough now so they could make out a form hunched over the wheel in the cockpit.

Suddenly it became obvious to them that the driver had been injured when the sloop's bowsprit swept away the windshield.

There was no time for shouted commands or warning blasts from the horn, no time for Yubari and Sakai to do anything but stand in frozen impotence like pedestrians on a street corner witnessing an accident in the making and helpless to prevent it.

They instinctively ducked as the hydroplane crashed square into the *Honjo Maru*'s port beam and erupted in an instantaneous, blinding sheet of gasoline flames. The engine flew from its mountings high into the air end over end before smashing onto the forecastle. Scattered bits of fiery debris splattered the ship like shrapnel from a bomb. Several of the wheelhouse windows were broken in. Things fell out of the sky for several seconds, raining about the ship and splashing in the river.

Miraculously no one was hurt on board the containership. Yubari ordered "all stop" on the engines. A boat was lowered to search the area astern, where oil was drifting up from the bottom and spreading on the low swells.

All that was found of the hydroplane's driver was a charred leather jacket and a pair of broken plastic goggles.

59

As the afternoon wore on, the mood of the *Ocean Venturer*'s crew began to be tinged with guarded optimism. A steady stream of men and equipment poured aboard from the *Phoenix* and the *Huron*. Soon auxiliary pumps stalemated the advance of the water gushing into the lower decks. And once the remains of the derrick were cut away, the list was reduced to nineteen degrees.

Most of the seriously injured, including Heidi, were transferred to the more spacious medical facilities on board the *Phoenix*. Pitt met her on deck as her litter was carried up from below.

"Wasn't much of a cruise, was it?" he said, brushing the ash-blond hair from her eyes.

"I wouldn't have missed it for the world," she replied, smiling gamely.

He leaned over and kissed her. "I'll visit you first chance I get."

Then he turned and climbed up the slanting ladder to the control room. Rudi Gunn met him in the doorway.

"A JIM suit was spotted floating downriver," he said. "The *Huron* is towing it in with their launch."

"Any word from the dive rescue team?"

"The team master, Art Dunning, reported in a minute ago. They haven't found the chamber yet, but he did say it looked as though the blast centered around the bow of the *Empress*. The entire forecastle has disintegrated. The mystery is, where did the explosives come from?"

"They were laid before we arrived," said Pitt thoughtfully.

"Or after."

"No way an amount large enough to create this kind of havoc could have been smuggled through our security ring."

"That ape of Shaw's beat the system."

"Once maybe, not several times, lugging heavy containers of underwater explosives. They must have stored the stuff in the bow section of the *Empress* until they could figure out where to place it throughout the ship to cause the greatest destruction."

"Blow the wreck and the treaty out of existence before we steamed over the horizon."

"But we showed up early and knocked them off their time schedule. That's why they stole the probe. They were afraid it might spot the explosives cache."

"Was Shaw so desperate to stop us he'd resort to mass murder?"

"That part throws me," Pitt admitted. "He somehow didn't strike me as the butchering kind."

Pitt's eyes wandered away and he caught sight of Chief Engineer Metz walking slowly into the control room. He looked like a man who was ready to drop. His face was drawn and haggard, clothes soaked from cap to boots, and he reeked of diesel oil.

"Guess what?" He smiled a tired smile. "The old girl is gonna make it. The *Venturer* ain't what it used to be, but by Jesus, it'll take us home."

It was the best news Pitt had heard since the explosion. "You've stopped the flooding?"

Metz nodded. "We're eight inches down from an hour ago. As soon as you can release a few divers, I can have the worst of the leaks sealed from the outside."

"The *Huron*," Pitt said anxiously. "Can you disengage the *Huron*'s pumps?"

"I think so," replied Metz. "Between our own equipment and that of the *Phoenix*, we should be able to cope."

Pitt wasted no more time. Skipping normal radio protocol, he roared into the microphone on his headset.

"Klinger!"

The reply took a few seconds, and when it came, the voice was slurred. "Hi there, this is Captain Nemo of the submarine *Nautilus* speaking. Over."

"You're who?"

"The guy in *Twenty Zillion Leagues Under the Sea*. You know. Great flick. Saw it when I was a kid in Seattle. Best part was the fight with the giant squid."

Pitt had to shake off a sense of unreality, and then he realized what was wrong. "Klinger!" he shouted, turning every head in the control room. "Your carbon dioxide level is too high! Do you understand? Check your air-scrubbing unit. Repeat. Check your air-scrubbing unit."

"Hey, how about that?" Klinger replied cheerily. "The indicator says we're breathing ten percent CO_2."

"Dammit, Klinger, listen to me! You've got to get down to point-oh-five percent. You're suffering from anoxia."

"Scrubber is on. How does that grab you?"

Pitt sighed with relief. "Hold on a little longer and activate your locator pinger. The *Huron* is coming to lift you on board."

"Whatever you say," Klinger replied, his tone like mush.

"How is the leakage?"

"Two, maybe three hours before the batteries are flooded."

"Increase your oxygen. Got that? Increase your oxygen. We'll see you for dinner."

He turned to speak to Gunn, but the little man had already anticipated him. He was halfway through the doorway.

"I'll direct the *Sappho I*'s retrieval from the *Huron* personally," he said, and then was gone.

Pitt looked through the open windows and saw a small boom lifting the JIM suit out of the water as a launch from the *Phoenix* stood by. The dome was unloosened and swung open. Three crewmen from the *Phoenix* reached it and lifted out a limp figure and laid him on the deck. Then one of them looked up at Pitt and gave a thumbs-up sign.

"He's alive!" came the cry.

Two men in the sub and one JIM suit operator safe, and the ship still afloat, Pitt summed. If only their luck held.

Dunning and his crew had found the saturation chamber almost two hundred yards from where it had been anchored. The hatch into the outer entry compartment had jammed in the closed position, and it took four of them grunting in unison with four-foot steel bars to muscle it open. Then they all stared at Dunning through their face masks, none expecting or wanting to be the first to enter.

Dunning swam up inside until his head burst into the pressurized air. He climbed to a small shelf and removed his breathing tank, hesitated and then crawled into the main chamber. The electrical cable to the *Ocean Venturer* had parted and at first he saw only blackness. He switched on his dive light and played its beam around the small enclosure.

Every man inside the chamber was dead; they were piled on top of one another like a cord of wood. Their skin had turned a deep purplish blue and the blood from a hundred open wounds had merged into one huge pool on the floor. Already it was coagulating from the cold. Dunning could see by the thin trickles from the ears and mouths that they had all died instantaneously from the frightening concussion before their bodies were battered nearly to pulp as the chamber was hurled in violent gyrations over the riverbed by the force of the explosion.

Dunning sat there coughing up the vomit that rose in his throat. He began to tremble from sickness and the smell of death. Five long minutes passed before he was able to call the *Ocean Venturer* and speak coherently.

Pitt took the message, closed his eyes and leaned heavily against a display panel. He felt no anger, only a vast sorrow. Hoker looked at him and read the sad drama in the lines of that strong expressive face.

"The divers?"

"That was Dunning," Pitt said, his eyes staring into nothingness. "The men in the chamber . . . there were no survivors. All died from concussion. Two are missing. If they were outside and exposed to the blast, there is no hope. He says they will bring up the bodies."

There were no words left in Hoker. He looked terribly old and lost. He went back to work on the video console, his movements slow and mechanical. Pitt suddenly felt too exhausted to carry on. It was a waste, the entire project a pitiful waste. They had accomplished nothing but the deaths of ten good men.

He did not hear the faint voice in the earphones at first. Finally it began to penetrate his despondency. Whoever was trying to reach him sounded weak and far away.

"Pitt here. What is it?"

The reply was garbled and unclear.

"You'll have to speak up, I can't make you out. Try increasing your volume."

"Is that any better?" a voice boomed through the receivers.

"Yes, I can hear you now." Pitt's own voice echoed back. "Who is this?"

"Collins." The next few words were distorted: ". . . been attempting to make phone contact since I came to. Don't know what happened. Suddenly all hell broke loose. Only now managed to splice my communications link."

The name Collins was not familiar with Pitt. In his few short days aboard the *Ocean Venturer,* he had been too busy to memorize and associate a hundred names with their respective faces. "What's your problem?" Pitt asked impatiently, his mind returning to other matters.

There was a long pause. "I guess you might say I'm trapped," the reply came back heavy in sarcasm. "And if it isn't inconvenient I would appreciate an assist in getting the hell out of here."

Pitt tapped Hoker on the shoulder. "Who is Collins and what's his capacity?"

"Don't you know?"

"If I did, I wouldn't be asking," Pitt growled. "He claims he's trapped and needs help."

Hoker looked at him incredulously. "Collins is one of the JIM suit operators! He was down during the explosion."

"Christ," Pitt muttered. "He must think I'm the prize idiot of the decade." He fairly yelled into the microphone. "Collins, give me your condition and precise location."

"The suit is intact. A few dents and scratches, nothing more. The life-support system indicates another twenty hours, providing I don't practice aerobic dancing." Pitt grinned quietly to himself at Collins' humorous spirits, felt regret that he didn't know the man. "Where am I? Damned if I know exactly. The suit is up to its crotch in mud, and there's trash hanging all over it. I can barely articulate the arms."

Pitt's gaze traveled to Hoker, who was staring back with a curious blank expression. "Any possibility he can jettison the lifting line, release his weights and make a free ascent like his partner?" Hoker asked.

Pitt shook his head. "He's half buried in silt and entangled in the wreckage."

"You did say he was in silt?"

Pitt nodded.

"Then he must have fallen through onto the second-class deck."

The possibility had also struck Pitt, but he was afraid to predict, to even express a hope. "I'll ask him," he said quietly. "Collins?"

"I haven't gone anywhere."

"Can you determine if you dropped into the target area?"

"Beats me," answered Collins. "I blacked out right after the big bang. Things were pretty well stirred up. Visibility is only now beginning to clear a little."

"Look around. Describe what you see."

Pitt waited impatiently for a reply, knuckles rapping unconsciously against a computer. His eyes roamed to the *Huron*, which was perched over the *Sappho I*, watched the crane on the afterdeck swing over the side. Suddenly his ear receivers crackled and he stiffened.

"Pitt?"

"I'm listening."

The self-assurance was gone and Collins sounded strangely subdued. "I think I'm where the bow of the *Storstad* struck the *Empress*. The damage around me is old. . . much corrosion and heavy growth—" He broke off, without completing the description. After a silence, he came back; his voice had a chill in it. "There are bones. I count two, no three skeletons. They're embedded in the rubble. God, I feel like I'm standing in a catacomb."

Pitt tried to visualize what Collins was seeing, how he would have felt if they could exchange places. "Go on. What else is there?"

"The remains of the poor devils, whoever they were, are above me. I can almost reach out and pat their heads."

"You mean skulls."

"Yeah. One is smaller, maybe a child. The others appear to be adults. I may want to take one home with me."

From the gruesome direction the conversation was turning, Pitt could not help wondering if Collins was losing his grip on reality. "What for? So you can play Hamlet?"

"Hell, no," Collins replied indignantly. "The jaws must have four thousand bucks' worth of gold in the teeth."

A bell rang in the back of Pitt's mind, and he reached back to recall an image on a photograph. "Collins, listen to me carefully. On the upper jaw. Are two large rabbit teeth in the upper center surrounded by gold caps?"

Collins did not answer immediately and the few moments' delay was maddening to Pitt. He could not know that Collins was too stunned to reply.

"Uncanny . . . positively uncanny," Collins murmured over the phone link in total bafflement. "You described the guy's bicuspids perfectly."

The manifestation struck with such abruptness, such incredibility, that Pitt was for the moment incapable of speech, capable only of the heart-stopping realization that they had at last discovered the burial vault of Harvey Shields.

60

Sarveux waited until the door had closed behind his secretary before he spoke. "I have read your report, and I find it deeply disturbing."

Shaw did not answer, for no answer was required. He looked across the desk at the Prime Minister. The man looked older in person than he appeared on camera. What struck Shaw were the sadness in the eyes and the gloves on the hands. Though he was aware of Sarveux's injuries, it still looked odd to see a man working at a desk wearing gloves.

"You've made very grave accusations against Mr. Villon, none of which are backed up with hard evidence."

"I'm not the devil's advocate, Prime Minister. I've only presented the facts as I know them."

"Why do you come to me with this?"

"I thought you should be aware of it. General Simms shared my view."

"I see." Sarveux was silent for a moment. "Are you certain this Foss Gly worked for Villon?"

"There is no doubt of it."

Sarveux sank back in his chair. "You would have done me a greater service by forgetting this thing."

A look of surprise came over Shaw's face. "Sir?"

"Henri Villon is no longer a member of my cabinet. And this Gly fellow, you say, is dead."

Shaw did not immediately answer, and Sarveux took advantage of his hesitation to continue. "Your hired assassin theory is vague and obscure to say the least. Based on nothing but conversation. There isn't enough circumstantial evidence here to prompt even a preliminary investigation."

Shaw gave Sarveux his best withering stare. "General Simms is of a mind that with a little more digging you may find that the infamous Mr. Gly was the mastermind behind your air crash and the recent demise of Premier Guerrier."

"Yes, the man was no doubt capable of—" Sarveux stopped in mid-sentence. His eyes widened and his face tensed. He leaned across the desk.

"What was that? What did you imply?" His voice was stunned, demanding.

"Henri Villon had the motive for wanting you and Guerrier dead, and he . . . I've proved to my satisfaction anyway . . . employed a known killer. I admit that two and two don't necessarily add up to four, but in this case even three may be an acceptable answer."

"What you and General Simms are suggesting is repugnant," Sarveux said in hoarse indignation. "Canadian ministers do not go around murdering one another to attain higher office."

Shaw saw that any further argument was fruitless. "I'm sorry I can't offer you more precise information."

"So am I," said Sarveux, his manner quickly becoming cool again. "I'm not convinced a blunder by you or one of your people didn't cause that nasty mess with the Americans on the St. Lawrence. And now you're trying to cover up by throwing the blame on someone else."

Shaw felt his anger rising. "I assure you, Prime Minister, that is not the case."

Sarveux stared at Shaw steadily. "Nations are not run on probabilities, Mr. Shaw. Please thank General Simms and tell him to consider the matter dropped. And while you're at it, please inform him I see no reason to pursue the North American Treaty business."

Shaw sat astounded. "But, sir, if the Americans find a treaty copy, they can—"

"They won't," Sarveux cut him short. "Good day, Mr. Shaw."

His hands balled into fists, Shaw got up and wordlessly left the room.

As soon as the door latch clicked, Sarveux picked up the phone and dialed a number on his private line.

Forty minutes later, Commissioner Harold Finn of the Mounties entered the room.

He was an unimpressive little man in rumpled clothes, the sort who is lost in a crowd or melts in with the furniture during a party. His charcoal hair was parted down the middle and contrasted with bushy white eyebrows.

"I'm sorry to have gotten you over here on such short notice," Sarveux apologized.

"No problem," Finn said stonily. He took a chair and began fishing through a briefcase.

Sarveux didn't waste time. "What are your findings?"

Finn unhinged a pair of reading glasses and held them in front of his eyes as he scanned a pair of opened folders. "I have the file on the autopsy and a report on Jean Boucher."

"The man who discovered Jules Guerrier's body?"

"Yes, Guerrier's bodyguard/chauffeur. He found the remains when he went to wake the premier in the morning. The coroner's report states that Guerrier died sometime between nine and ten the previous evening. The autopsy was unable to turn up a specific cause of death."

"Surely they must have some idea?"

"A variety of factors," said Finn, "none conclusive. Jules Guerrier was one step away from the grave. According to the forensic patholo-gist who conducted the autopsy, he was suffering from emphysema, gallstones, arteriosclerosis—the latter is what probably killed him—rheumatoid arthritis and cancer of the prostate gland." Finn looked up and smiled thinly. "It was a miracle the man lived as long as he did."

"So Jules died a natural death."

"He had a good excuse for it."

"What about this Jean Boucher?"

Finn read from the report. "Comes from a solid family. Good education. No record of arrests and nothing to indicate an interest in radical causes. Wife and two children, both girls who are married to honest wage earners. Boucher was hired by Guerrier in May of sixty-two. As far as we can determine, he was completely loyal to the premier."

"Do you have any reason to suspect foul play?"

"Frankly, no," replied Finn. "But the death of a well-known per-sonage demands strict attention to details so that no disputes arise at a later date. This case should have been routine. Unfortunately, Boucher threw a wrench into the gears of the investigation."

"In what way?"

"He swears Henri Villon visited Guerrier the night in question and was the last man to see the premier alive."

Sarveux looked bewildered. "That's impossible. Villon made the opening dedication speech at the performing arts center two hundred miles away. He was seen by thousands of people."

"Millions, actually," said Finn. "The event was on national television."

"Could Boucher have murdered Jules and then made up this fairy tale as an alibi?"

"I don't think so. We don't have a shred of evidence that Guerrier was assassinated. The autopsy is clean. Boucher needs no alibi."

"But his claim that Villon was present in Quebec; what purpose does it serve?"

"None that we can figure, yet his conviction is unshakable."

"The man was obviously hallucinating," said Sarveux.

Finn leaned forward in his chair. "He isn't insane, Mr. Sarveux. That's the catch. Boucher demanded to take truth serum and be placed under hypnosis and given a lie detector test." Finn took a deep breath. "We called his bluff, but the results proved conclusively he wasn't bluffing. Boucher was telling the truth."

Sarveux stared at him speechlessly.

"I wish I could say the Mounties have all the answers, but we don't," Finn admitted. "The house was swept by our laboratory people. With one exception, the only fingerprints they turned up belonged to Guerrier, Boucher, the maid and the cook. Regrettably all prints found on the bedroom door knob were smudged."

"You mentioned an exception."

"We found a strange impression from a right index finger on the front-door chime. We have yet to identify it."

"Doesn't prove a thing," said Sarveux. "It could have been made by a tradesman, a postman or even one of your people during the investigation."

Finn smiled. "If that were the case, the computer in our ID section would have a make in two seconds or less. No, this is someone we don't have on file." He paused to study a page in the folder. "Interestingly enough, we have an approximate time when persons unknown rang the chimes. Guerrier's secretary, a Mrs. Molly Saban, brought him a bowl of chicken soup to fight off the flu. She arrived around eight-thirty, punched the chime button, delivered the soup to Boucher and left. She was wearing gloves, so the next bare finger to come along left a clear impression.''

"Chicken soup," said Sarveux, shaking his head. "The eternal cure-all."

"Thanks to Mrs. Saban, we know that someone approached Guerrier's home sometime after eight-thirty of the night he died."

"If we accept Boucher's word, how could Villon be in two places at once?"

"I haven't a clue."

"The investigation, is it formally closed?"

Finn nodded. "There was little to be gained by continuing."

"I want you to reopen it."

Finn's only reaction was a marginal lift of one eyebrow. "Sir?"

"There may be something to Boucher's story after all," said Sarveux. He passed Shaw's report across the desk to Finn. "I've just received this from an agent in the British secret service. It suggests a connection between Henri Villon and a known killer. See if there is any substance to the possibility. Also, I'd like your people to conduct another autopsy."

Finn's other eyebrow came up. "Obtaining an exhumation order could prove a messy business."

"There will be no exhumation order," said Sarveux curtly.

"I understand, Prime Minister," said Finn, catching Sarveux's drift. "The affair will be handled under tight security. I'll personally see to the details."

Finn inserted the reports in his briefcase and stood up to leave.

"There is one more thing," said Sarveux.

"Yes, Prime Minister."

"How long have you known of my wife's affair with Villon?"

Finn's normally inscrutable features took on a pained look. "Well, sir . . . ah, it came to my attention nearly two years ago."

"And you did not come to me?"

"Unless we feel a treasonable act has been committed, it is Mountie policy not to become involved with the domestic privacy of Canadian citizens." Then he added, "That, of course, includes the Prime Minister and the members of Parliament."

"A sound policy," Sarveux said tightly. "Thank you, commissioner. That will be all . . . for the moment."

61

Daybreak found a dark pall over the St. Lawrence.

Two of the critically injured had died, bringing the death toll to twelve. The body of one of the missing divers washed up on the southern shore six miles downriver. The other man was never found.

Numb with exhaustion and sick of heart, the crew of the *Ocean Venturer* lined the railings in silence as their dead were solemnly carried aboard the *Phoenix* for the voyage home. To some it was a bad dream that would eventually fade; for others the tragedy would remain in vivid clarity forever.

After Collins was extricated and hauled aboard with only three hours of breathable air left in his JIM suit, Pitt closed down all further operations on the wreck. Metz reported that the engine room was reasonably dry and the *Ocean Venturer* was holding its own, the list now being only ten degrees. The damage control specialists from the naval ships were released and the long hoses of their support pumps withdrawn. The research ship would make home port under its own power, but on only one engine. The propeller shaft of the other had been bent out of alignment.

Pitt went down into the well-deck area and donned a thermal suit. He tightened his weight belt and was adjusting the harness on his air tanks when Gunn came up to him.

"You're going down," he said flatly.

"After all that's happened, it would be criminal to leave without getting what we came for," Pitt replied.

"Do you think it wise to dive alone? Why not let Dunning and his men go with you?"

"They're in no condition," said Pitt. "They went beyond repetitive dive limits bringing up the bodies. Their nitrogen buildup is excessive."

Gunn knew he could have moved the Matterhorn with greater ease than he could budge a stubborn Dirk Pitt. He shrugged off the abortive attempt and made a grim face.

"It's your funeral."

Pitt grinned. "I appreciate the joyous send-off."

"I'll keep an eye peeled on the monitors," said Gunn. "And if you're a bad boy and come home past curfew, I might even bring down the air bottles for your decompression stops myself."

Pitt nodded a wordless thanks. Unexcitably patient, quiet and unassuming, Gunn was the eternal insurance policy, the one who saw to the endless details overlooked by the rest. He never had to be asked. He planned with deep forethought and then simply accomplished what had to be done.

Pitt adjusted his face mask, threw Gunn a casual salute and dropped into the cold abyss.

At twenty feet he rolled over on his back and gazed upward at the bottom of the *Ocean Venturer,* which hovered above like a great dark blimp. At forty feet it faded into the murk and was gone. The world of sky and clouds seemed light-years away.

The water was dense and opaque, a dull green. As the increasing pressure tightened around his body, Pitt felt a prodding desire to turn back, lie down on his back in the sun, take a long nap and forget the whole thing. He shook off the temptation and switched on his dive light as the green dusk became black.

Then the enormous ship materialized out of the gloom in three dimensions.

An oppressive silence hung over the corpse of the *Empress of Ireland.* It was a phantom ship on a voyage to nowhere.

Pitt swam over the steeply sloping lifeboat deck, past the portholes and the eerie interior of the cabins beyond. He reached the edge of the excavation pit and hesitated. The water was noticeably colder at this level. He watched his air bubbles issue from the breathing regulator and rise to the surface in little clusters, merging and expanding upward. He pointed the dive light at them and they glistened like foam along a beach under a full moon.

He let himself glide slowly into the man-made cavity. Fifty feet down he settled as weightlessly as a leaf into the bottom silt. He was in the mangled womb of Harvey Shields' cabin.

An icy shiver ran down his spine, not from the frigid water—his thermal suit kept him reasonably comfortable—but from the specters of his imagination. He saw the bones described by Collins. Unlike the bleached white and connected skeletons in medical school classrooms, they had turned a tobacco shade of brown and become separated.

A mound of clutter had piled up in front of a small opening in the tangled steel behind the larger of the two skulls and was partly covered with mud. He moved in closer and began probing with his hands.

He touched a limp, round object. He pulled it free and a cloud of dustlike particles and tiny shreds of material billowed in front of his face mask. The object was an old life belt.

He worked himself into the opening and tore at the rubble. The dive light was nearly useless. The swirling disturbance in the water stonewalled the beam and reflected it like a thick bank of fog.

He came across a rusting straight razor, and nearby, a shaving mug. Then came a well-preserved shoe, an oxford by the look of it, and a small medicine bottle. The top was still sealed and the contents untainted by the water.

With the perseverance of an archaeologist sifting away the layers of time, Pitt explored the deteriorating junk with his fingers. He did not feel the cold seeping into his thermal suit. Without noticing, he had rubbed against sharp metal edges that sliced through the protective covering into his skin. Vaporlike trails of blood were issuing from several cuts on his back and legs.

His heartbeat quickened when he thought he saw his goal protruding from the silt. It was the arched handle of a piece of luggage. He wrapped his hand around it and gave a gentle tug. The badly corroded locking mechanism of a large suitcase came free. He shook away his false optimism and kept probing.

Two feet beyond, his eyes spotted another handgrip; this one was smaller. He paused and checked his dive watch. Five minutes of air were left. Gunn would be waiting. He took a long breath and slowly eased the handgrip out of the litter.

Pitt found himself staring at the remnants of a small hand case. The leather sides and bottom, though badly rotted, were still intact. Almost afraid to hope, he pried the hinges apart.

Inside was a muck-coated packet. Pitt knew instinctively that he held the North American Treaty.

62

Dr. Abner McGovern sat at his desk, stared thoughtfully at the cadaver stretched on the stainless steel table, and casually munched a deviled-egg sandwich.

McGovern was perplexed. The lifeless form of Jules Guerrier was not cooperating. Most of the tests on the corpse had been run four and five times. He and his assistants had analyzed the lab data endlessly, studied and restudied the results obtained by the police coroner of Quebec. And still the exact cause of death eluded him.

McGovern was one of those stubborn people who refuse to give up, the kind who stays up all night to finish a novel or add the last pieces of a jigsaw puzzle. He refused to give up now. A life did not simply cease without a reason.

Guerrier had been in pitiful physical condition. But the man was known to have a tremendous constitution. His will to live would never have extinguished like a lamp at the flick of a switch.

It had to be something other than a breakdown of bodily functions. It had to be from something induced.

Every test for poison had been run, even the exotics. All had proven negative. Nor was there evidence of the tiniest puncture from an injection needle under the hair or the nails, between fingers and toes, inside the orifices.

The possibility of suffocation kept returning to McGovern. Expiration from lack of oxygen left few telltale signs.

In the forty years he had served on the Mounties' forensic pathology staff, he could recall only a handful of cases where the victims were murdered by suffocation.

He slipped on a new pair of gloves and approached the stiff, as he referred to it. For the third time that afternoon he scrutinized the interior of the mouth. All was as it should be. No bruises, no paleness behind the lips.

Another dead end.

He returned to his desk and collapsed in the chair dejectedly, hands hanging loosely in his lap, eyes staring vacantly at the tile floor. Then he noticed a slight discoloration on the thumb of one glove. Idly he smeared it on a piece of paper, leaving a greasy pink smudge.

Quickly he bent again over Guerrier. Cautiously he rubbed a towel between the inner lips and outer gums. Then he peered at them through a magnifying glass.

"Ingenious," he murmured aloud as though conversing with the corpse. "Positively ingenious."

Sarveux felt terribly tired. His stand on noninterference with Quebec independence had met with a storm of opposition from his own party and the English-speaking loyalists in the west. The Parliament members from the Maritime Provinces had been especially indignant over his break with national unity. Their anger was to be expected. The new Quebec nation isolated them from the rest of Canada.

He was sitting in his study, sipping a drink while trying to wash away the day's events, when the phone rang. His secretary told him that Commissioner Finn was calling from Mountie headquarters.

He sighed and waited for the click of the connection.

"Mr. Sarveux?"

"Speaking."

"It was murder," Finn said bluntly.

"You have proof?"

"Beyond a doubt."

Sarveux gripped the receiver tightly. *God,* he thought, *when will it end?* "How?"

"Premier Guerrier was smothered to death. Damned clever of the killer. He used theatrical makeup to cover the evidence. Once we knew what to look for we found traces of tooth marks in the fabric of a bed pillow."

"You'll keep after Boucher."

"No need," said Finn. "Your report from British intelligence was most opportune. The print on the doorbell matches the right index finger of Foss Gly."

Sarveux closed his eyes. Perspective, he told himself; he must keep a perspective. "How is it possible Boucher mistook Gly for Villon?"

"I can't say. However, judging from the photo in the report, there is a slight resemblance. The use of makeup on Guerrier may be a key. If

Gly could fool our pathologists, he may be enough of a master of disguise to fix himself up to pass as the spitting image of Villon.''

"You're speaking of Gly as if he was still alive.''

"A habit of mine until I see the body,'' replied Finn. "Do you wish me to continue the investigation?''

"Yes, but I want everything kept confidential,'' said Sarveux. "Can you rely on your people to remain quiet?''

"Absolutely,'' Finn replied.

"Keep Villon under strict surveillance and get Guerrier back in his grave.''

"I'll see to it.''

"And one more thing, commissioner.''

"Sir?''

"From now on, report to me in person. Telephone communications have a way of being intercepted.''

"Understood. I'll be back to you shortly. Goodbye, Prime Minister.''

Several seconds after Finn hung up, Sarveux was still gripping the receiver. *Is it possible that Henri Villon and the slippery head of the FQS are one and the same?* he wondered. *And Foss Gly. Why would he masquerade as Villon?*

The answers took an hour in coming, and suddenly he wasn't tired anymore.

63

The trim executive jet, sporting the NUMA aquamarine colors, whined onto the landing strip and rolled to a stop within twenty feet of where Sandecker and Moon stood waiting. The door to the passenger compartment dropped open and Pitt climbed down. He carried a large aluminum container in both hands.

Sandecker's eyes mirrored a deep concern when he saw the haggard face, watched the slow faltering steps of a man who had lived too long with exhaustion. He moved forward and put his arm around Pitt's shoulder as Moon took the box.

"You look terrible. When was the last time you slept?''

Pitt peered at him through glazed eyes. "I've lost track. What's today?"

"Friday."

"Not sure . . . think it was Monday night."

"Good God, that was four days ago."

A car pulled up and Moon manhandled the box into the trunk. The three of them piled in the back seat, and Pitt promptly dozed off. It seemed he had hardly closed his eyes when Sandecker was shaking him. The driver had stopped at the laboratory entrance to the Arlington College of Archaeology.

A man wearing a white lab coat came through the doorway, accompanied by two uniformed security guards. He was sixtyish, walked slightly stooped and owned a face like Dr. Jekyll after he became Mr. Hyde.

"Dr. Melvin Galasso," he said without offering his hand. "Did you bring the artifact?"

Pitt gestured at the aluminum box as Moon lifted it from the rear of the car. "In there."

"You haven't allowed it to dry out, I hope. It's important that the outer wrapping be pliable."

"The travel bag and the oilcloth packet are still immersed in St. Lawrence River water."

"How did you find them?"

"Buried in silt up to the carrying handle."

Galasso nodded silently in satisfaction. Then he turned toward the doorway to the laboratory.

"All right, gentlemen," he said over his shoulder. "Let's see what you've got."

Dr. Galasso may have been sadly lacking in the social graces, but he had no shortage of patience. He used up two hours simply removing the oilcloth from the travel bag, describing in precise detail every step of the procedure as though lecturing to a class.

"The bottom mud was your savior," he elucidated. "The leather, as you can see, is in an excellent state of preservation and still quite soft."

With meticulous dexterity he cut a rectangular hole in the side of the travel bag with a surgical scalpel, extremely careful not to damage the contents. Then he trimmed a thin plastic sheet to slightly larger dimensions than the packet and eased it into the opening.

"You were wise, Mr. Pitt, not to touch the wrapping," he droned on. "If you had attempted to lift it out of the bag, the material would have crumbled away."

"Won't oilcloth stand up under water?" asked Moon.

Galasso paused and fixed him with a scholarly stare. "Water is a solvent. Loosely speaking, if given enough time it can dissolve a battleship. Oilcloth is simply a piece of fabric that has been chemically treated, generally on one side only. Therefore, it is perishable."

Dismissing Moon, Galasso went back to his work.

When he was satisfied that the plastic was correctly positioned under the packet, he began slipping it out a few millimeters at a time, until at last the still dripping, shapeless thing lay exposed and vulnerable for the first time in seventy-five years.

They stood there in hushed silence. Even Galasso seemed caught up in the awesome moment; he could think of nothing to say. Moon began to tremble and he clamped his hands on a sink for support. Sandecker pulled at his beard while Pitt sipped at his fourth cup of black coffee.

Wordlessly, Galasso began concentrating on unpeeling the wrapping. First he gently patted a paper towel against the surface until it was dry. Then he examined it from every angle, like a diamond cutter contemplating the impact point on a fifty-carat gem, probing here and there with a tiny marking pen.

At last he started the unveiling. With agonizing slowness he doggedly unraveled the brittle cloth. After what seemed an eternity to the men pacing the floor, Galasso came to the final layer. He paused to wipe the perspiration that was glistening on his face, and to flex his numbed fingers. Then he was ready to continue.

"The moment of truth," he said pontifically.

Moon picked up a nearby telephone and established a direct line to the President. Sandecker moved in closer and peered intently over Galasso's shoulder. Pitt's features were expressionless, cold and strangely remote.

The thin, fragile flap was lifted cautiously by degrees and laid back.

They had dared to confront the impossible and their only reward was disillusionment, followed by a crushing bitterness.

The indifferent river had seeped into the oilcloth and turned the British copy of the North American Treaty into a pastelike, unreadable mush.

Part V

THE MANHATTAN LIMITED

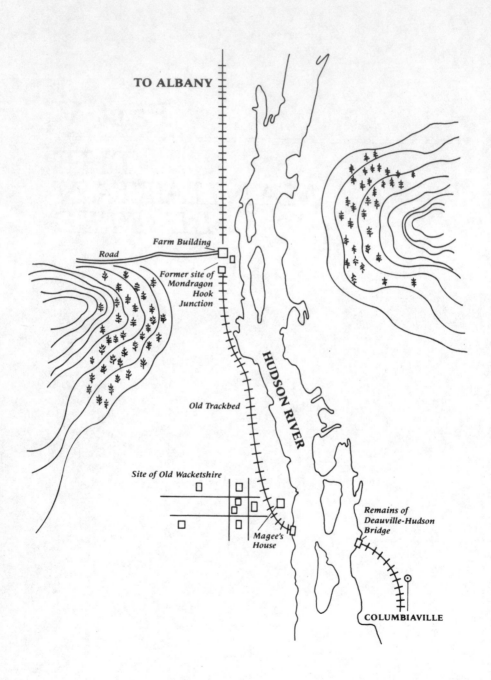

TO ALBANY

Road

Farm Building

Former site of
Mondragon
Hook
Junction

HUDSON RIVER

Old Trackbed

Site of Old Wacketshire

Magee's
House

Remains of
Deauville-Hudson
Bridge

COLUMBIAVILLE

64

The roar of the jet engines diminished soon after the Boeing 757 lifted from the runway of the Quebec airport. When the no-smoking sign blinked out, Heidi loosened her seat belt, readjusted the leg that was encased in an ankle-to-thigh cast to a comfortable position and looked out the window.

Below, the long ribbon that was the St. Lawrence sparkled in the sun and then fell away behind as the plane curved south toward New York.

Her thoughts wandered over the events of the past several days in a kaleidoscope of blurred images. The shock and the pain that followed the explosion beneath the *Ocean Venturer*. The considerate attention of the surgeon and sailors on board the *Phoenix*—her leg cast carried more drawings than a tattoo parlor sample book. The doctors and nurses in the Rimouski hospital where they had treated a dislocated shoulder, and laughed good-heartedly at her sorry attempts to speak French. They all seemed like distant figures out of a dream, and she felt saddened at knowing she might never see them again.

She did not notice a man slide into the aisle seat beside her until he touched her arm.

"Hello, Heidi."

She looked into the face of Brian Shaw and was too startled to speak.

"I know what you must think," he said softly, "but I had to talk to you."

259

Heidi's initial surprise quickly turned to scorn. "What hole did you crawl from?"

He could see her face flush with anger. "I can't deny it was a cold, calculated seduction. For that, I'm sorry."

"All in the line of duty," she said sarcastically. "Bedding down a woman to extract information and then using it to murder twelve innocent men. In my book, Mr. Shaw, you stink."

He was silent for a moment. American women, he mused, have an entirely different way of expressing themselves from that of British women. "A regrettable and completely senseless tragedy," he said. "I want you, and especially Dirk Pitt, to know I was not responsible for what happened."

"You've lied before. Why break your streak?"

"Pitt will believe me when you tell him it was Foss Gly who set off the explosives."

"Foss Gly?"

"Pitt knows the name."

She looked at him skeptically. "You could have stated your case with a phone call. Why are you really here? To pump more information out of me? To learn if we recovered the treaty copy from the *Empress of Ireland?*"

"You did not find the treaty," he said with finality.

"You're shooting in the dark."

"I know that Pitt left Washington for New York and the search on the Hudson River still goes on. That's proof enough."

"You haven't told me what you want," she persisted.

He looked at her, his eyes intent. "You're to deliver a message from my prime minister to your president."

She glared back at him. "You're crazy."

"Not the least. On the face of it, Her Majesty's government is not supposed to be aware of what yours is about and it's too early in the game for a direct confrontation. Because the situation is too delicate for two friendly nations to go through ordinary diplomatic channels, all communications must be handled in a roundabout fashion. It's not an uncommon practice; in fact, the Russians are particularly fond of it."

"But I can't just call up the President," she said, bewildered.

"No need. Just relay the message to Alan Mercier. He'll take it from there."

"The national security adviser?"

Shaw nodded. "The same."

Heidi looked lost. "What do I tell him?"

"You're simply to say that Britain will not give up one of its Commonwealth nations because of a scrap of paper. And we will conduct a strong military defense against any incursion from outside the nation's borders."

"Are you suggesting a showdown between America and . . ."

"You'd win, of course, but it would be the end of the Atlantic Alliance and NATO. The Prime Minister is hoping your country won't pay that high a price to take over Canada."

"Take over Canada," she repeated. "That's ridiculous."

"Is it? Why else are your people pulling out all stops to find a treaty copy?"

"There must be other reasons."

"Perhaps . . ." He hesitated as he took her hand in his. "But somehow I don't think so."

65

"So the train lies buried under the fallen bridge," said Pitt.

Glen Chase nodded. "Everything points in that direction."

"The only place it could be," added Giordino.

Pitt leaned over the railing of the catwalk that hung across the beam of the salvage barge. He watched the long projecting arm of the crane arc around and release a dripping mass of rusting girders into the main hold. Then it swung back and dipped its claw back into the river.

"At this rate it will take a week before we can probe the bottom."

"We can't excavate until the debris is out of the way," said Giordino.

Pitt turned to Chase. "Have one of your men remove a few fragments from the original truss connections with a cutting torch. I'd like to run them by an analytical chemistry lab."

"What do you expect to find?" Chase asked.

"Maybe why the bridge failed," Pitt replied.

A man with a hard hat held up a portable loudspeaker and shouted over the noise of the crane's diesel engine: "Mr. Pitt, you're wanted on the phone."

Pitt excused himself and entered the barge's command office. The call was from Moon.

"Any news?"

"None," Pitt answered.

There was a pause. "The President must have the treaty copy by Monday."

Pitt was stunned. "That's only five days away."

"If you come up empty-handed by one o'clock in the afternoon on Monday, all search activities will be canceled."

Pitt's lips pressed together. "Dammit, Moon! You can't set impossible deadlines on a project like this."

"I'm sorry, that's the way it is."

"Why such short notice?"

"I can only tell you that the urgency is critical."

The knuckles of Pitt's hand clenched around the receiver turned ivory. He could think of nothing to say.

"Are you still there?" queried Moon.

"Yes, I'm here."

"The President is anxious to hear of your progress."

"What progress?"

"You'll have to do better than that," Moon said testily.

"Everything hangs on whether we come across the train and the coach Essex was riding in."

"Care to give me an estimate?"

"There's an old saying among archaeologists," said Pitt. " 'Nothing is found until it wants to be found.' "

"I'm sure the President would prefer a more optimistic report. What should I tell him the chances are of having the treaty in his hands by Monday?"

"Tell the President," said Pitt, his voice like ice, "he doesn't have a prayer."

Pitt reached the Heiser Foundation analytic labs in Brooklyn at midnight. He backed the pickup truck against a loading dock and switched off the ignition. Dr. Walter McComb, the chief chemist, and two of his assistants were there, waiting for him. Pitt said, "I appreciate your staying up so late."

McComb, fifteen years older than Pitt and about seventy pounds heavier, hoisted one of the heavy bridge fragments without a grunt and shrugged. "I've never had a request from the White House before. How could I refuse?"

The four of them manhandled the steel scrap into a corner of a small warehouse. There the lab people used electric saws with moly steel blades to cut off samples which were soaked in a solution and cleaned by acoustics. Then they filtered away to different laboratories to begin their respective analytic specialities.

It was four in the morning when McComb conferred with his assistants and approached Pitt in the employees' lounge.

"I think we have something interesting for you," he said, grinning.

"How interesting?" Pitt asked.

"We've solved the mystery behind the Deauville-Hudson bridge collapse." McComb motioned for Pitt to follow him into a room crammed with exotic-looking chemistry equipment. He handed Pitt a large magnifying glass and pointed at two objects on the table. "See for yourself."

Pitt did as he was told and looked up questioningly. "What am I looking for?"

"Metal that separates under heavy stress leaves fracture lines. They're obvious in the sample on the left."

Pitt looked again. "Okay, I see them."

"You'll note that there are no fracture lines on the sample from the bridge to your right. The deformation is too extreme to have come from natural causes. We put specimens of it under a scanning electron microscope, which shows us the characteristic electrons in each element present. The results revealed residue from iron sulfide."

"What does it all mean?"

"What it all means, Mr. Pitt, is that the Deauville-Hudson bridge was cleverly and systematically blown up."

66

"A grisly business," Preston Beatty exclaimed with an odd sort of pleasure. "One thing to butcher a human body, but quite another to serve it for dinner."

"Would you care for another beer?" asked Pitt.

"Please." Beatty downed the final swallow in his glass. "Fascinating people, Hattie and Nathan Pilcher. You might say they came up with the perfect solution for disposing of the corpus delicti." He motioned around the bar, which was busy with the early evening two-for-one drinks crowd. "This tavern we're sitting in rests on the very foundations of Pilcher's inn. The townspeople of Poughkeepsie burned down the original in 1823 when they learned of the ghastly deeds that had gone on behind its walls."

Pitt gestured for a barmaid. "What you're saying is that the Pilchers murdered overnight guests for their money and then put them on the menu."

"Yes, exactly." It was clear that Beatty was in his element. He recited the events with relish. "No way to take a body count, of course. A few scattered bones were dug up. But the best guess is that the Pilchers cooked between fifteen and twenty innocent travelers in the five years they were in business."

Professor Beatty was considered the leading authority on unsolved crimes. His books sold widely in Canada and the United States and had on occasion touched the nonfiction best-seller lists. He slouched comfortably in the booth and peered at Pitt through blue-green eyes over a salt-and-pepper beard. His age, Pitt guessed from the stern, craggy features and the silver-edged hair, was late forties. He looked more like a hardened pirate than a writer.

"The truly incredible part," Beatty continued, "is how the killers were exposed."

"A restaurant critic gave them a bad review," Pitt suggested.

"You're closer than you know." Beatty laughed. "One evening a retired sea captain stopped overnight. He was accompanied by a manservant, a Melanesian he'd brought on board his ship many years before in the Solomon Islands. Unfortunately for the Pilchers, the Melanesian had once been a cannibal and his educated taste buds correctly identified the meat in the stew."

"Not very appetizing," said Pitt. "So what happened to the Pilchers? Were they executed?"

"No, while awaiting trial they escaped and were never seen again."

The beers arrived and Beatty paused while Pitt signed the tab.

"I've pored through old crime reports here and in Canada trying to connect their modus operandi with later unsolved murders, but they passed into oblivion along with Jack the Ripper."

"And Clement Massey," said Pitt, broaching the subject on his mind.

"Ah, yes, Clement Massey, alias Dapper Doyle." Beatty spoke as if fondly recalling a favorite relative. "A robber years ahead of his time. He could have given lessons to the best of them."

"He was that good?"

"Massey had style and was incredibly shrewd. He planned all his jobs so they looked like the work of rival gangs. As near as I can figure, he pulled off six bank holdups and three train robberies that were blamed on someone else."

"What was his background?"

"Came from a wealthy Boston family. Graduated Harvard summa cum laude. Established a thriving law practice that catered to the social elite of Providence. Married a prominent socialite who bore him five children. Elected twice to the Massachusetts senate."

"Why would he rob banks?" Pitt asked incredulously.

"For the hell of it," Beatty replied. "As it turns out, he handed over every penny of his ill-gotten gains to charity."

"How come he was never glamorized by the newspapers or old pulp magazines?"

"He had vanished from the scene long before his crimes were tied to him," Beatty replied. "And that came only after an enterprising newspaper reporter proved that Clement Massey and Dapper Doyle were one and the same. Naturally, his influential friends and colleagues saw to it that the scandal was quickly covered up. There wasn't enough hard evidence for a trial anyway."

"Hard to believe that Massey was never recognized during a holdup."

"He seldom went along," Beatty laughed. "Like a general directing a battle behind the lines, he usually stayed in the background. All the jobs were pulled out of state, and even his own gang didn't know his true identity. Actually, he *was* recognized on one of the few occasions he directed a robbery at first hand. But the witness' testimony was scoffed at by the investigating marshal. After all, who could believe that a respected state senator was a closet bandit?''

"Odd that Massey didn't wear a mask.''

"A psychological turn-on," said Beatty. "He probably flaunted himself just to experience the excitement that comes from crowding your luck. A double life can be a super challenge for some men. And yet deep down, they want to get caught. Like a husband cheating on his wife who throws lipstick-covered handkerchiefs in the family laundry hamper.''

"Then why the Wacketshire depot robbery? Why did Massey risk everything for a paltry eighteen bucks?''

"I've spent more than one night staring at the ceiling over that enigma." Beatty looked down at the table and moved his glass around. "Except for that caper, Massey never pulled a job that paid less than twenty-five grand.''

"He disappeared right after that.''

"I'd get lost too if I was the cause of a hundred deaths." Beatty took a long swallow of his beer. "Because he ignored the stationmaster's plea to stop the train and allowed women and children to plunge into a cold river, he became enshrined in the annals of crime as a savage mass murderer instead of a Robin Hood.''

"How do you read it?''

"He wanted to rob the train," Beatty answered matter-of-factly. "But something went wrong. There was a bad storm that night. The train was running late. Maybe he was thrown off schedule. I don't know. Something screwed up his plans.''

"What was on the train for a robber?" asked Pitt.

"Two million in gold coin.''

Pitt looked up. "I read nothing about a gold shipment on the *Manhattan Limited.*''

"St. Gaudens twenty-dollar gold pieces struck in nineteen fourteen at the Philadelphia mint. Bound for the banking houses in New York. I think Massey got wind of it. The railroad officials thought they were being clever by rerouting the gold car over half the countryside instead of dispatching it direct over the main track. Rumors were, the car was attached to the *Manhattan Limited* in Albany. No way to prove anything, of course. The loss, if there was a loss, was never reported. The bank bigwigs probably figured it better suited their image to hush the matter up.''

"That may explain why the railroad nearly went broke trying to salvage the train.''

"Perhaps.'' Beatty became lost in the past for a minute. Then he said, "Of all the crimes I've studied, in all the police archives of the world, Massey's penny ante robbery at Wacketshire intrigues me the most.''

"It smells for another reason.''

"How so?''

"This morning a lab found traces of iron sulfide in samples taken from the Deauville-Hudson bridge.''

Beatty's eyes narrowed. "Iron sulfide is used in black powder.''

"That's right. It looks like Massey blew the bridge.''

Beatty appeared stunned by the revelation. "But why? What was his motive?''

"We'll find the answers,'' said Pitt, "when we find the *Manhattan Limited*.''

Pitt drove mechanically on the return trip to the *De Soto*. A thought forced its way through the others: one he had ignored. At first he gave it a negative reception, but it refused to be shelved away. Then it began to come together and make sense.

He stopped at a phone booth in the parking lot of a supermarket and rang a number in Washington. The line buzzed and a gruff voice came on.

"Sandecker.''

Pitt didn't bother identifying himself. "A favor.''

"Shoot.''

"I need a sky hook.''

"Come again.''

Pitt could almost imagine the mouth as it clamped another notch on the cigar. "A sky hook. I've got to have a delivery by tomorrow noon.''

"What in hell for?''

Pitt took a breath and told him.

67

Villon eased the executive jet to the left of an afternoon cumulus cloud, the control yoke barely moving beneath his hands. Through the copilot's window, Danielle watched a carpet of Canadian pines glide past below.

"It's all so beautiful," she said.

"You miss the scenery in an airliner," Villon replied. "They fly too high for you to enjoy any detail."

She was in a deep shade of blue, a snug sweater and cotton knit skirt that circled around her knees. There was a sort of savvy look about her that could never quite overcome the feminine warmth that flowed under the surface.

"Your new plane is beautiful too."

"A gift from my well-heeled supporters. The title isn't in my name, of course, but no one touches it but me."

They sat in silence for a few minutes as Villon held the jet on a steady course over the heart of Laurentides Park. Blue lakes began to appear all around them like tiny diamonds in an emerald setting. They could easily make out small boats with fishermen casting for speckled trout.

Finally Danielle said, "I'm happy you invited me. It's been a long time."

"Only a couple of weeks," he said without looking at her. "I've been busy campaigning."

"I thought perhaps . . . perhaps you didn't want to see me anymore."

"Whatever gave you that idea?"

"The last time at the cottage . . ."

"What about it?" he asked innocently.

"You weren't exactly cordial."

He tilted his head lightly, trying to recall. Nothing materialized and he shrugged, writing it off to womanly touchiness. "Sorry, I must have had a lot on my mind."

He set the plane on a wide sweeping bank and dropped in the autopilot. Then he smiled. "Come on, I'll make it up to you."

He took her hand and led her from the cockpit.

The passenger cabin stretched twenty feet to the lavatory. There were four seats and a sofa, a thick carpeted floor, a fully stocked wet bar and dining table. He opened a door into a private sleeping compartment and bowed toward a queen-sized bed.

"The perfect love nest," he said. "Intimate, secluded and far from prying eyes."

The sunshine poured through the windows and spread over the bedsheets. Danielle sat up as Villon padded from the passenger cabin and passed her a drink.

"Isn't there a law against this sort of thing?" she asked.

"Sex at five thousand feet?"

"No," she said between sips of a Bloody Mary. "Letting an airplane fly around in circles for two hours without anybody in the cockpit."

"You going to turn me in?"

She stretched back seductively on the bed. "I can see the headlines now: NEW PRESIDENT OF QUEBEC CAUGHT IN FLYING WHOREHOUSE."

"I'm not President yet." He laughed.

"You will be after the elections."

"They're six months away. Anything can happen between now and then."

"The polls say you're a shoo-in."

"What does Charles say?"

"He never mentions you anymore."

Villon sat down on the bed and trailed his fingers lightly across her belly. "Now that Parliament has handed him a vote of no confidence, his power has evaporated. Why don't you leave him? Things would be simpler for us."

"Better I remain at his side a little while longer. There is much I can still learn of importance to Quebec."

"While we're on the subject, there *is* something that concerns me."

She began to squirm. "What is it?"

"The President of the United States is speaking to Parliament next week. I'd like to know what he intends to say. Have you heard anything?"

She took his hand and moved it down. "Charles talked about it yesterday. Nothing to worry about. He said the President was going to make a plea for an orderly transition of Quebec independence.''

''I knew it,'' Villon said, smiling. ''The Americans are caving in.''

Danielle began to lose control and reached out for him.

''I hope you filled the fuel tanks before we left Ottawa,'' she murmured in a slurred voice.

''We have enough for three more hours' flying time,'' he said, and then he came down on top of her.

''There is no mistake?'' Sarveux said into the phone.

''Absolutely none,'' replied Commissioner Finn. ''My man saw them board Mr. Villon's plane. We've tracked them on air force radar. They've been circling Laurentides Park since one o'clock.''

''Your man is certain it was Henri Villon.''

''Yes, sir, there was no doubt,'' Finn reassured him.

''Thank you, commissioner.''

''Not at all, Prime Minister. I'll be standing by.''

Sarveux replaced the receiver and paused a moment to rally his senses. Then he spoke into the intercom. ''You may send him in now.''

Sarveux's face tensed in the first conclusive moment of shock. He was certain his eyes were deceiving him, his mind playing tricks with his imagination. His legs refused to respond, and he could not gather the strength to rise from behind the desk. Then the visitor walked across the room and stood looking down.

''Thank you for seeing me, Charles.''

The face bore the familiar cold expression, the voice came exactly as he had known it. Sarveux fought to maintain an outward calm, but he suddenly felt weak and dizzy.

The man standing before him was Henri Villon, in the flesh, completely at ease, displaying the same aloof poise that never cracked.

''I thought . . . I thought you were . . . were campaigning in Quebec,'' Sarveux stammered.

''I took time out to come to Ottawa in the hope you and I might declare a truce.''

''The gap between our differences is too wide,'' Sarveux said, slowly regaining his composure.

''Canada and Quebec must learn to live together without further friction,'' said Villon. ''You and I should too.''

''I'm willing to listen to reason.'' There was a subtle hardening in

Sarveux's voice. "Sit down, Henri, and tell me what's on your mind."

68

Alan Mercier finished reading the contents of a folder marked MOST SECRET and then reread them. He was stunned. Every so often he flipped the pages backward, attempting to keep an open mind, but finding it increasingly difficult to believe what his eyes conveyed. He had the look of a man who held a ticking bomb in his hands.

The President sat across from him, seemingly detached, patiently waiting. It was very quiet in the room; the only sound was an occasional crackle from a smoldering log in the fireplace. Two trays of food sat on the large coffee table that separated the two men. Mercier was too engrossed to eat, but the President consumed the late dinner hungrily.

Finally Mercier closed the folder and solemnly removed his glasses. He pondered for a moment, then looked up.

"I have to ask," he said. "Is this mad plot for real?"

"Right down to the period in the last sentence."

"A remarkable concept," Mercier sighed. "I'll give it that."

"I think so."

"I find it hard to believe you took it so far in all these years without a leak."

"Not surprising when you consider only two people knew about it."

"Doug Oates over at State was aware."

"Only after the inauguration," the President acknowledged. "Once I possessed the power to put the wheels in motion, the first step, the obvious step, was to bring in the State Department."

"But not national security," said Mercier, a cool edge on his voice.

"Nothing personal, Alan. I only added to the inner circle as each stage progressed."

"So now it's my turn."

The President nodded. "I want you and your staff to recruit and organize influential Canadians who see things as I do."

Mercier dabbed a handkerchief at the sweat glistening on his face.

"Good God. If this thing backfires and your announcement of national insolvency follows on its heels . . . ?'' He let the implication hang.

"It won't,'' the President said grimly.

"You may have reached too far.''

"But if it is accepted, at least in principle, think of the opportunities.''

"You'll get your first indication when you spring it on the Canadian Parliament on Monday.''

"Yes, it'll be out in the open then.''

Mercier laid the folder on the table. "I have to hand it to you, Mr. President. When you sat silent and refused to intervene in Quebec's bid for independence, I thought you'd slipped a cog. Now I'm beginning to see the method behind your madness.''

"We've only opened the first door''—the President waxed philosophical—"to a long hallway.''

"Don't you think you're counting too heavily on finding the North American Treaty?''

"Yes, I suppose you're right.'' The President stared out the window at Washington without seeing it. "But if a miracle happens on the Hudson River by Monday, we may have the privilege of designing a new flag.''

69

The sky hook was just what its name suggested: a helicopter capable of transporting bulky equipment to the tops of high buildings and heavy equipment across rivers and mountains. Its slender fuselage tapered to a length of 105 feet and the landing gear hung down like rigid stalks.

To the men on the salvage site the ungainly craft looked like a monstrous praying mantis that had escaped from a Japanese science fiction movie. They watched fascinated as it flew two hundred feet above the river, the huge rotor blades whipping the water into froth from shore to shore.

The sight was made even stranger by the wedge-shaped object that hung suspended from the sky hook's belly. Except for Pitt and Giordino, it was the first time any of the NUMA crew had set eyes on the *Doodlebug*.

Pitt directed the lowering operation by radio, instructing the pilot to set his load beside the *De Soto*. The sky hook very slowly halted its forward motion and hovered for a few minutes until the *Doodlebug*'s pendulum motion died. Then the twin cargo cables unreeled, easing the research vessel into the river. When the strain slackened, the *De Soto*'s crane was swung over the side and divers scrambled up the ladder on the vertical hull. The cable hooks were exchanged on the hoisting loops and, free of its burden, the sky hook rose, banked into a broad half circle and headed back downriver.

Everyone stood along the rails gawking at the *Doodlebug*, wondering about its purpose. Suddenly, adding to their silent bewilderment, a hatch popped open, a head appeared and a pair of heavy-lidded eyes surveyed the astonished onlookers.

"Where in hell is Pitt?" the intruder shouted.

"Here!" Pitt yelled back.

"Guess what?"

"You found another bottle of snakebite medicine in your bunk."

"How'd you know?" Sam Quayle replied, laughing.

"Lasky with you?"

"Below, rewiring the ballast controls to operate in shallow water."

"You took a chance, riding inside all the way from Boston."

"Maybe, but we saved time by activating the electronic systems during the flight."

"How soon before you're ready to dive?"

"Give us another hour."

Chase moved beside Giordino. "Just what *is* that mechanical perversion?" he asked.

"If you had any idea what it cost," Giordino answered with an imperturbable smile, "you wouldn't call it nasty names."

Three hours later the *Doodlebug*, its top hatches rippling the water ten feet beneath the surface, crawled slowly across the riverbed. The suspense inside was hard to bear as the hull skirted dangerously close to the gnarled pieces of the bridge.

Pitt kept a close eye on the video monitors while Bill Lasky maneuvered the craft against the current. Behind them, Quayle peered at a systems panel, focusing his attention on the detection readouts.

"Any contact?" Pitt asked for the fourth time.

"Negative," answered Quayle. "I've widened the beam to cover a twenty-meter path at a depth of one hundred meters into the geology, but all I read is bedrock."

"We've worked too far upriver," Pitt said, turning to Lasky. "Bring it around for another pass."

"Approaching from a new angle," acknowledged Lasky, his hands busy with the knobs and switches of the control console.

Five more times the *Doodlebug* threaded its way through the sunken debris. Twice they heard wreckage scraping along the hull. Pitt was all too aware that if the thin skin was penetrated, he would be blamed for the loss of the six-hundred-million-dollar vessel.

Quayle seemed immune to the peril. He was infuriated that his instrument remained mute. He was particularly angry at himself for thinking the fault was his.

"Must be a malfunction," he muttered. "I should have had a target by now."

"Can you isolate the problem?" Pitt asked.

"No, dammit!" Quayle abruptly snapped. "All systems are functioning normally. I must have miscalculated when I reprogrammed the computers."

The expectations of a quick discovery began to dim. Frustration was worsened by false hopes and anticipation. Then, as they turned around for another run through the search grid, the river current surged against the exposed starboard area of the *Doodlebug* and swept its keel into a mudbank. Lasky struggled with the controls for nearly an hour before the vessel worked free.

Pitt was giving the coordinates for a new course when Giordino's voice came over the communications speaker.

"*De Soto* to *Doodlebug*. Do you read?"

"Speak," said Pitt tersely.

"You guys have been pretty quiet."

"Nothing to report," Pitt answered.

"You better close up shop. A heavy storm front is moving in. Chase would like to secure our electronic marvel before the wind strikes."

Pitt hated to give up, but it was senseless to continue. Time had run out. Even if they found the train in the next few hours, it was doubtful if the salvage crew could pinpoint and excavate the coach that carried Essex and the treaty before the President's address to Parliament.

"Okay," said Pitt. "Make ready to receive us. We're folding the act."

Giordino stood on the bridge and nodded at the dark clouds massing over the ship. "This project has had a curse on it from the beginning," he mumbled gloomily. "As if we don't have enough problems, now it's the weather."

"Somebody up there plain doesn't like us," said Chase, pointing to the sky.

"You blaming God, you heathen?" Giordino joked good-naturedly.

"No," answered Chase looking solemn. "The ghost."

Pitt turned. "Ghost?"

"An unmentionable subject around here," said Chase. "Nobody likes to admit they've seen it."

"Speak for yourself." Giordino cracked a smile. "I've only heard the thing."

"Its light was brighter than hell when it swung up the old grade to the bridge the other night. The beam lit up half the east shoreline. I don't see how you missed it."

"Wait a minute," Pitt broke in. "Are you talking about the phantom train?"

Giordino stared at him. "You know?"

"Doesn't everyone?" Pitt asked in mock seriousness. " 'Tis said the specter of the doomed train is still trying to cross the Deauville-Hudson bridge to the other side."

"You don't believe that?" Chase asked cautiously.

"I believe there is something up on the old track bed that goes chug in the night. In fact, it damn near ran over me."

"When?"

"A couple of months ago when I came here to survey the site."

Giordino shook his head. "At least we won't go to the loony bin alone."

"How often has the ghost called on you?"

Giordino looked at Chase for support. "Two, no, three times."

"You say some nights you heard sounds but saw no lights?"

"The first two intrusions came with steam whistles and the roar of a locomotive," explained Chase. "The third time we got the full treatment. The clamor was accompanied by a blinding light."

"I saw the light too," Pitt said slowly. "What were your weather conditions?"

Chase thought a moment. "As I recall, it was clear and blacker than pitch when the light showed."

"That's right," added Giordino. "The noise came alone only on nights the moon was bright."

"Then we've got a pattern," said Pitt. "There was no moon during my sighting."

"All this talk about ghosts isn't putting us any closer to finding the real train," said Giordino blandly. "I suggest we get back to reality and figure a way to get under the bridge wreckage in the next"—he hesitated and consulted his watch—"seventy-four hours."

"I have another suggestion," said Pitt.

"Which is?"

"To hell with it."

Giordino looked at him, ready to smile if Pitt was joking. But he was not.

"What are you going to tell the President?"

A strange, distant look came over Pitt's face. "The President?" he repeated vaguely. "I'm going to tell him we've been fishing in the air, wasting an enormous amount of time and money searching for an illusion."

"What are you getting at?"

"The *Manhattan Limited*," Pitt replied. "It doesn't lie on the bottom of the Hudson River. It never has."

70

The setting sun was suddenly snuffed out by the clouds. The sky went dark and menacing. Pitt and Giordino stood on the old track bed, listening to the deep rumbling of the storm as it drew closer. And then lightning crackled and the thunder echoed and the rain came.

The wind swept through the trees with a demonic whine. The humid air was oppressive and charged with electricity. Soon the light was gone and there was no color, only black pierced by brief streaks of white. Raindrops, hurled in horizontal sheets by wind gusts, struck their faces with the stinging power of sand.

Pitt tightened the collar of his raincoat, hunched his shoulders against the tempest and stared into the night.

"How can you be sure it will appear?" Giordino shouted over the gale.

"Conditions are the same as the night the train vanished," Pitt shouted back. "I'm banking on the ghost having a melodramatic sense of timing."

"I'll give it another hour," said a thoroughly miserable Chase. "And then I'm heading back to the boat and a healthy slug of Jack Daniel's."

Pitt motioned them to follow. "Come on, let's take a hike down the track bed."

Reluctantly Chase and Giordino fell in behind. The lightning became almost incessant and, seen from shore, the *De Soto* looked like a gray ghost herself. A great shaft of brilliance flashed for an instant across the river behind her and she became a black outline. The only sign of life was the white light on the mast that burned defiantly through the downpour.

After about half a mile, Pitt halted and tilted his head as if listening. "I think I hear something."

Giordino cupped his hands to his ears. He waited until the last thunderclap died over the rolling hills. Then he heard it too: the mournful wail of a train whistle.

"You called it," said Chase. "It's right on schedule."

No one spoke for several seconds as the sound grew closer, and then there came the clang of a bell and the puff of the exhaust. It was drowned out momentarily by another burst of thunder. Chase swore later that he could feel time grinding to a stop.

At that moment a light came around a curve and washed its beam on them, the rays eerily distorted by the rain. They stood there, each seeing the yellow reflections on the face of the others.

They stared ahead, disbelieving, yet certain it was not a trick of their imaginations. Giordino turned to say something to Pitt and was astounded to see him smiling, actually smiling at the expanding blaze.

"Don't move," Pitt said with incredible calm. "Turn around, close your eyes and cover them with your hands so you aren't blinded by the glare."

Instinct dictated they do just the opposite. The urge for self-preservation, to run or at least throw themselves flat on the ground tore at their conscious senses. Their only bond with courage was Pitt's firm words.

"Steady . . . steady. Be ready to open your eyes when I yell."

God, it was unnerving.

Giordino tensed for the impact that would smash his flesh and bones into a ghastly spray of crimson and white. He made up his mind he was going to die, and that was that.

The deafening clangor was upon them, assaulting their eardrums. They felt as though they had been thrust into some strange vacuum where twentieth-century reasoning lost all relevance.

Then, as if by magic, the impossible thing passed over them.

"Now!" Pitt shouted above the din.

They all dropped their hands and stared, eyes still adjusted to the dark.

The light was now aimed away and traveling down the abandoned track bed, the locomotive sound diminishing in its wake. They could clearly see a black rectangle centered in the glow about eight feet off the ground. They watched fascinated as it grew smaller in the distance and then turned up the grade to the bridge, where it blinked out and the accompanying clatter died into the storm.

"What in hell was that?" Chase finally muttered.

"An antique locomotive headlamp and an amplifier," answered Pitt.

"Oh, yeah?" grunted Giordino skeptically. "Then how does it float in mid-air?"

"On a wire strung from the old telegraph poles."

"Too bad there has to be a logical explanation," said Chase, sadly shaking his head. "I hate to see good supernatural legends debunked."

Pitt gestured toward the sky. "Keep looking. Your legend should be returning anytime now."

They grouped around the nearest telegraph pole and stared upward into the darkness. A minute later a black shape emerged and slipped noiselessly through the air above them. Then it melted back into the shadows and was gone.

"Fooled hell out of me," Giordino admitted.

"Where did the thing come from?" asked Chase.

Pitt didn't answer immediately. He suddenly stood illuminated by a lightning strike in a distant field; the flash revealed a contemplative look on his face.

Finally he said, "You know what I think?"

"No, what?"

"I think we should all have a cup of coffee and a slice of hot apple pie."

By the time they knocked on Ansel Magee's door they looked like drowned rats. The big sculptor cordially invited them in and took their wet coats. While Pitt made the introductions, Annie Magee, true to expectations, hurried into the kitchen to rustle up coffee and pie, only this time it was cherry.

"What brings you gentlemen out on such a miserable night?" asked Magee.

"We were chasing ghosts," Pitt replied.

Magee's eyes narrowed. "Any luck?"

"May we talk about it in the depot office?"

Magee nodded agreeably. "Of course. Come, come."

It took little urging for him to regale Chase and Giordino with the history behind the office and its former occupants. As he talked, he built a fire in the potbellied stove. Pitt sat silently at Sam Harding's old rolltop desk. He'd heard the lecture before and his mind was elsewhere.

Magee was in the midst of pointing out the bullet in Hiram Meecham's chessboard when Annie entered, carrying a tray with cups and plates.

After the last scrap of pie was gone, Magee looked across the office at Pitt. "You never did say whether you found a ghost."

"No," Pitt replied. "No ghost. But we did find a clever rig that fakes the phantom train."

Magee's broad shoulders drooped and he shrugged. "I always knew someone would discover the secret someday. I even had the local folks fooled. Not that any of them minded. They're all quite proud of having a ghost they can call their own. Sort of gives them something to brag about to the tourists."

"When did you get wise to it?" Annie asked.

"The night I came to your door. Earlier I was standing on the bridge abutment when you sent the phantom on a run. Just before it reached me the lamp blinked out and the sound shut down."

"You saw how it worked then?"

"No, I was blinded by the glare. By the time my eyes readjusted to the dark it was long gone. Baffled the hell out of me at first. My gut instinct was to search the ground level. That only added to my confusion when I failed to find tracks in the snow. But I'm a man with a curious streak. I wondered why the old railbed was torn up and hauled away down to the last crosstie, and yet the telegraph poles were left standing. Railroad officials are a tightfisted lot. They don't like to leave any reusable equipment behind when they abandon a right-of-way. I began following the poles until I came to the last one in line. It stands at the door of a shed beside your private track. I also noticed that the headlamp was missing from your locomotive."

"I have to give you credit, Mr. Pitt," said Magee. "You're the first to hit upon the truth."

"How does the thing operate?" asked Giordino.

"The same principle as a chair lift on a ski slope," Magee explained. "The headlamp and a set of four speakers hang suspended from a continuous cable strung along the crossbars of the telegraph poles. When the light and sound package reaches the edge of the old Deauville bridge, a remote switch shuts off the batteries and then it makes a hundred-and-eighty-degree turn and returns to the shed."

"Why was it that some nights we only heard the sound but saw no lights?" asked Chase.

"The locomotive headlamp is rather large," answered Magee. "It's too easily detectable. So on moonlit nights I remove it and run only the sound system."

Giordino smiled broadly. "I don't mind admitting, Chase and I were ready to take up religion the first time it paid us a visit."

"I hope I didn't cause you any unnecessary inconvenience."

"Not at all. It was a great source of conversation."

"Annie and I stand on the riverbank nearly every day and watch your salvage operation. Looks to me like you've experienced problems. Have any pieces of the *Manhattan Limited* been pulled up yet?"

"Not even a rivet," Pitt answered. "We're closing the project down."

"That's a shame," Magee said sincerely. "I was rooting for your success. I guess the train wasn't meant to be found."

"Not in the river at any rate."

"More coffee, anyone?" Annie came around with the pot.

"I'll take some," said Pitt. "Thank you."

"You were saying . . ." Magee probed.

"Do you own one of those little motorcars that railroad gangs ride on when they repair track?" Pitt asked, changing the subject.

"I have an eighty-year-old handcar that moves on muscle power."

"May I borrow it along with your phantom train gear?"

"When do you want to use it?"

"Now."

"On a stormy night like this?"

"Especially on a stormy night like this."

71

Giordino took up his station on the platform bordering the tracks. In one hand he held a large flashlight. The wind had died down to ten miles an hour, and by keeping to the corner of the depot he was sheltered from the sweeping rain.

Chase was not so lucky. He stood huddled atop the handcar a quarter of a mile up the track. For perhaps the tenth time he dried off the battery terminals and checked the wires leading to the locomotive headlamp and sound speakers that were jury-rigged on the front of the handcar.

Pitt stepped to the doorway and made a signal with his hand. Giordino acknowledged it and then jumped down onto the track bed and blinked his flashlight into the darkness.

"About damned time," Chase mumbled to himself as he pushed the battery switch and began pumping the hand levers.

The headlamp's beam glinted on the wet rails and the whistle shriek was swept ahead by a following gust of wind. Pitt hesitated, timing in his mind the advance of the handcar. Satisfied that Chase was approaching at a good clip, he reentered the office and absorbed the warmth from the stove.

"We're rolling," he said briefly.

"What do you hope to learn by recreating the robbery?" asked Magee.

"I'll know better in a few minutes," Pitt replied evasively.

"I think it's exciting," Annie bubbled.

"Annie, you act out the role of Hiram Meechum, the telegrapher, while I play the station agent, Sam Harding," Pitt instructed. "Mr. Magee, you're the authority. I'll leave it to you to take the part of Clement Massey and lead us through the events step by step."

"I'll try," Magee said. "But it's impossible to reconstruct the exact dialogue and movements of seventy-five years ago."

"We won't need a perfect performance," Pitt grinned. "A simple run-through will do fine."

Magee shrugged. "Okay . . . let's see, Meechum was seated at the table in front of the chessboard. Harding had just taken a call from the dispatcher in Albany, so he was standing near the phone when Massey entered."

He walked to the doorway and turned around, holding out his hand in simulation of a gun. The locomotive sounds drew nearer and mingled with the occasional boom of thunder. He stood there a few seconds listening, and then he nodded his head.

"This is a holdup," he said.

Annie looked at Pitt, unsure of what to do or say.

"After the surprise wore off," said Pitt, "the railroad men must have put up an argument."

"Yes, when I interviewed Sam Harding he said they tried to tell Massey there was no money in the depot, but he wouldn't listen. He insisted that one of them open the safe."

"They hesitated," Pitt conjectured.

"In the beginning," said Magee, his voice taking on a hollow tone. "Then Harding agreed, but only if he could flag the train first. Massey refused, claiming it was a trick. He became impatient and fired a bullet through Meechum's chessboard."

Annie hesitated, a blank look on her face. Then, carried away by her imagination, she swept the board off the table and scattered the chess pieces over the floor.

"Harding begged, tried to explain that the bridge was out. Massey would have none of it."

The headlamp beam on the handcar flashed through the window. Pitt could see that Magee's eyes were looking into another time.

"Then what happened?" Pitt prompted.

"Meechum grabbed a lantern and made an attempt to reach the platform and stop the train. Massey shot him in the hip."

Pitt turned. "Annie, if you please?"

Annie rose from her chair, made a few steps toward the door and eased down in a reclining position on the floor.

The handcar was only a hundred yards away now. Pitt could read the dates on the calendar hanging on the wall from the headlamp.

"The door?" Pitt snapped. "Open or closed."

Magee paused, trying to think.

"Quickly, quickly!" Pitt urged.

"Massey had kicked it closed."

Pitt pushed the door shut. "Next move?"

"Open that damned safe! Yes, Massey's very words, according to Harding."

Pitt hurried over and knelt in front of the old iron safe.

Five seconds later the handcar, with Chase pumping up a sweat, rolled by on the track outside, the bass of the speakers reverberating throughout the old wooden building. Giordino stood and swung the flashlight at the windows in a wide circular motion, making it seem to those inside that the beam was flickering past the window glass in the wake of the handcar. The only sound missing was the clack of the steel coach wheels.

A shiver crept up Magee's spine and gripped him all the way to the scalp. He felt as if he had touched the past, a past he had never truly known.

Annie lifted herself from the floor and put her arms around his waist. She looked up into his face, her expression strangely penetrating.

"It was so real," Magee murmured. "All so damn real."

"That's because our reenactment was the way it happened back in nineteen fourteen," said Pitt.

Magee turned and stared at Pitt. "But there was the real *Manhattan Limited* then."

Pitt shook his head. "There was no *Manhattan Limited* then."

"You're wrong. Harding and Meechum saw it."

"They were tricked," Pitt said quietly.

"That can't be . . ." Magee began, then stopped, his eyes wide in uncomprehension. He started over. "That can't be . . . they were experienced railroad men . . . they couldn't be fooled."

"Meechum was lying wounded on the floor. The door was closed. Harding was bent over the safe, his back to the tracks. All they saw were lights. All they heard were sounds. Sounds from an old gramophone recording of a passing train."

"But the bridge . . . it collapsed under the weight of the train. That couldn't be faked."

"Massey blew the bridge in sections. He knew one big bang would have alerted half the valley. So he detonated small charges of black powder at key structure points, coinciding the blasts with the thunderclaps, until the center span finally gave way and dropped in the river."

Magee, still puzzled, said nothing.

"The robbery of the station was only a sham, a cover-up. Massey had bigger things on his mind than a measly eighteen dollars. He was after a two-million-dollar gold-coin shipment carried on the *Manhattan Limited*."

"Why go to all the trouble?" Magee asked doubtfully. "He could have simply stopped the train, held it up and made off with the coins."

"That's how Hollywood might have filmed it," said Pitt. "But in real life there's always a catch. The coins in question were twenty-dollar pieces called St. Gaudens. They each weighed close to one ounce. Simple arithmetic tells us that it took a hundred thousand coins to make two million dollars. Then allow sixteen ounces to a pound, do a little dividing and you come up with a shipment weighing over three tons. Not exactly a bundle a few men could unload and haul away before railroad officials figured the cause of the train's delay and sent a posse charging down the tracks."

"All right," said Giordino. "I'll bite and ask the question on everyone's mind. If the train didn't pass through here and take a dive in the Hudson, where did it go?"

"I think Massey took over the locomotive, diverted the train off the main track and hid it where it remains to this day."

If Pitt had claimed to be a visitor from Venus or the reincarnation of Napoleon Bonaparte, his words couldn't have received a more dubious reception. Magee looked downright apathetic. Only Annie had a thoughtful expression.

"In some respects, Mr. Pitt's theory isn't as farfetched as it sounds," she said.

Magee stared at her as if she was an errant child. "Not one passenger or crewman who survived to tell the tale, or a robber confessing on a deathbed, not even a corpse to point a finger? Not a fragment from an entire train come to light after all these years . . . not possible."

"It would have to be the greatest vanishing act of all time," added Chase.

Pitt did not look as though he was listening to the conversation. He suddenly turned to Magee. "How far is Albany from here?"

"About twenty-five miles. Why do you ask?"

"The last time anyone saw the *Manhattan Limited* up close was when it left the Albany station."

"But surely you can't really believe . . . ."

"People believe what they want to believe," said Pitt. "Myths, ghosts, religion and the supernatural. My belief is that a cold, tangible entity has simply been misplaced for three-quarters of a century in a place where nobody thought to look.''

Magee sighed. ''What are your plans?''

Pitt looked surprised at the question. ''I'm going to eyeball every inch of the deserted track bed between here and Albany,'' he said grimly, ''until I find the remains of an old rail spur that leads to nowhere.''

72

The telephone rang at 11:15 p.m. Sandecker laid aside the book he was reading in bed and answered.

''Sandecker.''

''Pitt again.''

The admiral pushed himself to a sitting position and cleared his mind. ''Where are you calling from this time?''

''Albany. Something has come up.''

''Another problem with the salvage project?''

''I called it off.''

Sandecker took a deep breath. ''Do you mind telling me why?''

''We were looking in the wrong place.''

''Oh, Christ,'' he groaned. ''That tears it. Damn. No doubt at all?''

''Not in my mind.''

''Hang on.''

Sandecker picked out a cigar from a humidor on the bedside table and lit it. Even though the trade embargo with Cuba had been lifted in 1985, he still preferred the milder flavor and looser wrap of a Honduras over the Havana. He always felt that a good cigar kept the world at bay. He blew out a rolling cloud and came back on the line.

''Dirk.''

''Still here.''

''What do I tell the President?''

There was silence. Then Pitt spoke slowly and distinctly. ''Tell him the odds have dropped from a million to one to a thousand to one.''

''You found something?''

"I didn't say that."

"Then what are you working on?"

"Nothing more than a gut feeling."

"What do you need from me?" asked Sandecker.

"Please get ahold of Heidi Milligan. She's staying at the Gramercy Park Hotel in New York. Ask her to dig into old railroad archives for any maps that show New York & Quebec Northern Railroad tracks, sidings and spurs between Albany and the Deauville-Hudson bridge during the years eighteen eighty to nineteen fourteen."

"Okay, I'll take care of it. Got her number?"

"You'll have to get it from information."

Sandecker took a long puff on the cigar. "How does it look for Monday?"

"Grim. You can't rush these things."

"The President needs that treaty copy."

"Why?"

"Don't you know?"

"Moon clammed up when I asked."

"The President is speaking before the House of Commons and the Senate of the Canadian Parliament. His speech centers around a plea for merging our two countries into one. Alan Mercier let me in on it this morning. Since Quebec went independent, the Maritime Provinces have been considering statehood. The President is hoping to talk the Western Provinces into joining too. That's where a signed copy of the North American Treaty comes in. Not to coerce or threaten, but to eliminate the red-tape jungle of the transition and stonewall any objections and interference from the United Kingdom. His pitch for a unified North America is only fifty-eight hours away. You get the action?"

"Yes . . ." Pitt said sullenly. "I've got it now. And while you're at it, thank the President and his little group for letting me know at the last minute."

"Would it have mattered otherwise?"

"No, I guess not."

"Where can Heidi get in touch with you?"

"I'll keep the *De Soto* moored at the bridge site as a command post. All calls can be relayed from there."

There was nothing more to say. So Sandecker simply said, "Good luck."

"Thanks," Pitt came back.

And then the line went dead.

Sandecker had the number of Heidi's hotel in less than a minute. He dialed direct and waited for the connection.

"Good evening, Gramercy Park Hotel," a sleepy female voice answered.

"Commander Milligan's room, please."

A pause. "Yes, room three sixty-seven. I'll ring."

"Hello," a man answered.

"Is this Commander Milligan's room?" Sandecker demanded impatiently.

"No, sir, this is the assistant manager. The commander is out for the evening."

"Any idea when she'll return?"

"No sir, she didn't stop at the desk when she left."

"You must have a photographic memory," said Sandecker suspiciously.

"Sir?"

"Do you recognize all your guests when they pass through the lobby?"

"When they're very attractive ladies who stand six feet tall and wear a cast on one leg, I do."

"I see."

"May I give her a message?"

Sandecker thought a moment. "No message. I'll call again later."

"One minute, sir. I think she passed by and entered the elevator while we've been talking. If you'll hold on, I'll have the switchboard ring her room and transfer your call."

In room 367 Brian Shaw laid down the receiver and walked into the bathroom. Heidi lay in the tub, covered by a blanket of bubbles, her cast-enclosed leg propped awkwardly on the edge of the tub. Her hair was covered by a plastic shower cap and she lazily held an empty glass in one hand.

"Venus, born of the foam and the sea." Shaw laughed. "I wish I had a picture of this."

"I can't reach the champagne," she said, pointing to a magnum of Tattinger brut reserve vintage in an ice bucket perched on the washbasin. He nodded and filled her glass. Then he poured the remainder of the chilled champagne over her breasts.

She yelped and tried to splash him, but he ducked nimbly back through the doorway. "I owe you for that," she shouted.

"Before you declare war, you've got a call."

"Who is it?"

"I didn't ask. Sounds like another dirty old man." He nodded at a wall phone mounted between the tub and the commode. "You can take it here. I'll hang up the extension."

As soon as her voice came on the line, Shaw clicked the connection and then kept his ear pressed to the receiver. When Heidi and Sandecker finished their conversation, he waited for her to hang up. She didn't.

Smart girl, he thought. She didn't trust him.

After ten seconds he finally heard the disconnect as she placed the handset in its cradle. Then he dialed the hotel switchboard.

"May I help you?"

"Yes, could you ring room three sixty-seven in a minute and ask for Brian Shaw? Please don't say who you are."

"Nothing else?"

"When Shaw himself answers, just punch off the connection."

"Yes, sir."

Shaw returned to the bathroom and peered around the door. "Truce?"

Heidi looked up and smiled. "How'd you like it if I did that to you?"

"The sensation wouldn't be the same. I'm not built like you."

"Now I'll reek of champagne."

"Sounds delicious."

The phones in the suite jangled.

"Probably for you," he said casually.

She reached over and answered, then held the handset toward him. "They asked for Brian Shaw. Perhaps you'd like to take it in the other room."

"I have no secrets," he said, grinning slyly.

He muttered through a one-sided conversation and then hung up. He made an angered expression.

"Damn, that was the consulate. I have to meet with someone."

"At this time of night?" she asked.

He leaned down and kissed her toes that protruded from the end of the cast. "Revel in anticipation. I'll be back in two hours."

The curator of the Long Island Railroad Museum was an elderly retired accountant who nourished a lifelong passion for the iron horse.

He walked yawning through the relics on display while grumbling incessantly about being abruptly awakened in the dead of night to open the building for an FBI agent.

He came to an antique door whose glass was etched with an elk standing on a mountain, looking down on a diamond-stacked locomotive puffing a great billow of smoke as it rounded a sharp curve. He fished around with a large ring until he found the right key. Then he unlocked the door, swung it open and switched on the lights.

He paused and stuck out an arm, blocking Shaw's way. "Are you sure you're an FBI man?"

Shaw sighed at the stupid wording of the question and produced a hastily forged ID card for the third time. He waited patiently for the curator to read the fine print again.

"I assure you, Mr. Rheinhold . . ."

"Rheingold. Like the beer."

"Sorry, but I assure you the bureau wouldn't have put you to all this bother if the matter wasn't most urgent."

Rheingold looked up at him. "Can you tell me what this is all about?"

"Afraid not."

"An Amtrak scandal. I bet you're investigating an Amtrak scandal."

"I can't say."

"A train robbery maybe. Must be pretty confidential. I haven't seen any mention on the six o'clock news."

"Might I ask if we can get on with it," Shaw said impatiently. "I'm in a bit of a rush."

"Okay, just asking," Rheingold said, disappointed.

He led the way down an aisle bordered by high shelves crammed with bound volumes on railroading, most of them long out of print. He stopped at the end of one bookcase containing large portfolios, peered through the bottom lenses of his bifocals and read the titles aloud.

"Let's see, track layouts for the New Haven & Hartford, the Lake Shore & Michigan Southern, Boston & Albany . . . ah, here it is, the New York & Quebec Northern." He carried the portfolio over to a table and untied the strings on the cover. "Great railroad in its day. Over two thousand miles of track. Ran a crack express called the *Manhattan Limited*. Any particular section of the track you're interested in?"

"I can find it, thank you," said Shaw.

"Would you like a cup of coffee? I can make some upstairs in the office. Only take a couple of minutes."

"You're a civilized man, Mr. Rheingold. Coffee sounds fine."

Rheingold nodded and walked back down the aisle. He paused and turned when he came to the doorway. Shaw was sitting at the table studying the faded and yellowing maps.

When he returned with the coffee, the portfolio was neatly tied and replaced in its proper niche on the shelf.

"Mr. Shaw?"

There was no answer. The library room was empty.

73

Pitt felt inspired and determined, even exhilarated.

A deep sense of knowing he had opened a door that had been overlooked for generations acted on him like a stimulant. With an optimism that was not there before, he stood in a small, empty pasture and waited for the two-engine jet to float in for a landing.

Under normal procedures the feat would have been impossible: the field was pockmarked by old tree stumps and riddled with dry gullies. The longest flat spot ran no more than fifty feet before ending at a moss-covered rock wall. Pitt had expected a helicopter and he began to wonder if the pilot had a death wish or had brought the wrong aircraft.

Then he watched in fascination as the wings and engines began to slowly tilt upward while the fuselage and tail remained horizontal. When they reached ninety degrees and were facing skyward the plane stopped its forward motion and began to settle to the uneven ground.

Soon after the wheels touched the grass, Pitt walked up to the cockpit door and opened it. A boyish face with freckles and red hair broke into a cheery grin.

"Morning. You Pitt?"

"That's right."

"Climb in."

Pitt climbed in, secured the door and sat in the copilot's seat. "This is a VTOL, isn't it?"

"Yeah," the pilot replied. "Vertical takeoff and landing, made in Italy, Scinletti 440. Nice little flier, finicky at times. But I sing Verdi to it and it's putty in my hands."

"You don't use a helicopter?"

"Too much vibration. Besides, vertical photography works best from a high-speed airplane." He paused. "By the way, the name's Jack Westler." He didn't offer to shake hands. Instead, he eased the throttles toward their stops, and the Scinletti began to rise.

At about two hundred feet, Pitt twisted in his seat and stared back at the wings as they turned horizontal again. The craft began increasing its forward speed and soon returned to level flight.

"What area would you like to photo-map?" asked Westler.

"The old railroad bed along the west bank of the Hudson as far as Albany."

"Not much left."

"You're familiar with it?"

"I've lived in the Hudson River valley all my life. Ever hear of the phantom train?"

"Spare me," Pitt replied in a weary tone.

"Oh . . . okay," Westler dropped the subject. "Where do you want to begin rolling the film?"

"Start at the Magee place." Pitt looked around the rear cabin. It was void of equipment. "Speaking of film. Where is the camera and its operator?"

"You mean cameras, plural. We use two, their lenses set at different angles for a binocular effect. They're mounted in pods under the fuselage. I operate them from here in the cockpit."

"What altitude will you fly?"

"Depends on the focal lenses. Altitude is computed mathematically and optically. We're set to make our run at ten thousand feet."

The view of the valley from above was heady. The landscape unfurled and spread to the horizons, crisp and green, crowned by spring clouds. From five thousand feet the river took on the shape of a huge python crawling through the hills, with low islands sometimes dotting the channel like stepping-stones in a small stream. A vineyard country here, and an orchard land, broken by an occasional dairy farm.

When the altimeter read ten thousand, Westler made a sweeping turn to slightly west of north. The *De Soto* crept beneath, looking like a tiny model in a diorama.

"Cameras are rolling," Westler announced.

"You make it sound like a movie production," said Pitt.

"Almost. Each picture overlaps the next by sixty percent. That way, one particular object will show up twice at slightly different angles with varied highlights. You can detect things that are invisible from ground level, remnants of man-made disturbances hundreds or even thousands of years old."

Pitt could see very clearly the scar of the track bed. Then it abruptly stopped and vanished into a field of alfalfa. He pointed downward.

"Suppose the target is completely obliterated?"

Westler peered through the windshield and nodded. "Okay, there's a case in point. When the land over the area of interest was used for agriculture, the vegetation will assume a subtle color difference due to elements foreign to the native soil composition. The change might be missed by the human eye, but the camera optics and enhanced color tone in the film will exaggerate features in the earth beyond reality."

In no time at all, it seemed to Pitt, they were approaching the southern outskirts of New York State's capital. He gazed down at the oceangoing cargo ships docked at the port of Albany. Acres of railroad tracks fanned out from the storage warehouses like a giant spider's web. Here the old railbed disappeared for good under the heavy foot of modern development.

"Let's make another run," said Pitt.

"Coming around," acknowledged Westler.

Five more times they swept the fading New York & Quebec Northern tracks, but the faint, fragile line through the countryside still looked solitary, undivided by discernible offshoots.

Unless the cameras spotted something he couldn't detect, the only hope he had of finding the *Manhattan Limited* was Heidi Milligan.

The maps had vanished from the portfolio in the railroad museum, and Heidi had no doubt who had stolen them.

Shaw had returned to the hotel later that night, and they had made fluid and gentle love until early morning. But when she awoke, he was gone. Too late she realized that he had listened in on her conversation with Admiral Sandecker.

More than once, during their lovemaking, she had thought of Pitt. It was very different with him. Pitt's style was consuming and savage and impelled her to respond with savage intensity. Their time in bed had been a competition, a tournament that she never won. Pitt had drowned her, left her floating in a haze of exhausted defeat. Deep down it galled her independent ego and her mind refused to accept his superiority, and yet her body hungered for it with sinful abandon.

With Shaw the act was tender and almost respectful, and she could control her responses. Together they nurtured each other; apart they were like two gladiators circling, scheming for an opening to defeat the other. Pitt always left her spent and with a feeling she'd been used. Shaw was using her too, only for a different purpose, but strangely it didn't seem to matter. She longed to come back to him like someone returning from a stormy voyage.

She sat back in a chair in the library room of the museum and closed her eyes. Shaw thought he had forced her into a dead end by stripping the records. But there were other sources of railroad lore, other archives, private collections or historical societies. Shaw knew she could not afford the time-consuming journeys to check them out. So now she had to think of another avenue to explore. And what Shaw couldn't know, couldn't project in his scheming mind, was that she wasn't trapped at all.

"Okay, Mr. Smart-Ass," she muttered to the silent bookshelves, "here's where you get yours."

She called over the yawning curator, who was still grumbling about inconsiderate FBI agents.

"I'd like to see your old dispatch records and logbooks."

He nodded cordially. "We have cataloged samplings of old dispatch material. Don't have them all, of course. Too voluminous to store. Just tell me what you want and I'll be happy to search it out for you."

Heidi told him, and by lunchtime she had found what she was looking for.

74

Heidi stepped off the plane at the Albany airport at four o'clock in the afternoon. Giordino was there waiting for her. She brushed off an offer of a wheelchair and insisted on walking on her crutches to the car.

"How are things going?" she asked as Giordino pulled the car into traffic and turned south.

"Doesn't look encouraging. Pitt was poring over aerial photographs when I left the boat. No trace of a branch track showed up anywhere.''

''I think I've found something.''

''We could damn well use a piece of luck, for a change,'' Giordino muttered.

''You don't sound enthusiastic.''

''My school spirit has been bled out of me.''

''Things that bad?''

''Figure it out. The President goes before the Canadian Parliament tomorrow afternoon. We're dead. No way in hell we'll come up with a treaty by then . . . even if one exists, which I doubt.''

''What does Pitt think?'' she asked. ''About the train being some-place else besides buried in the river, I mean?''

''He's convinced it never reached the bridge.''

''What do you believe?''

Giordino gazed expressionless down the road. Then he smiled. ''I believe it's a waste of breath to argue with Pitt.''

''Why, because he's stubborn?''

''No,'' Giordino answered. ''Because he's usually right.''

For hours Pit had stared through binocular glasses at the photo blowups, his brain interpreting the detail in three dimension.

The zigzag rail fences separating pastures from bordering wood-lands, the automobiles and houses, a red-and-yellow hot-air balloon that made a colorful splash against the green landscape—they were all revealed in amazing clarity. Even an occasional railroad tie could be distinguished on the weed-strewn track bed.

Time after time he retraced the almost arrow-straight line between the destroyed bridge and the outskirts of Albany's industrial section, his eyes straining to pick out a minute detail, the tiniest suggestion of an abandoned rail spur.

The secret stayed kept.

He finally gave in and was leaning back in a chair resting his eyes when Heidi and Giordino entered the *De Soto*'s chartroom. Pitt stood tiredly and embraced her.

''How's the leg?'' he asked.

''On the mend, thank you.''

They helped her to a chair. Giordino took her crutches and leaned them against a bulkhead. Then he set her briefcase on the deck beside her.

"Al tells me you've drawn a blank," she said.

Pitt nodded. "Looks that way."

"I have some more bad news for you."

He said nothing, waiting.

"Brian Shaw knows everything," she said simply.

Pitt read the embarrassment in her eyes. "Everything covers a lot of territory."

She shook her head in frustration. "He stole the maps of the old rail line from the museum before I had a chance to study them."

"Do him damned little good unless he'd got a clue to their value."

"I think he's guessed," Heidi said softly.

Pitt sat thoughtful for a moment, rejecting any attempt at cross-examining Heidi. The damage was done. How Shaw came to lay his hands on the key to the enigma no longer mattered. Incredibly, he felt a tinge of jealousy. And he couldn't help wondering what Heidi saw in the older man.

"Then he's in the area."

"Probably sneaking around the countryside this minute," added Giordino.

Pitt looked at Heidi. "The maps may be worthless to him. Nothing resembling a rail spur shows on the aerial photos."

She picked up the briefcase, set it in her lap and opened the locks. "But there *was* a rail spur," she said. "It used to cut off the main line at a place called Mondragon Hook Junction."

The atmosphere in the chartroom suddenly galvanized.

Pitt said, "Where is that?"

"I can't pinpoint it exactly without an old map."

Giordino quickly glanced through several topographical maps of the valley. "Nothing here, but these surveys only go back to nineteen sixty-five."

"How did you discover this Mondragon Hook?" asked Pitt.

"Elementary reasoning," Heidi shrugged. "I asked myself where I would hide a locomotive and seven Pullman cars where no one could find them for a lifetime. The only answer was underground. So I began working backward and checked old Albany dispatch records before nineteen fourteen. I hit pay dirt and found eight different freight trains that hauled ore cars loaded with limestone."

"Limestone?"

"Yes, the shipments originated from a junction called Mondragon Hook and were destined for a cement plant in New Jersey."

"When?"

"In the eighteen nineties."

Giordino looked skeptical. "This Mondragon Hook could have been hundreds of miles from here."

"It had to be below Albany," said Heidi.

"How can you be sure?"

"New York & Quebec Northern records don't list ore cars carrying limestone on any freight trains that passed through Albany. But I did run across a mention of them in a dispatch log from the Germantown rail yard where there was a switch of locomotives."

"Germantown," said Pitt. "That's fifteen miles downriver."

"My next step was to search through old geological maps," Heidi continued. She paused and slipped one from her briefcase and flattened it on the table. "The only underground limestone quarry between Albany and Germantown lay here." She made a mark with a pencil. "About nine miles north of the Deauville-Hudson bridge and three-quarters of a mile west."

Pitt put the binocular glasses to his eyes and began scanning the aerial photos. "Here, due east of the quarry site, is a dairy farm. The house and barnyard have erased all remains of the junction."

"Yes, I see it," Heidi said excitedly. "And there's a paved road that runs toward the New York State Thruway."

"Small wonder you lost the trail," Giordino said. "The county laid asphalt over it."

"If you look closely," said Pitt, "you can pick out a section of old rail ballast as it curves from the road for a hundred yards and ends at the foot of a steep hill, or mountain as the natives would label it."

Heidi peered through the binoculars. "Surprising how clear everything becomes when you know what to search for."

"Did you happen to turn up any information on the quarry?" Giordino asked her.

"That part was easy," Heidi nodded. "The property and the track right-of-way were owned by the Forbes Excavation Company, which operated the quarry from eighteen eighty-two until nineteen ten, when they encountered flooding. All operations were halted, and the land was sold to neighboring farmers."

"I hate to be a wet blanket," said Giordino. "But suppose the quarry was an open pit?"

Heidi gave him a considering look. "I see what you mean. Unless the Forbes Company mined the limestone from inside the mountain, there'd be no place to hide a train." She scanned the photo again. "Too much growth to tell for sure, but the terrain appears unbroken."

"I think we should scout it out," Pitt said.

"All right," Giordino agreed. "I'll drive you."

"No, I'll go alone. In the meantime, call Moon and get some more bodies up here—a platoon of marines, in case Shaw brings in reinforcements. And tell him to send us a mining engineer, a good one. Round up any old-timers around the countryside who might remember any strange goings-on at the quarry. Heidi, if you feel up to it, kick the local publishers out of bed and dig through old papers for any relevant news items that were pushed to the back pages by the Deauville-Hudson bridge collapse. I'll know better where we stand when I inspect the quarry."

"Not much time left," Giordino said gloomily. "The President makes his speech in nineteen hours."

"I don't have to be reminded." Pitt reached for his coat. "All that's left for us now is to get inside that mountain."

75

The sun had set and was replaced by a quarter moon. The evening air was crisp and sharp. From his vantage point high above the old quarry entrance Shaw could see the lights of villages and farms miles away. It was a fair and picturesque land, he thought idly.

The sound of a piston-engined plane intruded on the silent countryside. Shaw twisted around and looked skyward, but could see nothing. The plane was flying without nagivation lights. He judged by the sound of the engines that it was circling at only a few hundred feet above the hill. Here and there the light of a star was blotted by what Shaw knew were parachutes.

Fifteen minutes later, two shadows moved out of the trees below and climbed toward him. One of the men was Burton-Angus. The other was stockily built. In the darkness he could have passed for a huge rolling rock. His name was Eric Caldweiler, and he was former superintendent of a coal mine in Wales.

"How did it go?" Shaw asked.

"A perfect jump, I'd say," Burton-Angus replied. "They practically landed on top of my signal beam. The officer in command is a Lieutenant Macklin."

Shaw ignored one of the cardinal rules of undercover night operations and lit a cigarette. The Americans would know of their presence soon enough, he reasoned. "Did you find the quarry entrance?"

"You can forget about it," said Caldweiler. "Half the hillside slipped away."

"It's buried?"

"Aye, deeper than a Scotsman's whiskey cellar. The overburden is thicker than I care to think about."

Shaw said, "Any chance of digging through?"

Caldweiler shook his head. "Even if we had a giant dragline, you're talking two or three days."

"No good. The Americans could show up at any time."

"Might gain entry through the portals," said Caldweiler, stoking up a curved briar pipe. "Providing we can find them in the dark."

Shaw looked at him. "What portals?"

"Any heavily worked commercial mine requires two additional openings: an escape way in case the main entrance is damaged, and an air ventilation shaft."

"Where do we start searching?" Shaw asked anxiously.

Caldweiler was not to be rushed. "Well, let's see. I judge this to be a drift mine—a tunnel in the side of the hill where the outcropping broke the surface. From there the shaft probably followed the limestone bed on a downward slope. That would put the escape way somewhere around the base of the hill. The ventilator? Higher up, facing the north."

"Why north?"

"Prevailing winds. Just the ticket for cross-ventilation in the days before circulating fans."

"The air vent it is then," said Shaw. "It would be better hidden in the hillside woods and less exposed than the escape portal below."

"Not another safari up the mountain," Burton-Angus complained.

"Do you good," said Shaw, smiling. "Work off the fancy buffets of those embassy row parties.'' He mashed out the cigarette with his heel. ''I'll go and round up our helpers.''

Shaw turned and made his way into a heavy thicket near the base of the hill about thirty meters from the old rail spur. He tripped over a root at the edge of a ravine and fell, arms outstretched for the slamming impact. Instead, he rolled down a weed-blanketed slope and landed on his back in a bed of gravel.

He was lying there gasping, trying to get his knocked-out breath back, when a figure materialized above him, silhouetted against the stars, and touched the muzzle of a rifle to his forehead.

''I rather hope you're Mr. Shaw,'' a polite voice said.

''Yes, I'm Shaw,'' he managed to rasp.

''I'm pleased.'' The gun was pulled back. ''Let me help you up, sir.''

''Lieutenant Macklin?''

''No, sir, Sergeant Bentley.''

Bentley was dressed in a military black-and-gray camouflaged night smock with pants that tucked into paratroop-style boots. He wore a dark beret over his head and his hands and feet were the color of ink. He carried a netted steel helmet in one hand.

Another man stepped out of the darkness.

''A problem, sergeant?''

''Mr. Shaw had a bit of a tumble.''

''You Macklin?'' asked Shaw, getting his breath back.

A set of teeth gleamed brightly. ''Can't you tell?''

''Under that minstrel makeup you all look alike to me.''

''Sorry about that.''

''Have you accounted for your men?''

''All fourteen of us, sound and fit. Which is quite something for a jump in the dark.''

''I'll need you to look for a portal into the hill. Some sign of excavation or depression in the earth. Begin at the base of the hill and work toward the summit on the north side.''

Macklin turned to Bentley. ''Sergeant, gather the men and have them form a search line ten feet apart.''

''Yes, sir.'' Bentley took four steps and was swallowed up in the thicket.

''I was wondering,'' Macklin said idly.

''What?'' asked Shaw.

''The Americans. How will they react when they find an armed force of Royal Marine paratroopers entrenched in upstate New York?''

"Hard to say. The Americans have a good sense of humor.''

"They won't be laughing if we have to shoot a few of them.''

"When was the last time?'' Shaw muttered in thought.

"You mean since British men-at-arms invaded the United States?''

"Something like that.''

"I believe it was in eighteen hundred and fourteen when Sir Edward Parkenham attacked New Orleans.''

"We lost that one.''

"The Yanks were angry because we burned Washington.''

Suddenly they both tensed. They heard the roaring protest of a car engine as it was shifted into a lower gear. Then a pair of headlights turned off the nearby road onto the abandoned rail spur. Shaw and Macklin automatically dropped to a crouch and peered through the grass that grew on the lip of the ravine.

They watched the car bump over the uneven ground and come to a stop where the track bed disappeared under the slope of the hill. The engine went quiet and a man got out and walked in front of the headlights.

Shaw wondered what he would do when he met up with Pitt again. Should he kill the man? A hushed command to Macklin, even a hand signal, and Pitt would go down under a dozen knife thrusts from men who were trained in the art of silent murder.

Pitt stood for a long minute, staring up at the hill as if challenging it. He picked up a rock and threw it into the darkness of the slope. Then he turned and climbed back behind the steering wheel. The engine came to life and the car made a U-turn.

Only when the taillights became dim red specks did Shaw and Macklin stand up.

"I thought for a moment that you were going to order me to snuff the beggar,'' said Macklin.

"The thought crossed my mind,'' replied Shaw. "No sense in prodding a hornet's nest. Things should get warm enough come daylight.''

"Who do you suppose he was?''

"*That,*'' said Shaw slowly, "was the enemy.''

76

It was good to capture a moment of togetherness. Danielle looked radiant in a bareback dinner dress of green shadow-print silk chiffon. Her hair was center-parted and swept back with a comb of gilded flowers decorating one side. A gold spiral choker adorned her throat. The candlelight glinted in her eyes when she glanced across the table.

As the maid cleared the dishes, Sarveux leaned over and kissed her softly on one hand.

"Must you go?"

"I'm afraid so," she said, pouring him a brandy. "My new fall wardrobe is ready at Vivonnes, and I made an early appointment for tomorrow morning to have my final fittings."

"Why must you always fly to Quebec? Why can't you find a dressmaker in Ottawa?"

Danielle gave a little laugh and stroked his hair.

"Because I prefer the fashion designers in Quebec to the dressmakers of Ottawa."

"We never seem to have a moment alone."

"You're always busy running the country."

"I can't argue the point. However, when I do make time for you, you're always committed elsewhere."

"I'm the wife of the Prime Minister," she smiled. "I can't close my eyes and turn my back on the duties expected of me."

"Don't go," he said tonelessly.

"Surely you want me to look nice for our social engagements," she pouted.

"Where will you be staying?"

"Where I always stay when I spend the night in Quebec City . . . at Nanci Soult's townhouse."

"I'd feel better if you returned home in the evening."

"Nothing will happen, Charles." She bent down and kissed him lukewarmly on the cheek. "I'll be back tomorrow afternoon. We'll talk then."

"I love you, Danielle," he said quietly. "My dearest wish is to grow old with you by my side. I want you to know that."

Her only reply was the sound of a door shutting.

The townhouse was in Nanci Soult's name, a fact that was unknown to Nanci herself.

A best-selling novelist and a native Canadian, she lived in Ireland to beat the staggering taxes brought on by inflation. Her visits to family and friends in Vancouver were infrequent, and she had not set foot in Quebec in over twenty years.

The routine never varied.

As soon as the official car dropped Danielle at the townhouse and a Mountie was stationed outside the entrance gate, she went from room to room slamming doors, flushing the toilet and setting the FM radio dial on a station that broadcast soothing music.

When her presence was secure, she walked into a closet and parted the clothes, revealing a door that led into a seldom used stairwell in the adjoining building.

She hurried down the steps to a single-car, interior garage that opened on a back alley. Henri Villon waited punctually in his Mercedes-Benz. He reached over and embraced her as she leaned across the front seat.

Danielle relaxed for the automatic response of his kiss. But the show of affection was fleeting. He pushed her back and his expression turned businesslike.

"I hope this is important," he said. "It's becoming more difficult to break away."

"Can this be the same man who recklessly made love to me in the Prime Minister's mansion?"

"I wasn't about to be elected President of Quebec then."

She withdrew to her side of the car and sighed. She could sense that the excitement and passion of their clandestine meetings was fading. There was no illusion to be shattered. She had never kidded herself into believing their special relationship could go on forever. All that was left now was to bury the hurt and remain cordial, if not intimate friends.

"Shall we go somewhere?" he said, breaking her reverie.

"No, just drive around."

He pressed the button to the electric garage door opener and backed into the alley. The traffic was light as he drove down to the riverfront and joined a short line of cars waiting to board the ferry to the east shore.

Nothing more was said between them until Villon steered the Mercedes up the ramp and parked near the bow, where they had a view of the lights dancing on the St. Lawrence.

"We have a crisis on our hands," she said finally.

"Does it concern you and me or Quebec?"

"All three."

"You sound grim."

"I mean to be," she paused. "Charles is going to resign as Prime Minister of Canada and run for President of Quebec."

He turned and stared at her. "Repeat that."

"My husband is going to announce his candidacy for President of Quebec."

Villon shook his head in exasperation. "I can't believe he'd do it. That's the dumbest thing I've ever heard. Why? There's no rhyme or reason for such a stupid decision."

"I think it stems from anger."

"He hates me that much?"

She lowered her eyes. "I think he suspects something between us. Perhaps even knows. He may be out for revenge."

"Not Charles. He's not given to childish reactions."

"I was always so careful. He must have had me followed. How else could he have caught on?"

Villon tilted his head back and laughed. "Because I as good as told him."

"You didn't!" she gasped.

"To hell with that fastidious little toad. Let him stew in righteous self-pity for all I care. There's no way the sniffling bastard can win the election. Charles Sarveux has few friends in the Parti Québécois. The mainstream of support belongs to me."

The ferry dock was only a hundred meters away when a man got out of the fifth car behind Villon's Mercedes sedan and joined the passengers returning to the parking deck after lining the railings to enjoy the view.

Through the rear window he could see two profiles in conversation, muffled voices seeping from the rolled-up windows.

Casually he moved alongside the Mercedes, pulled open the rear door as if he owned the car, and slipped into the back seat.

"Madame Sarveux, Monsieur Villon, good evening."

Confusion swept Danielle's and Villon's faces, replaced with disbelieving shock, then fear when they saw the .44 magnum revolver held in a rocklike hand, slowly wavering from one head to the other and back again.

Villon had genuine reason for his astonishment.

He felt as though he was staring in a mirror.

The man in the rear seat was his exact double, a twin, a clone. He could see every detail of the face from the spotlights on the landing dock that shone through the windshield.

Danielle let out a low moan that would have worked its way into a hysterical scream if the gun barrel hadn't whipped across her cheek.

The blood sprang from the gash in her otherwise flawless skin and she sucked in her breath at the instant agony.

"I have no qualms about striking a woman, so please spare yourself any senseless resistance."

The voice was a precise imitation of Villon's.

"Who are you?" Villon demanded. "What do you want?"

"I'm flattered the original cannot tell the fake." The voice took on a new inflection, one that Villon recognized in a horror-stricken flash. "I'm Foss Gly, and I intend to kill you both."

77

A light drizzle began to fall and Villon turned on the windshield wipers. The gun muzzle was pressed into the nape of his neck, the pressure never easing since they left the ferryboat.

Danielle sat beside him, holding a blood-soaked handkerchief to her face. Every few minutes she made little strange noises in her throat. She looked like a woman lost in a nightmare, a woman numbed by terror.

All questions and pleas had been met by icy silence. Gly opened his mouth only to issue driving directions. They were rolling through a rural area now, marked by the lights of an occasional farmhouse. Villon had no recourse but to do as he was told. He could only hope and wait for an opportunity to act, to somehow gain the attention of a passing motorist, or with luck, a cruising policeman.

"Slow down," Gly ordered. "A dirt road is coming up on your left. Take it."

With a sinking dread, Villon turned off the highway. The road had been recently graded, and it appeared well traveled by heavy construction equipment.

"I thought you were dead," Villon said, trying for a response.

Gly did not answer.

"That British intelligence agent Brian Shaw said you crashed a stolen boat into the side of a Japanese cargo ship."

"Did he tell you my body was never found?"

At last he had Gly in a talking mood. That was a start.

"Yes, there was an explosion . . ."

"Tied down the helm, set the throttles to FULL and jumped clear five miles before the collision. With all the traffic on the St. Lawrence, I figured it was only a question of time before the boat struck another vessel."

"Why are you made up to look like me?"

"Isn't it obvious? After you're dead, I'm going to take your place. I, and not you, will be the new President of Quebec."

Five seconds passed before the staggering disclosure penetrated Villon's mind.

"In God's name, that's madness!"

"Madness? Not really. Smart brains, I'd call it."

"You'll never get away with such a crazy scheme."

"Ah, but I already have." Gly's tone was calm, conversational. "How do you think I walked through Jules Guerrier's front door, past his bodyguard up to his room and murdered him? I've sat at your desk, met most of your friends, discussed political differences with Charles Sarveux, made an appearance on the floor of the House of Commons. Why, hell, I've even slept with your wife and with your mistress up there on the front seat."

Villon was dazed. "Not true . . . not true . . . not my wife."

"Yes, Henri, it's all true. I can even describe her anatomy, beginning with . . ."

"No!" Villon cried. He slammed on the brakes and snapped the steering wheel to the right.

The fates turned their backs on Villon. The tires failed to grip the damp earth, and the violent reaction he expected, he hoped for, never happened. There was no savage body-snapping motion from centrifugal force. Instead, the car slid slowly around in lazy circles.

Keeping his balance, his aim only slightly diverted, Gly pulled the trigger.

The .44 magnum shell shattered Villon's collarbone and passed through the windshield.

A scream poured from Danielle's mouth, and then died away into terror-choked sobbing.

The car gradually came to a gentle stop in the wet grass beside the road. Villon's hands jerked from the steering wheel. He threw his head against the backrest of the seat, tightly gripped the gaping wound and clenched his teeth in pain.

Gly stepped outside and pulled open the driver's door. He roughly shoved Villon toward Danielle and climbed in.

"I'll take it from here," he snarled. He crammed the gun barrel into Villon's side under the armpit. "Don't get cute again."

To Danielle it looked as if half of Villon's upper shoulder had been blown away. She turned and vomited on the door panel.

Gly made a U-turn and returned to the road. In half a mile a huge yellow-painted earthmover appeared in the headlights. Beside it was an excavated ditch ten feet deep and fifteen feet across. A high mound of earth was piled up along the opposite side. As Gly drove along the edge, Danielle could make out a large concrete pipe that stretched along the bottom of the ditch.

They passed a silent row of trucks and earthmoving equipment. The engineer's office, a battered old converted house trailer, sat dark and empty. The construction crew had gone home for the night.

Gly pulled up at a place where the new drainage line was being covered over. He braked, judging the angle of the incline down to the roof of the pipe. Then he gunned the engine and drove the Mercedes into the ditch.

The front bumper struck the circular concrete and sprayed sparks. The rear end slewed around until the car came to rest on its side, the headlights on a slight angle upward.

Gly took two pairs of handcuffs from his coat pocket. He clamped one to the steering column and Villon's left hand. He repeated the process on Danielle with the other set.

"What are you doing?" Danielle asked in a hoarse whisper.

He paused to stare at her. The raven hair was messed and the beautiful features were marred by the bloody tear. The eyes were those of a doe paralyzed with fright.

A hideous grin spread across his face. "I'm fixing it so you and your lover can spend eternity together."

"No reason to murder her," Villon groaned through the agony. "For God's sake, let her go free."

"Sorry," said Gly callously. "She's part of the bargain."

"What bargain?"

There was no answer. Gly slammed the door and began climbing up the sloping embankment. He rapidly reached the top and disappeared into the darkness. A few minutes later they heard the sound of a heavy diesel engine knocking to life.

The engine began to strain as though it was working under a heavy load. The throaty roar of the exhaust drew closer and then a huge silver scoop crept out over the rim of the ditch. Suddenly it tilted downward and three-and-a-half cubic yards of dirt rained down around the roof of the Mercedes.

Danielle let out a pitiful cry.

"Oh, Mary, mother of Jesus . . . he's going to bury us alive . . . oh, no, please no!"

Gly coldly ignored the pitiful plea and shifted the front-end loader into reverse, angling the bucket for the next bite of earth. He knew the position of every lever, their use and how to activate them. For two nights he had practiced, filling sections of the ditch so expertly that the dirt-moving crew had never noticed that an extra twenty feet of the open pipeline had been filled for them between work shifts.

Danielle fought frantically to break the chain on her handcuffs. The flesh around her wrists was quickly chafed into bloody shreds.

"Henri!" Her cry had become a gagging whimper now. "Don't let me die, not like this."

Villon did not seem to hear. The end would come sooner for him. He knew he was only a few seconds away from bleeding to death.

"Odd," he whispered. "Odd that the last man to die for Quebec liberty is me. Who would have ever thought . . ." His voice faded away.

The car was almost completely covered. The only parts that still showed were a portion of the shattered windshield, the three-cornered star emblem on the hood and one headlight.

A figure moved to the edge of the embankment and stood in the light. It was not Foss Gly, but another man. He looked down: his face was frozen in deep sorrow, and tears glistened on his cheeks.

For a brief instant, Danielle stared at him in horror. Her color turned ghastly. She placed her free hand against the glass in a pleading gesture. Then slowly, her eyes mirrored an understanding look, and her mouth formed the words 'Forgive me'.

The bucket was tipped again, the dirt fell and all sight of the car was blotted out.

At last the ditch was filled to ground level, and the exhaust of the front-end loader died into the night.

Only then did a saddened Charles Sarveux turn and walk away.

78

The airfield at Lac St. Joseph, deep in the hills northeast of Quebec City, was one of several belonging to the Royal Canadian Air Force that had been shut down because of budget cuts. Its two-mile runway was off limits to commercial aircraft, but was still used by the military for training and emergency landings.

Henri Villon's plane stood in front of a weathered metal hangar. A fuel truck was parked beside it and two men in raincoats were making a preflight check. Inside, in an office bare of furniture except for a rusting metal workbench, Charles Sarveux and Commissioner Finn stood in silence and watched the proceedings through a dirty window. The earlier drizzle had turned into a driving rain that leaked through the roof of the hangar in a dozen places.

Foss Gly was stretched out comfortably on a blanket. His hands were clasped behind his head and he was oblivious to the water that splashed beside him on the cement floor. There was an air of smugness about him, of complacency almost, as he gazed up at the metal-beamed ceiling.

The Villon disguise was gone and he was himself again.

Outside, the pilot jumped from the wing to the ground and dog-trotted to the hangar. He poked his head in the office door.

''Ready when you are,'' he announced.

Gly came to a sitting position. "What did you find?"

"Nothing. We inspected every system, every square inch, even the quality of the gas and oil. Nobody's tampered with it. It's clean."

"Okay, start up the engines."

The pilot nodded and ducked back into the rain.

"Well, gentlemen," said Gly, "I guess I'll be on my way."

Sarveux silently nodded to Commissioner Finn. The Mountie set two large suitcases on the workbench and opened them.

"Thirty million well-worn Canadian dollars," said Finn, his face deadpan.

Gly pulled a jeweler's eyepiece from his pocket and began studying a random sampling of bills. After nearly ten minutes he repocketed the eyepiece and closed the suitcases.

"You weren't joking when you said 'well-worn.' Most of these bills are so wallet-battered you can hardly read the denominations."

"As per your instructions," Finn said testily. "It was no simple matter scraping up that much used currency on such short notice. I think you'll find them all negotiable."

Gly walked over to Sarveux and held out his hand. "Nice doing business with you, Prime Minister."

Sarveux rebuffed Gly's gesture. "I'm only happy we caught onto your imposter scheme in time."

Gly shrugged and withdrew his empty hand. "Who's to say? I might have made a damned good President, better maybe than Villon."

"Pure luck on my part that you didn't," said Sarveux. "If Commissioner Finn hadn't known Henri's exact whereabouts when you brazenly walked into my office, you might never have been apprehended. As it is, my sad regret is that I can't have your neck stretched on the gallows."

"A good reason why I keep records for insurance," Gly said contemptuously. "A chronological journal of my actions on behalf of the Free Quebec Society, tape recordings of my conversations with Villon, videotapes of your wife in wild postures with your minister of internal affairs. The stuff major scandals are made of. I'd say that's a fair exchange for my life."

"When will I get them?" Sarveux demanded.

"I'll send you directions to their hiding place after I'm safely out of your reach."

"What assurances do I have? How can I trust you not to keep blackmailing me?"

Gly grinned fiendishly. "None, none at all."

"You're filth," Sarveux hissed angrily. "The excretion of the earth."

"Are you any better?" Gly snapped back. "You stood mute in all your sanctity and watched while I wasted your political rival and your cheating wife. And then you had the gall to pay for the job with government funds. You stink even worse than I do, Sarveux. The best of the bargain was yours. So save your insults and sermons for the mirror."

Sarveux trembled, the rage seething inside him. "I think you better get out . . . get out of Canada."

"Gladly."

Sarveux got a mental hold on himself. "Goodbye, Mr. Gly, perhaps we'll meet in hell."

"We already have," grunted Gly.

He snapped the suitcases shut, carried them outside and entered the airplane. As the pilot taxied to the end of the runway, he relaxed in the main cabin and poured himself a drink.

Not bad, he thought, thirty million bucks and a jet airplane. Nothing like making an exit in style.

The phone on the bar buzzed and he picked it up. It was the pilot.

"We're ready for takeoff. Would you care to give me flight instructions now?"

"Head due south for the United States. Stay low to avoid radar. A hundred miles over the border, come to cruising altitude and set a course for Montserrat."

"Never heard of it."

"One of the Leeward Islands in the Lesser Antilles, southeast of Puerto Rico. Wake me when we get there."

"Sweet dreams, boss."

Gly slumped in his seat, not bothering to fasten the safety belt. At that moment he felt immortal. He grinned to himself as he gazed through the cabin window at the two figures silhouetted against the lights of the hangar.

Sarveux was a fool, he thought. If he had been in the Prime Minister's shoes he would have hidden a bomb in the plane, rigged it to crash, or perhaps ordered the air force to shoot it down. The latter was still a possibility, though a slim one.

But there was no bomb and all the flight controls checked out from nose to tail.

He had done it. He was home free.

As the aircraft picked up speed and disappeared into the rainy night, Sarveux turned to Finn.

"How will it happen?"

"The automatic pilot. Once it's engaged the plane will begin a very gradual climb. The altimeters have been set to register no higher than 11,000 feet. The pressurization system and the emergency oxygen will not come on. By the time the pilot realizes something is wrong, it will be too late."

"Can't he disengage the autopilot?"

Finn shook his head. "The circuitry has been reset. He could beat the unit with an ax, but it would do no good. It is impossible for him to regain control of the aircraft."

"So they lose consciousness from loss of oxygen."

"And eventually come down in the ocean when they run out of fuel."

"They could crash on land."

"A calculated gamble," Finn explained. "Figuring the plane's range on full fuel tanks, and assuming Gly intends to fly as far away as possible before landing, it's eight to one they hit water."

Sarveux looked pensive for a moment. "The press releases?" he asked.

"Written and waiting to be handed to the wire services."

Commissioner Finn raised an umbrella and they began walking to the Prime Minister's limousine. Puddles were forming in the low spots of the taxi strip. One of Finn's men turned off the lights to the hangar and runway.

At the car Sarveux paused and looked up into the ebony sky as the last hum of the jet engines melted into the rain.

"Too bad Gly will never know how he was outsmarted. I think he would have appreciated that."

The next morning the following story ran on the international wire services.

OTTAWA, 6/10 (Special).— A plane carrying Danielle Sarveux and Henri Villon crashed in the Atlantic Ocean this morning 200 miles northeast of Cayenne, French Guiana.

The wife of Canada's Prime Minister and the presidential candidate for newly independent Quebec took off from Ottawa for a flight to Quebec City last night, and when they failed to make their scheduled landing the alert was given.

Villon was piloting his own plane and Madame Sarveux was the only passenger on board. All radio contact went unanswered.

Because Canadian air controllers did not immediately suspect the twin jet Albatross had flown into the United States, hours were lost on a fruitless search between Quebec and Ottawa. Not until an Air France Concorde reported an aircraft flying erratically south of Bermuda at 55,000 feet, 8000 feet above the maximum altitude for which Villon's Albatross was certified, did anyone begin to make a connection.

U.S. Navy jets were scrambled from the carrier *Kitty Hawk* near Cuba. Lieutenant Arthur Hancock was the first to spot the Albatross and reported seeing a man motionless at the controls. He followed until the plane went into a slow spiral dive and plunged into the ocean.

"We have no firm grasp on the cause," Ian Stone, a spokesman for Canadian Air Authority, said. "The only theory that makes any sort of sense is that Madame Sarveux and Mr. Villon became unconscious from lack of oxygen and that the plane, on autopilot, had flown itself over 3000 miles off course before running out of fuel and crashing." A search revealed no sign of wreckage.

Prime Minister Charles Sarveux remained in seclusion during the ordeal and had no comment.

79

An early morning mist quilted the Hudson Valley, cutting visibility to fifty yards. On the opposite side of the hill from the covered entrance of the quarry, Pitt had set up a command post in a motor home borrowed from a nearby fruit farmer. Ironically, neither he nor Shaw was aware of the other's exact location, although they were separated by only a mile of heavily forested hillside.

Pitt felt groggy from too much coffee and too little sleep. He longed for a healthy slug of brandy to clear the cobwebs, but he knew that would be a mistake. As inviting as it sounded, he was afraid it would cause a reverse reaction and slow his thinking, and that was the last thing he needed now.

He stood in the doorway of the motor home and watched Nicholas Riley and the diving team from the *De Soto* unload their gear while

Glen Chase and Al Giordino hovered over a heavy iron grating that was embedded in a rock-walled side of the hill. There was a popping sound when they lit an acetylene torch, followed by a spray of sparks as the blue flame attacked the rusted bars.

"I won't guarantee that opening behind the grating is an escape shaft," said Jerry Lubin. "But I'd have to say it's a safe bet."

Lubin had arrived a few hours earlier from Washington and was accompanied by Admiral Sandecker. A mining consultant with the Federal Resources Agency, Lubin was a small, humorous man with a pawnbroker nose and bloodhound eyes.

Pitt turned and looked at him. "We found it where you said it'd be."

"An educated guess," said Lubin. "If I had been mine superintendent, that's where I would have put it."

"Somebody went to a lot of work to keep people out," said Sandecker.

"The farmer who once owned the land." This from Heidi, who was perched on an overhead bunk.

"Where did you come by that tidbit?" asked Lubin.

"A kindly editor, a female I might add, got out of her boyfriend's bed to open local newspaper files for me. The story is that about thirty years ago, three scuba divers drowned inside the shaft. Two of their bodies were never found. The farmer sealed up the entrance to keep people from killing themselves on his property."

"Did you find anything about the landslide?" Pitt asked her.

"A dead end. All files prior to nineteen forty-six were destroyed by a fire."

Sandecker pulled at his red beard thoughtfully. "I wonder how far those poor bastards got before they drowned."

"Probably made it to the main quarry and ran out of air on the return trip," Pitt speculated.

Heidi spoke the same thought that suddenly crossed everyone's mind. "Then they must have seen whatever is in there."

Sandecker gave Pitt a worried look. "I don't want you to make the same mistake."

"The victims were undoubtedly weekend divers, untrained and underequipped."

"I'd feel better if there was an easier way."

"The air vent is a possibility," said Lubin.

"Of course!" Sandecker exclaimed. "Any underground mine needs air ventilation."

"I didn't mention it before because it would take forever to find it in this fog. Besides, whenever a mine is closed, the air portal is filled in and covered over. There's always the hazard of a cow or a human, especially a child, falling in and vanishing."

A knowing look crossed Pitt's face. "I have a feeling that's where we'll find our friend Brian Shaw."

Lubin stared quizzically. "Who's he?"

"A competitor," said Pitt. "He wants to get inside that hill as badly as we do."

Lubin gave an offhand shrug. "Then I don't envy him. Digging through a portal shaft the width of a man's shoulders is a bitch of a job."

Lubin would have got no argument from the British.

One of Lieutenant Macklin's men had literally stumbled and fallen on the scar in the earth that hid the ventilator shaft. Since midnight the paratroops had been feverishly laboring to clear the rubble-filled passage.

The work was backbreaking. Only one man at a time could dig in the narrow confines. Cave-in was a constant threat. Buckets hastily stolen from a neighboring orchard were filled and pulled to the surface by ropes. Then they were emptied and dropped for the next load. The mole dug as fast and as hard as he could. When he was ready to drop from exhaustion, he was quickly replaced. The excavation went on without pause.

"What depth are we?" asked Shaw.

"About forty feet," replied Caldweiler.

"How much further?"

The Welshman furrowed his brow thoughtfully. "I judge we should strike the main quarry in another hundred and twenty feet. How deep the ventilator was filled, I can't say. We could break through in the next foot or we might have to fight to the last inch."

"I'll settle for the next foot," said Macklin. "This mist isn't going to shield us much longer."

"Any sign of the Americans?"

"Only the sound of vehicles somewhere behind the hill."

Shaw lit another of his special cigarettes. It was his last one. "I should have thought they'd be swarming over the hillside before now."

"They'll get a jolly hot reception when they show," said Macklin, almost cheerfully.

"I hear American jails are overcrowded," Caldweiler muttered. "I don't relish spending the rest of my life in one."

Shaw grinned. "Should be a piece of cake for a man of your experience to tunnel out."

Caldweiler knocked the ashes out of his pipe. "Nothing like looking at the fun side. Though in all seriousness, I can't help wondering what in bloody hell I'm doing here."

"You volunteered like the rest of us," Macklin said.

Shaw exhaled a lungful of smoke. "If you live long enough to return to England, the Prime Minister himself will pin a medal on you."

"All for tearing up a scrap of paper?"

"That scrap of paper is more important than you'll ever know."

"For what it's going to cost us in blood and sweat, it'd damned well better be," groused Caldweiler.

A small convoy of armored personnel carriers rolled to a stop. An officer in battle dress leaped from the lead vehicle and shouted an order. A stream of marines, clutching automatic weapons, poured to the ground and began assembling in squads.

The officer, who had an eye for authority, walked straight up to the admiral.

"Admiral Sandecker?"

Sandecker fairly beamed at the recognition. "At your service."

"Lieutenant Sanchez." The arm snapped in a salute. "Third Marine Force Reconnaissance."

"Glad to see you." Sandecker returned the salute.

"My orders were unclear as to our deployment."

"How many men do you have?"

"Three squads. Forty including myself."

"All right, one squad to cordon off the immediate area, two to patrol the woods around the hill."

"Yes, sir."

"And Lieutenant. We don't know what to expect. Tell your men to tread with a light foot."

Sandecker turned and walked to the escape shaft. The last bar of the grating had been cut away. The diving team stood ready to pierce the heart of the hill. A curious silence fell over everyone. They all stared at the black opening as though it was a sinister doorway to hell.

Pitt had donned an exposure suit and was cinching the harness of his air tank. When he was satisfied everything was in order, he nodded to Riley and the dive team.

"Okay. Let's make a night probe."

Sandecker looked at him. "A night probe?"

"An old diver's term for exploring the dark of underwater caves."

Sandecker looked grim. "Take no chances and stay healthy . . ."

"Keep your fingers crossed I find the treaty in there."

"Both hands. The other is in case Shaw gets in before you do."

"Yes," said Pitt wryly. "There is always that."

Then he entered the beckoning portal and was swallowed up in blackness.

80

The old escape route from the main quarry sloped downward into the bowels of the hill. The walls were seven feet high and showed the scars from the miners' picks. The air was moist with the faint but ominous smell of a mausoleum. After about twenty yards, the passageway curved and all light was lost from the outside.

The dive lights were switched on, and Pitt, followed by Riley and three men, continued on, their footsteps echoing into the eternal darkness ahead.

They passed an empty ore car, its small iron wheels joined in rusting bond to narrow rails. Several picks and shovels stood neatly stacked in a chiseled niche as though waiting for calluosed hands to grasp their handles again. Nearby were other artifacts: a broken miner's lamp, a sledgehammer and the faded, stuck-together pages of a Montgomery Ward catalog. The pages were frozen open on advertisements displaying upright player pianos.

A jumble of fallen rocks blocked their way for twenty minutes until they cleared a path. Everyone kept a suspicious eye trained on the rotting timbers that sagged under the weight of the crumbling roof. No word was spoken while they worked. The uncommunicated fear of being crushed by a cave-in chilled their minds. Finally they wormed their way past the barrier and found the tunnel floor covered by several inches of water.

When their knees became submerged, Pitt stopped and held up a hand. "The water level will be over our heads before long," he said. "I think the safety team better set up operations here."

Riley nodded. "I agree."

The three divers, who were to remain behind in case of an emergency, began stacking the reserve air tanks and securing the end of an orange fluorescent cord that was wound around a large reel. As they arranged the gear, the dive lights danced spasmodically on the passage walls, and their voices seemed alien and magnified.

When Pitt and Riley had removed their hiking boots and replaced them with swim fins, they grabbed hold of the reel and continued on, unwinding the safety line as they went.

The water soon came to their waists. They halted to adjust their face masks and clamp their teeth on the mouthpieces of the air regulators. Then they dropped into the liquid void.

Below the surface it was cold and gloomy. Visibility was amazingly sharp, and Pitt felt a shiver of almost superstitious awe when he spied a tiny salamander whose eyes had degenerated to the point of total blindness. He marveled that any kind of life form could exist in such entombed isolation.

The quarry's escape shaft seemed to stretch downward like a great sloping, bottomless pit. There was something malignant about it, as though some cursed and unmentionable force lurked in the shadowy depths beyond the beams of the dive lights.

After ten minutes by Pitt's dive watch they stopped and took stock. Their depth gauges registered 105 feet. From beneath his face mask Pitt's eyes studied Riley. The divemaster made a brief check of his air pressure gauge and then nodded an okay to keep going.

The shaft began to widen into a cavern and the sides turned a dirty gold color. They had finally passed into a gallery of the limestone quarry. The floor leveled out and Pitt noted that the depth had slowly risen to sixty feet. He aimed his light upward. The beam reflected on what looked like a blanket of quicksilver. He ascended like a ghost in flight and suddenly broke into air.

He had surfaced in an air pocket below the ceiling of a large domed chamber. A crowd of stalactites fell around him like icicles, their conical tips ending inches above the water. Too late, Pitt ducked under to warn Riley.

Unable to see because of the surface reflection, Riley rammed his face mask into the tip of a stalactite, shattering the glass. The bridge of his nose was gashed and his eyelids were sliced. He would not know until later that the lens of his left eye was gone.

Pitt threaded his way through the cone-shaped trunks and gripped Riley under the arms.

"What happened?" Riley mumbled. "Why are the lights out?"

"You met the wrong end of a stalactite," said Pitt. "Your dive light is broken. I lost mine."

Riley did not buy the lie. He removed a glove and felt his face. "I'm blind," he said matter-of-factly.

"Nothing of the sort." Pitt eased off Riley's mask and gently picked away the larger glass fragments. The divemaster's skin was so numb from the icy water that he felt no pain.

"What rotten luck. Why me?"

"Stop complaining. A couple of stitches and your ugly mug will be as good as new."

"Sorry to screw things up. I guess this is as far as we go."

"You go."

"You're not heading back?"

"No, I'm pushing on."

"How's your air?"

"Ample."

"You can't kid an old pro, buddy. There's barely enough left to reach the backup team. You keep going and you forfeit your round-trip ticket to the surface."

Pitt tied the safety line around a stalactite. Then he clamped Riley's hand on it.

"Just follow the yellow brick road, and mind your head."

"A comedian you ain't. What do I tell the admiral? He'll castrate me when he learns I left you here."

"Tell him," Pitt said with a tight grin, "I had to catch a train."

Corporal Richard Willapa felt right at home stalking the damp woods of New York. A direct descendant of the Chinook Indians of the Pacific Northwest, he had spent much of his youth tracking game in the rain forests of Washington State, honing the skills that enabled him to approach within twenty feet of a wild deer before the animal sensed his presence and darted away.

His experience came in handy as he read the signs of recent human passage. The footprints had been made by a short man, he judged, wearing a size seven combat boot similar to his own. Moisture from the mist had not yet redampened the impressions, an indication to Willapa's trained eye that they were no more than half an hour old.

The tracks came from the direction of a thicket and stopped at a tree, then they returned. Willapa noted with amusement the thin wisp of vapor that rose from the tree trunk. Someone had walked from the thicket, relieved himself and walked back again.

He looked around at his flanks, but none of his squad was visible. His sergeant had sent him out to scout ahead and the rest had not caught up yet.

Willapa stealthily climbed into the crotch of a tree and peered into the thicket. From his vantage point in height he could see the outline of a head and shoulders hunched over a fallen log.

"All right," he shouted, "I know you're in there. Come out with your hands up."

Willapa's answer was a hail of bullets that flayed the bark off the tree below him.

"Christ almighty!" he muttered in astonishment. No one had told him he might be shot at.

He aimed his weapon, pulled the trigger and sprayed the thicket.

The firing on the hill intensified and echoed through the valley. Lieutenant Sanchez snatched up a field radio. "Sergeant Ryan, do you read?"

Ryan answered almost immediately. "Ryan here, go ahead, sir."

"What in hell is going on up there?"

"We stumbled on a hornet's nest," Ryan replied jerkily. "It's like the Battle of the Bulge. I've already taken three casualties."

Sanchez was stunned by the appalling news. "Who's firing on you?"

"They ain't no farmers with pitchforks. We're up against an elite outfit."

"Explain."

"We're being hit with assault rifles by guys who damn well know how to use them."

"We're in for it now," Shaw shouted, ducking his head as a continuous burst of fire raked the leaves above. "They're coming at us from the rear."

"No amateurs, those Yanks," Macklin yelled back. "They're biding their time and whittling us down."

"The longer they wait, the better." Shaw crawled over to the pit where Caldweiler and three others were still frantically digging, oblivious to the battle going on around them.

"Any chance of breaking through?"

"You'll be the first to know when we do," the Welshman grunted. The sweat was pouring down his face as he hauled up a bucket containing a large boulder. "We're near seventy feet down. I can't tell you any more than that."

Shaw ducked suddenly as a bullet ricocheted off the rock in Caldweiler's hands and took away the left heel of his boot.

"You better lay low till I call you," Caldweiler said calmly, as though remarking about the weather.

Shaw got the message. He dropped down into the shelter of a shallow depression beside Burton-Angus, who looked to be enjoying himself returning the fire that blasted out of the surrounding woods.

"Hit anything?" asked Shaw.

"Sneaky bastards never show themselves," said Burton-Angus. "They learned their lessons in Vietnam."

He rose to his knees and fired a long leisurely burst into a dense undergrowth. His answer was a rain of bullets that hammered into the ground around him. He abruptly jerked upright and fell back without a sound.

Shaw crouched over him. Blood was beginning to seep from three evenly spaced holes across his chest. He looked up at Shaw, the brown eyes beginning to dull, the face already turning pale.

"Bloomin' queer," he rasped. "Getting shot on American soil. Who would have believed it . . ." The eyes went unseeing and he was gone.

Sergeant Bentley slipped through the brush and looked down, his expression granite. "Too many good men are dying today," he said slowly. Then his face hardened and he cautiously peered over the top of the embankment. The fire that killed Burton-Angus, he judged, came from an elevation. He spotted a perceptible movement high in the leaves. He set his rifle on semiautomatic fire, took careful aim and ripped off six shots.

He watched with grim satisfaction as a body slipped slowly out of a tree and crumpled to the moist ground.

Corporal Richard Willapa would never again stalk the deer of his native rain forest.

81

Soon after the shooting had broken out, Admiral Sandecker put in an emergency radio call for doctors and ambulances from the local hospitals. The response was almost immediate. Sirens were soon heard approaching in the distance as the first of the walking wounded began filtering down from the hillside.

Heidi limped from man to man applying temporary first aid, offering words of comfort while fighting back the tears. The worst thing was their incredible youth. None of them looked as if they had seen their twentieth birthdays. Their faces were pale with shock. They had never expected to bleed or even die on their home ground, fighting an enemy they had yet to even see.

She happened to look up as Riley came out of the escape portal, led by two members of the diving team, his face masked in blood. A sickening fear rose within her when she saw no sign of Pitt.

Dear God, she thought wildly, *he's dead.*

Sandecker and Giordino noticed them at the same time and rushed over.

"Where's Pitt?" Sandecker asked, fearful of the answer.

"Still in there somewhere," Riley mumbled. "He refused to turn back. I tried, Admiral. Honest to God, I tried to talk him out of going on, but he wouldn't listen."

"I would have expected no less of him," Sandecker said lifelessly.

"Pitt is not the kind of man to die." Giordino's expression was set, his tone resolute.

"He had a message for you, Admiral."

"What message?"

"He said to tell you he had a train to catch."

"Maybe he made it into the main quarry," Giordino said, suddenly hopeful.

"Not a chance," said Riley, putting a dampener on any optimism. "His air must be gone by now. He's surely drowned."

Death in the stygian blackness of a cavern deep inside the earth is something nobody cares to think about. The idea is too foreign, too horrible to dwell on. Lost and trapped divers have been known to have literally shredded their fingertips to the bone, trying to claw their way through a mile of rock. Others simply gave up, believing they had re-entered the womb.

The last thing on Pitt's mind was dying. The mere thought was enough to instill panic. He concentrated on conserving his air and fighting against disorientation, the ever-present specter of cave divers.

The needle on his air pressure gauge quivered on the final mark before EMPTY. How much time did he have? One minute, two, perhaps three before he inhaled on a dry tank?

His fin accidentally kicked up a blinding cloud of silt that effectively smothered the beam of his light. He hung motionless, barely making out the direction of his air bubbles past the face mask. He followed them upward until he emerged into clear water again, and then began fly-walking across the ceiling of the cavern, pulling himself along with his fingertips. It was a strange sensation, almost as if gravity didn't exist.

A fork in the passage loomed out of the darkness. He could not afford the luxury of a time-consuming decision. He rolled over and kicked into the one on the left. Suddenly the light ray fell on a torn and rotting wet suit lying in the silt. He moved toward it cautiously. At first glance it appeared wrinkled and collapsed, as if its owner had dis-carded it. The light traveled up the legs and across the sunken chest area and stopped at the face mask, still strapped around the hood. A pair of empty eye sockets in a skull stared back at Pitt.

Startled, he began pedaling backward from the gruesome sight. The body of one of the lost divers had saved his life, or at least extended it for a brief space in time. The passage had to be a dead end. The bones of the second diver were probably somewhere deep within the gloom.

At the fork again, Pitt rechecked his compass. It was a wasted gesture. There was no place to go but to his right. He had already dropped the cumbersome safety reel. His air time was long past the point of no return.

He tried to contain his breathing, conserving his air, but already he could sense the lessening pressure. There were only a few precious breaths left now.

His mouth was very dry. He found he could not swallow, and he became very cold. He had been in the frigid water a long time and he recognized the initial symptoms of hypothermia. A strange calm settled over him as he swam deeper into the beckoning gloom.

Pitt accepted the last intake of air as inevitable and shrugged off the useless air bottles, letting them drop into the silt. He did not feel the pain when he bashed his knee on a pile of rock. A minute was all that was left to him. That was as far as the air in his lungs would take him. An abhorrence of ending up like the divers in the other passage flooded his mind. A vision of the empty skull loomed ahead, taunting him.

His lungs ached savagely, his head began to feel as if a fire was raging inside. He swam on, not daring to stop until his brain ceased to function.

Something glinted up the passage in the light. It seemed miles away. Darkness crept into the fringes of his vision. His heart pounded in his ears and his chest felt as though it was being crushed. Every atom of oxygen in his lungs was gone.

The final desperate moments closed in on him. His night probe had ended.

82

Slowly but relentlessly the net tightened as Macklin's dwindling force fought on. The bodies of the dead and wounded lay amid a sea of spent cartridge casings.

The sun had burned away the mist. They could see their targets better now, but so could the men surrounding them. There was no fear. They knew their chances of escape were impossible from the start. Fighting far from the shores of their island fortress was nothing new to British fighting men.

Macklin hobbled over to Shaw. The lieutenant had his left arm in a bloodstained sling and a foot wrapped in an equally bloody bandage.

"I'm afraid we've run our course, old man. We can't keep them back much longer."

"You and your men have done a glorious job," said Shaw. "Far more than anyone expected."

"They're good boys, they did their best," Macklin said wearily. "Any chance of breaking through that bloody hole?"

"If I ask Caldweiler one more time how he's doing, he'll probably bash my brains out with a shovel."

"Might as well toss a charge down there and forget it."

Shaw stared at him thoughtfully for a moment. Then suddenly he scrambled over to the edge of the pit. The men hauling up the buckets looked as if they were ready to drop from exhaustion. They were drenched in sweat and their breath came in great heaves.

"Where's Caldweiler?" asked Shaw.

"He went down himself. Said no one could dig faster than him."

Shaw leaned over the edge. The air shaft had curved and the Welshman was out of sight. Shaw yelled his name.

A lump of dirt shaped like a man came into view far below. "What now, damn it?"

"Our time has run out," Shaw's voice reverberated down the shaft. "Any chance of blowing through with explosives?"

"No good," Caldweiler shouted up. "The walls will cave in."

"We've got to risk it."

Caldweiler sank to his knees in total exhaustion. "All right," he said hoarsely. "Throw down a charge. I'll give it a try."

A minute later, Sergeant Bentley lowered a satchel containing plastic explosives. Caldweiler gently tapped the pliable charges into deep probe holes, set the fuses and signaled to be pulled to the surface. When he came into reach, Shaw took him under the arms and dragged him free of the pit entrance.

Caldweiler was appalled by the scene of carnage around him. Out of Macklin's original force, only four men were unwounded, yet they still kept up a vicious fire into the woods.

The ground suddenly rumbled beneath them and a cloud of dust spewed from the air shaft. Caldweiler immediately went back in. Shaw could hear him coughing, but his eyes could not penetrate the swirling haze.

"Did the walls hold?" Shaw yelled.

There was no answer. Then he felt a tug on the rope and he began pulling like a madman. His arms felt as if they were about to drop off when Caldweiler's dust-encrusted head popped up.

He sputtered incoherently for a moment and finally cleared his throat. "We're in," he gasped. "We've broken through. Hurry, man, before you get yourself shot."

Macklin was there now. He shook Shaw's hand. "If we don't see each other again, all the best."

"Same to you."

Sergeant Bentley handed him a flashlight. "You'll need this, sir."

Caldweiler had knotted three ropes together, increasing the length. "This should see you to the floor of the quarry," he said. "Now, in you go."

Shaw dropped into the pit and began his descent. He paused briefly and looked up.

The dust from the explosion had not settled, and all view of the anxious faces above was obscured.

On the perimeter's rim, Lieutenant Sanchez' men still crouched behind trees and rocks, maintaining an intense rate of fire into the thicket-covered gully. Since the first shots he had lost one dead and eight wounded. He also had been hit, a bullet passing through his thigh and out again. He tore off his battle jacket and wrapped the entry and exit holes with his undershirt.

"Their fire has slackened," commented Sergeant Hooper, between spits of tobacco.

"It's a miracle any of them are still alive in there," Sanchez said.

"Nobody fights that hard but fanatical terrorists."

"They're well trained. I have to hand them that." He hesitated, listening. Then he scratched an ear and peered between two large boulders that shielded him. "Listen!"

Hooper's brow furrowed. "Sir?"

"They've stopped firing."

"Could be a trick to sucker us in."

"I don't think so," said Sanchez. "Pass the word to cease fire."

Soon a strange silence settled over the battle-scarred woods. Then slowly a man rose out of the thicket, his rifle held high over his head.

"Son of a bitch," Hooper muttered. "He's wearing full battle dress."

"Probably bought it at war surplus."

"Smug-looking bastard."

Sanchez rose to his feet and casually lit a cigarette. "I'm going in. If he so much as picks his nose, cut him in two."

"Stay off to the side, sir, so we have a direct line of fire."

Sanchez nodded and walked forward. He stopped a yard or two away from Sergeant Bentley and looked him over. He noted the blackened face, the netted helmet with the twigs sticking out of it and the enlisted man's insignia. There was no trace of fear in the face. In fact, there was a spreading smile.

"Good morning to you, sir," greeted Bentley.

"You in charge here?"

"No, sir. If you will please follow me, I'll take you to him."

"Are you surrendering?"

Bentley nodded. "Yes, sir."

Sanchez leveled his rifle "Okay, after you."

They stepped through the bushes defoliated by bullets and into the gully. Sanchez' eyes took in the scattered bodies, the gore-sopped earth. The wounded stared back at him with indifferent interest. Three men who looked unscathed snapped to attention.

"Straighten up the line, lads," said Bentley sternly.

Sanchez was at a loss. These men didn't fit the picture of terrorists, not any he'd seen or heard about. They appeared to be uniformed soldiers, highly disciplined and trained for combat. Bentley led him up to two men resting beside an excavated hole in the ground. The one who looked like he'd been rolling in dirt for a detergent commercial was bent over the other, cutting away a boot that was filled with blood. The man stretched beside him on the ground gazed up at Sanchez' approach and threw a jaunty salute.

"Good morning."

A cheerful lot, thought Sanchez. "Are you in command here?"

"Yes indeed," replied Macklin. "May I have the honor of your name, sir?"

"Lieutenant Richard Sanchez, United States Marine Corps."

"Then it's diamond cut diamond. I'm Lieutenant Digby Macklin of Her Majesty's Royal Marines."

Sanchez stood there open-mouthed. All he could think of to mumble was "Well, I'll be damned."

The first thing Shaw noticed as he eased himself down the ventilator shaft was the dank and musty stench that welled up to meet him. After about twenty yards he could no longer reach out with his feet and touch the encircling earth walls. He clutched the rope in a near death grip and beamed his light into the dark.

Shaw had dropped into a vast cavern, at least forty feet from floor to ceiling. It was empty except for a large pile of debris in one corner. The rope ended twelve feet from the ground. He shoved the flashlight under his armpit, took a deep breath and released his grip.

He fell like a pebble falling down a well through the blackness, a frightening experience he would never care to repeat.

A gasp was squeezed from his lungs when he landed. He should have struck clean, his legs taking most of the impact. But when he fell to one side, his outflung wrist smashed against something hard, and he heard the sickening crack as it fractured.

Shaw sat there for two or three minutes, lips tightened in agony, feeling sorry for himself. Finally, he snapped abruptly to his senses, realizing it was only a question of minutes before the Americans would be coming down the air shaft and struggled to a sitting position.

Groping in his waist for the flashlight, he pushed the switch. Thank God, it still worked.

He found himself next to railroad tracks of a narrow gauge that ran from the cavern into a tunnel carved at one end.

Awkwardly he one-handedly slipped off his belt and made a crude sling, then rose to his feet and struck out along the track into the tunnel.

He walked between the rails, careful not to trip on the raised ties. The tracks ran level for fifty yards and then started to slant up a slight incline. After a while he stopped and played the beam into the darkness ahead.

What seemed like two monstrous red eyes reflected back at him.

Cautiously he moved forward, stubbed his toe against something solid, looked down and saw another set of rails. They were spiked at a much wider gauge, even wider than the ones British trains ran on, Shaw judged. He came out of the tunnel into another cavern.

But this was not an ordinary cavern. This was an immense crypt filled with dead.

The red eyes were two lanterns mounted on the rear of a railroad car. On the observation platform were two bodies, mummies really, still fully clothed, their blackened skulls staring into the eternal dark.

The hair on the back of Shaw's head raised and he forgot about the stabbing ache in his wrist. Pitt had been right. The underground quarry had yielded the secret of the *Manhattan Limited*.

He glanced around, half expecting to see a shrouded figure holding a scythe, beckoning with a bony finger, beckoning for Shaw. He passed alongside the coach, noting that it was surprisingly free of rust. At the boarding steps, where the next car was coupled, another grotesque bundle lay, its head propped against the six-wheeled truck. Out of morbid curiosity, Shaw stopped and studied it.

Under the flashlight the skin showed a dark brownish-gray color and had the consistency of leather. As the months and years passed, the body had desiccated and hardened and become naturally mummified by the dry air of the quarry. The round visored cap still resting on the head indicated that this man had been the conductor.

There were others, scores of them, scattered around the train, frozen in the final posture of death. Most had died sitting up; a few were lying outstretched. Their clothing was in a remarkable state of preservation and Shaw had no trouble telling the men from the women.

Several of the dead were stiffened in warped positions below the open door to the baggage car. In front of them a jumbled stack of wooden crates sat partly loaded into an ore car. One of the mummies had pried open a crate and was holding a rectangular-shaped block against his chest. Shaw rubbed away the grime on the object and was stunned to see the smear turn the color of gold.

My God, he thought. By today's prices there must be over three hundred million dollars' worth of the stuff lying about.

Tempting as it was to linger and contemplate the riches, Shaw forced himself to push on. Sweat was soaking his clothes, yet he felt as if he were in a refrigerator.

The engineer had chosen to die in the cab of his locomotive. The great iron monster was blanketed under a century of dust, but Shaw could still decipher the fancy gold numerals "88" and the red stripe that ran down the side.

Thirty feet in front of the cowcatcher there was a massive fall of rock that had buried the main entrance of the quarry. More dead were strewn about here; having dug frantically with their final breath, their gnarled hands still clutched around picks and shovels. They had actually moved several tons of stone, but it had been only an exercise in futility. A hundred men couldn't have dug through that mountain of rubble in a month.

How did it all happen? Shaw trembled unconsciously. There was an undeniable horror about the place. Helplessly trapped in a cold and dark underground prison, what tortures of the mind had they all endured before death ended their suffering?

He continued around the locomotive and coal tender, then mounted the steps of the first Pullman car and walked down the aisle. The first sight he saw there was a woman lying in a berth, her arms embracing two small children. Shaw turned away and kept moving.

He rummaged through any and all hand cases that remotely looked like they might contain the North American Treaty. The search went with frustrating slowness. He began to rush as the cold fingers of panic touched his mind. The flashlight was dimming, the batteries would not last but a few minutes longer.

The seventh and last Pullman car, the one with the grisly occupants on the observation platform, bore the emblem of the American eagle on the door. Shaw cursed himself under his breath for not starting here. He laid his hand on the knob, turned it and passed inside. For an instant he was taken back by the opulence of the private coach. *They certainly don't make them like they used to,* he mused.

A figure wearing a derby hat with a yellowed newspaper covering his features was sprawled in a red velvet revolving chair. Two of his companions sat folded over a mahogany dining table, their heads in their arms. One was dressed in what Shaw identified as an English-cut coat and trousers. The other wore a tropical worsted suit. It was the second who grabbed Shaw's interest. A withered hand clutched the grip of a small travel case.

Almost as if he was afraid of waking its owner, Shaw painstakingly removed the case from under the rigid fingers.

Suddenly he froze. Out of the corner of his eye he thought he caught an imperceptible movement. But it had to be an illusion. The wavering shadows on the walls were causing his inborn fears to run wild. If it was left to his imagination, the feeble light could make anything come alive.

Then his heart stopped. A cardiologist would say that's impossible. But his heart stopped as he stared paralyzed at a reflection in the window.

Behind him, the cadaver with the derby in the revolving chair was straightening to a stiff-backed position. Then the hideous thing lowered the newspaper from its face and smiled at Shaw.

83

"You won't find what you're looking for in there," Dirk Pitt said, nodding at the travel bag.

Shaw would never deny that he'd been rattled out of his wits. He sagged into a chair, waiting for his heart to pump again. He could see now that Pitt wore an old coat over a black wet suit. When he finally collected his senses, he said, "You have a disconcerting way of announcing your presence."

Pitt added to the dim illumination by turning on his dive light and then nonchalantly turned his attention back to the old newspaper. "I always knew I was born eighty years too late. Here's a used Stutz Bearcat Speedster with low mileage for only six hundred and seventy-five dollars."

Shaw had used up all his emotional reactions in the past twelve hours and was hardly in the mood for idle levity. "How did you manage to get in here?" he demanded more than asked.

Pitt continued to study the classified automobile ads as he answered. "Swam in through the escape shaft. Ran out of air and almost drowned. Would have too if I hadn't lucked onto a pocket of stale air under an old submerged rock crusher. One more breath enabled me to break into a side tunnel."

Shaw motioned around the coach. "What happened here?"

Pitt pointed toward the two men at the table. "The man with the travel case is, or rather was, Richard Essex, undersecretary of state. The other man was Clement Massey. Beside Massey is a farewell letter to his wife. It tells the whole tragic story."

Shaw picked up the letter and squinted at the faded ink. "So this fellow Massey here was a train robber."

"Yes, he was after a gold shipment."

"I saw it. Enough there to buy the Bank of England."

"Massey's plan was incredibly complex for its time. He and his men flagged the train at an abandoned junction called Mondragon Hook. There they forced the engineer to switch the *Manhattan Limited* onto an old rail spur and into the quarry before any of the passengers realized what was happening.''

"Judging by this, he got more than he bargained for.''

"In more ways than one,'' Pitt agreed. "Overpowering the guards went off without a hitch. That part of the plan had been well rehearsed. But the four army security guards who were escorting Essex and the treaty to Washington came as a rude surprise. When the gunfire died away, the guards were all dead or wounded and Massey was minus three of his own men.''

"Apparently it didn't stop him,'' said Shaw, reading on.

"No, he went ahead and faked the Deauville-Hudson bridge accident; then he returned to the quarry and set off black powder charges that sealed off the entrance. Now he had all the time in the world to unload the gold and flee out the escape exit.''

"How was that possible if it was filled with water?''

"The best laid plans, et cetera,'' said Pitt. "The escape shaft runs on a higher level than the deep end of the quarry where the original flooding occurred. When Massey hijacked the *Manhattan Limited,* the way out was still dry. But after he blew the entrance, the shock waves opened underground fissures and water seepage gushed into the shaft and cut off any chance of escape, condemning everyone to a slow, horrifying death.''

"The poor devils,'' said Shaw. "Must have taken them weeks to perish from cold and starvation.''

"Strange how Massey and Essex sat down at the same table to die together,'' Pitt mused aloud. "I wonder what they found in common at the end?''

Shaw set his flashlight so that its beam illuminated Pitt. "Tell me, Mr. Pitt. Did you come alone?''

"Yes, my diving partner turned back.''

"I must assume you have the treaty.''

Pitt gazed at Shaw over the top of the paper, his green eyes inscrutable. "You assume correctly.''

Shaw slipped his hand from a pocket and aimed the .25 caliber Beretta. "Then I'm afraid you must give it to me.''

"So you can burn it?''

Shaw nodded silently.

"Sorry,'' Pitt said calmly.

"I don't think you fully comprehend the situation.''

"It's obvious you have a gun.''

"And you haven't," Shaw said confidently.

Pitt shrugged. "I admit it didn't occur to me to bring one."

"The treaty, Mr. Pitt, if you please."

"Finders keepers, Mr. Shaw."

Shaw exhaled a breath in a long silent sigh. "I owe you my life, so it would be most inconsiderate of me to kill you. However, the treaty copy means far more to my country than the personal debt between us."

"Your copy was destroyed on the *Empress of Ireland,*" Pitt said slowly. "This one belongs to the United States."

"Perhaps, but Canada belongs to Britain. And we don't intend to give it up."

"The empire can't last forever."

"India, Egypt and Burma, to name a few, were never ours to keep," said Shaw. "But Canada was settled and built by the British."

"You forget your history, Shaw. The French were there first. Then the British. After you came the immigrants: the Germans, the Poles, the Scandinavians and even the Americans who moved north into the western provinces. Your government held the reins by maintaining a power structure run by people who were either born or educated in England. The same is true of your Commonwealth countries. Local government and large corporations may be managed by native employees, but the men who make the major decisions are sent out by London."

"A system that has proven most efficient."

"Geography and distance will eventually defeat that system," said Pitt. "No government can indefinitely rule another thousands of miles away."

"If Canada leaves the Commonwealth, so might Australia or New Zealand, or even Scotland and Wales. I can think of nothing more distressing."

"Who can say where national boundaries will lie a thousand years from now. Better yet, who the hell cares?"

"I care, Mr. Pitt. Please hand over the treaty."

Pitt did not respond, but turned his head, listening. The sounds of voices faintly echoed from one of the tunnels.

"Your friends have followed me down the air vent," said Shaw. "Time has run out."

"You kill me, and they'll kill you."

"Forgive me, Mr. Pitt." The gun muzzle pointed directly between Pitt's eyes.

A deafening, ringing clap shattered the silent gloom of the cavern. Not the sharp, cracking report of a small-caliber Beretta, but rather the booming bark of a 7.63 Mauser automatic. Shaw's head snapped to one side and he hung limp in his chair.

Pitt regarded the smoldering hole in the center of his newspaper for a moment, then rose to his feet, laid the Mauser on the table and eased Shaw to a prone position on the floor.

He looked up as Giordino charged through the door like a bull in heat, an assault rifle held out in front of him. Giordino jerked to a halt and stared fascinated at the derby still perched on Pitt's head. Then he noticed Shaw.

"Dead?"

"My bullet creased his skull. The old guy is tough. After a nasty headache and couple of stitches, he'll probably come gunning for my hide."

"Where'd you find a weapon?"

"I borrowed it from him." Pitt motioned to the mummy that was Clement Massey.

"The treaty?" Giordino asked anxiously.

Pitt slipped a large piece of paper from between the pages of his newspaper and held it in front of the dive light.

"The North American Treaty," he announced. "Except for a charred hole between paragraphs, it's as readable as the day it was signed."

84

In an anteroom of the Canadian Senate chamber, the President of the United States nervously paced the carpet, his face betraying a deep sense of apprehensiveness. Alan Mercier and Harrison Moon entered and stood silently.

"Any word?" asked the President.

Mercier shook his head. "None."

Moon looked strained and gaunt. "Admiral Sandecker's last message indicates that Pitt may have drowned inside the quarry."

The President gripped Mercier's shoulder as if to take strength from him. "I had no right to expect the impossible."

"The stakes were worth the gamble," said Mercier.

The President could not shake the heavy dread in his gut. "Any excuse for failure has a hollow ring."

Secretary of State Oates came through the door. "The Prime Minister and the Governor-General have arrived in the Senate chamber, Mr. President. The ministers are seated and waiting."

The President's eyes were sick with defeat. "It seems time has run out, gentlemen, for us as well as for the United States."

The 291-foot Peace Tower forming the center block of the Parliament building gradually grew larger through the windshield of Scinletti VTOL aircraft as it banked toward the Ottawa airport.

"If we don't get backed up by air traffic," said Jack Westler, "we should land in another five minutes."

"Forget the airport," said Pitt. "Set us down on the lawn in front of Parliament."

Westler's eyes widened. "I can't do that. I'd lose my pilot's license."

"I'll make it easy for you." Pitt slipped the old Mauser pistol out of Richard Essex's travel case and screwed the business end into Westler's ear. "Now take us down."

"Shoot . . . shoot me and we crash," the pilot stammered.

"Who needs you?" Pitt grinned coldly. "I've got more hours in the air than you do."

His facial color bleached brighter than a bedsheet, Westler began the descent.

A crowd of tourists who were photographing a Royal Canadian Mounted Policeman lifted their faces to the sky at the sound of the engines, and then parted like a reverse whirlpool. Pitt dropped the gun in his seat, shoved open the door and leaped out before the landing wheels settled in the turf.

He ducked into the converging onlookers before the astonished Mountie could stop him. The door of the tall Peace Tower was jammed with cordoned lines of tourists waiting to catch a glimpse of the President. Pitt bulled his way through, ignoring the shouts of the guards.

Once inside the memorial hall, he was momentarily confused about which direction to take. Two dozen cables snaked across the floor.

He followed them at a dead run, knowing they would end at the videocameras taping the President's speech. He almost made it to the door of the Senate chamber before a Mountie the size of a small mountain, ablaze in scarlet ceremonial tunic, blocked his way.

"Hold it right there, mister!"

"Take me to the President, quick!" Pitt demanded. As soon as he spoke he realized the words must have sounded absurd.

The Mountie stared incredulously at Pitt's strange attire.

Pitt had only had time to remove his wet-suit top and borrow Giordino's jacket—two sizes too short—before dashing to Westler's plane. He still wore the wet-suit bottoms and his feet were bare.

Suddenly two more Mounties clutched Pitt from flanking sides.

"Watch him boys. He might have a bomb in that satchel."

"There's nothing in there but a piece of paper," said Pitt, maddened to the core.

The tourists began to gather around them, clicking their cameras, curious to see what the disturbance was about.

"We better get him out of here," said the Mountie, who snatched the travel bag.

Pitt had never felt such despair. "For God's sake, listen to me—"

He was in the process of being none too gently jerked away when a man in a conservative blue suit shouldered past the crowd. He gazed briefly at Pitt and turned to the Mountie.

"Having a problem, constable?" he asked, displaying a U.S. Secret Service ID.

"Some radical trying to break into the Senate chamber—"

Pitt suddenly broke loose and lurched forward. "If you're Secret Service, help me." He was yelling now but didn't realize it.

"Take it easy, pal," blue suit said, his hand snapping to the holstered gun under his armpit.

"I have an important document for the President. My name is Pitt. He's expecting me. You've got to get me through to him."

The Mounties pounced on Pitt again, this time with fire in their eyes. The Secret Service agent held up a restraining hand.

"Hold on!" He stared at Pitt skeptically. "I couldn't take you to the President even if I wanted to."

"Then get me to Harrison Moon," Pitt snarled, getting fed up with the absurdity of it all.

"Does Moon know you?"

"You better believe it."

Mercier, Oates and Moon were sitting in the anteroom of the Senate, watching the President on a television monitor, when the door burst open and a horde of Secret Service men, Mounties and building guards, dragging Pitt with at least a half-dozen set of hands, flooded into the room like a tidal wave.

"Call off the hounds," Pitt shouted. "I've got it!"

Mercier spun to his feet, open-mouthed. He was too stunned to react immediately.

"Who is this man?" Oates demanded.

"My God, it's Pitt!" Moon managed to blurt.

His arms pinned, an eye swelling from a sneak punch, Pitt nodded toward the battered old travel bag held by the Mountie. "The treaty copy is in there."

While Mercier vouched for Pitt and swept the security people from the room, Oates studied the contents of the treaty.

Finally he looked up hesitantly. "Is it real? I mean, there's no chance of a forgery?"

Pitt collapsed in a chair, tenderly probing the growing mouse under his eye, the long mission seemingly finished. "Rest easy, Mr. Secretary, you're holding the genuine article."

Mercier turned from closing the door and quickly thumbed through a copy of the President's speech. "He's about two minutes away from his closing statement."

"We better get this to him, fast," said Moon.

Mercier looked down at the exhausted man in the chair. "I think Mr. Pitt should have that honor. He represents the men who died for it."

Pitt abruptly sat up. "Me? I can't go in front of a hundred million viewers watching the Canadian Parliament and interrupt a presidential address. Not looking like a masquerade party drunk."

"You won't have to," said Mercier, smiling. "I'll interrupt the President myself and ask him to step to the anteroom. You take it from there."

In the deep red setting of the Senate chamber, the leaders of the Canadian government sat stunned at the President of the United States' invitation to begin negotiations for merging the two nations. It was the first any of them had heard of it. Only Sarveux sat unperturbed, his face calm and unreadable.

A wave of mutterings coursed through the chamber as the President's national security adviser stepped to the lectern and whispered in his ear. An interruption of a major address was a break in custom and was not to be taken without a minor fuss.

"Please excuse me for a moment," the President said, heightening the mystery. He turned and stepped through the doorway to the antechamber.

In the President's eyes, Pitt looked like a derelict from hell. He came forward and embraced him.

"Mr. Pitt, you don't know how happy I am to see you."

"Sorry I'm late," was all Pitt could think to reply. Then he forced a crooked smile and carefully held up the holed paper. "The North American Treaty."

The President took the treaty and carefully scanned its contents. When he looked up, Pitt was surprised to see tears rimming his eyes. In a rare instance of emotion he muttered a choked "Thank you," and turned away.

Mercier and Moon sat down before the TV monitor and watched the President return to the lectern.

"My apologies for the interruption, but a document of great historical significance has just been handed to me. It is called the North American Treaty . . ."

Ten minutes later, the President concluded solemnly ". . . and so for seventy-five years, under the terms set forth, Canada and the United States have unknowingly been existing as two nations while under international law they were only one . . ."

Mercier let out a long sigh. "Thank God, he didn't slap them in the face by saying they belonged to us."

"The future will not look upon us kindly," the President continued, "if we fail to consider the tremendous potential our former leaders have laid before us. We must not stand separate from one another as we have in the past. We must not look upon ourselves as English-Canadian or Anglo-American or French-Canadian or Mexican-American. We must all look upon ourselves as simply Americans. Because that's what we are, North Americans . . ."

The ministers of Parliament and the premiers of the provinces reflected varied degrees of emotion. Some sat quietly enraged, some showed thoughtful contemplation, others nodded as though in agreement. It was clear the President was not holding the treaty over their heads like a club. He made no demands or threats. But they never doubted for a moment that the power was there.

". . . our histories are closely entwined, our people strikingly similar in life-styles and outlook. The only fundamental difference between us is a viewpoint toward tradition . . .

"If the provinces of Canada decide to go separate ways, they face a long and difficult journey that can only end in collision with others. For the good of all, this must not happen. Therefore, I call upon you to join with me in building the mightiest nation on earth . . . the United States of Canada."

In the Senate chamber the applause was mild and scattered after the President's address. The listeners sat numb, unsure of how to take his proposal for a single nation. The unthinkable had at last been brought out in the open.

Mercier sighed and turned off the TV monitor. "Well, it's begun," he said softly.

Oates nodded. "Thank God the treaty got here in time, or we might have witnessed a political disaster."

Instinctively they all turned to voice their thanks to the man who had done so much to incur their debt.

But Dirk Pitt had fallen sound asleep.

85

The Prime Minister's Rolls braked to a stop before the huge jetliner bearing the presidential seal. Secret Service men exited the cars behind and discreetly placed themselves around the boarding ramp.

Inside, Sarveux leaned forward and unfolded a burled walnut vanity table from the rear of the front seat. Then he opened a cabinet, produced a crystal decanter of Seagrams Crown Royal whiskey and poured two small goblets.

"Here's to two old and close friends who have covered a long haul."

"That we have," said the President, with a weary sigh. "If anyone ever found out how you and I secretly worked together all these years to formulate a single-nation concept, we'd both be shot for treason."

Sarveux smiled faintly. "Drummed out of public office perhaps, but surely not shot."

The President thoughtfully sipped the whiskey. "Strange how a casual conversation between a young minister of Parliament and a freshman senator in front of a fireplace at a hunting lodge so many years ago could change the course of history."

"The right time and place for a chance meeting of two men who shared the same dream," said Sarveux, thinking back.

"The merging of the United States and Canada is inevitable. If not in the next two years, then in the next two hundred. You and I simply worked together to advance the timetable."

"I hope we don't live to regret it."

"A unified continent with nearly the population and land mass of the Soviet Union is nothing to regret. It may well prove to be the salvation of both countries."

"The United States of Canada," said Sarveux. "I like the sound."

"How do you read the future?"

"The Maritime Provinces—Newfoundland, Nova Scotia and New Brunswick—are now cut off from the rest of Canada by an independent Quebec. They'll see it in their best interests to apply for statehood in the coming months. Manitoba and Saskatchewan will follow. An easy decision for them, because they've always had close ties with your northwestern farm states. Next, my guess is that British Columbia will open negotiations. Then with the Pacific and Atlantic ocean ports gone, the other provinces will gradually fall into line."

"And Quebec?"

"The French will temporarily exult in their independence. But in the cold light of unavoidable economic hardship, they'll come to accept statehood as a pretty good bargain after all."

"And Britain. How will they react?"

"Same as they did with India, South Africa and the other colonies. Bid a reluctant goodbye."

"What are your plans, my friend?"

"I shall run for President of Quebec," Sarveux answered.

"I don't envy you. It will be a hard, dirty fight."

"Yes, but if I win, we win. Quebec will be one step closer to joining the union. And most important, I'll be in a position to guarantee the flow of electrical energy from James Bay and make sure that you are included and benefit from the development of your oil-field discovery in Ungava Bay.''

The President set his empty goblet on the vanity table and looked at Sarveux. "I'm sorry about Danielle. The decision to tell you about her liaison with Henri Villon didn't come easy. I wasn't certain how you'd take it or if you'd even believe me."

"I believed you," said Sarveux sadly. "I believed you because I knew it to be true."

"If only there had been another way . . .''

"There wasn't.''

Nothing was left to say. The President opened the car door. Sarveux took hold of his arm and held him back.

"One final question must be settled between us,'' he said.

"Go ahead.''

"The North American Treaty. If all else fails, will you force Canada to abide by the terms?''

"Yes,'' the President replied, and there was a hard glint in his eyes. "There is no turning back now. If I have to, I will not hesitate to enforce the treaty.''

86

It was raining when Heidi limped into the TWA passenger boarding lounge at Kennedy Airport, a drenching New York downpour that tore away leaves and slowed rush-hour traffic to a caterpillar crawl. She wore her navy uniform under a blue raincoat, and her water-specked hair spilled from below a regulation white cap. She dropped a large shoulder bag to the carpet and, carefully balancing on her good leg, eased into a vacant seat.

After the whirlwind events of the past several weeks, the prospect of returning to the routine of duty depressed her. She had not seen Pitt since he rushed off to Ottawa, and the marines guarding Brian Shaw had refused to let her near him before he was carried unconscious into an ambulance that sped away to a military hospital. In the excitement she had been nearly forgotten. It was only through the thoughtfulness of Admiral Sandecker that she had been driven to New York for a well-deserved sleep at the Plaza Hotel and booked first-class on a flight back to her station in San Diego the following day.

She stared through the window at the rain forming lakes on the runway and reflecting the multicolored lights in two dimensions. If she had been alone she would have allowed herself the indulgence of a good cry. She felt a deep sense of longing as she remembered how Shaw touched her. He had invaded her life and she was resentful now of the love he had taken. But there was no remorse, only annoyance with herself for losing control.

Blind and deaf to the people milling around her, she tried to put her feelings and the shameful actions of the past few weeks from her mind.

"I've seen melancholy creatures before," said a familiar voice beside her, "but, lady, you take the prize."

"Does it show that much?" she asked, surprised at how calm her voice sounded.

"Like a black cloud over a sunset," replied Pitt with his devilish smile. He was dressed in a navy-blue sport jacket with red Breton slacks and wallaby shirt. He looked down at her over a monstrous bouquet of mixed flowers. "You didn't think I was going to let you slink away without saying goodbye?"

"At least somebody remembered." She felt damp and straggly and tired and hurt and rejected. "Pay no heed if I sound bitchy. This is my night for self-sympathy."

"Maybe these will help." He laid the flowers in her lap. The bouquet was so immense she could hardly see over the top.

"They're gorgeous," said Heidi. "I think I'll cry now."

"Please don't." Pitt laughed softly. "I've always wanted to buy out a flower store for a beautiful girl. Embarrass me and I may never do it again."

She pulled Pitt down, kissed him on the cheek and fought back the tears. "Thank you, Dirk. You'll always be my dearest friend."

"A friend?" He feigned a hurt look. "Is that the best I can do?"

"Can we ever be anything else to each other?"

"No . . . I suppose not." His face went gentle and he took her hand. "Funny how two people who had so much going for them couldn't find it in their hearts to fall in love."

"In my case, it was because of someone else."

"The fickleness of women," he said. "They fall for the guy who treats them like trash, and yet they wind up marrying John Q. Square."

She avoided his gaze and stared out the window. "We've never learned to deny our feelings."

"Does Shaw love you?"

"I doubt it."

"You love him?"

"I'm not my usual practical self when it comes to Brian. Yes, I love him for all the good it'll do me. We consumed each other. He had his reasons, I had mine. If he wanted me, I'd run to him like a shot. But it'll never happen."

"There comes that sad face again," Pitt said. "I refuse to send a whimpering female on board an airplane. You leave me no choice but to cheer you up with one of my magic tricks."

Heidi laughed softly through watery eyes. "Since when did you practice magic?"

Pitt took on a mock hurt look. "You've never heard of Magnificent Pitt, the Illusionist?"

"Never."

"All right for you, nonbeliever. Close your eyes."

"You're joking."

"Close your eyes and count to ten."

Heidi finally did as she was told. When she opened her eyes, Pitt was gone and Brian Shaw was sitting in his place.

The cry that she had kept bottled away burst from her as she embraced him, and the tears rolled down her cheeks and dropped from her chin.

"I thought you were locked away," she blurted between sobs.

Shaw lifted the folded raincoat that was draped across his lap and revealed the handcuffs. "Pitt arranged for me to come."

She tenderly touched the bandage that showed beneath a tweed cap. "Are you all right?"

"My double vision is almost gone," he answered, smiling.

The airline attendant behind the check-in counter announced that Heidi's plane was ready to board.

"What will happen to you?" she asked, afraid to release him.

"I suspect I'll spend some time in one of your federal prisons."

"Would you think me maudlin if I said I love you?"

"Would you think me a liar if I told you the same?"

"No," she said. And she felt a rush of relief because she knew he wasn't lying.

Shaw said, "I promise you that someday we'll be together."

That part could never be true. It tore painfully, deep in her chest. She pulled away. "I must go," she whispered.

He read the hurt in her eyes and understood. He lifted her up and onto the crutches. A helpful flight attendant came over and took Heidi's travel bag and the flowers.

"Goodbye, Heidi."

She kissed him lightly on the lips. "Goodbye."

After Heidi had disappeared through the boarding gate, Pitt walked up and stood beside Shaw.

"An awfully good woman," he said. "Be a shame to lose her."

"A good woman," Shaw agreed wistfully.

"If you don't hurry, she'll leave without you."

Shaw looked at him. "What are you talking about?"

Pitt shoved a packet in Shaw's breast pocket. "Your boarding pass and ticket. I fixed it so you have adjoining seats."

"But I'm under arrest as an enemy agent," said Shaw, his thoughts at a loss.

"The President owes me a favor." Pitt shrugged.

"Does he know what you're doing?"

"Not yet."

Shaw shook his head. "You're asking for trouble, setting me loose."

"I've been there before." Pitt held out his hand. "Don't forget, you promised me a backgammon lesson."

Shaw shook with both his hands. Then he held them up, displaying the steel bracelets. "Most aggravating, these things."

"Picking the lock should be child's play for a secret agent."

Shaw made a series of movements under the raincoat. Then he held up the cuffs, his hands free. "I'm a bit rusty. I used to do it much faster."

"James Bond would have been proud of you," Pitt said dryly.

"Bond?"

"Yes, I hear you two were quite close."

Shaw exhaled his breath in a long sigh. "He exists only in fiction."

"Does he?"

Shaw shrugged, then stared at Pitt for a long moment. "Why are you doing this after the pain I've caused Heidi?"

"She loves you," Pitt said simply.

"What do you get out of it?"

"Nothing that will add to my bank account."

"Then why?"

"I enjoy doing things out of the ordinary."

Before Shaw could reply, Pitt had turned and mixed into the flowing crowd on the concourse.

The rain had stopped, and Pitt put down the Cobra's convertible top. He drove toward the lights of Washington that glowed ghostlike against the low-hanging clouds. The breeze whipped his hair, and he deeply inhaled the sweet fragrance of wet grass that rose from the fields beside the highway.

Pitt tightened his grip on the wheel, pressed the accelerator to the floor and watched the tachometer needle as it crept slowly into the red.

ABOUT THE AUTHOR

CLIVE CUSSLER lives the same sort of adventurous life as his hero, Dirk Pitt. In addition to his writing, Cussler has tramped through the Southwest in search of gold mines, gone scuba diving in isolated Rocky Mountain lakes for missing aircraft, and now leads expeditions searching for America's historic shipwrecks. On one such, John Paul Jones' *Bonhomme Richard* was discovered, and more recently Cussler excavated the sunken wreck of one of the *Monitor*'s sister ships. The *Monitor*'s famous nemesis, the *Merrimack*, is another ship whose artifacts have been recovered from the sea by Cussler. He is currently searching for the *C.S. Hunley*, the famous Confederate submarine which was the first of its kind ever to sink a warship in combat.

A noted collector of classic automobiles, Cussler writes his bestselling thrillers at his home in the foothills of the Rocky Mountains overlooking Denver, Colorado.